INSIDE THE

Ballerina

keep smiling

Chloe Openshaw

Claire

Thanks so much for
being part of the
tour!

Love Chloe xx.

Edited by Lolli Molyneux-Dixon
Cover design by Ken Dawson
Typesetting by Book Polishers

Acknowledgements

JO ~ Thank you so much for encouraging me to finish this book despite the difficult year in which it was written.

WO ~ Thank you for always believing in me, and for continuing to be my greatest supporter.

Lolli ~ Thank you for your dedication to this project. I really appreciate your guidance and expertise.

To all my Instagram followers ~ Thank you for your support and encouragement, and for providing my work with a platform on which to stand.

1

NESTLED DEEP WITHIN THE SLEEPY VILLAGE OF PERTH, Scotland, a cluster of heavy clouds rumbled above a quaint row of houses lining Pembroke Road, a secluded side street located on the outskirts. The imposing meteoric masses dripped over the roof slates with midnight darkness, their irregular form hanging from the heavens like a string of blackened corpses, and the once tranquil sky became pierced with blasts of thunder.

Kitty Twist cowered beneath the eye of the storm in her kitchen, her attention drawn towards the windows where the rain clattered against the flimsy panes of glass. Her ear drums detected the clock's notification that the hour had come, and although the thunder above continued to intimidate, it was the persistent sound of the clock, marking every passing second, which ignited her fear. Beneath her floral, flimsy blouse, Kitty's chest pounded in anticipation of her fiancé's return. Just the thought of hearing his approaching footsteps caused a snake of apprehension to work its way up from the base of her spine, and anxiety to scratch at her skin. Amid mounting levels of panic, her lungs contracted and caused a lightheadedness to further rock her composure. She gazed at her trembling hands in bewilderment, unable to recall a time when they felt steady. Through her tears, the scars dotting her skin appeared magnified and the sight of her engagement ring was the final catalyst which induced a fresh plume of tears to fall. A noise outside diverted her attention and caused her body to gravitate towards the window.

Kitty heard her fiancé's voice the moment it echoed its way in through the open kitchen window. 'Evening, Tim. Awful weather, isn't it?' she heard him comment to a neighbour outside, the sound of his voice filled her stomach with dread. A car door slammed, causing her entire body to jolt. Upon hearing the double beep of Stevie's car as the doors were locked, like every other evening, her body froze. The wrought-iron gate, behind which sat number 67, kissed the garden wall. The wind carried the sound of Stevie struggling with his keys, and Kitty fought the urge to throw herself towards the front door and secure the chain in place, knowing that, although it wouldn't offer the permanent protection that she craved, it would perhaps provide her with a few more precious moments alone.

After a pause, she heard the clunk of his brass key enter the lock, drowning her insides with more stomach-churning dread. Having spent all day cleaning the house, she realised her eyes were now darting around the room in a last-minute search for any errors she had made, which Stevie would be sure to spot. The interior of their home looked immaculate, thanks, in part, to Kitty placing herself, fully clothed, in the bathtub for the latter half of the afternoon, just to ensure that every inch of carpet remained pristine. The raw skin on her hands burned and wept – a testament to the hours she had spent scrubbing every wipeable surface in the house.

'I'm home,' announced Stevie, slamming the door behind him. The floorboards creaked, causing Kitty's body to tense. Stevie paused at the front door and listened, just like he did every day upon returning from work. 'What a busy day,' he added in a neutral tone. From the kitchen came the sound of a knife hitting a wooden chopping board in steady, rhythmic strokes. Stevie's face broke into a thin smirk. 'Have you missed me?' he called, loosening his tie and pacing towards the kitchen.

Hearing his strides, Kitty sensed an irritability in her fiancé by the way that his feet navigated the hallway, his footsteps hitting hard against the wood floor. Her heart plummeted to new depths along with any remaining scraps of hope that this evening might be different. With her back to the room, she failed to witness his sprawling, tense expression. He paced further into the room. 'What the hell is that?' he spat.

She didn't dare turn around as she replied. 'It's sirloin steak and salad, like you requested.' She felt his imposing stance the moment he stepped forward, his day-old aftershave whipping her insides into a sickening frenzy.

'Not the salad, you stupid idiot,' he replied, his words firing like daggers into her back. She moved closer to the cumbersome, kitchen island, allowing it to bear more of her weight the moment her legs felt unstable. Her hand clenched around the knife, turning her knuckles white. She resolved to keeping her head lowered, avoiding eye contact, and flicked through her mental checklist, trying to pinpoint her apparent error. *I've put his slippers out. The post is on the table. His beer is ready. Tea is prepared, and he wanted steak, didn't he? I've cleaned the house. What have I missed?* Her whole body seized when Stevie's hand skimmed the side of her body. He picked up the bottle of beer, and backed away.

'Oh, I've forgotten to chill your glass, haven't I? I'm sorry. I'll do it now.' Kitty reached over to grab Stevie's glass, but he intersected, grabbing her hand and slamming her palm against the wall. Kitty's whole body jolted, the corner of the island digging into her side the moment he dragged her like a puppet towards the wall. A loose nail pressed hard into her soft skin, causing her palm to bleed and mark the olive paintwork with dots of red.

Kitty's other hand clenched into a fist surrounding the knife. 'Stevie, please stop,' she begged. 'You're hurting me.' The severity of the pain shot through her body, the colour drained from her face and her eyes stung as she fought back tears. She felt the weight of the blade and tried desperately to find the strength to turn and stab it deep into his body. Her hands trembling, the knife escaped her grip and the steel blade clattered against the floor, forcing her to accept a gut-wrenching defeat.

Stevie's eyes fell to the knife on the floor, then rose to land on Kitty's hand. 'What is this?' He ignored the trail of blood that was now snaking its way down her arm, his temples pulsating. With her hand firmly trapped beneath his, he moved himself closer to her, his mousey-coloured hair brushing past Kitty's face as she held her breath.

She followed his gaze with reluctance, and then it dawned. 'I can remove it,' she cried, cursing herself for not having realised sooner. His problem had never been the warm pint glass – it was the ruby-red polish she had used to paint her nails. 'I thought you'd like it,' she whispered. 'I did it especially for you.'

'They look awful,' he spat. 'Such a slutty colour.' With his own nails, he scratched away hard at the polish. 'Who's this meant to impress, eh? Nobody's going to look at you just because you have this sort of shit on,' he hissed. His eyes remained locked on Kitty's shimmering fingertips, the veins in his forehead bursting.

Kitty's inherent good nature oozed through her apologetic body language, her demeanour deflated. Her head hung in a manner which portrayed defeat in its rawest form. 'I'm sorry,' she cried, her body braced for a scolding. Her tears left a trail of guilt smeared over Stevie's hand. 'You're hurting me,' she whimpered.

Stevie released his grip before tossing her hand away. He stormed out of the kitchen and down the hallway. He opened the front door and paused. 'Get it off before I get back,' he muttered, before stepping back out into the rain.

The front door slammed and the racket echoed through the two floors of the now quiet rented semi, the sound of silence Kitty's greatest friend. She remained muted, her limbs weary like those of a puppet on a string. Overcome with fatigue, she felt her knees buckle beneath her, and the cool wood of the floor was soon against her back. Her bloody palm throbbed, and Kitty made a silent prayer in the hope that she would be released from the pain. She cradled her torso, listening carefully for signs of his return, fearing that this time, he would cause more damage than she could possibly recover from. She peered towards the front of the house. The sound of Stevie's car engine roared, his wheels spinning with haste. He was gone, for now.

Whilst droplets of fresh blood trickled down her wrist, Kitty gathered herself and slowly managed to get back onto her feet. She looked at her body, assessing the damage. Her left hand lay limp, her tiny bones recovering from the threat of fracture. The bloody wound on her palm painted an ugly picture against her porcelain skin, adding another scar to what now amounted to a large collection obtained in their short, six-month relationship. She scrambled out of the kitchen and heaved herself down the hallway towards the front door, silently weighing up her options. With an unstable stance, she clasped both hands on the handle and contemplated turning it.

Her fear reignited at the thought of his return, and she convinced herself she could hear the sound of a car approaching. She reluctantly released her grip and thrashed her hands against the door with scraps of mustered energy, punishing herself, as always, for failing to fully defend herself in the heat of the moment. All she could do was echo the faintest of mumbles, 'Help.'

She let the door bear the weight of her forehead for a few seconds, enjoying the cool of the wood against her reddened skin, before turning her face to the side. Slowly, she allowed her body to fold in on itself, until she lay in a heap on the floor. She reached out and clawed at the door, her fingernails tracing the familiar ridges previously etched in the grain of the wood.

Although she was desperate to leave, Kitty knew deep down that now would not be the right time for her to escape - not yet. If she walked out now, there would be no going back. In order for the moment to be right, she would need to have everything in place, her life beyond the garden gate all set up, ready and waiting for her. At this second, with blood seeping from her hand and a sense of disorientation following her traumatic evening, she simply wasn't prepared. She needed a plan; somewhere to go where Stevie would never find her.

The sound of the gate creaking forced her eyes to open wide, and the tears seemed to form almost automatically, alongside the lump in her throat. Her skin tingled with discomfort in anticipation of another violent encounter, and beneath the surface, anxiety wrapped tight around her chest. Kitty listened to the sound of approaching footsteps with a sense of dread buried in the pit of her stomach. After a brief pause, there came a knock at the door. She held her breath and remained silent. Another moment passed before a louder knock came.

'Kitty, it's me, Millie. I know you're home so let me in.' Millie rattled her knuckles against the door again. 'Kitty, why won't you talk to me?' she shouted. Millie stepped back, trying to see past the closed curtains in the lounge window, the entire room obscured from view. She knelt on the doormat and parted the letterbox to allow a small gap.

Kitty shifted her body to the side, her breath escaping in erratic bursts. She could smell her friend's perfume the moment it seeped through the gap, the soft, delicate scent more comforting than a warm blanket. She closed her eyes, in one moment willing Millie to leave, and in the next, praying for her to force entry and take her away, to safety, and to freedom.

'Kitty, please come to the door. I'm worried about you. I need to know you're alright.' Millie peered through the gap, witnessing nothing except the empty hallway and dark interior, the dim lighting hiding the trail of blood dotting the floorboards. 'Kitty, please. Come to the door. Just let me know that you're alright and then I'll leave, if that's what you want.'

Only a few inches separated the two best friends, both their heads pressed against the door, a look of sadness etched in their eyes. Kitty heard the upset reverberating through her friend's words, Millie's voice choked with emotion, and yet the fear instilled in her bones prevented her from opening the door. The letterbox slammed shut before opening a few seconds later to allow a card to fall to the floor. The sound of Millie's footsteps became faint the further she walked away, the creaking gate signalling her departure. Kitty reached out and took hold of the card, pressing it to her chest before reading. She closed her eyes and willed her friend to return, convincing herself that she would find the strength and force herself to open the door. Through tear-soaked eyes, Kitty looked at the item clenched in her hand, the simplicity of the handwritten note causing a raft of tears to fall from her cheeks. *I promised your mum I would look after you. I won't break my promise. Call me. Otherwise, I'll be back.*

With Millie's card clenched in her hand, Kitty pulled herself onto her knees and parted the letterbox, the whites of her eyes shining through the narrow gap. Outside, the doomsday clouds dispersed, the burnt-looking masses now releasing torrents in the distance. Just as her fingers pulled away, she spotted the stretched arches of a vivid rainbow through stinging eyes. Cherished recollections from her past transpired into faint mumbles, her mother's voice echoing in through the letterbox. Kitty listened to the words running through her mind with a longing intensity, the same way she once listened to her mum as a frightened child. *Don't be afraid of the storm, Kitty, search the sky for rainbows instead.*

Kitty blinked to encourage her tears to fall so that she could admire the nostalgic image before it vanished. For the first time in months, a humbling feeling consoled her broken heart, leaving her with a renewed energy to survive, and escape.

2

SNIPPETS OF EARLY SPRINGTIME DANCED OVER THE QUAINT TOWN of St. Ives, Cornwall. A few weeks previous, the town had borne witness to the exchanging of the seasonal baton, encouraging winter to hunker down and new scents to awaken. Fresh, vibrant foliage flourished on naked tree branches and the surface of the sea glimmered beneath a fresh season sunrise. A myriad of dusty-pink blossom added to the perfect morning backdrop, a scene well suited to an art display in a seaside gallery.

The view beyond Charlotte Pendlebury's bridal suite looked edible. Cotton-wool clouds paired with a buttery, melting sunshine to set the perfect tone for the day ahead. With some reluctance, the pesky, cool breeze played along with the romantic ambience and tucked itself back into hibernation, allowing a serene stillness to shimmer over the coastal town. Everything favoured an outdoor wedding ceremony, perfect for Charlie Pendlebury to marry the man she boasted to be the love of her life.

From the age of seven, Charlie yearned to get married. One sunny July morning whilst the sun warmed her delicate skin, seven-year-old Charlie discovered her mum's wedding dress whilst rooting with curiosity in the attic. When she lifted the lid on the tattered box, her expression sparkled. She cast away her own clothes and slipped herself into her mum's bridal gown. Her nostrils inhaled a pungent mustiness and dust particles fell like dirty rain over the disused, cramped attic. Despite the weight of the dress bearing down on her frame, Charlie hoisted herself onto a wobbly stool. With her t-shirt sat lopsided in place of a veil, she declared her love to her imaginary husband, at which point she tossed her bouquet of dreary, garden-picked daisies.

Now twenty-five, Charlie swapped her imaginary someone for her handsome bachelor, Ben Fox; a local Cornish artist and all-round good guy. Charlie had devoted her heart to Ben from the moment they first met in primary school.

'Have the caterers arrived?' Charlie asked whilst sat in the middle of wedding day headquarters, her hairdresser, make-up artist and nail beautician all working at a feverish pace. Nobody answered her question, so she repeated. 'Can somebody find out if the caterers have arrived?' She studied the colour-coordinated notepad resting on her lap - her bridal bible. With her free index finger running down her scribbled list, a stream of questions followed. 'Are all the chairs in place? Are the flowers complete? Have the balloons been delivered? Where's my bouquet?'

Pippa rocketed out of her seat. She snatched the book and flung it through the air, post-it notes cascading in the fashion of premature confetti. 'Bloody hell, you've got to stop.' Pippa positioned herself in front of Charlie, her stance unapologetically rigid. 'It's all in hand, Charlie. Leave the bloody book alone and just enjoy your day. You're missing out on everything that's going on because you're fretting, even though you're paying a wedding planner an extortionate fee. Let her fret, that's her job.'

Pippa never held back. 'You're obsessing, and I bet you haven't even noticed how beautiful it is out there,' she added, pointing towards the bridal suite balcony to see gentle sea waves dancing in the distance. 'Have you noticed that the sky is a perfect shade of blue, or that the birds are singing? Have you seen that there's blossom on the trees, just like you'd hoped? These are the things you should be taking notice of.'

Charlie took an exaggerated sip from her champagne flute and for the first time that morning, drank in the day ahead with a fresh pair of eyes. She peered around Pippa's hands-on-hips stance and admired the horizon, witnessing for herself that the conditions couldn't have been more perfect. She brought her attention back inside and nibbled on the strawberries that had been especially delivered for her breakfast, the juicy fruits purposefully arranged in the shape of a heart. 'Who on earth did this?' she laughed, lightening the mood and permitting others in the room to exhale.

'You've probably paid an extra fifty quid for someone to do that sort of nonsense,' Pippa added. 'I love you, more than anything, and Ben,' she continued, kissing her best friend on the cheek. 'But you've got to enjoy this day, every second of it, because I'm not going through this bloody charade again.' She walked over and took hold of the dress hanging from the wardrobe. 'I've starved myself for two whole weeks just so that I can fit into this slither of a dress, and I've listened to my fair share of wedding talk. So, please, let's just enjoy the day without the bloody book, okay?'

Charlie held her flute aloft in Pippa's direction and with an extended pinkie, cleared her throat before replying, 'I love you too, Pip, and thanks for being such a wonderful Maid of Honour.'

Pippa let her dressing gown fall. 'And another thing, whilst I'm on a roll; if you blow that bloody whistle once more, I swear I'll deny being your best friend and I'll abandon you at the altar myself,' she threatened whilst yanking up the zip on her dress, struggling to navigate the section covering the curvy contours of her hips.

Charlie got down from her seat. 'That's fine,' she replied. She bent down and took hold of a flamingo-pink whistle. 'But, as the bride, I should be allowed one last blowout,' and with that, Charlie pressed the plastic against her honey-glossed lips.

In a room opposite the bridal suite, Benjamin Fox adjusted the collar on his ash-grey tuxedo for at least the third time in under half an hour. He heard the screech of his wife-to-be's whistle and felt the onset of a headache. A river of doubt washed through his mind and his face flushed. 'Is it me, or is it warm in here?' he mumbled, his blood pressure skyrocketing.

'Feeling a bit hot under the collar, are we?' mocked his Best Man. Ruben opened a few windows, allowing the cool, morning air to spill into the stifling room.

Ben looked down to find his hands were trembling and tried to shake it off, his heart beating hard beneath his shirt and causing his breath to become laboured. 'This is all just pre-wedding jitters, isn't it?' he asked Ruben, the only other person in the room. 'Everyone feels terrible just before they get married, don't they?'

Ruben's body juddered at the ridiculous nature of the statement. 'This is meant to be the best day of your life. Is that not how you're feeling?' He tried his best to hide the doubt in his voice, knowing full well that his friend was about to make a huge mistake.

Ben failed to hear the question, too wrapped up in his own tangle of thoughts. 'And in any case, she won't use the whistle once we're married, so that's one less thing to worry about.'

Good luck getting it off her, thought Ruben. Seeking to calm his own nerves, he grabbed a chilled bottle of Bud and plunged it into his best friend's hand. 'Just nerves,' he reassured, before glugging a beer himself, going through his Best Man's speech for the umpteenth time, not wanting to do his pal anything but proud.

Ben necked his drink; his second of the morning. 'I'm not sure it is just nerves,' he confessed in one quick breath, alcohol fuelling the bravery.

'What do you mean? Talk to me.'

'Well, I love her, of course I do. I've known her since primary school, you know that, and we've been together forever.' Ben took another exaggerated swig of his beer. He and Charlie had lived only a few streets away from one another their whole lives, and although temporarily separated whilst attending different universities, they had remained a couple since the age of seventeen.

'But, because I've known her almost my entire life, it feels like we're just best pals, not, you know, lovers… if that makes sense.' Ruben looked around the room, now adjusting his own collar, willing someone else to come along and take charge of steadying the quivering groom.

Ben turned to face his Best Man, flinging his arms in the air. 'I have no comparisons to draw upon. I've never dated anyone else, so I don't know if these feelings are normal. Is this how it's *meant* to feel?' Ruben took another glug of his drink, allowing Ben an opportunity to continue. 'I know she's great, incredible even. She's always been faithful and she's going to make a great wife, isn't she?' Ben lowered his head. 'Why does it feel like I'm trying to convince myself?'

Ruben asked the only question that he could think of. 'What's making you question everything?' He already knew the answer, he'd shared enough pints with Ben down at the pub to know what went on behind his best friend's front door.

'She's got everything I'm looking for.' Ben drained his bottle before continuing. 'She's compassionate, funny and generous.' His churning stomach urged him to splurge the painful, deep-rooted truth, and yet he couldn't force the words out.

'You asked her to marry you, you must've felt sure in that moment.'

Ben lowered his head again whilst shaking away his shame. 'I don't remember proposing.' The confession echoed around the room, refusing to silence.

'What? You've always said that you did it whilst in Venice, in that posh restaurant that was extortionate.'

'*She* said that I did it in the restaurant, but I was too bloody drunk to remember my own name. And I couldn't argue about it in the morning, even though I knew it wasn't something I was planning.'

Ruben covered his face. 'So, what you're saying is, Charlie's tricked you into getting married?'

Ben shook his head. 'I'm saying that I proposed, but I don't remember doing it. She's been wanting to get married for years, you know that.'

'And what about a ring? You wouldn't have had one.'

'Apparently I wanted her to choose her own, knowing that I'd pick the wrong style, which does sound like me.'

'I know, but…' began Ruben, taking a glance at his watch.

'And she's already talking about starting a family,' Ben interrupted, shaking his head again and rubbing his temples. 'But for me, I need time to get the studio up and running. Things are going well, and I can feel things starting to happen, and if I let that slip, I'd never forgive myself. I've wanted this my whole life. I've never really wanted to be a dad, and I've told Charlie that, but she doesn't listen, or she doesn't want to hear the truth.'

'What are you going to -'

Ben held his hands up. 'You know what, don't say anything else,' Ben began, speaking over Ruben. 'It's all just jitters. Could you go and check that everything's okay? I'll be down in a few, once I've washed these nerves away with another quick beer.'

Ruben placed his hands on his friend's shoulders. 'You sure? There's still enough time to change your mind. You can still walk away if you don't think it's the right decision.' Ben wasn't sure at all, but signalled with his head towards the door, encouraging Ruben to leave.

'I'm fine, honest.'

With reluctance, Ruben agreed. 'Okay then, see you down there,' he said, before leaving the room and closing the door.

Stood in the empty suite, Ben was left alone with his thoughts, which were now spinning around in his mind. He cracked open another beer, his stomach twisting with anticipation. He thought through his doubts one last time, imagining how it would feel to call the wedding off, and the hurt it would cause to Charlie and her family.

He stood before the mirror and spoke aloud to himself. 'She's so possessive, and you know it,' he blurted in one quick breath. He forced more beer down his throat, the cool liquid paving the way for more declarations. He fidgeted some more with his collar, trying to loosen it so that his airways didn't feel strangulated. But once one revelation escaped, a flood of emotions followed and he spoke directly at his own reflection, his hands gesticulating. 'She opens your post, and she reads through all your emails. She rummages in your wallet and workbag. She checks your phone like it's hers, and she knows all your passwords. That's just not normal.' He closed his eyes and ran his hands through his hair, shuddering at the sound of his own voice. He thought back to the time when he'd actually summoned up the courage and left Charlie having caught her rooting through his workbag. 'Why did you go back?' he mumbled to himself, opening his eyes and staring into the mirror, noting his drawn facial expression.

He could hear the clock on the wall ticking, the hands counting down to what was supposed to be a pivotal moment in his life. He stretched out his crow's feet with his fingertips and drew in a long breath. 'Stop dwelling on the past,' he told himself. He closed his eyes and imagined how pretty Charlie would look in her wedding dress.

Ben straightened out his tuxedo and for the last time as a bachelor, took a swig of beer and walked towards the window, inhaling the fresh, Cornish air. He admired the sea view, the perfect backdrop for his wedding day. He dragged his shoulders back, lifted his chin, and repeated the same string of words until they became fluent: *I do. I do. I do.*

3

TWELVE MONTHS AGO, WHEN KITTY TWIST FIRST CROSSED PATHS with Stevie Best, it had appeared as though the universe had attempted to deliver several warning signs, although unfortunately, each one had gone unnoticed. Clouds of misfortune had blemished the skyline; the calendar had marked out the date – Friday 13th. That morning, her compact mirror had smashed the moment it slipped out of her hands, and her schedule had been thrown off after the lock in her front door had broken, leaving her trapped inside her own house, waiting impatiently for a locksmith, who arrived an hour late.

'I'll have a tall, non-fat latte with a caramel drizzle,' said Stevie when he called in at Millie's Café that Friday morning. Rude and stand-offish with the barista, he had failed to properly acknowledge Kitty, too engrossed in his social media feeds. With his usual coffee shop temporarily closed due to refurbishment, Millie's just happened to be the next café to appear on his daily commute to the office where he worked as a solicitor.

Kitty recited Stevie's order, recalling nothing but his first three words. 'Millie, you got a sec?' she called over her shoulder, turning to witness nothing but piles of unbaked pastries, with Millie nowhere in sight.

'Erm,' she stammered, rummaging around on the counter to try and find a pencil. 'Sorry, could you just repeat that? I didn't quite catch your order,' Kitty added, chancing a glance up at Stevie.

From the moment his eyes had met Kitty's, he had felt a strong pull of infatuation. He didn't usually take notice of anybody in the morning, his mind too preoccupied with running over the day's meetings and the tasks stacked up on his desk. But Kitty had grabbed his attention - her engaging blue eyes, quiet charm and natural beauty had knocked him off his stride.

'Sorry, I got chatting to the delivery driver. Here, let me take over,' offered Millie, appearing behind the counter. 'You go and put the pastries in the oven.'

Stevie dropped his phone into his pocket and relished the nervous way Kitty bit her bottom lip and twirled a pencil in between her fingers. 'Actually, I'll just have a tea to go, please. Milk, one sugar,' he requested.

'Are you okay?' Millie whispered, placing her arm around her friend's waist. Kitty produced an encouraging smile, at which point Millie walked off and tended to the unbaked chocolate croissants and cinnamon swirls.

'Tea with milk and one sugar, I can certainly do that,' she replied to Stevie. Whilst making his order, Kitty couldn't help but notice the dimples accentuating Stevie's smile. She noted his tall stature and admired his smart attire, all tailored to fit his frame. When he caught her looking, her cheeks flushed with deep shades of red, an inner glow awakening long forgotten emotions. Whilst adding the sugar to his drink and stirring for longer than required, she relished the fluttering feelings warming her insides. She failed to hear her favourite song playing on the radio, or the whizzing siren of a dashing ambulance. The smell of something sweet burning drifted past her nose without detection, and although a queue emerged, Stevie stole all of Kitty's attention.

'Here you go,' she said, placing the tea on the counter. Stevie handed over his money, along with an extended smile that failed to fade.

'I think this is going to be the best cup of tea I've ever tasted,' he commented. 'Thank you, Kitty,' he added, noticing her name badge. 'Hopefully see you again for more tea,' he concluded before walking away. Once out of the café and heading up the road, he turned to take one last look at Kitty before she vanished from sight, catching her looking over at him. In a way seldom experienced thus far in her life, her heart skipped.

Every subsequent morning, Stevie called in to Millie's on his way to work, his phone wedged in his pocket. He manipulated the queue, only stepping forward when Kitty became free.

'Hello, again,' tended to be his standard opener, locking eyes with her and producing a wry smile – the kind of smile that translated more than a casual greeting. 'How are you?' he asked, prolonging the amount of time spent in her company, much to the dismay of the queue of aggravated, impatient customers snaking behind.

'I'm good, thank you for asking. What can I get you today – the usual?' also tended to be Kitty's standard reply, which she usually had to offer in an attempt to rein in her inner glow. The pair engaged in polite exchanges, nothing too flirtatious - that wasn't Kitty's style. But she did revel in their fleeting conversations, and Stevie's chattiness always left her with crumbs of curiosity to nibble on for the rest of the day. For the first time in months, she became impatient for the next day, finding herself basking in a morning giddiness that soon became her daily highlight.

One Friday night on his way home from work, only a few weeks after initially meeting Kitty, Stevie popped back into Millie's, just before closing time.

'Sorry, but we're all switched off for the day,' said Millie, pushing the door to prevent Stevie from entering.

'Oh, I wasn't actually after buying anything,' he protested, wedging his foot in the crack. 'I just wanted to have a quick chat with Kitty, if that's alright?'

'Oh, okay. Wait here, I'll just go and grab her before she leaves.'

Kitty appeared from out the back, her coat and bag flung over her shoulder, her embarrassment and apprehension cementing her feet behind the counter.

'Hi. We're actually closed, everything is switched off. Sorry,' she said, pointing to the silenced coffee machines. Stevie stepped further in.

'Oh, that's alright, I wasn't after a drink. I, erm, just wanted to ask you something.' Millie appeared behind the counter.

'You shoot off. I'll lock up tonight,' she insisted, giving her pal an encouraging glance.

'Oh, well, if you're sure. See you tomorrow,' she replied whilst walking towards Stevie, who held the door open, allowing her to step outside. It was one of those early April evenings just as the clocks sprung forward. The sudden change in the seasons became apparent, the sky still splattered with middle-of-the-day shades of blue towards late afternoon. The pair walked side by side, neither one knowing quite how to behave, the conversation a little harder to navigate outside of their usual café context. Kitty admired the swooshing birds above, whilst Stevie's eyes scoured the pavement, searching for conversation inspiration.

'So,' he began, turning to look at Kitty. 'I have a confession.' She met his gaze, her raised eyebrows venturing a silent question. Stevie produced his signature smile, a grin and fine set of dimples that she couldn't help but admire.

'I think, because of you, I now have a serious addiction to tea. I normally only have one a day, on my way to work, but since meeting you, I find myself buying cups of tea three times a day, just so that I can see you.' Stevie didn't avert his gaze, waiting for Kitty's all-important reaction. After a few tense seconds, he caught sight of her blushed cheeks, and her nervous bottom lip once again gave her away.

Kitty didn't reply, not initially. She digested his kindness like a moist, oven-baked cookie, relishing how it wrapped around her heart, warming her insides. Overcome with a mental fuzziness, her mind cavorted with his words. A quivering sensation traced through her nerves and she worked hard to subdue an urge, her childhood twinkle toes itching to dance anytime she experienced feelings of such happiness.

'So, I was wondering if I could take you out for a drink, preferably not to a coffee shop, maybe a pub or bar in town instead?' The question hung in the air. Sensing her apprehension, Stevie relaxed his shoulders as they strolled. 'Nothing formal, just a drink. You can't beat a cool beer and packet of peanuts, or a cocktail and olive, if you're fancy,' he added. 'I'd like to be able to talk to you without a queue of people huffing on my shoulder,' he concluded, a train of sincerity delivering his sentiment.

She didn't reply, her thoughts far away, preventing an answer from arriving. They reached a natural fork in the road, their stride coming to a conclusion. Stevie's impatience made him press for a reply. 'So, Miss Twist, what do you think?' he asked again, ending the pause in conversation. His words momentarily dragged Kitty out of the past and into her future.

'Well, the thing is,' she began, ready to brush Stevie off, knowing deep down that she wasn't ready to begin dating, not yet.

'What's the thing?' he added, encouraging her to elaborate on her halted sentence.

'The thing is, now isn't really a great time.'

'I knew you'd say that, so I have another confession,' he added. 'You see, I asked your friend, Millie, a few days ago if she thought me asking you out was a good idea, and she said that although you'd say no, that I shouldn't take anything but yes for an answer.'

Kitty smiled and shook her head, imagining the kind of smirk plastered all over Millie's face.

Stevie lowered his head and caught her gaze. 'So, Kitty Twist. I'll meet you at Leicester's Lounge tonight. You know the place, that bar at the end of Victoria street?' She gave the faintest of acknowledgements. 'Perfect. Seven o'clock.' Stevie caught Kitty off-guard and kissed her on the cheek before strolling off into the distance. He turned around once, the pair exchanging mutual, child-like grins.

Upon arrival at Leicester's Lounge that evening, Stevie

waited with impatience for his date to arrive. 'Hi,' he said with a welcoming smile upon witnessing Kitty strolling towards him. 'I'm so glad that you decided to come,' he added, wrapping his arms around her to offer a prolonged embrace. 'The thought did run through my mind that I might end up spending the night in my own company.'

Kitty allowed herself to relish the delicious embrace, an initial closeness she couldn't recall ever experiencing with former partners. 'Well, there wasn't much on telly tonight so I thought why not,' she replied once their bodies parted. Before she became lost in the depths of Stevie's sapphire eyes, she diverted her gaze.

'I remember one of our previous conversations about how you used to be a textiles teacher, so I thought this was more appropriate than a bunch of fresh flowers,' he commented, pulling from his pocket a hand-stitched corsage. 'Not that guys even do this sort of stuff anymore, but I guess I'm different.'

Kitty held out her hand. 'It's lovely, thank you so much,' she replied, her face aglow whilst she admired the flower. 'Crafted by yourself?'

Stevie shook his head and laughed. 'No, I'm afraid not,' he explained, grabbing the door handle so that Kitty wouldn't spot the barrage of nerves shaking through his hands. 'Shall we head inside?' He held the door ajar, admiring Kitty's floral choice of clothes the moment she brushed past him - a dress that buttoned the length of her body, the material nipped in at the waist by a delicate, beaded belt.

'Let's sit over there,' he suggested once inside. 'There's a secluded snug over in the far corner,' he added, pointing to a quaint booth illuminated by dripping candles and a dimmed, miniature table lamp.

'It's so nice here, I feel like I should have been before,' Kitty commented, admiring her surroundings and feeling at ease within minutes, her sprinkling of nerves dancing their way out of the door.

'Well, cheers. Here's to what I hope will be the first of many drinks shared in your company,' he toasted once the waitress had delivered their order, his smouldering eyes burning through any of Kitty's final layers of apprehension.

Their first date passed by in a whirl, hours of effortless conversation washed down by three or four rounds of punchy cocktails. The fancy, fluted glasses brimming with sweet-spiked alcohol helped Kitty to recall what it felt like to dip her feet back into the dating scene. She didn't pay attention to her everyday worries and she didn't think about what tomorrow would bring; the rest of the world became insignificant and she lived in the moment. Her smitten mind lost itself in Stevie's stream of effortless conversation, and by the end of the evening, she found herself relishing the moments that Stevie nudged himself closer.

'Shall we get going?' he asked, noting the emptiness of the surrounding tables.

'Sure,' she replied, though she could have stayed in the moment forever, basking in the aftermath of a spectacular first date. Whilst escorting her home, purposefully meandering the side streets of Perth just to extend their walk, Stevie took hold of Kitty's hand. 'I'll try and keep your fingers warm.'

Although she flinched at first, his gesture encouraged a seed to bloom within her heart, the first shoots of happiness to sprout since her personal tragedy. Once they arrived at her place - a rented semi-detached on the outskirts of town, only a few streets away from where she grew up - Stevie placed his arms at either side of her body, securing her against the wall. His infectious smile made her explode with giggles, his passionate kiss stealing her breath. 'Can I see you tomorrow? That's if I can wait that long,' he asked, brushing her hair behind her ears.

Kitty nodded. 'I'd like that.'

'Maybe I could take you for dinner. What do you think?'

Kitty beamed. Her balance felt unstable and her legs weakened. She lifted her head to make eye contact and placed her hand on his arm with a light touch. 'That sounds perfect.'

'Well, it's a date then, Miss Kitty Twist. I'll come and collect you tomorrow,' he concluded before walking away. Kitty snuck inside, revelling in a raft of emotions. She peered around, ready to share her excitement, only to recall her reality.

She took out her phone. 'He's amazing, Mills,' she boasted to Millie. 'I can't thank you enough for pushing us together,' she added, caving into the strong desire to share her happiness with the only other person in her life that mattered.

'You can thank me when you ask me to be your Maid of Honour,' Millie joked, revelling in the sound of happiness that had once again found its way back into her friend's life.

'He's asked me out again tomorrow.'

'Blimey, he is keen,' Millie replied. 'Just enjoy yourself, you deserve it.'

'Love you, see you tomorrow,' she replied, before hanging up. Kitty scrunched herself into the oversized cosy chair in the lounge and admired a photo of her mum, the one person she had once told everything. She thought about Delilah, wondering what her mum would have made of her date, and to her core, resented the illness that had taken her mum's life.

4

DELILAH TWIST HAD PASSED AWAY JUST FOUR MONTHS PRIOR to Kitty and Stevie meeting, and Kitty's heart continued to break with every memory of her mother that presented itself. The moment she opened her eyes each morning, Kitty told herself that the new day ahead would be better. Today would be the day that she wouldn't cry. Today would be the day that her heart would stop aching. Today would be the day that she could contemplate a future that didn't involve her mum. Today would be the day that she would tackle the grim task of sorting through her mum's belongings.

At the time of diagnosis, Kitty's dad, Ernest Twist, spent much of his time on the golf course in a desperate attempt to escape the reality of losing his wife to cancer. The news arrived one tranquil, autumnal day without warning, like a plane falling from the sky.

'Come and sit down, Kitty, I have something to tell you,' Delilah insisted one Friday morning, just as Kitty suggested baking some chocolate brownies to satisfy her afternoon sugar cravings. 'You know I went for my routine mammogram, don't you, a few weeks ago?' One sentence in, Kitty's heart seized. Her vocal cords became too twisted to speak and all she could do was nod. 'Well, I got called back to see the consultant, and yesterday he told me that I have cancer.' An immediate anger rushed over Kitty.

'You went to an appointment like that without me? How could you?' she replied, getting up and marching towards the lounge window. 'I should have been there with you. You shouldn't have kept this from me. I thought we shared everything?'

'I needed to hear the diagnosis alone, so that I could react however I needed to without worrying about upsetting you, or your dad,' defended Delilah, patting the seat. 'Please, come and sit down,' she encouraged. Kitty followed the request and took a tentative seat, scooping her mum's hands into her own as she did. She felt scared for the first time in her adult life, fighting back the tears she felt welling beneath her eyelids. She wanted to press rewind, or to pause time completely. She wanted to hold her mum's hand without feeling afraid. She wanted to be able to look into her mum's eyes without anticipating what pain or suffering may be waiting on the horizon.

'Tell me everything. What did they say?'

'The specialist cancer nurses told me that it's always best to be honest with loved ones and not skirt around the facts. And so that's what I'm going to do.'

'Oh, God, Mum. You're scaring me now.' A twisted sensation grappled with Kitty's stomach and lungs, stealing her breath.

'The cancer is what they call stage four. That means it has already spread to other parts of my body,' declared Delilah.

At this point in the conversation, Kitty urged her mum to continue in the hope that she might be able to end the sentence by saying something positive. But Delilah remained silent, taking hold of Kitty's hands and pressing them between hers. Her head lowered in a bid to shield her own fears, before she concluded her sentence. 'It's terminal.'

The words *stage four* and *terminal* rang through Kitty's ears like a piercing alarm that refused to silence, and her mum's devastated expression explained any immediate, unanswered questions that Kitty may have had. Kitty's head dropped and a trail of tears dripped off her face and onto her mum's delicate hands.

Delilah looked up, a warm beam radiating from her lips, her tone soothing. 'Do you remember what I told you as a child whenever a thunderstorm scared you?' Kitty nodded, the memory vivid in her mind. She pictured herself glued to the window as a child, looking beyond the dark clouds that intimidated and instead gazing with hope towards the horizon skyline, searching for rainbows.

'I would tell you not to be afraid of the storm and to focus all your energy on searching for things that made you feel happy, like a bright rainbow that shines through troubled times.' Kitty felt Delilah's hands shaking beneath her own, and looked up to find her mum looking back at her with pain in her eyes. 'I know that even now, on those days that are showery and sunny, we both still find ourselves searching for rainbows.' Delilah held her daughter's hand tight. 'The storms that tear through your life will still always pass, Kitty, just like they did when you were a child, and with or without me, there will be plenty more rainbows in your future.'

'How long do you have?' Kitty asked.

Delilah's skin bunched around her eyes and a pained stare emanated from her face. Her muscles jumped beneath her skin whilst her fingers played with her wedding ring. She recalled her own mental promise never to lie, or exaggerate. 'Weeks. Maybe a month, if I'm lucky,' she replied, an audible stress echoing through her voice. Kitty bottled up her breath, a pained jolt coursing through her body at the news. She flung her arms around her mum and secured her in a tight embrace, taking a moment to hide her anguish and replace her pained expression with something more hopeful.

'I love you, Mum,' she whimpered into Delilah's ear, 'And we'll get through this together. I'll be right here, by your side.'

In the aftermath of the diagnosis, Kitty refused to leave Delilah's side for more than a couple of hours. She quit her job as a textiles teacher, enabling her to savour every moment with her mum, which turned out to be just a few weeks.

'There's something I need to tell you,' Delilah began early one morning upon waking. She sensed her time approaching, her whole body ached and her mind struggled to remain lucid amid the barrage of numbing, end-of-life drugs. Her whisper caused Kitty to stir, her heavy head leaving an indentation where it had rested on the edge of her mum's bed as she'd slept, their hands pressed together all the while.

'What did you say, Mum? Do you need more painkillers?' she replied, her mind still lumbered with the fog of sleep. Sitting upright, she rubbed her eyes and glanced toward the clock to find it was still the middle of the night.

'I want you to know that you'll always be looked after financially.'

'Mum, I don't want to talk about money, it isn't important.'

'Yes, it is. Your dad and I have set up an account so that when you turn twenty-five, everything we ever wanted for you will be yours,' she began, adding as much clarity to her voice as she could muster. 'This house is paid for and is already in your name, so I don't want you worrying.'

'All I want is you, I don't want anything else,' she replied, shaking her head in protest.

Delilah remained still in her bed, blinking slowly as she tried to resist the embrace of sleep. 'There's something else, and I'm just sorry I haven't told you sooner, but I promised your dad I wouldn't.'

'Told me what?'

Delilah's eyes closed under the weight of her exhaustion.

'Mum? What is it?' she asked, wiping away a few loose strands of Delilah's fine, wispy hair. Kitty watched an unfamiliar expression cast dark shadows over her mum's face. 'Mum?'

Delilah forced her eyes to open, the menial task requiring strength her body could no longer produce. 'I want you to look in -' she began, before her sentence ceased. Her head tilted softly to the side and her breath became shallow.

'Mum, whatever it is, it can wait. I need you to rest and get some sleep. We can talk in a little while.' Kitty pulled up the covers and tucked her mum in, ensuring she felt warm, and comfortable. But Delilah felt her time in life expiring. She pulled at Kitty's hand until she moved closer, so that their faces were almost touching.

'You need to know something,' she whispered. 'I have wanted you to know for such a long time and I always intended on telling you, I promise.' She closed her eyes for a few seconds, gaining the strength to continue, a tear escaping from the corner of her eye. 'I have hated keeping this secret from you,' she added, her eyes parting just enough to admire Kitty's face. 'You and I never keep secrets, do we?' The strength of her voice tailed off at the end of her sentence, her lack of breath and energy sabotaging the volume of her words. 'And when you find out, I need you to remember how much I love you. I will always love you, Kitty.'

Kitty's throat constricted and a pained, watery gaze appeared in her eyes. 'Mum, what is it?' You can tell me anything, you know that. We're best friends and always will be, no matter what.' She wiped away her mum's tears, placing a gentle kiss on her clammy forehead.

A haunting grimace spread across Delilah's face, her inner turmoil combining with her intense physical pain. 'Look inside,' she mumbled, the pain preventing another word to be spoken. 'Look in…' she tried to speak again, but her eyes drifted closed, and her dry lips pressed themselves together against the pain.

'Mum, look in what?' she asked, propping her mum's face up with her palm. A moment passed in which Delilah's breath became ever more laboured, and Kitty realised her mum was gone forever.

'Dad!' she screamed. 'Dad.' After a few moments by her mum's side, Kitty rushed downstairs, searching for her dad. She barged into the lounge, only to find him unconscious in his chair. 'Dad,' she shouted again, crouching by his side and shaking his unresponsive body. She searched for a pulse, her trembling hands pulling loose the shirt collar around his neck, and yet the tips of her fingers were unable to detect the crucial sign of life. 'Dad, wake up,' she cried, struggling to ease his body onto the floor.

She scrambled across the room and grabbed his mobile, pressing the emergency icon before returning to his side. With the phone resting on the chair arm and on loud speaker, she remained on her knees by her dad's side, performing heart compressions and giving him the kiss of life. She could hear the call handler's voice on the other end of the phone, reassuring her that help was on the way, and yet it felt like a lifetime before the paramedics finally arrived. All the while, her weary arms continued to pound against her dad's chest, and her tears fell from her face upon witnessing his life slipping away. She screamed for help, and yet nobody heard her cries. She pressed her ear against her dad's lips, feeling for his breath, her dad's mouth feeling cold against her warm skin.

Upon hearing the approaching sirens, she ran to open the front door and then remained crouched on the floor whilst the ambulance crew took over, the shock of the situation stealing her ability to move. She watched the paramedics from afar with baited breath and knew from their expression alone, that her father had also been taken away from her.

5

AFTER THEIR INITIAL FIRST DATE, THE SECLUDED NOOK AT Leicester's barely lost its warmth, Stevie and Kitty spending many an evening snuggled up in what they considered to be their corner booth.

'Shall I stay the night?' Stevie asked one Friday night, a couple of weeks after they'd first met, their extended, goodnight kiss rolling into the night.

Upon opening her eyes the following morning, Kitty lay awake, watching Stevie sleep, and for the first time in months, the grief she had become so accustomed to carrying was no longer her first thought of the day.

'Good morning,' he smiled, reaching over to her side of the bed, delivering a kiss. 'How did you sleep?'

'Good,' she replied, finding herself suddenly shy. 'Can we just stay here forever?' she joked, relishing the happiness she felt tingling all over her body.

Stevie smiled and stroked her face. 'We certainly can. I'd stay here forever if you were by my side. Why don't you call Millie, say you're not going in today?'

'I was only joking. We can't stay in bed all day.'

'I don't want you working in that café when I know deep down, it's not the career you want,' he began. 'Didn't you say that Millie only offered you the job as an attempt to encourage you to get on with life, you know, after losing your parents? Well, you're doing that now, with me, aren't you?'

Kitty raised her eyebrows, her mind lost in thought. 'I'm not sure she'll be able to cope without me, and although you're right - it's not my forever job - it's really helped me because it's been forcing me to leave the house,' she replied, getting out of bed and reaching for her uniform.

'But you're happy now, aren't you? Here, with me,' he said, grabbing her hand and pulling her back onto the bed. 'You don't need a reason to leave the house anymore.'

'I know,' she reassured, taking hold of his hand. 'It's just a big step to give up my job when I don't have any plans.' She lowered her head and distracted herself by fidgeting with her apron tassels.

'It's a big step for me too, you know. I've pretty much abandoned my flat and my friends since I met you. But to me, it feels right,' he added, dejection in his body language.

Kitty adored the fact that once again, somebody cared so deeply for her. 'Give me five minutes, then I'll come and get back in bed,' she said, before grabbing her phone and making her way downstairs.

'What do you mean you're handing in your notice?' Millie questioned, the shock in her voice hard to disguise. 'Are you sure that's what you want? What are you going to do all day by yourself? I haven't seen you outside of work all week, it feels like you've abandoned me already for a man,' Millie joked, the underlying truth in her words getting caught in the emotional lump lodged in her throat.

Kitty shook her head. 'I'm not abandoning you, Millie. It's just I've got Mum and Dad's stuff to sort through and I've put it off for long enough,' she began. 'I'm scared to find out what she wanted to tell me, you know that, but I have to look through her things sooner or later, so now seems like a good time. I finally feel ready.' She paused, a sickening feeling returning whenever she thought about her mum's last words. 'I can also take some time to figure out if I want to go back into teaching,' she explained. 'And Stevie wants to spend some more time together. So why not?'

'But, what about your bills? What about maintaining some routine in your life? I thought that's what you wanted, what you needed?'

Kitty sighed in an all too familiar way. 'Thanks to Mum and Dad, I've got enough in the bank, and even if I don't like the reason that it's there, I may as well use some of it. It's what they would have wanted.' Kitty paused and admired one of her favourite photos of her mum that sat on the lounge windowsill. 'He makes me happy, Millie.' There was no reply.

'Anyway, I best let you go, I don't want you burning anything because of me. I love you, Millie,' Kitty said, before ending the call.

In the weeks that followed, Stevie worked to manipulate Kitty's life, stealing more of her freedom, until it worked out that she had very little time to herself when he wasn't at work. 'Hasn't this past month or so been amazing?' he asked, holding her face and kissing her forehead before he left for work one morning. He paused near the front door, taking hold of her hands. 'Don't go out today,' he requested before leaving for work. 'Then, when I get a minute, I can phone you here and we can have a chat without having to battle the awful reception,' he said, his gentle touch slipping underneath Kitty's shirt. He pressed his lips against hers whilst sliding his hand further up her torso.

'With a kiss like that, I'll do whatever you ask today,' she joked, her balance unstable after he released his embrace. 'I've still got things to sort up in the attic and if I stop popping to Millie's for a chat, I'll get it done much quicker.'

'I was going to do this tonight,' he continued, pausing his words in order to take a breath. 'But now seems like the perfect time.' He lowered his hand into his pocket, taking out a tiny, royal blue jewellery box, before bending down on one knee. 'Kitty Twist, I will promise to love you forever and take care of you forever,' he began to declare, 'if you will do me the honour of marrying me.' Kitty hid her face in her palms, her features flushing with various shades of pink.

'Yes, I will marry you,' she beamed. Stevie placed the ring on her finger before scooping her into his arms and swinging her round in an extended moment of celebration. Beneath the glow of a late April sunshine, Kitty stood and admired the understated nature of the precious gem now decorating her finger, knowing that she would have chosen the exact same style.

'I can't believe it. Just wait until I show Millie,' she declared. 'She'll never believe that we're engaged. I might pop over and show her whilst you're at work.'

Stevie placed his hands on Kitty's face. 'Let's wait a while before we tell the world. Let it be our secret, just for now. And I'd like you to be at home, remember, for when I call you from work during the daytimes.'

Through a physical display of displeasure, Kitty's shoulders slumped into her body, her face mauled by frown lines. 'You want me to stay home every day?'

Stevie moved away and plunged his hands into his pockets. 'Is that a problem?' he asked, his inner anger seeping into the extremities of his fingers.

Kitty wrapped her arms around him. 'I just can't wait too long to tell Millie, she and I don't have secrets. And anyway, I'll get bored staying in all day every day.'

'The house is always a mess, so that'll keep you busy for most of the time,' he said. Kitty looked around the pristine room, knowing that since he'd been staying over, every room in her home had been kept obsessively tidy.

'I best get going, Mrs Best-to-be. I'll call you later on,' he said, wrapping his arms around her body and landing a kiss on her nose. 'I'm going to get used to calling you that.'

Kitty watched Stevie's car pulling away and listened as the sound of his engine tore down the road. She ignored his request and instead grabbed her coat and bag, heading out of the door and slamming it behind her.

'Blimey, and what do I owe this pleasure?' Millie asked the

moment Kitty walked into the café.

'I just thought I'd stop by and say hello. I know you think I've abandoned you since meeting Stevie, so I just wanted to see you and check that you're alright.' Kitty walked up to the till and rested her body against the counter.

Millie smiled. 'Well, you have abandoned me but I'll forgive you, that's what best friends do,' she explained. 'And you do seem so happy, how could I be cross at that?'

'I am happy, more than I've ever been,' she replied, holding her left hand so that the ring became visible. 'Do you notice anything?'

Millie couldn't hide the shocked expression that appeared on her face the moment she caught sight of the engagement ring, her words failing her. 'You're engaged, already? You barely know him,' she finally announced. Millie remained behind the counter, turning her face away, and continued to fill the coffee machines.

'I know that he makes me happy. I know that I love him, and that he loves me. Isn't that all there is to know?' Kitty lowered her hand, feeling her excitement draining.

'Your mum would never have approved.'

'Is that what you're going to say every time I make a decision that you don't agree with?' Millie ignored the reply, shaking her head with disappointment.

'Don't you have anything positive to say?'

Millie turned to face her friend. 'I've got a busy day ahead. We're a staff member down since you left, so I best get on.' At that point Millie walked through to the back kitchen, and waited until she heard the café door shutting.

Kitty walked away and headed into town, spending a few hours shopping by herself before returning home, noting Stevie's car parked outside the house.

'Oh, hi. You're early,' she said as she opened the door, her face ruby from the bitter wind whipping through the streets. She spotted three pairs of Stevie's shoes aligned by the front door, two additional coats hanging from the rack, plus three of his empty sports bags in the hallway. Kitty made her way down the hall towards the kitchen doorway, noting the way his body leaned against the frame. 'I went to do a little retail therapy,' she explained, holding out her shopping bags and craning her neck to give him a kiss.

Stevie arched his head backwards. 'I called to have my chat with you, but you weren't home,' he snapped. 'You decided to leave the house, even though I asked you not to. Where exactly have you been?' he asked, failing to make eye contact. 'I thought I told you to stay at home?'

'I just nipped into town. I wanted to see Millie, but turns out she was too busy to chat,' she commented in a light-hearted manner, shielding her sadness. 'Moving in, are we?' she asked, pointing towards his raft of personal belongings littering the hallway, before pushing past him to enter the kitchen.

Stevie turned slowly towards her. 'I told you not to leave and you went and did it anyway.' He paced towards her, a flash of anger in his eyes.

'I wasn't gone for very long. I had my mobile with me if you were worried. I wanted to ring you, but I didn't want to disturb your afternoon meetings, so I messaged you instead. Did you not get it?'

Stevie's nostrils widened, his teeth grinding with purpose in the back of his mouth. He grabbed Kitty's hand, snatching her keys and mobile, then in a deeper tone spat, 'If I say don't do something, then I mean don't do it.' He smashed her phone against the floor. 'You won't be needing this,' he said as the screen crunched under the heel of his shoe. Kitty flinched, his anger urging her to step backwards until her back rested against the wall. She watched his body draw closer, his arms pinning her at either side of her body. The outburst was so out of character for him that she expected him to break out into rumbles of bottomless laughter at any minute, his irrational reaction all part of an ill-conceived joke.

'You're all mine now, Kitty Twist, and I won't share you with anybody,' he stated, smothering her with a kiss so deep she felt suffocated. 'And don't think that you can leave, because I'll always find you,' he whispered steadily into her ear. He pressed her cheeks together with his hands and looked deep into her eyes.

Kitty remained trapped against the wall. She watched the intensity of Stevie's anger flood into his face, snake-like trails of red blood infusing the whites of his eyes. His dimples vanished, his rage swallowing all traces of his former self. She spotted, for the first time, a dark, malicious glaze tarnishing his eyes. His upper body remained rigid whilst his foot kicked the wall.

'Get out of my sight, Kitty, before I do something I'll really regret,' he insisted, thrashing his hands through the air in frustration.

Kitty spent the night alone in the bedroom, listening from behind the door, hoping that Stevie wouldn't follow her upstairs, preferring her own company. The sight of all his belongings made her feel sick, and so she fell asleep, hoping to wake up in the morning and put the incident behind her.

'Doesn't it look much better like this?' Stevie asked the following morning when Kitty crept downstairs. She stood in the hallway, frozen, as a sense of dread crept up her spine and she felt her bones shudder. Whilst her feet remained nailed to the floor, a pained, slack expression painted itself across her features. Her hair fell across her face, forming a curtain across her reddened eyes. 'What have you done?' she asked, the moment she walked into the lounge.

'Just tidied things up a bit,' he replied.

Kitty absorbed each alteration, noting how all her belongings had been moved, the tranquillity of her home destroyed. 'Where's the photo of me and Mum?' she questioned, a sinking feeling further dislodging her composure.

'It's over there,' he replied, pointing to a secluded part of the room. The photograph captured the moment she and her mum had both worn white tutus to perform ballet poses in the garden one summer afternoon – one of her favourite childhood memories.

Kitty turned to face Stevie. 'I can't really see the photos of mum when they're like this,' she said. Her eyes then spotted the jug of daffodils that had been resting on a side table, all the delicate petals had been deliberately scattered and torn, creating a patch of yellow to appear on the floor.

'But I'm living here as well now, so shouldn't it feel like home to both of us?' he asked. 'I haven't touched all your rubbish in the attic, it's a bloody disgrace up there.'

Kitty jumped on the statement. 'It's not rubbish,' she felt quick to defend, hurt at the accusation made against her parents' belongings. She paced through to the kitchen, wanting to hide her visible upset, only to be greeted by more changes. Her hotchpotch rack of spices now rearranged so that each label faced forwards, no more than three jars sitting together.

'It's a bit organised for me, I don't think I'll be able to keep it like this,' Kitty laughed, running her hand across the spices, purposefully throwing off the injected symmetry.

Stevie's pupils dilated, his tone of voice lowering to a level she had yet to experience. 'You will keep it like this,' he replied, his hands repositioning the jars. 'I know you will.' He took hold of Kitty's hand, pulling it close to his lips, his fingers squeezing her delicate bones with an uncomfortable force. An evil look spiralled in his eyes, and Kitty closed her eyes, shutting him out.

'Open your eyes,' he demanded, taking hold of her face. 'You don't want to know what I'm capable of if you ever do something like that again,' he threatened, squeezing together her cheeks until the soft inner skin pressed with an uncomfortable force against her teeth. With a slow reluctance, Kitty opened her eyes and witnessed first-hand the dramatic end of her romantic dream. 'Do you understand? Nod your head if you do,' he demanded, retaining a firm grip of her face. Kitty produced a meek nod and tried to mask the fear she felt in the pit of her stomach, but the only emotion conveyed by her face was sadness.

'Next time, I won't be so understanding,' he threatened, tossing her face to one side, his fingertips leaving spots of white where they had pressed so forcefully into her cheeks. He turned and walked out of the room, pausing in the doorway. 'Don't do it again,' he threatened, staring at her blotchy face. He opened the front door and then left, slamming it behind him.

Kitty ran down the hallway and began a desperate search for her mobile. She spotted the phone on a side table, and found she was unable to even turn it on after Stevie had smashed it the previous day. She peered out of the lounge window from behind the curtain, a sickening feeling overwhelming her stomach. She walked towards the front door ready to leave, and yet her hand froze on the handle, Stevie's threats causing her to become trapped inside her own home.

6

THE OUTSIDE WORLD EMBRACED STEVIE BEST, VIEWING HIM AS a good guy; the perfect bachelor. He melted with charm in social settings, presented himself as a caring neighbour and, over the years, had perfected the role of an astute solicitor. The only people that knew a dark side to his character existed were his parents, Celia and Sidney.

'Mum, are you home?' shouted Stevie upon letting himself in to his parents' house, calling in unannounced on his way home from work. Before wandering through to the lounge to see his mum, he quickly called Kitty to let her know that he would be late home, and to tell her to delay tea by half an hour. When she failed to answer the house phone, he left a voice message on the machine.

'Mum?' he called out again, the house remaining eerily silent. Stevie meandered from room to room. When a reply failed to come, he made his way up the stairs and reached the bathroom, pushing the door ajar.

'Bloody hell. Mum, what are you doing?' he shouted, finding Celia slumped on the floor, her hands bleeding after cutting herself with a pair of kitchen scissors.

'I just want it to stop,' she cried, shaking her head. 'I want the voices in my mind to stop.'

Stevie helped his mum off the floor and sat her on the edge of the bath. 'Are you okay? Where are you hurt?' he asked, examining the few surface wounds scattering her left hand. 'Promise me, Mum, that you won't do this again,' he begged, wrapping her hand in bandages, just like he had done on many occasions in the past. 'We've talked about this before, haven't we? You need to try and ignore the voices.'

'I'm exhausted,' she cried, peering at her hands. 'I don't want to obsess about things all day, really I don't. And my silly behaviour makes your dad so angry, you know that. But I can't help it. My mind just doesn't switch off,' she explained. 'It's so hard to ignore.'

'Thank goodness I decided to pop over. You just need to call me when you start to feel like this, and I'll come straight over.' Stevie kissed his mum on the forehead, knowing that his words didn't have the power to silence her inner demons.

'I don't like disturbing you at work, you know that. You've worked so hard to get to where you are now, and I'm not about to spoil that for you,' Celia cried, watching the blood seep through the cotton bandages. 'Your dad doesn't understand, and he doesn't listen, no matter how many times I try to talk to him about it,' she explained, looking up at Stevie. 'But I know you understand, you know that it just makes me feel better when everything is in the right place.'

Stevie loved his mum, adored her, but deep down, he also resented the fact that he had learned all of his traits through watching her, his obsessive behaviour now mirroring that of his mother's.

'I'm going to nip out and get some more bandages. Stay here and don't move until I get back, okay?'

Celia nodded, watching her son disappear from the room. The front door closed with a loud thud shortly after.

Stevie grabbed his phone the moment he got in the car. Whilst driving, he rang Kitty again, leaving another message and lying about where he was, stating that the last meeting of his day had overrun. Embarrassed about his family, Stevie had always maintained that he had little contact with his parents, citing that they had never really got along very well, and that he chose to move up to Scotland to further his career, leaving his family behind in Nottingham, where he had grown up as a child.

Still waiting in the bathroom, Celia heard the front door open, and assumed Stevie had returned. 'That was quick,' she shouted.

'What's this?' Sidney Best raged within seconds of stepping through the door, noticing that his house, once again, had been meticulously arranged despite his specific instructions to the contrary. 'She's lost her mind,' he ranted to himself downstairs, running his hand across everything that his wife had taken hours to perfect. He refused to tolerate her obsessive behaviour. With bulging, wide eyes, he scanned the next room. His rage bubbled upon sight of the three photo frames on the windowsill, the three strategically placed coasters on the table, the three cushions on the sofa and the three wicker hearts hanging on the wall. When he had left for work that morning, his house looked like anyone else's, a little haphazard but tidy. He stormed up the stairs.

'Where are you?' he shouted, the anger in his voice impossible to hide.

'Please don't hurt me,' Celia cried, watching her husband pace towards her, a look of fright evident in her glossy eyes. She backed herself into a corner and covered her head with her arms, unwilling to plead with the man she now despised, yet couldn't leave.

'Please, Sid, don't hurt me,' she whimpered.

'You're crazy,' he spat, kicking Celia in the stomach, his rage taking over. 'Gone in the head, you are. You've lost your bloody marbles,' he added, thrashing his anger over his wife's face, unaware that Stevie had entered through the open front door, bandages in hand.

'They lock people like you up.' Sidney bent down on his knees, staring at his wife straight in the eyes. 'This will stop, do you hear me?' he hissed, ending the beating by thrashing Celia's face with the back of his hand, his gold ring branding itself onto his wife's skin. He stood upright, towering over her and shaking his head.

Downstairs, Stevie could smell Sidney's aftershave, and then came the sound of his dad's raised voice. He bolted up the stairs, reaching the landing in only five strides, unaware that in his pocket, his phone had accidentally made a call to Kitty.

'Hello?' she answered on the other end, knowing it would be Stevie, as he was the only person who ever called her on the landline phone. She heard shouting in the background, and muffled noises, like someone was fighting. 'Stevie, is that you?' she asked when nobody replied. The shouting became louder, and she could hear Stevie's voice as he swore. Her hand began to shake, and she placed the phone in the cradle, putting the call on loudspeaker, and then backed away, listening as an invisible spectator to the argument unfolding on the other end of the line. Tears welled in her eyes, the sound of her fiancé's voice instilling fear into every one of her nerves. Her frame slid down the wall, her legs unable to support her weight.

Back at Stevie's parents' house, all parties remained unaware that they were being listened to.

'Get off her, you bastard!' Stevie shouted, leaping to his mum's defence and punching his dad on the side of the face, causing Sidney's body to crash to the floor. 'Mum, are you okay?' he asked, helping her to her feet and escorting her out of the room, leaving his dad squirming on the floor.

'Tell me you're okay,' he said, entering his parents' bedroom and sitting Celia on the bed, cupping her face with his hands. 'You've been lying to me, haven't you? You said that he doesn't do this anymore. But he never stopped, did he?'

Celia closed her eyes. Stevie guided her head towards his body, kissing the top of her hair whilst she rested on his chest. Flashbacks from his childhood surged through his mind, painful experiences he'd tried so hard to forget. As a child, Stevie had witnessed first-hand some of the abuse taking place in the family home, all because of his mum's deep-rooted desire to keep things in a certain place.

'Please don't hurt me,' Celia had cried that day, watching her husband charge towards her upon witnessing the ordered nature of the kitchen cupboards. Peeking out from behind the sofa, eleven-year-old Stevie had watched the terrifying scene unfold, soiling his trousers in the process.

'Please, Sidney, don't hurt me,' he heard his mum whimper.

'There's something wrong with you,' Sidney had spat, kicking Celia until her limbs became weak. 'You're an embarrassment to this family,' he'd added, striking his hand against his wife's face.

Stevie had shouted out, leaping to his mum's defence. 'Dad, stop, you're hurting her!' he had pleaded, grabbing hold of his dad's arm before being cast aside. He scrunched himself on the floor next to his mum when his dad's foot continued to strike, the force now walloping them both, knocking the wind from his lungs and producing bloody gashes and bruises on his face. 'It's alright, Mum, I won't leave you.'

Over a decade had passed since that first beating, and yet little had changed. Stevie moved his mum's face away so that he could look her in the eye. 'Mum, my flat is empty. I'm not staying there at the moment, so why don't you move in? Leave Dad, whilst you still can.' Celia pulled her face away, looking up at her son.

'I love him, Stevie, and deep down, I know he loves me too.' Celia wrapped her arms around her son. 'He's not usually like this, honestly, he isn't. And I'm going to stop all this silliness, I promise I am. So, please don't worry about me, I'll be fine,' she whispered into his ear.

'Then promise me something. If he ever lays another finger on you, you will call me, straight away.' Stevie maintained eye contact, unwilling to let his mum avoid agreeing to his request. Celia nodded, despite knowing that she would never pick up the phone.

'Please don't hate him. He loves you, Stevie, I know he does. He just has a hard time showing it,' she replied, holding her son's hands in hers. Stevie held his mum tight, wrapping his arms around her slight frame. 'I don't care how he feels about me. I only care how he treats you. You're my mum, and I won't let him hurt you.'

Celia listened for Sidney, peering towards the door. 'You've shown him how you feel, I think he'll have got the message.'

Stevie glanced down at his watch. 'I need to get going. Are you sure you're going to be alright?'

Celia nodded, and produced the most convincing smile she could muster.

'Give me a call later on.' Stevie kissed her again and walked out of the bedroom and back through to the bathroom, finding his dad assessing his wounds in the mirror.

'You bastard, I knew you were still beating her,' he began, closing the door behind him. 'Don't ever hit her again,' he threatened, grabbing hold of his dad's arm and wrenching it behind his back. 'Otherwise, I'll snap this off. Do you understand?' Sidney's face grimaced under the strain, Stevie continuing to pull until his dad nodded in agreement. 'I'll be watching you,' he concluded, before walking out the door.

Outside, Stevie got back into his car, taking his phone out of his pocket and witnessing for the first time that he had accidentally called the landline at home, the call still showing as connected. 'Are you there, Kitty?' he asked. When no reply came, he terminated the call and sped off down the street. Still upset after seeing how frightened and distraught his mum was, deep down, Stevie acknowledged that he never wanted his fiancé to feel the same way. Like he had done so many times previously, he vowed to have more patience, knowing that he loved Kitty, and that she had once loved him. He told himself that never again would he get as angry as his dad had, or lash out without thinking.

Back on Pembroke Road, Kitty remained crouched on the floor. She now knew that her fiancé was lying to her, leading some sort of double life that she remained unaware of, making her fear him more than ever before. The sound of a car pulling up outside made her body flinch, and her eyes darted towards the front of the house. In an all too familiar way, the garden gate creaked, making

Kitty dash into the kitchen. As the sound of footsteps travelled up the garden path, Kitty made an effort to busy herself and act like nothing had happened.

'I'm home,' Stevie announced upon opening the front door. He spotted the fresh vase of daffodils sat on the hallway table, and felt immediate anger and jealousy, the promise he had made to himself already threatening to be broken. It wasn't that he hated daffodils, he just hated what they represented to Kitty – a reminder of her mum and the wonderful relationship that she had shared with both of her parents, something that he had never experienced. With his anger mounting, he convinced himself that he was nothing like his dad, and that his relationship with Kitty was totally different to that of his parents.

He looked at the phone, noticing that there were no new message notifications. His footsteps fell loud and heavy as he paced down the hallway. 'I rang you earlier, twice actually. Why didn't you answer the phone? Where were you?' he quizzed, lingering in the kitchen doorway and trapping Kitty inside.

'I was upstairs cleaning and had the radio on, sorry.'

Stevie digested her excuse. 'Well, maybe you shouldn't have it so loud. Did you get my messages?'

Kitty maintained her composure. 'Yes, I saw them when I came downstairs to get tea ready, so I delayed putting it in the oven.' She prayed the line of questioning would stop there, not confident that her composure would withstand a barrage of questions about what she may or may not have overheard only a handful of moments ago.

'Did you receive any other calls today?' he asked, checking his phone to see how long his accidental call had been connected.

'Just yours at lunchtime, that's it.'

Stevie knew that she was lying. He walked over to where she was standing, and wrapped his arms around her body, kissing the back of her exposed neck. 'I'm sorry I'm late home from the office. I'll make it up to you,' he whispered into her ear, trying his best to suppress his anger and jealousy. His arms secured with an uncomfortable tightness, and he used all of his strength to restrain himself from shaking the truth out of her, or thrashing her for even daring to lie to him. For once, he chose to bide his time before confronting Kitty, his mind too distracted with thoughts of his mum.

Kitty looked down at his arms as they met at the front of her body, her eyes spotting the fresh patches of blood splattered on his shirt sleeve. She closed her eyes and pretended she hadn't seen it.

'Why don't you go upstairs and change whilst I get tea out?' she suggested, wriggling free and tending to the food. 'You don't want it to go cold.'

'Good idea,' he agreed, before leaving the room and walking up stairs.

The moment Stevie disappeared, she placed her hands over her face, trying to calm her fraught nerves. She wondered how much more she could take, and prayed for a miracle to come along and save her life.

7

From her attic window, Kitty admired the view from across the rooftops. She gazed at the park, where a collection of kites mottled the sky with more vibrancy than a kaleidoscope of tropical butterflies. Like she had done every day for the previous eight months, Kitty pictured in her mind grabbing hold of one of the kite strings, allowing her body to swirl through the sky before landing in someone else's shoes, someone else's life. She dreamt of being a child again, casting her memory back to the happiest period in her past. She transported herself back to the Twist family home, specifically to the many sunny afternoons spent in the garden with her mum, both of them dressed in their matching ballet outfits, twirling like they had been performing lead parts in the Royal Ballet. She could feel the warmth of those summers gone by on her face, and the way her mum's hand felt when pressed against hers, comforting and safe. But as soon as she opened her eyes, the memories faded.

Wishing she could continue with her daydreaming forever, she dragged her sight away from the window, pulling it back into her own secret world. Her line of vision landed on her arms, the sunlight accentuating the assortment of bruises dotting her exposed skin. With the argument still fresh in her mind that she had overheard between Stevie and his dad, Kitty tore herself away from the window with listless limbs, and tried to think of a way out. She crouched on the floor with her arms outstretched, imitating the act of preparing to pray, and thought about leaving the house, like she imagined every day, but Stevie's constant threats nailed her to the floor.

Alone in the attic - her secret refuge whilst Stevie worked at the office - Kitty once again searched through the remaining boxes belonging to her mum, seeking comfort, and closure. The dimly-lit, dusty attic was the only space that Stevie refused to alter, the thick layers of dirt coating every surface working to keep him at bay. Kitty sat in the middle of the floor with boxes surrounding her, and with a gentle touch, took out each item, recalling the attached memory. She searched through her mum's old purses and looked in every zip compartment of her handbags, already familiar with the contents. Digging through a pile of old books, she picked out her mum's well-thumbed copy of *Anne of Green Gables* and thumbed through the pages, spotting an envelope tucked into the spine. Her heart pounded, tingles alighted her skin and she became woozy. Her eyes blinked out of sync and her fumbling hands took hold of the envelope, seeing that it had been addressed to her mum. Kitty pressed the envelope against her chest, her hopes skipping. She took a deep breath and attempted to regain her sudden sense of breathlessness. Her fingers eased out the letter, and she held the delicate paper between her fingertips, fearful of damaging it. Her heart welled with emotion, and heavy tears made the words difficult to read. She wiped her cheeks with her shoulder and steadied her shuddering hands.

After digesting the contents of the letter - twice - Kitty put it in her pocket and dashed downstairs. She hastily grabbed her keys and some loose change, before diving out of the door onto the street. Breaking into a run, her legs carried her down the road with the speed of an escaped prisoner. Shocked with herself after making such a sudden attempt at freedom, she checked over her shoulder and was elated to find no one in pursuit. Spurred on by the fresh air in her lungs and the sensation of the pavement pounding beneath her feet, she reached the end of the road and hid herself away in the shabby public phone box, gasping in the stale air to catch her breath. Shaking, she fumbled with the coins, stuffing them into the slot, and took out the letter, punching in the phone number.

After three rings, someone answered.

'Hello, Mel speaking. How can I help?'

'Hi. My name is Kitty and I'm calling about a business that was for sale about a year ago. Flourish, in St. Ives,' she spluttered in one breath.

'Erm, yes, I remember, it was myself that dealt with the listing, but the sale fell through.'

'I know,' Kitty interrupted. 'I think my parents were the ones who were attempting to purchase, but they passed away not long after. Their names were Delilah and Ernest Twist.' Kitty fought to control her emotions. 'I know this is a long shot, but would you be able to call the owner and check if the business is still for sale, or at the very least, pass on my number? I'd very much like to speak with the seller, if at all possible.'

'I haven't heard from the seller since, and the business failed to be relisted, so I assume it's no longer on the market, but I will make a call for you, if that's what you'd like.'

'I would. That's great, thank you so much. I don't have a mobile or easy access to email. So, please could I call you back in a few minutes and see if you've had any luck?'

The faint, muffled sounds of a sigh could be heard on the other end of the phone, followed by a long pause. 'Give me ten minutes, then call back,' confirmed Mel, before ending the call.

Kitty took a glance at her wrist, encouraging the seconds to pass at a greater speed. She peered up the road, begging not to see Stevie's car, dimples of sweat scattering her forehead. Inside her mouth, her teeth clenched to create a hard jawline. Her neck and shoulders stiffened, and she teetered on unsteady feet. A headache pounded at her skull and her breathing grew heavy. After a ten-minute wait, she picked up the receiver and once again punched in the digits.

'Hi, it's Kitty Twist.'

'Hi Kitty, it was myself you spoke to.' There was an extended pause. Kitty could hear the sound of voices in the background. 'I actually managed to get hold of the owner and, as it happens, she would still be interested in selling. It appears that today is your lucky day.'

Kitty closed her eyes and tilted her head upwards, taking a moment to admire the brightness of the sky.

'I can arrange a viewing. When would be the most convenient time for yourself? The sale does come with a flat on the same street, I'm not sure if that was detailed in the original documents you have from your parents.'

'I won't need a viewing and I'd like to purchase the flat too,' Kitty replied without hesitation. Although she couldn't see Mel's reaction, she sensed it down the line.

'You want to buy a business and a flat without viewing them beforehand?'

'Crazy, I know. But yes, I do. I'm living in Perth, up in Scotland, so it's not easy to travel down. You can post me all the details so that I can go through everything, but if my parents wanted to buy the business and thought it a worthy investment, so do I.'

The conversation paused before Mel spoke. 'Okay then. I'll get the process started and send you some up-to-date information, and we can go from there. Does that sound alright?'

'That sounds wonderful, thank you so much.' Kitty provided Mel with her address before placing the phone in its cradle, noticing the state of her shaking hands. A smile spread across her face, a smile that no matter how hard he tried, Stevie would never erase. The sun edged its way across the sky, shining beams of warmth into the phone box which each came to rest on Kitty's face.

A bang on the phone box door caused her heart to leap into her mouth.

'Hi,' said Millie, pulling the door free with a puzzled expression on her face. 'Still not allowed a phone of your own, I see,' she added, shaking her head with exasperation when all she really wanted was to grab Kitty and deliver her a warm, protective hug. 'I'm surprised you're even allowed out without him. When was the last time we saw each other alone?' Kitty couldn't answer, knowing that since her engagement, she hadn't left the house by herself.

'I can see it in your eyes, Kitty. I know something isn't right. You're huddled in a phone box during the middle of the day looking petrified. This isn't normal.'

'Don't, Millie,' Kitty said in a pleading voice. 'He just doesn't like how people become so lost in their phones. You can't blame him for that.'

'You're right, I can't. But I can blame him for the fact that I never see you anymore. I can blame him for the fact I'm never allowed over to your place. I can blame him for the fact that you never come out anymore.' Millie wedged her foot into the gap between her friend and the cumbersome door. 'I blame myself, you do know that, don't you? This is all my fault. I encouraged you to meet up with him in the first place because I promised your mum I would make sure you were happy, and that I would always take care of you, like a sister. And I feel like I'm failing in my promise.' Millie lowered her head and supported herself against the side of the phone box. A pained expression washed over her face and her eyebrows knitted themselves together.

Kitty put her hand on Millie's shoulder. 'Please don't cry,' she began, loathing herself even more. 'I don't want to argue. I just need to get home,' she explained.

'See, this is exactly what I mean. This isn't normal, Kitty,' Millie replied, her hand gesticulating at Kitty's frightened appearance. 'Enough is enough. So what if he gets mad? What's he going to do? I promised your mum I'd look after you and yet I can't see you. I can't message you. I can't even talk to you,' she said, holding up a finger each time she rolled off another issue. 'It's not normal. This is not normal,' she added, pointing out each time Kitty cast a worrying glance up the street. 'What's going on, Kitty? I can help. If he's acting like a bastard, then tell him to leave. Finish the relationship and give him the ring back. Or come and stay at mine and if he pesters you, then I'll tell the bastard to leave you alone, no problem.' Millie looked at the ground when Kitty failed to respond, her shoulders drooping with a heavy sense of hopelessness. She looked up with pleading eyes and exposed palms, 'Why won't you just leave him?'

Kitty didn't have an answer, so she turned her head away in avoidance. She'd asked herself the same question for more than six months, but like others in similar situations, leaving felt impossible. 'I love him,' she mustered. 'He's my fiancé.'

Millie took hold of her friend's hand, refusing to believe her words. 'Kitty, look at me. This isn't how love should feel,' she began. 'I'm worried about you. I never get to speak with you anymore. What am I meant to think? I feel like involving the police, I really do, but I don't want to make it worse for you.' Millie caught sight of some bruises peeking out from under Kitty's top, evoking an immediate stream of tears. 'Tell me he's not physically hurting you,' she cried. She pulled the door open wider, wanting to hold her friend tight and never let go. 'Come with me now. Leave him, Kitty, please, you have to leave him.' Millie stroked Kitty's face with her hand.

Kitty moved away, pulling her sleeve down. 'He's not hurting me. I'd leave if he was. I love Stevie and he loves me,' she reassured, plastering a fake smile across her face. 'And anyway, only yesterday I told him that I wanted a girly night out, just me and you, and he was fine with it,' she lied. 'So, we'll get a date sorted, maybe next month, and then we'll be able to celebrate your birthday too. We can have a proper chat, okay?' she begged, tilting her head and nodding.

Millie shrugged her shoulders. 'Okay. But there's one condition, and I mean it, Kitty. If we don't have a night out by this time next month, I'll be back,' Millie pointed her finger, partly in jest, partly serious. 'And then I'll be banging on your door and I won't care if he's in or not, I'll insist on you coming out with me. Alone.'

'That's a deal. Now, please go, otherwise you'll have a queue of customers snaking the pavement, and we can't have a cake crisis, can we?' Kitty looked at her watch, knowing that at any moment, Stevie would be home.

Millie flung her arms around Kitty and squeezed her tightly before dragging herself away. She stopped part way down the street and shouted back at the top of her lungs, 'I love you, Kitty.'

'I love you, Millie,' she shouted back, the moment her friend turned the corner. She looked at her watch before running back up the road, holding her breath every time a vehicle tore around the corner. No sooner had she closed the front door than the sound of Stevie's car became audible as he pulled up outside. Kitty's feet bounced up the stairs, two at a time, her mum's letter stashed beneath her top. She knew she had run out of time to tidy the house. She knew that things were out of place, but it was too late.

'I'm home,' he announced, walking in through the front door. He immediately spotted that the collection of shoes beneath the rack weren't straight. He paced down the hallway and into the kitchen, seeing that the three oven gloves weren't positioned on their hooks and that the tea, sugar and coffee pots weren't perfectly aligned. Like a struck match, his anger ignited. 'Kitty? Where are you?' He opened the fridge and saw that nothing had been placed correct. He slammed the door and walked through to the lounge, spotting the two haphazard cushions on the sofa, and noticing that the photos on the wall had been moved.

'Gosh, is that the time? I didn't realise it was so late,' Kitty replied whilst navigating the attic stairs. 'I've been sorting stuff out.'

Stevie made his way upstairs and paused on the landing. 'What's all this?' he interrupted, peering into the bathroom, the open door revealing Kitty's toothbrush left on the side of the sink, and his three bottles of aftershaves knocked out of line by her randomly placed can of deodorant.

'What's all what?' she asked, trying desperately to retain the lightness in her voice. She stepped onto the landing and turned to witness his furious face, his jaw tightening. His eyes narrowed and his fingers fidgeted by the side of his body before rolling themselves into a tight ball. A flashback to his childhood raged through his mind and he recalled the time that his dad callously thrashed through all his mum's hard work – like Kitty had done to his.

'How many times do I have to tell you about keeping things tidy? What part of that don't you understand?' he erupted, lashing his hand out and striking Kitty across the face. She fell to the floor and her body landed in the corner. Stevie swung his leg back and thrust it towards Kitty's body, allowing his foot to bury itself into her soft skin.

'I'm sorry,' she cried, shielding her stomach with her hands.

Through the bathroom door, which sat ajar, Stevie caught sight of his flushed facial features in the mirror, noting his bloodshot eyes. 'Don't do it again,' he concluded before stomping downstairs and slamming the lounge door shut.

Kitty dragged her beaten body into bed, her swollen lips and face too sore to attempt speaking. Her eyes settled with a comforting gaze on the single photo frame that rested on her bedside table. She admired a picture of her and Delilah whilst on holiday, mother and daughter sat on a beach with their legs buried beneath the sand. Their faces beamed with a natural, ingrained happiness, their hands clasped together and their giggles infectious. Desperate to escape the pain, Kitty closed her eyes tight and smiled as her mum's laugh filled her ears. Taking herself back to that summer day, she felt the warmth of the sun on her face, and her nostrils filled with the flowery scent of her mum's perfume.

Weeping silently into a blood-stained pillow, Kitty took solace in her planned disappearance from Perth, which she ran through meticulously in her mind. With access to the remaining inheritance set aside by her parents imminent, she allowed herself to feel excited at the prospect of life beyond her existence on Pembroke Road.

8

BEFORE SUNRISE, MANY OF THE BUSINESSES DOTTED AROUND the centre of St. Ives showed signs of activity; deliveries being accepted, ovens switched on in preparation for breakfast orders, and market stalls fully stocked ready for a busy day of trading. By contrast, the shop owners located on the side street of Ladysmith Lane embraced life at an alternative pace. The quaint street appeared abandoned until the sun appeared in the sky, and the faint hustle of tourists could be heard descending from their holiday houses, at which point, the shop doors opened ready to seduce the passing patrons.

'Have you heard the news?' asked Ruben whilst he opened up the shutters to Legumes, chatting to Agnes, who happened to arrive on the street at the same time.

Agnes searched in her oversized bag for her shop keys whilst juggling all the stuff cradled in her arms. 'I assume you're talking about Peggy, and that she's selling up again?' she replied, pulling out the keys from her dungaree pocket. 'It was only a matter of time, if you ask me. We knew that she wanted to sell the shop last year.' Struggling to carry all her stuff through the door without something toppling, Ruben offered a hand.

'Here, let me,' he said, taking the keys and opening the door to Agnes' jewellery shop. 'You seem okay about it, like it's no big deal,' added Ruben, shrugging his shoulders and slumping himself on a chair whilst peering across the street through a bewildered gaze. 'Just because we knew she wanted to sell, doesn't make the thought of it any easier. It just won't feel right without her across the road. She's the glue that holds this street together.'

Agnes put on some music and flipped the door sign to '*Open*'. 'We shouldn't rely on Peggy so much. And anyway, what can we do? We can't stop her from selling, and if she's not happy here anymore, if her heart isn't in it, then she's better off leaving and finding something that does bring happiness back into her life.' Ruben's extended sigh informed Agnes that he agreed, though he couldn't bring himself to admit it aloud.

Flourish had been Ladysmith Lane's pioneer shop, and although some businesses had changed hands over the decades, Flourish had always remained in the safe hands of Peggy Maltby. As the trusted confidant of everyone on the lane, Peggy epitomised the kind of adorable human being that people couldn't help but love. On the outside, she wore a warm smile as part of her daily attire, ready to offer comfort to friends and strangers. But, despite working closely with her for a number of years now, no one on the street was aware that hidden beneath her smile was a long-kept secret.

At the age of sixteen, and after one naïve night spent in the park with Aaron Wilding, Peggy learnt of her pregnancy. She kept the news to herself for as long as possible, hiding her growing bump. And only a matter of months after the news became public, Aaron moved away from Cornwall, unwilling to let the rest of his life be decided for him. For Peggy, despite knowing that the road ahead as a single, teen parent would be tough, she displayed an unwavering desire to keep her unborn baby. But her parents had disagreed.

'How can you be a mother when you're only a child yourself?' her father shouted each time Peggy spoke about becoming a mother. 'You wouldn't know where to start! And how will you support yourself? You don't even have a job. Your mother and I will be the ones lumbered with a bloody baby, and we just won't do it.'

'I can do it, Dad, I know I can,' she cried, placing her hands across her swollen abdomen. 'Just let me prove it to you. I'll make a wonderful mum, I know I will, and I'll provide my baby with all the things that it needs.'

Crisscrossing the room, her mother joined in. 'You don't have a job. You don't have any money. You're not married - you're not even in a relationship. You're just a child, Peggy,' her mum shouted. 'The baby will be better off with a family who can take proper care of it, and give it a better chance in life. You're too young to throw your whole life away, Peggy, and we won't let you do it, not if you want to remain here, living under this roof.'

During the sleeping hours of one chilly, Saturday night, Peggy Maltby pushed her way through the ordeal of a prolonged, difficult childbirth. Without the support of her parents, Peggy lay alone in the delivery room and held her new-born baby girl for a few precious minutes. She felt the warmth radiating from her tiny, premature bundle and drank in her baby's features, knowing that she would never see her daughter again. Peggy's arms naturally cradled her baby, the gentle vibration causing the girl's eyes to close. Her steady trail of tears fell onto the baby girl's face - the girl with no name. 'I love you,' she whispered, holding the child so close that their noses kissed. 'And I always will,' she added, before placing a soft kiss on her baby's cheek. 'And I'm sorry that I can't take you home with me where you belong, and I'm sorry that I didn't try harder to be your mummy,' she added, stroking the baby's face and inhaling her distinctive aroma. 'I'll never stop thinking about you, and I'll never stop being your mummy. I know that one day we'll be together again, and I just hope that you will have the ability to offer me the forgiveness I know I don't deserve.'

The adoption mediator knocked on the door and entered the room, ready to take Peggy's baby away. 'It's time,' said the man wearing the grey, pinstriped suit. His features became embedded into Peggy's memory, the same features that, twenty-something years later, still stalked her dreams like unwanted ghosts.

Peggy ignored the man and carried on gazing into her baby's eyes, as though nobody else in the world existed. 'They've come to take you away from me now, but please know that I didn't want this. The only thing I want in the whole world is to be your mummy.' The man paced towards the bed and reached out his arms, removing the baby from Peggy's embrace before turning to leave the room.

'Please don't take her away from me,' she broke down. 'Please, I'm begging you - don't take my baby.'

'She'll be well cared for, Peggy. Her new parents already love her so much and are ready to provide her with everything that she's going to need in life.' The moment the door slammed shut, Peggy dragged herself out of bed and lunged her weary body towards the door. Out in the corridor, she fell to the floor in a flood of tears. For years, decades, Peggy suffered in silence, trying to deal with the painful aftermath of an enforced adoption.

After marrying in her twenties and trying unsuccessfully for years to start a family of her own, Peggy diverted her focus and set up a business - Flourish. The haberdashery shop didn't compensate for her inability to have any more children, but it did offer Peggy a distraction, and a new purpose in life.

For the first couple of weeks after opening, nobody walked through the shop door, or even passed the window – tourists didn't know it existed because it remained tucked away down a side street off the beaten track. Day after day, Peggy sat behind the counter waiting for customers, and, after three long weeks, the footfall increased, albeit by a trickle. In a bid to spread the word about her quaint shop, Peggy offered her customers cups of tea to warm up their insides during the nippy, dreary days, or glasses of fresh lemonade to cool their brows on scorching afternoons. She took in homemade cakes and placed them on her countertop, offering a slice to anyone who walked through her door. And her plan worked. Before the year was out, there wasn't a day that went by where the shop wasn't brimming with customers.

Ruben dragged himself off Agnes' chair and made his way to the door. 'It's just not going to be the same on the street without her,' he explained, pressing on the handle.

'We just need to hope that whoever buys it will bring as much to the street as Peggy did. Big shoes to fill though,' replied Agnes, casting an admiring gaze over at Flourish, revelling in all the hours that she'd spent watching Peggy welcome the passing tourists of St. Ives. 'Anyway, there's no time to stand here gassing with you.'

'Bloody hell, you're right,' Ruben agreed, taking a look at his watch. 'I've got lunches to prepare and I can feel in my bones that it's going to be another busy one.'

'See you later, and bring me a brew round at eleven with a slice of that chocolate and beetroot cake, if you don't mind.'

The sky over Ladysmith Lane glistened, the sun providing a taster of the day's forecast. The smell of a new tourist season hung in the air, anticipation sweeping through the street. Ruben stood outside his café, listening to the background sound of the waves tumbling onto the shore. He could see the sun stretching above the horizon, creating a wonderful glow. 'I don't understand why anybody would want to leave here,' he muttered, the warmth of the morning sun landing on his face.

'Morning, Ruben! What did you say?' shouted Vera. Ruben raised his hand in acknowledgement, but instead of stopping to chat, continued to scurry inside his café.

'I can't stop, Vera, I need to get the ovens switched on and the cake mixers turning. It's going to be a busy one today, I can just sense it,' he shouted across. 'I'll bring a coffee over later for you and Alfred.'

With no transport access, both sides of Ladysmith Lane were lined with a handful of shops. Crook Antiques sat on one side at the far end, owned by Vera and Alfred Crook. By her own admission, Vera looked like a bit of an antique. Always wearing her trademark rainbow sock-and-odd-shoe combination, Vera embodied an oddball. Outside their shop, a fully-functioning gramophone played, offering a musical experience that either ensured patrons returned, or put them off ever wanting to hear a gramophone again.

Ruben's vegan café, Legumes, sat opposite to the antique shop. The boho-chic-style café offered scrumptious food that didn't come out of a packet, or off a conveyor belt. Whether it was a Sri Lankan braised roots stew with coconut dhal dumplings, a beetroot and red onion tarte, or a vegan lemon drizzle cake, Ruben's food always hit the mark with customers.

Next door to Legumes was Pebble & Sand – the jewellery shop owned by Agnes Mather. 'Are you taking requests today, Vera?' she asked, popping her head through a crack in her open shop door and watching as the gramophone took up its usual spot on the street.

'Anything for you,' Vera replied, the scratchy sounds of Arthur Collins soon drifting over the cobbles. Agnes wedged her door open, allowing the music to be carried in. 'Eh up, here she is, late as usual,' she mocked, spotting Susie rushing up the street. Susie Blue owned Past Times, a vintage boutique selling every fashion trend from the 1920s onwards.

Susie looked flustered. 'Hi, Agnes. I had a late one last night and couldn't get out of bed this morning,' she said, pushing her shop door open with her thigh.

'Bring me a coffee, Ruben, about eleven,' Susie added, already feeling the desperate need for caffeine.

The final shop in the quaint little cluster on Ladysmith Lane was Hair by Lily, a salon owned by eccentric trendsetter, Lily Owen. 'Morning, Ruben, my usual please. I'm flagging already so can you give me an extra shot?' requested Lily, pushing her way into Legumes. 'I'm feeling a bit tired today.'

Ruben smirked. 'You're not on your own. Blimey, it looks like you've got an eager one waiting already,' he signalled with his head to where a customer was trying to get into Lily's salon across the road. 'Going to be a busy one today!' He handed over the steaming double expresso. 'Hopefully this will help.'

'Oh, bloody hell. I best get going.'

'Heard anything from Peggy?' asked Ruben, just before Lily vanished.

She shook her head, looking over towards Flourish, the shop hanging in unusual darkness. 'Not since she told me she'd found a new buyer,' Lily squinted, 'I think there's a new sign in the window though,' she announced as her body was drawn across the road.

Ruben followed Lily, pausing outside Flourish. Vera, Agnes and Susie soon noticed the commotion and so they too followed. The gang of friends huddled around the front door to Peggy Maltby's shop. Lily read aloud the little hand-written sign.

'Under new management,' announced Lily. 'It's really happening.'

9

For the eighth consecutive hour, Kitty remained perched in the lounge window, just out of sight, conscious to keep herself hidden behind the curtain. From the moment Stevie had left for work that morning, she had taken to her position. She willed the postman to arrive and prayed that today would be the day that he delivered her letter, but at just gone 4 o'clock in the afternoon, her hopes had begun to diminish. Ignoring the ache now swelling in the base of her spine and neck, she continued to run through the details of her planned escape. Over the past few days, she had thought about little else. She felt like her life depended on the arrival of the letter, and every day that had passed since she had spoken with the property agent in Cornwall, Kitty prayed that her plan would work. She had continued to tolerate Stevie's foul behaviour, knowing in the back of her mind that she wouldn't have to suffer for too much longer. With a last look at the clock, she admitted defeat, and peered up to the top of the road, bracing herself for Stevie's return, when, at last, she spotted the postal worker walking casually around the corner.

Kitty jumped down from her perch and crouched behind the door, glaring at the clock in the hallway. She listened for the creaking gate as her heart pounded in her chest. After a tense wait, the gate creaked and she heard the sound of heavy footsteps approach. The letterbox opened to admit a large brown envelope, which fell to the floor, before the footsteps retreated and Kitty was alone once more with the echo of the ticking clock. She picked up the envelope, turning it over in her hands to see her name displayed on the front in block capitals. With quivering hands, she struggled to peel back the glued edge. Finally breaking the seal, she pulled free the contents, her blurred vision skimming the sea of words until landing on a phrase of emboldened text: *Sale complete.* Her eyes blinked at an unusual pace in an attempt to see past her tears, and she reviewed the words over and over, ensuring that she'd read them correctly. Allowing the news to take hold, she felt a warmth swell in her chest and allowed herself to enjoy this brief moment of happiness. Dropping her shoulders back, she pressed the letter close to her chest and took a deep breath.

Her momentary tranquillity was suddenly interrupted with the sound of a car engine dying out just outside the house, before the familiar clang of metal against brick came as the gate was forced open, and her sense of dread returned once more. Sprinting down the hallway towards the kitchen, her eyes darted around the room in a frantic search for a safe place to hide the letter. In her haste, she dropped the envelope and it slid beneath the kitchen table. She dropped to her knees and scrambled to reach out and grab hold of the letter at the exact moment that she heard the front gate slamming to a complete shut. Struggling to her feet, Kitty's eyes once again darted around the space, desperate to find somewhere to hide her letter. As the sound of Stevie's key turning in the lock of the front door echoed through the house, she resorted to stuffing the letter hastily into the breadbin, before hurriedly straightening out her hair and clothes in anticipation of her fiancé's arrival, making every effort to fend off the ocean of nerves threatening her composure. She busied herself in the kitchen, rushing to take the casserole out of the oven.

The front door slammed to a complete shut.

Stevie dropped his work satchel and coat with purpose. 'I'm starving,' he announced, upon entering the kitchen.

'Hi,' Kitty replied, keeping her back to the room whilst she continued to prepare the food. The moment she felt his arms wrapping around her waist, she resisted the urge to flinch, her whole body desperate to reject his attempt at physical contact. 'Good day at work?' she asked, moving away from his embrace so that she could butter some bread.

'Busy, busy, busy,' he replied, checking his phone before slipping it back into his trouser pocket. 'But I don't want to talk about my day, I want to know what you've been up to.' Stevie sat at the table, waiting to be served.

Kitty forced a smile upon her face and attempted to respond in a bright tone. 'Well, after you left this morning, I did the dishes and cleaned the house. I then carried on sorting the attic.' Kitty paused, she could feel Stevie's eyes watching, making sure that she ladled the hotpot into his dish without spilling any on the circumference of the white porcelain. 'I then started to get tea ready.' The script Kitty recited failed to alter day after day, the previous eight months all sounding the same.

'You surely must be getting close to finishing sorting through your parents' things,' he replied through a mouthful of succulent steak. 'How much rubbish did you store up there?' he added.

'All of it, a lifetime's worth of belongings. And it's not rubbish, it's all precious to me,' she replied, forcing some food down her throat, pretending to concentrate on her meal. Her twisted insides made her sickly whilst her anxiety destroyed her appetite, and she felt nothing but an emptiness in the pit of her stomach. Beneath the table, her knee bounced in time with her cantering heart, and she attempted to wipe away some of the moisture which was gathering in her palm on the leg of her trousers.

Stevie curled his lip and the skin over his knuckles tightened. 'It's a waste of time if you ask me. You should just get rid of it all, be done with it. It's not like they passed away yesterday. What can you possibly want with it all? I should just go up there and get rid of it for you.'

Kitty dropped her fork. She felt her words catch in her throat before she managed to respond. 'You don't need to do that. I've nearly finished. Soon it will all be gone.'

'I hope so, otherwise I will do it for you. We don't want to be taking a whole load of rubbish from your past and moving it into our new home once we're married. We'll want a fresh start, won't we?'

Kitty ignored his question, and instead yawned and rolled her neck. 'I didn't sleep very well last night so I think I'll get an early one tonight.'

Stevie cast a hard stare, watching his fiancée get up from the table and fumble with the dishes, his eyes burning into her back. He wiped his mouth and dropped his folk in his bowl. 'Maybe an early night would do you good,' he suggested, standing and positioning himself right up against her back, his warm breath skipping over her ear.

Kitty plunged her shaking hands into the sink, concealing her tremble beneath the bubbles. 'I think that's a good idea.'

He kissed her on the neck before asking, 'Is my bath ready?'

'Won't be long.'

'Fancy joining me? We could talk weddings.'

'Erm,' she stumbled, her composure wavering. 'I best get all these dishes sorted, but how about I join you tomorrow, when I'm not so tired. I'll make it extra deep for the both of us.'

'Your loss,' he replied, turning to leave the kitchen. Seconds later, the slam of the bathroom door resonated through the house, followed by a splashing noise the moment his body sunk into the steaming tub.

Like a dart, Kitty grabbed the letter from the breadbin and left the dirty dishes, rushing upstairs. She scampered into the bedroom, closing the door with care behind her. She fell to her knees next to their double bed and pulled free her bedside table. Reaching behind the narrow gap in the drawers, she pulled off the loose, flimsy backboard, revealing beneath a stash of papers. She took out her most recent letter and read those two emboldened words once more, before adding it to the collection. Her shaking fingers fumbled, flicking through each piece of correspondence. After spending a number of weeks going back and forth to the phone box and post office, she held in her hands the deeds to the new business and flat she now owned in St. Ives. All the solicitor letters, all her banking details, plus the estate agent correspondence, were bundled together with her passport, driving licence, birth certificate, and her parents' original letter about Flourish.

'Bring me a beer,' Stevie hollered from the bathroom, making her jump. She dropped all of the paperwork and quickly scrambled to gather everything together again and return it to the safety of the cavity in the back of the bedside table, failing to notice that two letters had fallen free.

'Okay, I won't be a minute,' she replied, her flustered voice echoing across the landing. Kitty dashed downstairs and grabbed a beer from the fridge, tripping over her feet as she darted back upstairs.

'What are you doing?' Stevie questioned, hearing her stumble.

Kitty creaked the bathroom door open. 'Here you are.'

'Are you okay? I thought I heard a banging noise?'

Kitty patted down her top. 'I dropped a mug whilst washing up, that's all.'

'Are you sure you don't want to have a soak? I could wash your back - it's been a while since I admired your tattoo.' Flashbacks blew through Kitty's mind and she remembered the incessant buzzing sound of the tattoo gun, the smell of the ink, the sickly-sweet scent of the aftershave worn by the tattoo artist. She remembered the stabbing sensation she had felt burning across her shoulder blades each time the needle had punctured her skin, and felt a swell of anger rising in her chest.

'I need to finish off getting your things ready for work, but tomorrow I'm all yours,' she said with a smile, masking her anger. She left the bathroom and gently closed the door behind her, shutting her eyes tightly as she willed the tears not to form behind her eyelids. Trying hard to compose herself, she was confronted with the realisation of what might await the following day should her plan fail, and she could no longer hold the tears back.

'I'll enjoy my lunch even more tomorrow knowing what will be waiting for me at home,' shouted Stevie, the sound of his beer bottle clattering against the ceramic bath echoing through the house.

Wiping her tears away, Kitty crept back into the bedroom, closing the door behind her. In a moment of panic, she noticed one of the stray pieces of paper that she had accidentally dropped on the floor. Through clouded vision and a scrambled brain, she grabbed hold of it and reached behind her drawers to try and place it with the others. She heard the sound of water draining and then the stomping of Stevie's feet landing on the bath mat. She stuffed the letter back behind the bedside table and pushed it against the wall.

'I knew you were up to something,' Stevie hissed, easing the bedroom door ajar with a stealthy hand. He paced into the room, his eyebrows pulling together the moment he caught Kitty scrunched on the floor. 'What are you doing?'

Kitty swung around to face him, catching a glimpse of white out of the corner of her eye, the other letter she had dropped. 'I was just looking for the back to one of my earrings, it's fallen off somewhere,' she replied, fiddling with her left ear. 'I'll just take it out, so I don't lose the stud. I'm sure I'll find it tomorrow whilst I'm cleaning.' Getting herself up off the floor, she discretely reached out to push the other stray piece of paper further beneath the bed. 'Shall I go and get you another beer ready?'

Stevie paced round to her side of the bed, his eyes scouring with a heightened sense of suspicion. 'I'll help you look for it.'

Kitty walked towards the bedroom door. 'Well I've searched everywhere in here, so I doubt you'll find it. I'll go and look in the lounge, I was lying on the sofa this afternoon because I was tired, so it's most likely fallen behind one of the cushions.' With her heart cradled in her palms, she walked out of the room and headed downstairs and into the kitchen. She held her breath and closed her eyes, pressing her back against the wall. She heard Stevie getting dressed, the drawers slamming shut, so she took out another beer in anticipation of his return.

'Is my beer ready?' Stevie bellowed, the bedroom door opening.

Kitty rushed to place it in the lounge for him, on his coaster next to the television control.

Stevie appeared in the lounge. 'The match is about to start,' he said, slumping himself in front of the television and switching on the football.

'Right, well I'm off to bed, so I'll let you enjoy it in peace,' she announced, placing a kiss on his cheek. He grabbed her face, pressing his lips against hers.

'I deserve more than a peck, don't I?' he said, threads of anger lining his words.

Kitty stepped closer and kissed him in a way she once loved, but now loathed. She tasted the beer in his mouth and felt suffocated by this forced, prolonged exchange.

She pulled herself away. 'Let's save this for our bath tomorrow,' she was quick to suggest, 'When I'm not so tired. An early night tonight will do me good.' She walked away and prayed that he'd let her go, the football her rescue.

'I love you, Kitty.'

Kitty forced out a reply whilst walking up the stairs, 'I love you more, Stevie Best.'

Kitty shut herself in the bathroom and locked the door. Her body collapsed with relief and it took every ounce of remaining energy to stop herself from falling to the floor. Behind the safety of the closed door, her fake smile vanished, and her hands trembled freely. Leaning against the sink to steady herself, she caught sight of her haunting reflection, a ghostly stranger staring back. She splashed her face with water and took several deep breaths in an attempt to regain some composure.

Once she had collected her nerves, she opened the door and

tiptoed across the landing and into the bedroom. She grabbed the fallen letter from under the bed and pulled her drawer free so that she could take hold of all her hidden documents, stuffing them into one of her mum's dainty handbags. Listening at the top of the stairs, she heard Stevie shouting insults towards the television, and so took the opportunity to creep back into the bathroom whilst he was distracted, closing the door behind her. She placed her handbag and a change of clothes into the bottom of the laundry basket, using a pile of dirty towels to conceal what lay beneath. Her haunting expression couldn't be concealed, a look of panic evident on her face, and so she turned out the light and made her way back into the bedroom.

She eased her slight frame into a spotty, two-piece pyjama set then buried her body beneath the cool, crisp sheets, her makeshift cocoon offering some level of protection. With the curtains drawn and the door secured in place, the room closed its eyes, offering complete darkness. Kitty lay on her left side and curled into the foetal position, facing away from Stevie's side of the bed. She told herself to be strong and survive one more night; tomorrow, freedom awaited. The hours passed painfully slowly as she watched each minute pass on the alarm clock at the side of the bed.

On the verge of sleep, she heard the door creak open and suddenly felt her limbs stiffen beneath the sheets.

'Are you still awake?' Stevie asked through the darkness. Wearing nothing but his underpants, he climbed into bed.

Please, not tonight, she thought, remaining as still as she could.

Stevie leant over, 'Are you awake?' His beer breath drowned her face, threatening her dormant demeanour. He gave her body a nudge, and still, Kitty maintained her sleeping stance.

'Bloody typical,' he huffed, leaning back over to his side of the bed and took hold of his phone, opening up his work emails. Kitty's eyes opened in the darkness, the whites shining brighter than satellites in the sky.

10

*C*HARLIE LISTENED AS THE ELEMENTS OUTSIDE HER BEDROOM window engaged in lively conversation. The sea lapped in the distance and the early morning chorus of ambient noises informed her a new day awaited. She remained in bed, worms of anxiety eating away at her optimism for the outcome of her impending test. Her hands grabbed hold of the covers and she pulled up the duvet, closed her eyes, and allowed her heightened senses to embrace the sounds that surrounded her. She tuned in to the orchestra of rustling leaves, the fallen foliage skipping across the ground each time the wind lifted. The constant echo of birdsong fell easy on her ears, heightening her spirits and hopes. She heard the faint, distant hum whenever a new wave eased itself onto the sandy shore, and she felt blessed to own an apartment situated on the seafront of picturesque St. Ives.

On tiptoes, she skipped across to the bathroom, revitalised by the cool breeze that was drifting in from the open window. Taking a deep breath, she eased down her knickers and perched herself on the toilet.

'Right, here goes,' she said to herself, holding the ovulation test between her legs. 'Rest on a flat surface and wait three minutes,' she read aloud having performed the test, placing the instructions in the bin and the ovulation stick on the windowsill. 'Don't look,' she snapped at herself after only thirty seconds had passed, and she had felt her eyes pull towards the window. Distracting herself with

73

washing her hands and brushing her teeth, once the tasks were complete, she collected the stick from the window and tried to steady her nerves. The shock of seeing the positive result made her hands fumble, and the stick fell from her grip into the toilet. 'Oh my God!' she exclaimed, her face still beaming. Her eyes became blurred with tears, her heart locking in the fleeting feeling of hope. She hurriedly dialled Ben's number and jumped from foot to foot as she waited for him to answer. 'Bloody hell, just pick up!' she willed, flustered. Before his voicemail permitted the opportunity to leave what was bound to be an excited and barely comprehensible message, she threw on some clothes and headed outside. Striding towards Ladysmith Lane, bundled against the wind in a trench coat, she unlocked her phone and scrolled through her list of favourite contacts. 'Pip, it's me. Bit of an emergency. Can you call my 9.30 appointment and reschedule? Maybe my 10 o'clock too, just in case. So sorry. I'll explain later. Be there as soon as I can.'

The distance from her apartment to Ben's studio, which took up the quaint attic space above Agnes' shop, Pebble & Sand, didn't take long to walk, and even less when power-striding. With a dishevelled expression on her face, flyaway hair crisscrossing above her head and her lungs panting for breath, she barged her way through Ben's studio door, reserving just enough energy to make it to the top of the stairs. 'I hope you're ready,' she shouted upon nearing the top. The thirteen steps leading up to her husband's place of work granted Charlie just enough time to leave a trail of clothes. By the time she reached the summit, she sported nothing but her finest lilac knicker and bra set - lingerie that promised volume and support. 'Look what we've got,' she announced, opening the studio door at the top of the stairs and holding her phone out in front of her, the photo of the ovulation stick floating in the toilet on full display.

Ben, plus his prospective early-morning client, looked immediately to the source of interruption - a beautiful woman standing half-naked in the doorway.

'What on earth?' Ben stammered, his jaw agape.

Careful to avoid eye contact with both Charlie and Ben, his client resumed his assessment of one of the paintings.

'Oh!' Charlie gasped, her cheeks flushing a deep shade of crimson.

'Give me a moment won't you, Steve, I won't keep you a second,' said Ben, before ushering his wife into the back office. 'What the bloody hell are you doing? And why aren't you wearing any clothes?' he added, closing the door behind him.

'I didn't think you'd have anyone here at this time, you didn't tell me you had an early appointment,' Charlie replied, holding her phone so that Ben could see the picture. 'It wasn't in your diary.'

Ben ignored her phone and instead, ran his hands through his hair in frustration. 'I didn't think I needed to tell you every time I book in a potential client, and I'm awful with keeping my diary up-to-date, you know that better than me,' he added. 'In any case, this wasn't a pre-booked meeting, he walked in the moment I arrived.'

Charlie shook her head and took a sharp intake of breath, her eyes blinking to a rapid pace. 'Why are you being so snarly?'

Ben anchored his hands on his hips. 'You turn up here, practically naked, and on a workday morning, and you wonder why I'm cross when I have a potential client with me. How exactly would you like me to react, Charlie? We're not on our honeymoon.'

Charlie arched her shoulders back. 'Well, I didn't know you had a client, otherwise I wouldn't have surprised you like this,' she began. 'But I thought you might have been pleased to see me.' She placed her arms on her hips, and twirled. She maintained eye contact, raising her eyebrows, waiting for the expected reaction.

Ben shook his head, his gaze falling to the floor, breaking the moment of eye contact.

Charlie cast her hands in the air. 'Well, aren't you at least going to ask me what was so important now that I'm here? It's not every day that I turn up wearing just my underwear.'

'I'm actually wondering why you're not at work, and who's seeing *your* clients.'

'Don't worry about my clients, it's all in hand. We have other business to tend to. Look, we're ovulating, Mr Fox, right now,' she said, holding out her phone as evidence. She moved closer to Ben so that she could whisper into his ear, placing a gentle kiss on his neck. 'Right now is the perfect time to make a baby - our baby.' Ben side stepped his new bride and looked out of the window, his hands still cemented to his hips, his back facing the office.

'You've got to be joking,' he muttered, moving his hands to the windowsill for support. 'We haven't even been married a month. We agreed to wait. The business is just getting going. It's not the right time and we agreed to hold off, or at least I thought we'd agreed.' He turned to face Charlie. 'What did you expect me to do? Whip off my clothes and do it right here in the studio?' Ben shook his head before turning away.

A fiery mixture of emotions ignited in Charlie's stomach.

'I told you I didn't want to wait. We've been together forever, Ben. I told you I wanted a baby. I've always wanted a baby.' The volume of Charlie's now hysterical voice rose. 'You're using the business as an excuse, aren't you?'

Ben moved away from the window and pulled Charlie close to his body. 'I'm not using the business as an excuse, I just don't want to have a baby right now, that's all. I want us to enjoy being married. I want us to go on some more holidays, just the two of us, before we're responsible for another human being. And the business is picking up, it's not an excuse. People are finally taking an interest in my work and in another year, we'll be in a much better financial position to think about bringing another person into the world.' He ran his hands up and down her naked arms, offering warmth and comfort.

'Once I've got my name out there and word spreads, I know my work will fly off these walls,' he added with a real sense of belief, imagining the feeling of his dream coming true. 'I need to make this pay, it has to start paying, otherwise I'll have no job and we'll have no way of paying all the bills. The deposit for this place has eaten our savings, we've got nothing to fall back on.' A look of worry wrinkled Ben's brow and his posture stooped. 'Steve, the client out there, works for a chain of hotels, and he's talking about placing a big order. This could be the break I've been working so hard to secure.' Ben looked over her shoulder and tried to see through the frosted panel in the door. 'That's if he's still here.'

After standing for so long without any clothes, Charlie felt a chill, her limbs trembling.

'Here, let me warm you up.' Ben rubbed his hands up and down his wife's arms again in a vain attempt to provide warmth. 'Lift your arms up,' he instructed, grabbing his polo sweater and slipping it over her upper half. 'You'll freeze if you stand like that any longer.' Charlie was uncharacteristically quiet.

'Why don't you sit down for a minute. Let me see if I can save this potential sale,' Ben suggested whilst straightening out his shirt, combing his hair with his hands and wiping off the lipstick smeared over his lips.

Charlie slumped herself onto a seat, cupping her hands on her lap. Her pedicured toes sparkled in the morning sun. 'You just don't get it, do you?' she began, stopping Ben before he left, his hand resting on the door handle. 'I want a baby more than anything. I don't care about money and I don't want to wait.'

Ben dipped his head, the weight of sadness bearing down. He leaned against the door. 'Don't do this, Charlie. Not now.'

'Do you love me?' she asked without looking up.

Ben paused before replying. 'I do love you.'

'But?'

Ben lifted his head, scared to turn around and face his wife. 'But I'm just not sure that I want to start a family.' His words fell heavy.

'Ever?' Charlie asked.

'I've said it before, but you just don't listen, you don't want to hear it. You make me happy, but I can't hide the way I'm feeling.

It's not fair on you.'

His words punctured Charlie's hope-filled heart. 'You don't mean it. I know you don't,' she protested, shaking her head. 'I swear you've never mentioned this before.'

He looked up. 'I have. You just don't listen,' he began, holding his hands out with frustration. 'But it is the truth, Charlie. I love you and our life together, but that's enough for me.' Ben drew in a prolonged breath. 'I need to go and see this client, let's talk about this tonight.' He clasped his fingers around the door handle.

'I swear, if you walk out that door, you'll regret it.'

He pressed his head against the door. 'Don't do this, Charlie. Please, don't do this.'

Charlie stood, trying to retain her dignity despite her lack of clothes. 'If you let me leave, I might not be there when you get home.'

'Please, Charlie. Let's just talk about it tonight when we've both calmed down.'

'It'll be too late tonight, Ben.'

He thought for a moment before pressing down on the handle and opening the door. The warmer air from the heated studio drifted in. 'It didn't have to be like this, Charlie,' he said, unwilling to turn and face his wife.

'I mean it, Ben. It will be too late.'

Ben shook his head. 'Sorry about that, Steve,' he announced to the room, before stepping forward and closing the door behind him.

Charlie's disappointment weighed heavily on her shoulders, and she placed both hands on the desk for support. With tears streaming down her face, she removed her wedding rings, placing them on top of Ben's wallet. 'I deserve better,' she told herself. She opened the door and scurried down the stairs, scooping up her clothes and getting dressed with haste. She made her way out onto Ladysmith Lane, and with the back of her hand wiped away the tears. In anticipation of Ben running after her, she slowed her pace and paused at the end of the street. Ben always apologised first after an argument, no matter who was to blame, and so she waited for him to follow.

After a moment of waiting, wrapping the trench coat tightly around her to combat the wind, she felt her heart sink to new depths. She willed his studio door to open and prayed for Ben to run down the street, shouting his apologies and promising to make their marriage work by agreeing to start a family. But the studio door remained closed, no matter how hard she willed, and as the seconds passed, a nauseating feeling in her stomach became more potent. Realising her marriage was on the edge of collapse, she erupted in a torrent of tears, and so turned the corner and walked away.

Back at the studio, Ben caught sight of Charlie out of the window the moment she had left. He could see that she was crying, and noticed the way that her longing expression was willing him to chase after her, a look of desperation visible in her eyes. Loathing to see her upset, all Ben wanted to do was make his wife stop crying. His heart and his mind engaged in a battle as he debated the appropriate action, his heart having always won in the past. This time, he allowed his heart to go with Charlie as she turned the corner, and it took all of his strength not to bolt out of the studio and chase after her. Resolving that they had grown apart, both of them wanting different things out of life and now heading down different paths, he let out a sigh and returned his attention to his work, a bittersweet moment of relief washing over him that he had finally been able to express his true feelings, no matter how much it hurt.

11

KITTY LAY AWAKE, FIDGETY, LIKE THE ELEMENTS OUTSIDE HER window. The breeze clattered weakened tree branches against the roof, rain showers fell in sheets, cars rattled sporadically down the road, and other more ambiguous noises rumbled in the distance. With tired eyes, Kitty watched the clock. She saw each hour come and go and waited for the hands to rest on 12:45, 90 minutes after Stevie had fallen asleep that evening. Kitty had done her research and learned that a person is most difficult to rouse an hour and a half after falling asleep. She diverted her gaze away from the clock knowing that staring at its face wouldn't make time pass any quicker. Her gaze rested on the outline of the photo frame resting on her bedside table. She urged herself not to forget to pick up the only personal item that she intended on taking with her when the time to escape finally arrived.

After battling fatigue, she had fallen asleep, only to be awoken by a cat wailing loudly outside. Kitty's eyes opened wide as she witnessed the alarm clock digits stating that it was 12:57. Flustered by having fallen asleep, her heart leapt into her throat the moment the hysterical feline screeched for a second time, the noise penetrating the panes of glass and ringing like an alarm in her bedroom. She turned to look at Stevie's side of the bed, the duvet tucked snug around his neck, his breathing deep and consistent.

Kitty forgot about reaching for her photo frame, and instead peeled back the duvet to expose her lower limbs, revealing her shivering skin. She waited for a few seconds, ensuring that that her jostling hadn't disrupted Stevie's slumber. With a delicate movement, she pulled her body upright and waited again, holding her breath in the burrows of darkness and checking that Stevie hadn't flinched. In a practiced manner, she swung her feet and eased herself off the bed. Poised on her tiptoes, she crept across the room, releasing the bedroom door from its frame, thankful that the oil she had added to the hinges seemed to be doing its job.

Just as the door pulled free, the sound of a deep voice resonated through her ears from behind. Kitty's body froze against the door. She closed her eyes and lingered beneath the shadows of darkness, holding her frantic breath captive. The jumbled words subconsciously released by Stevie stopped the moment his body rolled over, a chorus of genteel snores ringing through the air. Kitty remained glued to the door, her nerves on edge.

The snoring continued and developed into a consistent pattern. Kitty released her breath and made a move, slipping out through the gap before easing the wood back into the frame. Her feet teetered into the bathroom, her quivering fingers securing the door in place. Manoeuvring herself quietly over to the washing basket, she removed the lid and took out the few items of clean clothing she'd hidden the previous evening.

In a moment of lapsed concentration whilst undressing, her shoulder nudged the shampoo bottle resting on the edge of the bath, and the bottle came crashing down into the tub. Standing still in the darkness, Kitty's face flushed and her feet remained planted to the cool, tiled floor. Her eyes welled and she drove her face into the bundle of clothes gripped in her hands, cursing her carelessness. She pressed her ear to the door, listening intently for the rustling of bed covers.

She could no longer hear the sound of snoring.

Across the hallway in the bedroom, Stevie awoke, befuddled after a deep sleep. His eyes opened with reluctance, trying to bring into focus the time displayed on his phone. He peered over to

Kitty's side of the bed, noting her empty pillow. 'Kitty?' he called out, his ears listening for sounds coming from the bathroom. 'Are you alright?' His disgruntled face scorned through the darkness at having been woken, his tiredness drawing his heavy head back down onto the pillow. His eyes closed and yet he remained awake. In his mind, he counted the number of times over the previous few weeks that Kitty had woken him during the night, just to use the toilet. He thought about how he would be sure to mention this problem to her the following morning, and waited with a growing lack of impatience for a reply to his question.

In the bathroom, Stevie's words caused a wave of hysteria to rumble through Kitty's core, warm beads of panic pouring through her eyes. 'Sorry, just having a wee,' she replied, her finger flicking the bathroom lock, securing the door in place. 'Go back to sleep, I'll be in in a minute.' She waited, pressing her ear back against the door. She thought back to the previous occasions where she purposefully woke during the middle of the night, practicing how genteel she needed to be in order to avoid detection. On the three occasions Stevie had stirred, he had fallen back to sleep within a few minutes. She rolled her head so that her forehead pressed against the door, her jaw clenched, her teeth grinding away the mounting peaks of tension.

A couple of minutes passed without noise, and she concluded that he had fallen back asleep.

Shivering and cold to the core, Kitty slid a knee-length skirt up over her legs and lowered a blouse over her head, a beige belt securing both in place. Beneath the clothes in the washing basket, she fumbled in the dark and took hold of her only luggage – her mum's vintage shoulder bag and bundle of precious documents inside. With the bag tossed over her shoulders, she looked down and took a breath.

After a few moments, she reached out and pulled open the door, stepping carefully onto the landing. From behind the bedroom door, she heard the creaking sound made by the wooden bedframe.

'Are you alright? You've woken me up, again,' Stevie snarled, his words travelling through the gap at the bottom of the door.

Kitty's heart leapt into her mouth. She took a sharp intake of breath and collected her broken composure before forcing out a calm reply. 'I've got a tickly throat, just going to go and get a glass of water.' She pressed her hand over her mouth, trapping inside the fear brimming in her throat.

In the bedroom, Stevie lay himself down again, hoping to supress his mounting aggravation. He thought about the meeting pencilled in his diary for first thing in the morning, and how he didn't want to go into the office tired. Then, he thought about how good it would feel to get out of bed and release his frustrations, knowing that the following night, Kitty would be less inclined to disturb his sleep. 'Be quick and don't make a noise,' he grumbled, pulling back Kitty's side of the covers ready for her return. His weary eyes closed, and he slid back into a light sleep before he had managed to convince himself to drag his body out of bed.

In the hallway, with a cardigan in hand, Kitty listened, her skirt dancing around her legs from the breeze swooping in through the gap in the front door letterbox. Her legs felt heavy and unsteady, burdened by the flood of anxiety swamping her body. Just as she took a step forward, her chin dropped. She thrashed her head from side to side amid a mixture of frustration and disappointment, picturing in her mind the precious photo frame still resting on her bedside table. Reluctant to leave the precious memory behind, she crept back up the stairs.

With the silence of the night providing a small sense of encouragement, she placed her hand on the bedroom door, and braced herself for entering the room. But the sounds from the other side of the door, along with the weight of anxiety that had buried itself in her chest, told her that Stevie hadn't yet sunk back into a deep sleep. His breathing sounded erratic and the absence of any snoring caused her to pause with reluctance. She released her grip, retracting her hand in a slow and guilty movement.

Promising herself she would one day be able to come back and collect her precious keepsakes, she crept down the staircase, a trail of her tears soaking into the carpet.

She peered into the lounge, thinking that maybe she could take one of her other photos with her, but the bunch of dead daffodils diverted her attention. As had happened on a number of occasions throughout their relationship, the butchered petals lay scattered on the floor following another of Stevie's callous outbursts. She suffered the beatings, but she refused to accept his purposeful act of spite every single time she chose to pick a bunch of daffodils from the garden. For Kitty, the vibrant flowers acted as a poignant reminder of her mum, something Stevie was well aware of, which made his act of sabotage unforgivable in her eyes.

She arched her neck, picturing where he lay above, imagining how it would feel to inflict the same level of pain. With a look of finality, her eyes scanned the ceiling whilst her ears listened once more for sounds of movement. The bed wasn't creaking. The floorboards lay undisturbed. The cats outside were now silent. And then came the confirmation she felt desperate to hear; a rumbling chain of snores echoing through the bedroom door and down the stairs. Kitty looked down at her feet and severed the invisible shackles wrapped around her legs, allowing herself to move towards the front door.

She slipped her feet into a tattered pair of shoes that she'd hidden at the back of the rack, leaving behind her usual pair of pumps, and took hold of an old coat. With the door key resting between her fingers, she eased it into the lock. With her hand placed on the handle, she took a final glance back at the unhappy home in which she had been kept prisoner for too long. Images of all the beatings she'd endured played like an old-fashioned cinema reel, the memories cascading through her mind.

Pulling her shoulders back, she breathed deeply and turned towards the door. The deluge of tears sliding off her face ran dry. Her fingers twisted the doorknob, and the door permitted a silent release. She opened it as slightly as she could manage and squeezed her body through the narrow gap, closing the door behind her.

With just the clothes on her back, Kitty Twist stepped outside and submerged herself into the shadows of the night.

12

OUT ON THE STREET, KITTY DRANK IN THE COOL, CRISP AIR. She took one last look at her front door before easing the gate open. With a heart that ached to its core, she tore herself away from everything she cherished, a place that had once felt like home. She wrapped her coat around her body and pulled her shoulders up, protecting her neck from the snappy chill biting at her skin. She scurried down the street as though hot coals burnt beneath her shoes, an eagerness to escape pushing her away.

The further she walked, the more it felt like multiple pairs of spying eyes haunted the streets, the sensation sending shivers of paranoia coursing down Kitty's spine. Her head turned in all directions whilst her feet continued to move, her dilated pupils watching for twitching curtains and lurking shadows.

The sulky sky hung heavy overhead, but then the spotlights in the canopy took their turn to illuminate, the wind ushering away the stagnant clouds to reveal the stars beneath. Kitty crossed the road and made her way further down Pembroke Road, turning back to look up at her open bedroom window one last time. She watched the curtains move in the breeze and shook away the illusion of the figure behind them. As the sound of a door being opened rang through the night, she kept her head low and continued to march forwards. Heavy footsteps echoed in the distance, triggering a wave of panic. Without thought, she bolted as fast as her legs would carry, turning the corner before hiding in the shadowy crevice of a secluded shop doorway. Her body clung to the wall, trying to blend in with the architectural contours. Her warm breath fired white mist through the cool air. The footsteps drew closer, the sound of stomping feet now just around the corner from her hiding spot. She covered her mouth with her sleeve, trapping in her misty breath. She watched a man stride past, his eyes too focused on his phone to spot her.

Once the man had vanished, she continued to walk. Frosty fragments of the early April night cluttered the air and made the hairs on her body stand on edge. Kitty walked with increased speed down the street, the brisk pace making her breathless by the time she reached the main road, the taxi rank coming into view. Roy Barrister sat at the front of the queue, awaiting his next passenger.

Kitty knocked on the passenger-side window, and Roy wound it down.

'Hello, darling. Where can I take you?'

Kitty gulped, summoning up the courage to state her faraway destination. 'St. Ives.'

A look of bewilderment spread across Roy's face. 'I'm sorry, love, that's a new one on me – never heard of a town called St. Ives round here. But it's alright, you can tell me which way to go and I'll do the driving. How about that?' Roy turned the key and adjusted his seat in preparation for departure.

'St. Ives, Cornwall, I mean.' Kitty corrected, looking over her shoulder. 'Name your price.' Kitty knew that the journey from Perth to St. Ives would be close to six hundred miles, taking up to ten hours, maybe more – a fee never calculated by Roy.

He scratched his head and looked at Kitty, trying to gauge her level of alcohol consumption. Impatient, Kitty raised her eyebrows and displayed a look of desperation hard to fake.

'Round trip?' he asked.

'No. I'm not returning, but I'll pay you anything if you take me – just name your price.'

'£800.' Roy hoped his plucked price would deter her, knowing that a train journey would be cheaper, and quicker. Then, he could close the window, put the radio back on and wait for the next, more regular customer.

'Perfect,' replied Kitty. 'Plus, I'll give you an extra £100 if you deny ever seeing me tonight.' Kitty waited for a reply, shielding herself behind the car, her eyes darting around in the darkness.

Taken aback, Roy searched Kitty's pleading eyes, the look of desperation on her face enough to make his own heart ache. He reached over into the back, opening the passenger door. 'You best get in.'

With another look over her shoulder, Kitty stepped into the safety of the black shell. She sank into the seat, hiding within its leather folds.

'Thank you,' she said, her hand reaching out and pressing the lock, the sound of safety permitting a breath to release. She took a glance over her shoulder once the engine roared, the line of chimneypots becoming hazy beneath the dim backdrop of sporadically lit lampposts.

'I'll give you this now, then you don't need to worry about payment at the other end,' she insisted, rummaging in her bag for the bundle of cash.

Roy held up his hand. 'There will be no need for that, you can pay me upon arrival. And I won't be accepting any additional payment, all my passengers' journeys remain confidential,' he added, taking a look at Kitty in the rear-view mirror. 'My job is to deliver you safely to your chosen destination, nothing more, nothing less.' Roy turned on the radio. 'But there is one crucial thing that we *must* agree on before we leave town.' Kitty's concerned expression encouraged Roy to elaborate. 'And that's what radio station we'll be listening to. I like a bit of rock 'n' roll. How about yourself?'

Kitty smiled. 'Fine with me.'

The car crept away into the night, and Kitty's tears of relief saturated her lap, her tired body easing down the seat. Her face developed a slow smile and she pressed her palm against her heart, offering a reassuring salute to its future safety. She then turned her head again, inspecting her rear view and periphery.

'I've been watching to make sure that we weren't followed, and there hasn't been a car behind us for at least five minutes', reassured Roy, his words encouraging Kitty to turn back around and face the front window. 'Nobody saw us leave the rank.' Kitty's head dropped, appreciation pouring from her face.

'Are you ok?' he asked. 'Here, take these.' He passed her a box of tissues just as they joined an A-road that navigated them directly out of Perth. 'They're the fancy ones that aren't meant to hurt your nose.' He looked in the rear-view mirror again, repeating his question once Kitty dried her eyes. 'Are you ok?' His sincere tone struck against Kitty's heart.

She lifted her head so that she could see him in the mirror and took a breath before answering. 'I am now, thank you.'

Roy nodded, acknowledging his part in his passenger's journey, a strange sense of honour taking hold of his emotions.

For Kitty, the realisation sank in. She thought about her parents and the sentimental items she had been forced to leave behind, which amounted to all her worldly possessions.

'Let me know when you need a comfort break, then I can stop at the services,' Roy suggested, taking a slurp from his can of pop.

'Okay, thank you,' she replied, at which point a song begun to play on the radio.

'It's meant to be lovely in Cornwall, you know. Beautiful beaches,' he added. 'My Auntie owned a holiday house not far away from St. Ives, in a little place called Carbis Bay. During every summer holiday, when I was off school, I used to travel down on the train to visit. Of course, it's probably all changed since then, we're talking forty years ago.' Kitty smiled, thinking back to her own childhood memories of summer holidays with her parents littered with ice creams, sand between her toes and ill-taken photos.

'Here, have some sweets,' he offered, handing back a bag of sugar-coated rocks. 'They're terrible for your teeth, but they do taste good,' he added, doing his best to halt the flow of Kitty's tears.

'Thanks,' she replied, smiling. 'Thanks, Roy,' she added upon sight of his cabbie ID badge. Roy reciprocated with a smile.

'There's plenty more where they came from. I hide them all in here, in my glove compartment, away from my wife.'

Kitty lay back and closed her eyes, recent lack of sleep forcing her body to shut down. The road's imperfections created an artificial heartbeat in the cavity of the car, sending her to sleep. After a few comfort breaks along the way, Kitty awoke in the early hours of the morning, the creamy lampposts of the Cornish coast welcomed her eyes with a warm salute.

13

'I FANCY BACON INSTEAD OF CEREAL,' SHOUTED STEVIE FROM THE top of the stairs. 'Get me some ready - I'll be down in ten.' He powered up the shower, steam filling the room like a sauna, anger filling his body at the sight of the fallen shampoo bottle. He returned it to its rightful place and tried to let his frustration go and instead, thought about the day ahead, the scheduled meetings at work he would have to endure before coming home to a shared bath with his fiancée. 'Don't you dare make me late,' he shouted, unable to smell the meaty aromas drifting through the house. His temper rumbled at the thought of Kitty disobeying him, the chance of him being in a good mood already hampered by being woken during the night. He left his dirty clothes scattered in the bathroom and the bed covers strewn across the floor, and rushed to get changed. 'Why can't I smell breakfast? Didn't you hear me shouting?' he asked, making his way downstairs. His body paused near the front door, his face realigned with a tightened jaw and ugly twist to his mouth. He crept down the hallway, easing the kitchen door open.

Upon sight of the empty, dark kitchen, his blood boiled. His fists tightened until his knuckles turned white. With force, he lashed out at the crockery decorating the breakfast island, sweeping it onto the floor with the back of his arm, the subsequent smashing sound permeating the thick, Victorian walls. He took a sharp intake of breath, and his feet paced the kitchen.

'Where are you?' he whispered, pacing back down the hallway

and through to the lounge. The curtains were still drawn and the room as he left it the previous evening. 'You're going to regret this when I get my hands on you,' he spat.

After a few minutes of checking each room, he knew Kitty wasn't home. 'Bloody bitch. Where are you?' he snarled. With the spirit of a fighting bull, he charged upstairs and pulled open Kitty's chest of drawers, puzzled by the brimming selection of clothes. He scattered all her underwear over the floor, frantically searching. He pulled open the wardrobe doors, all of Kitty's clothes hanging with usual precision. Stevie dropped to his knees, scooping out the contents of the bottom of the wardrobe, nothing but shoes, shorts, bikinis and pyjamas falling free.

'She can't have gone far without any clothes,' he muttered to himself. He scrambled over to her bedside table, noticing her precious picture still positioned at the side of her bed. He tossed the items to the floor in one swift movement and then looked through the drawer, spotting her parents' jewellery box. He smirked, knowing that Kitty wouldn't go far without her collection of precious sentimental items. He grabbed the jewellery box and his fingers eased the stiff lid apart to reveal the gold bands held within. 'She definitely can't be far away,' he grinned, a secret sense of satisfaction seeping through his veins. Stevie tossed the rings across the room before running downstairs.

'Where's the little bitch gone?' he asked himself, grabbing hold of Kitty's usual handbag and tipping the contents out onto the kitchen island. He rummaged haphazardly through the mess; her purse, a lip balm, a packet of tissues, and a half-eaten packet of chocolate covered peanuts littered the surface. He took hold of her smashed mobile phone, checking that she hadn't managed to get it fixed behind his back, and had been using it all along. But the broken screen prevented it from being used, and so he threw it across the room.

With the house upended and no clue unearthed that could hint at Kitty's whereabouts, Stevie grabbed his laptop from his satchel, pressing hard on the keyboard. 'She must have logged on,' he muttered to himself, urging to find her location so that he could drag her back, just like he had always threatened. The slow connection of his Wi-Fi ignited his impatience.

'Riley. Cancel all my morning meetings, something's come up,' he instructed, calling the office from his mobile. Before Riley could ask if everything was alright, he hung up. Stevie looked at his phone, searching through his call history, his Google search history, his sent emails, but nothing stood out to him; not a single clue as to Kitty's whereabouts.

'Finally,' he announced, hearing the ping the moment his device powered into life. His fingers clicked from one system to the next, scouring the screen for any electronic footprint Kitty may have left. After ten minutes of frantic searching, he tossed the laptop onto the floor. He stood in the middle of the room and for the first time since meeting Kitty, felt he'd lost control.

He grabbed his keys and headed out the front door.

'Haven't seen Kitty this morning, have you, Billy?' he asked his neighbour.

'I haven't, Stevie. Come to think of it, I haven't seen your Kitty for days, maybe weeks. I saw her some time ago cleaning that front door of yours, gave it a right good scrub she did.' Stevie held his hand up in appreciation.

'Thanks anyway. She's probably just nipped to get some fresh bread, we're running a bit low this morning. See you later.' Stevie straightened up his tie, tucked in his shirt and ran his hands through his hair whilst pacing down the street.

'Hi,' he announced upon entering the corner shop, taking a passport-sized photo out of his wallet. 'Have you seen my fiancée this morning? We live up the road and I'm a little worried about her.' The scruffy lad behind the counter didn't take much notice of the photo, providing nothing more than a shrug of the shoulders.

Stevie reached over and grabbed the lad's t-shirt. 'Listen, Liam,' he began, noting the boy's name badge. 'This is important, so why don't you take a look at the photo and then go and check your cameras,' Stevie instructed, looking towards the security system.

'I can't leave the counter unattended, and I'm the only one here,' Liam spluttered.

'You stay here,' instructed Stevie, releasing Liam's clothes before walking off through to the back office. 'I'll take a quick look, it'll only take a minute.' Stevie didn't wait for a reply, and before Liam could protest, Stevie found himself scrolling through the latest footage. His eyes scanned each person that entered, looking closely to see if it was Kitty, but after ten minutes of scrutinising the footage, he soon caught up to the present time. Without saying anything to Liam, he stormed out of the shop.

'Morning Stevie, how's things?' asked Jerry, Stevie's other immediate neighbour. 'Haven't seen you for a while. Keeping well?'

'I'm alright, thanks, Jerry,' he replied, stopping in his tracks, somewhat annoyed at having to partake in polite chit-chat. 'In a bit of a rush this morning, got a meeting first thing. I'll catch you later,' Stevie said, fobbing off the conversation and walking away.

'No worries. Send my regards to Kitty,' said Jerry, hauling his bike on his shoulder and walking up his front steps. 'I was going to say hello to her last night, but she seemed in a bit of a rush so I didn't bother.' Stevie froze, and he slowly turned to face Jerry. His eyes thinned and his nostrils flared.

'What did you just say?' Stevie paced back towards his neighbour.

'I saw your Kitty, oh, must've been close to one, maybe one-thirty in the morning. I'd been late to bed, all work and no play at the moment with assignments to mark, and when I was out checking that I'd locked the car, I saw her walking down the road.' Jerry reached his front door and propped his bike against the wall, searching in his pocket for his keys.

Beneath his calm exterior, Stevie's rage spiralled into a tornado. 'Which way was she walking?'

Jerry pointed. 'That way, down towards Victoria Road.'

'Did she have any bags with her?' Was she alone?' Stevie's face grimaced with anger.

'You alright?'

'Did Kitty have any bags with her? Was she alone?' he repeated, his temper frazzled and his words spilled out abruptly.

'No, not that I can remember,' replied Jerry in a flippant manner, unwilling to continue the conversation that had now taken a sour turn. 'Anyway, I best get going, busy day ahead, just like you,' he added, opening his front door. But Stevie darted, wedging his foot in the gap to prevent it from closing.

'What are you doing?'

'I just need to know some more information,' he replied through a forced, friendly expression. 'I expected Kitty home before I left for work this morning, so I'm a little concerned.' The fake façade didn't wash with Jerry.

'Well, I don't know any more than what I've already told you. I saw her walking down the road, that's all. If you're that worried, I suggest you call her mobile and ask her yourself.' Jerry forced his front door shut, shook his head and brushed off the unusual, frosty exchange with a neighbour he'd once shared regular pints with in the garden.

Stevie jumped into his car and, without fastening his seatbelt, sped off down Pembroke Road, tearing around the corner and heading towards town.

At the same moment, the coffee machines in Millie's café were steaming, ready to go, and the early morning delivery of sweet pastries were now in the display counter, ready for opening. Millie sat at one of the tables in the middle of the café, just having a sip of her milky, weak tea and a bite of buttery toast before the crowds descended.

Stevie abandoned his car in front of the shop.

'Where is she?'

Millie looked around at the sound of a raised voice, catching sight of Stevie stood at the door, his fists banging against the glass, threatening to smash it through.

'What the bloody hell are you doing?' Jumping up from her chair, she rushed towards the door and turned the key hanging in the lock.

'Where is she?' Stevie asked again, pushing past Millie once the door opened and heading towards the back of the café.

'Where's who?' Millie remained in the front of the shop.

Stevie reappeared seconds later.

'Kitty. Where is she?'

'I have no idea.'

'Don't lie to me,' Stevie slammed his fist onto the counter, the cups clattering beneath the sudden force. 'You're her best friend, she must've told you where she's gone. She tells you bloody everything.'

'She hasn't told me anything, Stevie. I have no idea where she is.'

'A neighbour saw her leaving in the middle of the night. She didn't have any bags and she hasn't left a note.'

Millie peered outside, urging someone to come in. 'If she's left, there must've been a good reason. And there must be a reason why she hasn't told you.'

'And what's that supposed to mean?' Stevie paced back towards Millie, an intimidating expression plastered across his face.

'Leaving a loved one during the middle of the night without any explanation isn't normal, is it?' Millie manoeuvred herself towards the front door. 'If she wants to come home, Stevie, she will do. It's a pity you took away her mobile, otherwise you could call her, or try and track her whereabouts, I'm sure you had a tracking App downloaded onto her phone, or followed her movements on Google Maps,' she concluded, raising her eyebrows and opening the door, indicating for him to leave.

'Have a good day, Millie,' he replied when a few customers entered the café. 'Be sure to let me know if you hear from her because I will be back,' he concluded, walking out and getting into his car, the wheels spinning the moment his foot pressed the accelerator.

'Hot-headed people should be bloody banned from driving,' the first customer entering the café commented, watching with disgust as the car spun away down the street.

Back inside the café, Millie took out her mobile, willing to see a missed call, or a text message from her friend. She scrolled through all her social media accounts, searching for any hidden interaction, but finding nothing. Millie opened up her gallery, clicking on her favourite photo of the pair during a trip to London, Kitty wearing an oversized Union Jack Beefeater hat along with some garish sunglasses. 'Where are you?' she whispered to herself, a nauseating sense of worry rocking her composure.

Less than ten minutes later, a stream of ambulances and police cars tore down the street past the café.

'What's happened?' Millie asked a customer who entered the café.

'There's been a bad accident. A car has overturned near the crossing. I heard someone say that the driver and a pedestrian have both been badly injured.' Millie couldn't concentrate on the commotion occurring only a few hundred yards away from her café. Instead, she walked through to the back office and diverted her attention back to her phone. Her fingers scrolled through her social media accounts again, hoping to find a hidden message from Kitty, and yet despite her best efforts, uncovered nothing but a flood of cherished memories. She tried to call Kitty's number, only to be disappointed when the call failed to be connected. Feeling like she had failed in her role as Kitty's best friend, Millie covered her face with her hands and cried. A wave of guilt rocked her composure, and she felt helpless. A sickening feeling flooded her stomach, knowing deep down that she had failed to be there for Kitty in what appeared to have been her darkest hours.

14

IN THE BACK OF THE TAXI, A GROGGINESS HUNG HEAVY OVER Kitty's body. She manoeuvred herself, her neck feeling stiff whilst her legs felt riddled with pins and needles. The car came to a halt and the engine was switched off.

'Are we really here?' she asked, peering out of the window and noticing the lapping turquoise sea in the distance.

'We are, my love,' Roy grinned, his own tired eyes admiring the crisp, morning view.

Kitty stepped out of the car and stretched her legs, taking in a breath so deep her lungs filled to capacity with salty, seaside air. She gazed out towards the horizon, welcoming the initial feelings of freedom. The breeze brushed past her face, tickling her skin, and the smell of the ocean flooded into her nose. Her eyes admired a world that had all the trimmings of a picturesque postcard.

Roy followed suit and stepped out, shaking his weary legs. 'What a long journey.'

Kitty dragged her vision away from the coastline, and turned to Roy. 'Thank you so much,' she replied, digging in her bag, pulling out a bundle of notes and stretching out her hand. 'For everything. I really can't thank you enough.'

'My pleasure,' he said, pushing away Kitty's hand. 'I want you to keep it, put it towards whatever it is you need,' he added. 'All that matters to me is that I've done as you asked, driven you to safety and away from Perth.' Roy put his hands in his pockets. 'I won't mention this trip to anyone, you have my word,' he added. Having watched her in his rear-view mirror for hours whilst she slept, he had spotted the bruises on her arms and the scattering of scars on her hands. 'Just look after yourself.'

'Thank you, Roy, but please take the money. I'm going to be alright now and that's all thanks to you,' she replied.

Roy stepped closer and gave Kitty a hug, placing his arms around her shoulders. 'Take care of yourself,' he whispered into her ear, before getting back into the car and starting the engine.

'Thank you,' she said once again, watching the car disappear into the distance. Roy's hazard lights flashed in one last acknowledgement and farewell gesture.

Kitty wrapped her coat around her body and followed the winding path that led down to the seafront. She arched her neck, the rising sun acting as a guide, the misty, pink sky whisking her into its embrace. A rush of adrenalin caused her heart to beat haphazardly, and for the first time in over a year, a feeling of giddiness blossomed its way to the surface of her face, and she caught herself smiling.

The morning hadn't yet awoken, and only a handful of joggers, dedicated dog walkers and eager surfers dotted the harbour beneath a hazy sky. A scattering of boats bobbed about on the surface of the sea, a few rogue gulls gliding past Kitty on their hunt for breakfast. At the end of the path, she blended in with the morning backdrop and slipped off her pumps, the sand providing a soft, comforting platform as each grain felt cool against her naked feet. The sea looked polished; the surface shimmering in the sunlight. Kitty sat on a bench and allowed herself to drink in the air, a subtle blend brought about by the shifting of the seasons creating a perfect, crisp morning. To Kitty, the calm, clear sea, the pearly sand, and the dotting of surfers made the view feel quintessentially Cornish, and she wanted to stay in the blissful moment for as long as she could.

With her hand outstretched, Kitty eased off her engagement ring, her swollen, warm skin releasing the band with painful reluctance. The sun reflected off the chiselled edges of the diamond, and her mind recalled the initial excitement she had felt when Stevie had presented it to her. She got up and walked towards the edge of the surf, opening her hand and tipping the ring into the sand, watching it sink briefly before being carried out to deeper waters. She cast her gaze towards the distance, comforted by the sound of the sea, each lapping wave creating its own unique melody. Never had she felt so free, or so comfortably alone in the world. She turned away and took a seat back on the bench, her head lowered.

'Morning,' announced a male voice from behind. 'I'm so sorry, I didn't mean to scare you,' added Ben Fox the moment he witnessed her startled expression. With a coffee in hand and what looked like a book of some description wedged under his arm, he walked down the few steps so that he stood just before Kitty. 'I come and sit on this bench every morning, have done for the past couple of weeks. I've not had to fight for the space before,' he said with a smile.

'Oh, I'm sorry, I didn't realise,' she replied, vacating the bench with an overly polite haste.

Ben held out his hand. 'I'm teasing. Please, sit. It'd be nice to have company - it's usually just me, a cup of coffee and my sketch book.' Kitty turned to walk away, offering the stranger nothing but a polite smile.

Ben offered out his hand just before Kitty scarpered. 'I'm Ben,' he said, presenting a more formal means of introduction.

'Hi,' she replied, turning back and shaking his hand with a light, flimsy grip.

'I come down here in the morning, before it gets too busy. It helps to clear my mind before the start of another inevitably crazy day,' he looked down at the sand, spotting his fidgeting feet. 'I'm sorry, I'm not sure why I'm offloading any of this on to you,' he added, feeling his toes curling with embarrassment. He willed his concentration to tear itself away from her warming blue eyes. He felt captivated by Kitty's presence, and found himself admiring her conker-coloured hair, the glossy locks rippling down her back. Even though he'd only just met her, Ben found her subtle smile immediately comforting. He took a seat on the bench, shuffling his body to one side until it clung to the edge, offering as much space as possible in the hope she would follow.

Noting Ben's moment of awkwardness, and for the first time in years feeling like she wanted to laugh, Kitty warmed to the conversation. 'Nice to meet you, Ben,' she said, taking a seat at the opposite end of the bench.

'How do you sketch without a pencil?'

Ben patted down his pockets, peering at his book. 'Good point. I promise I do usually draw. I'm an artist, or at least I'm trying to be an artist.'

Kitty smirked, before casting her gaze back out to sea in an attempt to collect her muddled thoughts.

'I haven't seen you around these parts before, and I'm pretty good with faces. Do you live locally?' he asked, looking out towards the moored boats and using all his willpower not to stare directly at the beautiful woman he was now keeping company with. 'I find that all the tourists seem to merge into one unidentifiable face.' Ben turned back to look at Kitty. 'And I don't think you fit into that mould.'

Kitty admired the motley selection of tourists that were now starting to pepper the beach. 'Their faces do merge, don't they?' she laughed, before turning to face him. 'You're right. I'm not a tourist and you won't have seen my face before,' she began to explain. 'I've just moved to the area,' she confirmed with a brimming sense of pride. 'My first day actually.'

'Exciting. Where've you moved from?'

Kitty scrunched her face, though she didn't realise. 'Erm, up North.'

'Why here? Why St. Ives?' asked Ben, intrigued. 'Apart from the obvious,' he added, holding out his hand and gesturing towards the canvas of scenery.

'It's a place that my mum and dad loved. They always dreamt of moving to Cornwall.'

Ben sensed the sadness beneath the surface of Kitty's words, her voice heavy and laden with it.

'It's a wonderful place to live, and I have no doubt that you'll be very happy here. Do you want a tip from a local?' Ben paused, crossing his legs and facing the sea, the choppy waves tumbling onto the shore with gay abandon.

'Sure.'

'The best place to be, if not sitting right here, on this very patch of beach, is Ladysmith Lane. I have it on very good authority that there's a top-notch café and a few quirky shops that are worth a look at.'

Without looking at Ben, Kitty replied. 'I've actually heard the same,' she said, smiling and closing her eyes, the salty, ocean air dancing on her skin, awakening her hibernating senses. 'Seems I've done my homework,' she added. The pair locked gazes for a brief, yet meaningful moment, before Kitty looked away. The breeze snapped at her delicate cheeks, creating shivers all over her body.

Off in the distance, a weather front drew in, the early morning rising sun sulking behind the mounting clouds and casting ominous shadows onto the sand below. The sea began to act with a defensive edge, throwing up barriers and thrashing waves, intimidating the harmless, bobbing boats.

Ben stood, noticing the town awakening. 'I didn't know we were expecting stormy weather today. I best be going. A soggy sketchbook isn't going to make me rich.'

Kitty admired the incoming clouds with a nostalgic fondness, her mind diverting to comforting thoughts of her mum. 'During a storm you should look for rainbows. That'd make a nice picture to sketch,' Kitty replied, her cheeks plumping the moment a smile crept onto her face.

Ben pulled up the collar on his t-shirt, trying to hide his smitten smile. 'I will, thanks for the artistic inspiration,' he replied.

'I've enjoyed my bench for long enough, it's their turn now,' he said, turning his head towards the early-morning surfers dressed in wetsuits and carrying boards beneath their arms. 'It was nice chatting to you. I hope I'll bump into you again.' He paused, slightly embarrassed by his out-of-character forward approach. 'I'm sorry, I never asked your name.'

Kitty paused, nets of apprehension containing her words. A sense of vulnerability made her throat feel dry, and a watery gaze concealed her eyes. Her posture stooped, and before replying, she took in a deep, purposeful breath in an effort to restore calm. 'My name is Kitty.'

'Well, it's nice to have met you, Kitty,' Ben concluded, turning to walk away. Kitty stood up and caught his attention before he had travelled too far.

'You couldn't help me, could you? I'm sorry to ask but you'll probably know the answer to my question.'

'Of course.'

'Would you know where Farrington Road is? I have an appointment and no clue which direction I should head in.'

'Yeah. If you head over there and then make a right,' he began, pointing towards the far end of the path. 'You know what. It's not far, why don't I show you? It'd be much easier.' Ben's smile radiated from his face, and he held out his hand, offering to assist Kitty up the steep steps. She reached out with a nervous hesitation and took hold of his hand, noting how warm and soft his skin felt whilst appreciating the gentlemanly gesture.

'Thanks,' she said, releasing her grip when she reached the top.

'No problem. Any excuse to delay starting work.'

The pair walked towards the awakening hullabaloo of the bustling tourist town. The narrow side streets of St. Ives were dotted with people eager to enjoy another coastal day in the early-spring sunshine. Delivery drivers were unloading fresh batches of fruit to the cafés, and floral scents drifted through the air the moment the doors to a florist swung open. Kitty listened with intrigue to all the chattering occurring around her like she had never experienced it before, like she had been asleep her whole life and was now witnessing the simplicities of life for the very first time.

Ben witnessed in Kitty's eyes how she had become lost in the moment, and a million questions surged through his mind. He was eager to learn about the girl responsible for making his heart skip, the girl who had managed to bring a smile to his face for the first time in weeks.

'You don't have much luggage for someone moving to the area,' he said, noting the tiny handbag hung over her shoulder.

Kitty turned to look at him. 'I like to travel light.'

'Less to carry,' he smiled. 'And, hopefully, you'll need to wear fewer layers down here. It's true what they say, you know - the weather is much better in the South. I don't know how you Northerners cope with so much rain.' The thought ran through Ben's mind to take Kitty the long way to Farrington Road, extending the amount of time spent in her company, but she spotted the church in the distance.

'Oh, I think I know where I am. It's just behind the church, is that right?'

'Sure is.'

Kitty paused on the pavement, ready to cross the road. 'Well, thank you so much for walking me this far.' An awkward moment lingered whilst Ben tried to summon up the courage to ask for her number.

'Take care,' she added before walking away, eliminating his opportunity to pluck up the courage. Ben watched Kitty as she blended into the backdrop of the morning, kicking himself for not speaking up, her figure disappearing the moment she turned the corner.

Kitty made her way up Farrington Road, both sides of the street lined with period properties full of seaside character. She looked for number 333; a quaint-looking house set back off the main road, the frontage protected by a trio of magnolia.

She paused just to the right of the property and checked the address on her paperwork before opening the rusty iron gate. The sound as it banged against the wall transported Kitty back to Perth, back to 67 Pembroke Road, and rattled her composure. A toxic, deep-rooted sense of fear infested her bones that no matter how far she travelled, and no matter where she hid, wouldn't easily be shaken. She closed the gate and entered the property, her white pumps blending in with the fallen boat-shaped leaves off the magnolia tree the moment she made her way up the winding path that snaked to the front door.

She spotted the coaster-size key safe box on the wall, concealed by a blooming hanging basket. She took out the bundle of paperwork stuffed into her bag, looking for the safe code that the solicitor had provided. With fumbling fingers, she punched in the four digits. A noise rustled from behind, footsteps making her flinch and check her periphery. Noting the increased pace in her heartbeat, she turned to see a jogger striding up the street, and urged herself to dismiss the paranoia which hung over her like a constant shadow.

The cover of the key safe released, allowing her to open the box. *It's all yours now – enjoy!*, read the handwritten note attached to the keys. An excited, jittery feeling encouraged the ingrained frown to fall from Kitty's face, and she took a second look at the note, before cupping the keys in both hands and turning to walk away. As she opened the garden gate to leave the property, a pair of eyes remained fixed on her back as Kitty was observed from an upstairs window.

Inside the house, Peggy Maltby watched on. She whispered to herself whilst watching Kitty walk away. Tears welled behind her weathered eyes, her wrinkled hands trembling. She urged herself to remain silent, but her heart poured, haemorrhaging with an abundance of love that had remained hidden for so long.

'Hello, I'm Peggy,' she announced upon opening the window, her words travelling up the street to meet Kitty's ears. 'Would you like to come inside?'

Up the street, Kitty paused and turned her head, looking up at the woman. Although she'd never met Peggy, or spoken with her before, a strange feeling drew her back, an odd sense of familiarity. The estate agent had only released snippets of information about the seller of Flourish, and yet when Kitty first set eyes upon Peggy Maltby, it somehow felt like their two worlds had already collided. 'Hello. Yes, of course. Thank you.'

15

'I'LL COME DOWN AND OPEN UP. PLEASE, DON'T LEAVE,' REPLIED Peggy, witnessing a haunting expression clinging to Kitty's face. Peggy closed the window and disappeared from view, scurrying down the stairs and towards the front door.

Kitty remained planted at the other side of the gate, her heart pounding against her chest.

'Hi,' repeated Peggy, standing in her doorway, a worn pair of slippers and a knitted shawl protecting her against the morning chill. 'Do you want to come in for a cup of tea? I'd really love to get to know a bit more about you, and chat about the shop. My solicitor told me that they would sort everything on my behalf, but I'd like to be involved with the process which is why I suggested that the keys could be collected from here.'

The offer of a warm cup of tea and the ability to rest her weary body encouraged Kitty to accept the invitation. She released the gate. 'Absolutely, that would be lovely, thank you,' she replied, wiping her pumps on the doormat and stepping over the threshold.

Kitty entered the property to find herself overwhelmed by its contents – a clear reflection of what Peggy had been occupying herself with in Flourish for so many years. A collection of embroidery projects and paintings decorated each wall, with antiquities, china collections, and an array of eclectic teapots decorating every side table. 'My mum loved tea pots,' Kitty commented, signalling to one particular piece on the dresser in the hallway. 'She was constantly adding to her collection, even though she knew my dad would grumble about it.'

Peggy admired the collection she had amassed. 'I just can't resist a good teapot. The more shapes and styles I own, the happier I feel,' she joked.

'You have a lovely home,' added Kitty as the pair weaved themselves through to the sitting room; a cosy snug located at the back of the property. 'So similar in style to the photos I've seen of Flourish.'

'Go and take a seat, I'll bring in the tea,' suggested Peggy, indicating which door Kitty should follow. 'Make yourself at home.'

Kitty gazed around the living room. The space felt lived in and homely, soft furnishings and trinkets adding a personal touch. Yet the more time she spent admiring the room, the more she begun to realise there was something missing – evidence of a family. She looked around the room in search of a photograph of a smiling partner, children, or family of any description, but found none. Then she spotted a single photo resting at the side of what looked to be Peggy's favourite chair, given how worn the fabric had become. The heart-shaped cream frame enclosed a dated photo, the colour and quality of the picture poor. Kitty stepped closer, noting the smile on the woman's face, her arms cradling a tiny bundle, the pink blanket swaddled around a baby's tiny frame.

'Here we go,' announced Peggy, entering the room with a tray.

'You and your family really do have a beautiful home.'

Peggy sighed with an extended heaviness. 'It's just me here,' she replied, closing the door behind her.

'Oh, I'm sorry. I saw the photo and just assumed.' As soon as she had uttered the words, she regretted them, noting Peggy's reaction.

Peggy placed the tray down and sunk her body into the chair next to the photo. 'Don't apologise. That is a picture of me and my daughter. She's all grown up now,' she replied, pausing to admire the photo that had by now become ingrained into her memory. 'Help yourself,' she added, nudging the kitchen tray towards Kitty.

'Biscuits at breakfast time. Lovely, thank you,' Kitty commented, taking a bite out of the crumbly shortbread.

'I wasn't going to ask you in because I know in all the correspondence from the estate agent and the solicitor, this wasn't part of the original arrangement. But, for me, it feels like I'm handing over a family member. It's the end of an era for me and I wanted to meet in person the individual who's bought the shop, you know, to feel at ease that it's going to be in good hands.'

'After so many phone calls, it's nice to be able to put a face to the name,' Kitty began. 'Can I ask, if you don't mind, why you decided to sell to me? I understand that the shop went on the market a year or so ago, but I believe that the sale fell through. So, why now? Why me?'

Peggy eased herself back into her chair and the cushion moulded itself snugly around the contours of her body. 'Well, you're right, in part. I did put the business up for sale about a year ago, wanting to hang up my knitting needles and enjoy an early retirement. My knees aren't what they used to be and it's hard in winter, you know, when it's dark and cold outside.' She took another sip of her tea. 'So, I decided about a year ago to sell up and, whilst still in reasonable health, try to achieve a few things on my bucket list.' Peggy picked up a postcard, turning it to face Kitty. 'I've always wanted to travel to India and experience the sights and sounds that I've spent so long reading about. A friend of mine visited not so long ago, but I couldn't go because of the shop.' Peggy savoured her tea, preparing herself for what she anticipated would follow. 'And it didn't take long for the business to sell the first time. The buyers were a lovely couple. They were passionate about the shop and I admired their reasons for buying, so I knew the business would have been in good hands.' She placed her mug down and cupped her hands on her lap. 'Everything was set, the paperwork almost complete. But then it all fell through at the last minute, really. I believe that one of the purchasers had been diagnosed with cancer.'

Kitty could feel a sudden sadness mounting. 'This may come as a bit of a surprise, but that lady was my mum.' She lowered her head, a sharp, familiar pain stabbing at her chest. The sense of loss flooding Kitty's heart made it feel like Delilah had passed away only days ago.

Peggy stood up and walked over to sit next to Kitty. 'I thought as much,' she began, shaking her head. 'When I found out your surname from the estate agent, I knew it was too much of a coincidence – it had to be you.' Peggy's hands fumbled with a tissue. 'The very moment I received that call out of the blue from the estate agent informing me that a young lady from Perth seemed interested in buying the shop, I knew it had to be you, I just knew it.'

Kitty shook her head and allowed her eyes to close. Plump tears dripped off her face each time her head moved from one side to another. 'I found out about my parents' intentions to purchase Flourish in a letter my mother had written before she passed. I just don't understand why my parents didn't tell me about this at the time. I don't understand why they kept such a big secret from me. We were so close. My mum and I were the best of friends. We told each other everything, and yet they chose to keep this life-changing decision from me. It just doesn't make any sense.' Kitty dabbed her blotchy face, her tissue saturated with sadness, and disappointment.

'Your mum and dad were planning on buying the shop, for you. They were planning on moving down here, to St. Ives, and in the hope that you'd want to follow them, they invested in Flourish, plus the flat. They wanted to keep it a secret until we exchanged contracts, and I guess because of what happened, they never got to tell you, because the contracts were never exchanged.' Peggy diverted her own saddened eyes. 'One day I got a call from your dad, from him personally, not just a message through the solicitors, which, given the circumstances, would have been understandable. And he wanted to explain and apologise. It broke my heart. I sobbed with him down the line. I recall the day so well.' Peggy fought back her emotions, her memory haunted by the way that Ernest's voice had sounded that day.

Kitty closed her eyes tightly and willed the pounding in her head to ease. Her thoughts were scrambled, and she couldn't stop crying. 'I'd have followed them here in a heartbeat, even without the shop,' she began, gathering up her emotions. 'My mum and dad were my life and it still hurts like they were both only taken from me yesterday.'

Peggy's eyebrows pulled together. 'They?'

'My dad passed away too, on the same night as my mum, just before Christmas. He suffered a massive stroke.'

Peggy shook her head at the cruelness of the tragedy. 'Oh, Kitty, I'm so sorry. How on earth did you cope?'

'I didn't,' she confessed. 'I was a mess. I was so lonely, and I felt my life was no longer worth living.' She paused, taking a deep breath in an effort to force the following utterance. 'And then I met someone, and even though I knew something wasn't right, I allowed myself to remain in a bad relationship,' she paused again. There were so many words to describe her experience with Stevie, and yet embarrassment prevented any poignant descriptions from being revealed. 'I just wanted someone to take away the hurt of losing my parents and, in a way, he did, but in exchange, I was left with more pain than what I started with.' Kitty shrugged. 'He was a distraction, a terrible distraction, and I know that now. It was like I was blinded, brainwashed almost, I guess, but he enabled me to push away the grief, like the whole thing with my parents had never happened. And when I realised who he really was, it was too late. I felt trapped, and even though I was scared, I couldn't leave. Pathetic, I know.' Kitty smiled in a way that revealed her deepest sadness, and her greatest regrets.

Peggy was rushed with a mixture of emotions – anger, rage, helplessness, frustration. She reached out and took hold of Kitty's hands. 'And have you made the trip down here alone?' she asked, noticing the scars and the petrified expression that rose to the surface the moment Kitty allowed herself to reflect upon her past.

A meek smile broke through to the surface. 'Yes, I have.'

Peggy's face sparkled. 'Then you are definitely brave, and now you have a new start in life to look forward to,' she announced. 'And you can follow any path you like.' Peggy indicated for Kitty to pick up her cup. 'This deserves a toast. To new beginnings, for both of us.'

Kitty clinked cups before taking a gentle sip. 'Did you actually meet my parents?'

Peggy nodded through a warm fondness. 'I did, just once. It was a very strange day really. They came down to St. Ives to take a look at the shop and go through the accounts, but after only half an hour with the estate agent, I got a call requesting that I go and meet them.' Peggy reached over and grabbed a book off the coffee table. 'I was worried because I thought something was wrong, that they'd found an issue with the business or flat. But when I got there, all they wanted to do was take me out for lunch. I guess they wanted to sort of thank me for selling, although I was the one who felt indebted.' Peggy opened the book that was resting on her lap, taking out a few hidden photos. 'We all went to a café located down on the front and sipped on glasses of chilled rosé while sharing stories.' Peggy handed the photos to Kitty.

Resting them in her palms, Kitty studied the two pictures. The first captured both Delilah and Ernest stood in front of Flourish, their faces beaming. Their smiles leapt out from the picture and Kitty could almost hear their giggles of excitement. 'I remember them going away for the weekend not that long before mum got her diagnosis, but they told me they were staying in York. I guess that must have been the weekend they came down,' Kitty replied, studying every inch of the photo.

'They took a copy of those too, and planned on giving it to you along with the keys, whenever the right moment came for them to reveal their plans, which we now know never happened.'

Kitty couldn't take her eyes off Delilah, drinking in the happiness that was exuding from the photograph. 'I can't remember a time she ever looked happier,' she confessed. 'All I see in my memories now is the final days of pain that did nothing but drown her eyes.' Kitty dragged her attention away from the photo and peered out into the garden. 'Memories can be so cruel,' she added, searching her long-term memory for happier recollections and willing them to rise to the surface.

'From what I gathered that day, your mum enjoyed a wonderful life. All she spoke about was you, Kitty, and her face lit up every time she did. After your parents had left, I felt like I'd met you too.' Peggy took hold of Kitty's hand once more. 'You must remember the good times. The happy memories are still there, they're just trapped beneath your pain, and that will ease, given enough time. Take these photos with you and every time you can't see past the grief, look at your mum's beaming smile and remember everything she wanted for your future.'

Kitty held her hands out and nodded. 'It's all starting to make sense, now,' she began, turning to face Peggy, a look of contentment easing itself across her face. 'On the day that my mum passed away, she wanted to tell me something, only her voice just couldn't get the words out - at that stage a terrible weakness had taken hold of her body, preventing her from speaking more than a few words at a time. She was trying to tell me to look in something, I think,' she explained with a puzzled expression. 'I searched through everything, through all her things and yet I couldn't find anything. And then not long ago, I came across the letters from the solicitors. She must have been trying to tell me about their plans down here. And now that you've explained the story, it all makes perfect sense,' she concluded, smiling with comfort at uncovering her mum's secret.

Kitty looked up at Peggy, their eyes meeting. 'Are you alright?' she asked, noting a peculiar expression presenting itself on Peggy's face.

Peggy stood up and meandered over to the window, peering out over her mature, spacious garden.

'Please, if there's something else you know, Peggy, please tell me,' begged Kitty.

Peggy paused before replying. 'Your mum did want to tell you something, Kitty, but not just about the shop.' Peggy remained facing the garden, shielding her emotions with her back towards the room.

'Then what?' Kitty asked, placing her cup on the table. She noticed the way that Peggy's body stiffened, causing a rigidity to stiffen her own spine. 'Peggy, what is it?'

'I made a promise to your mum, Kitty, and I can't betray her trust, I just can't. I gave her my word and I want to keep it. I owe it to her.' Peggy swung her body around, her face flooded with ripples of tears. Kitty stood up and walked over towards the window.

'I didn't mean to upset you, I'm so sorry, that was never my intention,' she began, placing her arms around Peggy's shoulders. 'This is all just so overwhelming. I'm meeting you for the first time and yet you seem to know so much about my parents, information that I didn't even know myself, and I'm their daughter.' Kitty moved away and stood in the window, noting the garden flourishing with daffodils. 'It's so much to deal with and now I feel like there's something else that I don't know.'

Peggy stood alongside Kitty, and they both looked out over the garden. 'I wanted your mum to tell you herself, and I know she planned on doing just that, but it didn't happen because she became so poorly, so quickly.' The pair remained shoulder to shoulder. 'But I beg that you don't give up. Don't let go of what your mum said in her final hours, and discover for yourself her last wish.'

Kitty's lip quivered. 'Even though I don't fully understand, I love that you won't betray my mum. She must have trusted you, Peggy, and so I do too.' Kitty burrowed her head into the palm of her hands. 'I had to leave everything behind to escape. I don't have any of my mum's belongings down here with me to search through.'

Peggy guided Kitty until her shielded face landed on the softness of her shoulder. 'And you did the right thing, Kitty. But when the time is right, when it's safe, you can return to Perth and search again. Your mum never wanted to hurt you, Kitty, that I can tell you. She loved you so much and did everything she could to protect you. And I know that you'll find the answers that you're looking for, I know you will.'

Kitty wiped her face, dabbing her cheeks with a tissue. 'Thank you, Peggy,' she began, after taking a few deep breaths. 'Thank you so much for being there for my mum. And thank you for selling your business to me. I'll take good care of it, I promise I will.'

'Oh, I know it's in the very best of hands, I wouldn't have sold it otherwise. And, once you've got yourself set up, I'll come down and take a look, see what wonderful things you've been up to.' Peggy released a calming breath. 'And don't be scared to inject some new life into the shop. After all these years, it's what the place deserves.'

'I'll try my best. I think I might head over there now, if you don't mind. I'd like to take a look around and see for myself what my mum and dad fell in love with.' With some reluctance, Kitty made her way out of the room. 'Thank you again, Peggy, for everything. I'll make sure that I keep in touch, if that's okay with you?' Kitty navigated her way through the narrow, winding hallway towards the front door.

'Of course. I'd love nothing more.' Peggy followed Kitty to the door. 'If there are any issues with the shop, be sure to call me, anytime. The key does tend to stick a little, but I'm sure you'll soon get the knack. The flat is fully furnished, but if there is anything missing, I'm sure we can get it sorted.'

Kitty paused by the front door. 'I appreciate all that you've done, Peggy, for my family, too, not just for me.'

'My pleasure.' Instead of shaking Kitty's hand, Peggy held out her arms. 'Nice to have finally met you, Kitty.' The pair savoured the embrace, each one loathing to part. After a few seconds, Peggy opened the front door, allowing the rising temperatures to seep in and the sunshine to rest upon her face.

Kitty admired the snippets of sun-drenched sky that she saw peeking out beyond the budding trees scattering Peggy's garden. 'Thank you, Peggy. I hope we'll see each other soon.'

Peggy waved goodbye, a plethora of raw emotions tumbling through her mind. She felt like shouting for Kitty to come back, and to prevent her from leaving. She wondered whether she should have broken her promise and taken the opportunity to tell Kitty the truth. But the moment had passed, and although it broke her heart, she stood at the door and watched Kitty leave.

16

KITTY TURNED THE CORNER AND MADE HER WAY DOWN TO Ladysmith Lane. She admired the quaintness of the street and the history etched into the rustic cobbles. The lack of uniformity in the architecture added a quirkiness, along with the traditional-style lampposts that lined the street. An injection of colour was provided by the mismatch of front doors, and the zigzag rows of traditional bunting that dressed the street in the most appropriate manner.

Kitty approached Flourish with a heavy heart, like she was meeting a long-lost relative after spending a lifetime separated. She stood across the road, her feet teetering on the edge of the pavement, not quite ready to cross. She admired the two large, wooden bay windows sat either side of the door, both painted olive and framing the contents behind. The display could have been mistaken for a scene out of someone's home; a scattering of plum knitted cushions, a collection of handmade soft toys all accentuated by drapes of stitched bunting. Even without signs of life or internal lighting to illuminate it, the vibrant, cosy window display worked to entice wandering eyes.

Kitty took out one of the photos that Peggy had given to her and made her way across the street, standing in the exact same spot as her parents in the picture. She felt an immediate closeness to her mum and dad and a sense of comfort at the thought of stepping into their dream, and her future. Without her phone, a desire to capture an image of the poignant moment came and went.

She took out the keys, and struggled as the lock jammed in the door. 'Just open,' she muttered after a few seconds of fumbling.

'Hi,' Lily announced, noticing who she assumed to be her new business neighbour standing at the door to Flourish. Kitty spotted Lily in her periphery, the stranger now lingering in close proximity. Kitty had hoped to make it through the door undetected, allowing her a few private moments to breathe and absorb her new life in privacy.

'Hello,' she replied, only half turning to acknowledge Lily, still grappling with the door and willing it to accept her entrance. 'What's wrong with this thing?'

Lily sensed the apprehension in Kitty's half-hearted attempt at a menial greeting and out of the corner of her eye, watched Kitty struggling with the stubborn door. 'Here, let me help,' she insisted, walking the few paces to the shop attached to hers. 'This door always gets jammed, and I'm not sure why, but Peggy, the previous owner, always said that I had the magic touch.'

'Oh, thank you,' Kitty replied, moving aside and watching how Lily did nothing more than jiggle the key about in the lock, at which point, it released.

'See, there you go.' Lily stepped aside and smiled. 'With practice, you'll soon get the hang of it,' she added, before turning and walking away. Kitty pushed herself to extend the olive branch.

'Thank you.'

The two words were sufficient in preventing Lily from entering her salon, her hand pausing on the handle.

'I'm Kitty. It's my first day and it's all a bit daunting to be honest, especially when I can't even open the door.' The words tumbled out the moment she peered inside and the enormity of this new chapter now starting in her life overwhelmed her. Embarrassed by her sudden outburst in front of a stranger, her face quickly became crimson and she wished she could somehow rewind time and remake her first impression.

Lily sympathised. 'On *my* first day, I gave someone the wrong shade of highlights. I just lost my brain and somehow mixed up the bottles. My hands shook the entire day, and I don't think I completed one straight hair cut for my entire shift.'

Kitty felt a tightness in her chest, her downcast expression and shuffling feet indicators of her inner turmoil. 'Good to know it happens to others and not just me,' she finally replied, looking Lily in the eyes before her attention gravitated back towards her shop. 'What have I done?' she mumbled, still stood on the pavement, gazing into her shop and not having a clue what to do first.

Lily also remained stood on her doorstep. 'The good thing is, all of us are happy to help,' she said. 'Whatever you need, just ask and someone will know the answer,' she explained, pointing up and down the street with her hands. 'Everyone on the street is super friendly, and helpful in any kind of crisis.'

Kitty shook her head. 'What makes me think I can do this?' she muttered, feeling her tears mounting. She suddenly found herself craving the warm embrace of her mum, and her words of reassurance.

'Are you alright?'

Kitty felt silly, too intimidated to step foot inside the shop she now owned. Waves of doubt rolled in off the sea, unsteadying her balance and threatening to topple her remaining strands of confidence.

'I think I need another cup of tea, if you could help with that? I'd really appreciate it.'

Lily jumped at the opportunity, sensing many commonalities and a kindred spirit. She signalled for Kitty to follow her inside. 'Of course. Come on in and I'll put the kettle on.' Kitty locked her shop door and meandered the few paces up the street to the hair salon.

'Here. Take a seat,' Lily offered, moving the strewn gowns off all the seats in the window waiting area before disappearing out the back to fill the kettle. Kitty sat with such a stillness and blank expression that she resembled part of the display; a human mannequin.

'I've been wondering who'd bought the shop. The notice hasn't been up too long, you know, saying under new management, and Peggy didn't really provide many details, so I didn't want to pry. It all seemed to happen in a bit of a flash.' A natural chatterbox, Lily filled the pockets of silence despite not being in the same room. 'Did she tell you why she's sold up?' she added, stepping into the salon whilst fastening her accessories belt.

'I think it just felt like the right time for her.'

The shop door opened, the person walking in failing to spot Kitty's figure perched in the window.

'Thought I'd treat you today, Lily,' announced Ben, pushing his way through the door with a cup of coffee in both hands. 'I'm in an exceptionally good mood, do you want to ask me why?' Lily attempted to introduce Kitty, but he didn't allow time for a response before elaborating on his statement. 'I'll tell you why. It's because I met someone this morning and I can't quite put my finger on what it was about her, and we didn't even talk for that long, but there was just something… something so quintessentially wonderful about her.' He placed one hand dramatically across his heart after handing Lily her coffee, and steadied himself against the wall with the other. 'She took my breath away.'

Lily threw Kitty an apologetic look in the mirror, holding up her finger to indicate that this would just take a minute.

'And I know what you're gonna say,' Ben started speaking through a nagging tone. 'It's not the right time, it's too soon after everything that's happened.' His usual voice then returned. 'But I can't help the way that I felt, the way that *she* made me feel.' He finally stopped talking, exhausted by his own emotional outpour. He slumped himself down in one of the styling chairs facing an elongated mirror, and was shocked to find Kitty's reflection.

Unawares of their previous acquaintance, Lily began formal introductions. 'Ben, this is Kitty. She's the new owner of Flourish. And Kitty, this is Ben Fox, Ladysmith Lane's finest artist. His studio is just over there, above Pebble & Sand.' Lily pointed across the road before noting the look on Ben's face. 'You alright? You look a little flushed.'

Ben and Kitty exchanged a mutual look of embarrassment. Unable to escape the shame and awkwardness of the situation, Ben made a move by standing up and jabbing his friend in the back with his finger. 'Very nice of you to say so, Lily, but I'm actually the only artist on the lane, which automatically makes me the best,' he replied, a slight flush refusing to subside from his cheeks.

Kitty stood up too. 'I still struggle to colour within the lines so I'm in awe of anyone that can paint freestyle.' She held her hand out, saving Ben from further social meltdown. 'Nice to meet you.' She delivered him a grin and slight nod.

'Nice to meet you, Kitty, and welcome to the street.' The moment his hand merged with hers, his heart ignited. He felt his eyes becoming lost in hers, his thoughts mesmerised by her natural beauty. 'Well, I can't stand around here chatting, there are blank canvases that require attention. Plus, there's another cup of coffee with my name on it losing steam as we speak. Have a nice day, ladies.' And with that, Ben bolted up the street, kicking himself for behaving like such a fool.

'Well, that felt a little odd. HHe doesn't normally act so weird.'

'Lily,' Kitty began, changing the subject and embracing a fleeting moment of bravery. 'I do need help, or more of a favour really.'

'Of course, anything.'

Kitty scanned herself in the mirror from top to bottom. She loathed all elements of familiarity in her reflection, wanting to erase the ghosts attached to her appearance. 'I need a makeover, if you have time. I've just come out of a relationship and, you know how it is, I need a fresh look.'

Lily whipped out a cape like she was a Spanish flamenco dancer and flung it around Kitty's body. 'Then take a seat. What can I do for you today? It looks like my first appointment is a no-show, which means I'm all yours until eleven-thirty, at which point I have the adorable Vera in for her monthly perm.' Lily ran her hands through Kitty's deep auburn locks, each strand straightened to eradicate any natural curl. 'Are we thinking just a little tidy-up?'

'I want to go blonde.'

Lily raised her eyebrows so high they almost jumped off her face. 'Excuse me?'

'I mean it,' Kitty replied, smiling and nodding with a firm sense of reassurance.

'Why would you want to do such a crazy thing? You have such wonderful hair, hair that most women who walk through my door would die for.'

'I'm ready for a change, a complete change. I was blonde as a child and my hair is still very curly naturally, if you can believe it. So, either I pay you to do a proper job, or I buy a do-it-yourself kit and end up with hair that's green.'

'Why on earth would you have spent what must've been so much time killing all of those natural curls?'

Kitty's evasive edge resurfaced. 'We've all done some silly things just to try and please a man, haven't we?'

Lily exhaled and nodded in agreement. 'My list of mistakes could fill a notebook cover to cover. Well, if you're sure, and I mean really sure, because once the bleach is applied, there's no turning back…'

Kitty nodded with encouragement. 'Let's do it,' she encouraged.

In between slurps of tea, Lily applied the colourant, her hands weaving with the brush, hatching out Kitty's brand-new identity.

'So, apart from being unable to open the door, which is only a minor issue that I am certain that you can overcome,' Lily mocked, 'are you excited about opening up next door?'

Kitty felt hesitant and cleared her throat. 'I've never owned a business before, but how hard can it be, right?' she mocked. 'I have a fashion degree and can craft just about anything out of fabric, if I put my mind to it. And I'm pretty good with numbers, too. What more is there to running a haberdashery business?'

Lily admired Kitty's free-spirited nature. 'Exactly,' she laughed, examining the transformation already taking place under the foils. 'So, are you local?'

Kitty raised her eyebrows. 'No. This is my first day in St. Ives and, so far, it's going well, apart from the door issue, of course.'

'I'm not sure whether you're crazy, or the cleverest person that's ever walked through my door. Now, how about I get us both a crumpet whilst we wait? I missed breakfast and I'm starving.' Kitty couldn't recall the last time she'd eaten a meal and yet didn't feel any sensation of hunger.

'I'm alright, thank you. I need to go food shopping after we've finished here anyway.'

Lily walked through to the back office. 'I won't be a minute then, you just relax,' she called. Whilst Kitty sat, waiting with patience for her hair to be transformed, she glanced down at her ring finger, the absence of her engagement ring feeling odd. Her thoughts wandered back to Perth and she imagined the potential scenes unfolding at home, the images sending a shiver to coarse through her body that was so strong, Lily captured her reaction.

'You okay?' she asked upon returning into the room. 'You looked like you've just seen a ghost.'

'Looking at my reflection right now is pretty scary,' she mocked.

'Well, while we're waiting, why don't I cover up the mirrors? That way, your post-relationship transformation will hopefully be a nice surprise.' Lily spent a good deal of time securing ripped magazine pages to every single mirror in the salon, all the while, chatting to Kitty about everything from holidays and hangovers, to sea side life and love.

'Right, let's get you rinsed off,' she said, indicating for Kitty to move over to the basin.

'How's it looking?' she asked with hesitance on her way back over to the styling chair.

Lily removed the towel and began combing through the long, wavy strands of wet hair. 'You'll see once it's dried. Now, tell me again, you don't want any cutting, spraying, straightening or styling – am I right?' Lily plugged in her diffuser and applied some curl-boosting crème to Kitty's hair.

'Maybe just scoop it round into a flimsy plait to take it off my face.'

The din from the dryer commanded silence, permitting Kitty some private time to anticipate the result. After a handful of minutes, Lily placed down her dryer. She spun the chair round so that she could be the first to witness the new person now sat in her salon, all traces of the old Kitty unrecognisable with her clothes hidden beneath the cape.

'It looks perfect. Just perfect,' announced Lily, finishing off a waterfall-style braid that swooped round the side of Kitty's ears, a few, delicate, curly strands framing her freckle-dotted face.

The salon door swung open.

'I can't believe I made such an idiot of myself earlier,' Ben announced, this time checking for clients in the salon before opening his mouth, noticing only a blonde lady in the seat, her back facing him. Without seeking visual confirmation, Kitty recognised Ben's voice, soft and caring with a deep, masculine undertone.

'I just wanted to pull my hoodie over my face and run.'

'What *are* you talking about?' asked Lily, adding the final touch to Kitty's new style. 'This is the second time you've rushed in here today, acting all weird, and I have no clue what it is you're actually going on about. The only thing I do know is that you were prodding me in the back,' she said, twisting to try and examine her back for bruises.

Ben flung his arms in the air. 'The girl. The girl I was telling you about that I met on the beach, the girl with the incredible blue eyes and a smile that could light up the whole of St. Ives. She was sat over there, on that very chair.' Ben turned and pointed at the now vacant window seat.

'Oh, then I assume that you're talking about this lady who is now sitting here,' Lily swung the chair around so that Kitty faced the room.

'I asked Lily for a red colour with some light, copper highlights. How does it look? Be honest,' Kitty asked in an attempt to squash the awkwardness, directing her question at Ben.

'Erm.'

'She's teasing you, you idiot,' Lily intervened, prodding Ben in the stomach. 'She's trying to make light of feeling awkward in your presence.' Lily bent down to look at Kitty, the mirrors still covered with magazines. 'I promise you, not all men in St. Ives are so utterly terrible when it comes to romance.' Lily stood up straight. 'Well, let's address this moment of embarrassment right now and get rid of any future awkwardness because you're going to bump into one another working on the same street. I'm just nipping to make a brew, so I'll leave you to it. Back in a mo.' When just out of sight from Kitty, Lily gave Ben the thumbs up, accompanied by an erratic stream of signals with her head, offering silent encouragement.

Ben plunged his hands into his pockets. 'I'm so sorry.'

'Really, there's no need to apologise,' interrupted Kitty. 'I've just arrived in town, as you know – literally only a few minutes before I first met you on the beach this morning,' she began, feeling the need to state her situation. 'I've bought the shop next door and I also need to move into my new flat, which is next door to here, but that way,' she explained, pointing to her left. 'So, you can imagine how busy my life is going to be in the upcoming months, no time for anything really, apart from work.'

Ben felt a weight of disappointment in his heart. 'So that there's no more awkwardness, I feel we should start over, if that's okay with you? You do look totally different to the person I met on the beach this morning, so it's kind of like I'm meeting you for the first time anyway.'

Kitty stood and smiled. 'Great idea. I'm Kitty, lovely to meet you, Ben.' She held out her hand and offered him a hand shake.

Lily re-entered the salon. 'I see you two have sorted things out,' she commented, noting the handshake. 'Now to more important matters. Are you ready to see the transformation for yourself?' she asked, tearing away the newspaper and magazine pages to reveal the mirrors.

An audible gasp released from Kitty's mouth the moment she caught sight of her reflection, her blond, curly hair inducing fond recollections, her look so similar to her natural, childhood appearance. Her eyes welled, a feeling of safety igniting in her soul. 'Blimey. If any of my friends from home were to walk past me now, I'm not sure they'd recognise me.' Kitty stepped closer to the mirror and touched her hair.

'See, I told you I don't always get it wrong,' Lily proclaimed, admiring her work.

'Thank you so much,' she replied, providing Lily with an impromptu embrace, swept up by the enormity of the moment, with gratitude pouring from her heart. 'You don't know how much this means.'

'You're welcome. New look, new start,' she whispered into Kitty's ear.

Kitty unstrapped her cape. 'Lily says that everyone on this street is super helpful, willing to lend a hand. Is that right?' she asked, directing the question at Ben.

'Sure.'

'Well, I'm opening my shop tomorrow and it turns out that I can't even open the door. So, I might need a few helpers, you know, just in case I have any more disasters. Can I count you two in?'

Ben jumped in first with his reply. 'I'm free. I'm good at anything, other than painting,' he joked.

'Yep, I'll be there too. I can act as the official door opener.'

'Perfect, I'll see you both tomorrow then. And thanks again, Lily.' She placed the money on the counter and left the salon. With her old identity washed away with the outgoing tide, a gentle breeze swept through her ripples of blonde, curly hair. She meandered down the street and blended into the background of life in St. Ives like a true chameleon.

17

Upon leaving the salon, a curiosity encouraged Kitty to cross the road and peruse the adjacent businesses on Ladysmith Lane. She caught sight of her reflection in a shop window and a subtle smile spread across her face.

'Hi. Are you open?' she asked after pushing open the door to Past Times and popping her head through the gap.

'Oh, course, come in!' Susie encouraged.

Kitty stepped inside and closed the door behind her. 'Thanks.'

'Are you after anything particular? Everyday kind of stuff, or maybe something for a night out?' asked Susie from behind the counter, running her eyes over Kitty's figure to try and gauge her dress size.

Kitty ran her hand across the assortment of clothes on the rails, a real dolly mixture of colours on offer.

'Everyday kind of stuff.' She picked out some flares and held them up to her waist. 'I quite like these.'

'They're a great choice. There's a changing cubicle over there in the corner, go and have a try-on if you like.' Before she headed into the changing room, Kitty grabbed a rainbow t-shirt with the word *love* stitched into the fabric, along with a chunky, fuchsia jumper dotted with snazzy buttons. Once behind the curtain, she peeled off her clothes and allowed them to fall to the floor. Early on in their relationship, Stevie had replaced much of Kitty's wardrobe, her quirky sense of style replaced with a selection of drab clothes that all worked to conceal her enviable shape.

'Are you enjoying your holiday?' asked Susie, hearing the zip fastening on Kitty's trousers.

'I'm not on holiday. I've bought the shop across the road. It will be my first day opening tomorrow.'

'Sorry, I just assumed.'

Kitty pulled back the curtain and stepped out, her new blonde curls looking more radiant without her gawky, beige skirt and blouse. 'Don't worry about it. I quite like the fact I look like a tourist. What do you think?' Kitty turned back to admire her look in the cubicle mirror, her inner bohemian once again blooming. Her new pair of waist-high, floral flares and off-the-shoulder t-shirt teased out her innate individuality, and in front of the mirror she flourished with more vibrancy than a field scattered with bluebells.

Susie nodded her head in agreement. 'You look amazing. Is that a tattoo I can see hiding beneath your t-shirt?'

'Just a silly mistake,' she explained with a strained voice. She took another look through the rails, picking out a handful of other items to try on.

Susie wandered over towards the window and peered across the road. 'It's felt so strange looking across and seeing Flourish all locked up and the lights turned off. I'm so excited that it's going to be reopening.'

Kitty appeared from out of the changing room and approached the till. 'Me too,' she replied. 'But right now, I'm more nervous than excited.'

'You'll be fine. If I can run a shop, then pretty much anyone can. I failed in every subject at school and I'm not really very business-minded, yet here I am,' Susie explained, holding out her hands and admiring her shop.

'I'll take all these, please. I'll keep the flares and t-shirt on, if that's alright?' Kitty placed her old clothes in one of Susie's boxes labelled *Recycling*, then rummaged in her purse.

'Great. Cash or card?'

'Cash, please. Here you go,' she replied, rooting in her bag and handing over the money. 'Thanks so much, and please feel free to pop across tomorrow, I'm going to need all the support I can get. At the very least, I'll make sure there are cakes and refreshments – I've heard that counter-top goodies have gone down well in the past at Flourish.'

'I'll be there, and it's been lovely to have met you. I think you'll fit right in with us on the lane.'

'Super. I best get going. I've a million things to do before tomorrow morning.'

Upon leaving Past Times, Kitty walked back across the road and took out her shop key, wiggling it in the lock until it permitted entry. 'Here we go,' she said to herself, walking into the shop for the very first time. She closed the door behind her and ripped off the piece of paper that stated the shop was 'Under new management'.

With her back pressed against the door, Kitty took a moment to admire the interior. Scanning the room as it lay beneath a gloomy darkness, the first thing she noticed was a wonderful aroma. The comforting, delicate and yet undistinguishable smell of lavender hung like fine cotton threads in the air, tickling her nostrils and making the fine hairs inside her nose dance.

She reached out her hand and flicked the light switch, the two rows of large, copper lights illuminating the shop's interior with more pizazz than a West End production. Sat central in the space was a large wooden measuring desk, positioned to greet anyone who entered the shop. A single stool sat behind the desk, the wooden seat worn after years of accommodating weary bodies. To the left, one huge, zonal storage unit decorated the wall, each segment full of folded fabrics. Below it were multiple wooden wheelbarrows, each bed brimming with offcuts.

To the right, balls of wool every shade of the spectrum were bundled into hanging baskets, producing a kaleidoscope of colour. White wicker baskets dotted the three side tables, each one brimming with knitting accessories. On a shabby-chic style dresser, there were hundreds of small mason jars, each filled with a different colour, shape and size of decorative button.

Dangling above the desk, dozens of ribbon reels and organza strips hung like a vibrant, summer downpour. The two main windows filled the shop with generous amounts of natural light, allowing midday rays to illuminate the gems on offer inside. More retro wheelbarrows full of offcuts sat in the window displays, each framed by pastel-coloured bunting. A strategic scattering of patchwork cushions, along with a mannequin, completed the enticing shop window. The mannequin sported a handmade, chunky yellow jumper, the words *Please Come In* embroidered on the front in a vibrant shade of pink stitching. Even if you weren't a knitter, and even if you weren't out shopping for fabric, if you walked past Flourish, you'd be drawn in by its quaint charm.

Kitty edged her way in, running her hand across the counter and acquainting herself with its ingrained contours. She meandered to the left, running her fingers across the fabrics, feeling the various textures each piece of material offered. Ideas popped into her mind as to how she could add her own personality to the shop's already wonderful offerings, and what item she might craft first. *A patchwork tablecloth for a children's tea party,* she thought, upon spotting a pink and white polka dot pattern. *Or maybe a range of vintage-style hair bands,* she pondered, upon catching sight of some cream beading and organza, which was dangling right in front of her eyeline. With her creative instincts now awoken and flowing, she felt eager to wave her crafty, magic wand, and to embellish the shop with her own sprinkle of charm.

Then, the door swung open. 'Have you got any umbrellas, love? It looks like the clouds are rolling in,' asked an elderly lady, a trolley brimming with fresh-cut flowers being pulled behind her.

'Erm,' replied Kitty, fumbling over her words. 'I'm not actually open today, but let me see what I can do.' She rooted under the counter, finding everything a person could ever need in life; a plaster, multiple pairs of scissors, cups, biscuits, even an old toaster. 'Ah, here we go,' she announced, spotting an umbrella, the attached tag stating *Left in shop by unknown, 23rd July.* 'Here, you can take this.' She walked to the door and handed the lady the umbrella. 'For free, I mean,' she added when she saw the elderly lady rooting in her purse, counting up a handful of coins. 'Come back tomorrow and I'll make you a nice cup of tea,' she added, noting how the lady looked cold, her lips dry and chapped.

'Oh, that would be nice, thank you.' Kitty closed the door and locked it, watching the lady hobble off into the distance. She noted how the lane still appeared to be dotted with people despite it being late afternoon, each couple or individual meandering in the same carefree manner. Kitty walked away from the window and sat herself behind the desk. She played with the till, like she had imagined when playing a game of shopkeeper as a child. After an hour of making sure that she could operate the sewing machine and other gadgets, and familiarising herself with the products, she turned off the lights, ready as she ever would be to open to the public the following morning.

'You managed to get inside then?' shouted Lily from the salon door, spotting Kitty locking up.

'First attempt, too.'

'And the hair is still looking great, five hours in. And the flares - nice, very nice.' Lily twizzled her hand, requesting Kitty to spin. 'Perfect,' she added, admiring Kitty's new look from all angles. 'You know what, you wouldn't even know you were the same person. I hope your family and friends are ready for the shock – they might not even recognise you!' The comment made Kitty's knees buckle, a slow smile appearing on her face.

'Really?'

'Kitty, you look completely different to when I first met you this morning. It's like you've undergone an extreme makeover.' Kitty's eyes sparkled and she took another quick glance at her own reflection.

'I'm going to go and get a takeaway. I can't be bothered cooking tonight. Fancy joining me? There's a great place down by the front,' invited Lily. 'They make the best steak sandwiches I've ever tasted.'

'Thank you so much, but there's still a million things I need to do before tomorrow,' she replied, running through the list of jobs in her mind. 'I need to pop to the shop and buy a new phone because mine broke. I need to grab some supplies from the supermarket and then I'm going to check out my flat before crawling my weary body into bed. It's been quite a day. Another time maybe?'

'Of course, no problem. I'll see you tomorrow then,' waved Lily, heading up the lane.

After calling in at a few shops, and with her hands laden with shopping bags, Kitty headed home, her body aching with each stride having taken the toll of the day. She unlocked the door to her flat and snuck herself away, taking refuge inside. With her back pressed against the front door, her body sank to the floor. The shopping bags slipped free from her hands and whilst peering up the stairs, the enormity of everything that she'd done in the past twenty-four hours rattled her composure. With her hands, she covered her face and sobbed, the world which she'd fled now feeling so far away, and yet her fear still felt raw and very much close by. Her thoughts drifted back to Millie the moment she took out her new mobile phone, wanting to send a simple text confirming she was now safe and well. Yet the thought of connecting with her abandoned world felt risky, and she returned her phone to the little pocket within her bag.

After a few moments, she walked up the stairs, familiarising herself with the quirks of the space she was now to call home. She meandered through each perfectly presented room, her fingers knocking the soft furnishings and her hips nudging each chair until everything looked more haphazard, removing any shred of symmetry. Taking out a fresh bunch of daffodils from one of her shopping bags, Kitty filled a pint glass with water and eased the stems into the cavity, resting them on the windowsill. The petals added a lovely touch of brightness to the otherwise plain room, and Kitty smiled at the realisation that her latest bunch of daffodils would finally be permitted the opportunity to bloom as nature had intended, without being purposefully destroyed. In her mind, the moment felt like a small victory in what had felt like a very long, and personal war.

Through fresh eyes and a clear mind, the sight of the vibrant flowers made her recall how, at this time of year, daffodils had once scattered the family garden in an abundance, the flowers blooming year after year, a sea of yellow petals shining brighter than the summer sun. Delilah always placed bunches of daffodils in each room during the early spring months, a tradition that Kitty continued despite learning that Stevie sought pleasure from destroying them, and she now resented him more than ever for tarnishing one of her precious memories.

Her gaze diverted to the scene beyond the window, noticing how the sky over St. Ives displayed its best summer suit, a perfect evening azure. Her ears detected the sound of birdsong, the choir perched in the trees performing like a well-strung instrument. Kitty could see and hear spring on the cusp of mushrooming, the trees outside her window heavy with buds, all ready to flourish. Her thoughts drifted back to Delilah, imagining how she and her mum may have spent such a wonderful evening together, the pair perhaps chatting whilst sipping on cool drinks, or tending to the garden, planting the first flowers of the season.

With a sense of exhaustion, she slumped her body into the oversized single chair near the window and released an extended breath. She pulled up her legs until her knees met her chest, resting her head back. At the side of her chair, an envelope rested on the table, her name handwritten on the front. She admired the sketch of the house, before opening the card to read its message – *Welcome to your new home, Kitty* – written in Peggy's hand. With her eyes lingering on the words, she smiled and felt so grateful for the personal touch. The perfect timing of the card made her smile, and held it to her chest, Peggy's words helping to cast away some of Kitty's worries and fears for her future. She eased her head back and relished the momentary sense of peace following the storm she had now escaped.

18

DROPLETS OF EARLY MORNING SUNSHINE WASHED INTO KITTY'S bedroom, a stark brightness resting on her eyes, easing them open. For a brief moment, fright wrapped itself around her body until she rolled over, spotting the empty pillow. 'I did it,' she smiled, whilst kicking the soles of her feet against the mattress. With a contented purr, she lay her head back down and hid beneath the duvet before throwing it back and releasing a high pitch scream. 'I did it.'

She peered around her bedroom, a wave of tranquillity flooding in off the sea. For the first time in months, she stepped out of bed and swung the curtains wide open, ready to greet the new day. She crept through to the kitchen and sipped on a cool glass of water, her body gravitating towards the window. The soundwaves from Vera's gramophone below eased their way through, encouraging Kitty to swing back the lounge curtains too, and open the window to amplify the quirky music. She caught sight of the rows of bunting crisscrossing the street, each fabric offcut hanging like a colourful cloud above the lane. She spotted Ruben down in his café, his hands kneading what looked like a fresh batch of dough, her nose detecting the subtle aroma of coffee trickling through the air.

Despite the captivating nature of the new world beyond her window, she couldn't help but take hold of her new phone and tap in the memorised digits for Millie's café. Without the aid of her old phone to act as a prompt, Kitty could only recite three

135

phone numbers by heart; Millie's mobile, the café, and Stevie's mobile. A dialling tone streamed into her ear the moment she took a seat, her knees bouncing.

'Hello, Millie's café, how can I help?' a flustered voice on the other end of the line asked. Kitty felt nauseous, her pupils dilating.

'Hello?' the person asked again. In the background, Kitty heard her friend's faint voice, singing.

'Can you tell me which postcodes you deliver to?' Kitty asked, knowing the requested information would need to be looked up, buying her more time to hear Millie's voice, the only person in the whole world that she desperately wanted to speak to.

'I'll just go and check, I won't keep you a moment,' the assistant replied, placing the phone on the counter. Kitty pressed her eyelids together, heightening her sense of hearing. She listened to Millie singing in the background, the familiar tone of her voice making Kitty weep.

'I can't find the delivery leaflet, so I'll just pass you over to the manager, she'll know off the top of her head,' said the girl on the other end of the phone.

'Hello, can I help? I'm Millie, the manager.' Kitty's hand quivered against her ear. She closed her eyes and pressed her free hand against her face, capturing her falling tears. Hearing Millie's voice felt so wonderful, and yet Kitty couldn't reply.

'Hello. Is there anybody there?' Millie asked again before hanging up.

Kitty looked out over the street again, the increased activity out on the lane encouraging her to put aside her thoughts of Perth, and to quickly get ready for the day ahead. After eating a few slices of toast and showering, she tossed her pearl bag over her shoulder and headed downstairs. She lingered in her doorway, her fuchsia jumper providing the perfect level of warmth for the awakening day. Despite having never been a caffeine addict, the aroma of freshly ground coffee beans that drifted through the air drew Kitty across the street like a magnet, straight into Legumes.

'Morning, what can I get for you?' asked Ruben, flour clinging to the fine, spiky hairs on his arms.

'I'm thinking coffee,' began Kitty, scanning the menu board behind the counter and quickly becoming flummoxed by the raft of choices. 'You have so many options. I'm not a coffee connoisseur, despite having worked in a café for a short period of time, but I feel like this morning could be the perfect time to kick start my own coffee education.'

'Oh, and why is this education required today? Big day ahead?' Ruben asked, in his typical chirpy manner.

'It's my first day opening a new business. I'm already feeling nervous and I haven't even opened the door to greet my first customer.' The bell rang as somebody entered.

'I promise, I'm not stalking you. I come in here every morning for a coffee,' announced Ben in a jovial way, holding up his hands with innocence. 'I'm defending myself too much, aren't I?'

Ruben produced a puzzled expression. 'Do you two know one another?'

Ben took the opportunity to offer up some witty commentary. 'We do, although we have only met recently. This is Kitty. She's the new owner of Flourish and is our new business neighbour. We met yesterday, and she soon learnt what an absolute idiot I am.'

'Well, nice to meet you, Kitty, and congratulations on being so astute. Ben here really is a bit of a loser,' replied Ruben, flicking flour.

Kitty felt awkward. 'Could I have a cup of whatever you think will get me through the day?' she requested, at which point Ruben started clattering around with his favourite machine.

'I'll get you a latte, followed by a double-shot expresso. So, where did you two meet yesterday?'

Ben jumped to answer the question. 'We just happened to cross paths a few times, that's all.'

Ruben laughed and turned to face Ben. 'I'm sensing by your body language that you've already made an ass of yourself and now you're trying to cover your tracks,' he said before turning to look at Kitty. 'Tell me the truth so I can tease him for a few days - has he made an idiot out of himself?'

'He's telling the truth. We bumped into one another, that's all,' she replied. She took a sneaky glance in Ben's direction, doing her best to hold in the smile itching to break through. 'I also met Lily and Susie, who, along with Ben, have agreed to come to the shop later just to make it look like I have some customers. I'm hoping to recruit some more actors. Maybe you could pop across too?' she asked, catching Ruben's eye when he turned around.

'Count me in. What do I have to do?' he asked.

'Look like a customer, you know, mingle, blend into the background and just make it look like my shop is busy.'

'I can do that. I spend most of my life blending into other people's backgrounds'

'You're going to be busy, I'm sure of it. It's a great little touristy shop,' encouraged Ben. 'Just offer up loads of freebies and then once they're inside, encourage them to empty their pockets.' Ben's naturally playful conversation coaxed Kitty out of the invisible shell she had placed around herself for protection.

'Sounds like a form of bribery to me,' she replied.

'This is a business masterclass you're hearing right now, from the guy who's just landed a major contract from one of the biggest tourism hitters in St. Ives.' Ruben tapped the counter with a baguette, commanding attention from his meagre audience. 'Go into any hotel in and around Cornwall, and you'll no doubt be admiring one of this gentleman's paintings pretty soon.'

Embarrassed, Ben shuffled his feet, dipping his head to hide his reddening cheeks. 'The guy's eyes were glassy when he placed the order so he was probably hungover and unaware of what he was actually buying.'

'You're way too humble. It's a brilliant achievement - be proud!' declared Ruben, placing Kitty's coffees on the counter. 'Anyway, before his head gets too big, let's bring him back down. He may be alright at business, but if you're seeking romantic advice, then avoid him like a weak cup of coffee and come to me instead.' Ruben threw the tea towel over his shoulder with a swagger. 'Isn't that right, Ben?'

Ben looked down and shook his head.

'He knows I'm right, that's why he's gone so quiet.'

Ben looked down at his phone, re-reading the only two text messages from Charlie since she had left him, the first stating *our marriage is over,* the second, *stop calling me.*

Ben placed the exact change on the counter for his usual order. 'That may be true, but you're no dating expert,' he began, before looking at Kitty. 'What you should really do is ignore both of us, and then I can guarantee you'll be much better off. Now, please can I have my usual? There's my money. I have paintings to paint and this can only be achieved with the aid of caffeine.'

'Well, I best get going. Hopefully I'll have some customers to serve today, too,' Kitty added. 'Before I do, would it be possible to have two pitchers of lemonade, plus two large cakes of whatever flavour you have prepared? All to take away, please.'

'So, you're going with the bribery option – great choice,' confirmed Ruben, taking out a lemon drizzle and a coffee and walnut cake and placing them on the counter top. 'With these in your arsenal, your first day is bound to be a smash.'

'Thanks, let's hope so,' she replied, handing over the money and taking hold of what she could. Struggling to carry the hoard, Ben offered to escort her down the street, a bake balancing in each hand, whilst Kitty carried the two pitchers of tangy lemonade.

'I'll follow you down with the coffees,' Ruben insisted, wanting to witness for himself the exciting moment that the doors to Flourish re-opened.

'Somehow, it appears that I have now tasked myself with the most important job of all,' announced Ben. 'If the cakes fall, you can blame any subsequent catastrophes of the day on me.' As the three new friends made their way down the lane, Lily and Susie meandered over.

Kitty looked at the ladies who she also hoped would become new friends. 'Thanks for coming.'

'You can do this,' encouraged Lily, sensing Kitty's apprehension at even getting over the threshold without a hiccup. 'You did it yesterday and you can do it again today.'

For Kitty, opening the door for the first time and inviting strangers into her world felt brave, and she questioned if she could summon enough courage to proceed. Without further thought or time to second guess herself, she handed Lily one of the lemonade pitchers and inserted the key, giving it a wiggle and then pushing open the door.

'Here we go,' she announced, more to herself than anyone else. She switched on the lights and turned the sign to *Welcome. Please come in.* 'I'm officially open.'

'Congratulations,' said Lily, placing the lemonade on the counter the moment she stepped inside. 'I've got a client booked in at nine, so I best get going. But I'll stop by later to see how you've got on.' Susie offered her congratulations too, before walking away and opening up her own shop that sat directly opposite.

Before Kitty could take off her jumper, the shop door opened and in walked her first, genuine customer. Ruben and Ben shuffled backwards, both giving Kitty the thumbs up and mouthing *good luck*. She waved as they walked away, leaving her to try out her new role of shopkeeper for the first time.

'Hi. Do you do alterations? I've just bought this dress which is a bit baggy, and I'd like the size adjusting, if possible.'

'Let's take a look,' Kitty began, taking out the dress to assess the work involved. 'I think we can make it work.' The lid on her box of crafty skills opened for the first time since her parents had passed away and since she'd left her teaching job, and although a little rusty, she took out a measuring tape from under the counter. 'Let's get you sized up and then we'll know how much to take it in.' Like a summer bouquet basking beneath the sun, in her new role, Kitty flourished. 'Can I get you a piece of cake? I haven't tried it myself yet, but if that icing is anything to go off, it's going to taste amazing.'

A steady stream of customers trickled through all day, keeping Kitty's mind occupied, and although she felt her heart flutter each time the bell over the door jingled, she relaxed and threw herself into Cornish life like a seasoned expert. The latter end of the working day approached when the bell once again rang.

'Hello, Kitty? Are you here?' she heard a familiar voice announce. Kitty appeared from out of the back office.

'Oh, hi, Peggy,' she replied, a wave of gratitude washing over at the sight of a new, yet familiar face. 'I'm so glad you stopped by.' The pair didn't just hug, they shared a comforting, heartfelt embrace.

'I wouldn't have missed it for anything. I know how important today was for you, and for your parents.' Peggy gazed around the shop, and despite the fact the interior hadn't yet been altered, the shop somehow still displayed a new identity. 'Kitty, your parents would have been so proud. I'm so proud of you too, and I've only known you a couple of days.'

'Thank you, Peggy,' she replied, holding out her hand, and taking comfort in the reciprocated, sincere affection of another human being. Peggy's hand felt delicate to the touch, the tiny bones protruding through her aged skin, just like Delilah's once had. 'It's been a real success, better than I could've hoped. I'm not saying it's been easy, because it hasn't. But I never expected this journey that I have found myself taking to always run smoothly.'

Peggy fiddled with the silver brooch fastened to her shawl, the knitting needles and yarn pin sparkling beneath the spotlights. 'When I spent the day with your mum, she noticed this brooch and said it reminded her of you because you could always be found knitting or sewing. I explained that I'd worn it every day in the shop, as a sort of uniform, if you like. My mother gave it to me because I loved knitting. I told your mum that when you all moved down here, I would pass this over to you.' Peggy paced forwards and pinned the brooch onto Kitty's jumper, admiring how it glimmered with an effortless elegance. 'Take a look in the mirror, see what you think.'

Kitty walked over to the mirror, pressing her fingers against the metal, feeling honoured at the sentiment. 'Peggy, it's beautiful. Are you sure you don't want to keep it?'

'I'm quite sure. It belongs to you now. It belongs in this shop.'

'Well, thank you so much. I'll wear it every day.'

The doorbell jingled. 'How's it going?' asked Ben, calling in on his way home, and failing to spot Peggy at first. 'Peggy! Ah, I can't believe you're here.' Ben wrapped his arm around her. 'We've all missed you so much.'

'I've missed you all, too. I've just popped over to see how Kitty is getting on and it already feels like she's been here forever. She's the perfect fit for the shop, wouldn't you agree?'

Ben willed his cheeks not to flush. 'Couldn't agree more,' he said through a smile, unable to prevent himself from beaming whenever in Kitty's presence.

'Well, I'm going to get going.' Peggy gave Kitty a hug before opening the door. 'Bye folks, I'll come and visit you all soon. Pass my love onto everyone, won't you?' she added before walking off up the street.

Kitty took a look at the time. 'Are you done for the day?'

'Sure am. I'm my own boss, so there's nobody to fire me,' he replied, walking up to the counter. 'So, how's it been? I see there is no cake left - always a good sign.'

'It's been great, better than I expected. And I can still sew, which is a bonus!' she jested. 'I have a proposition for you, if you're interested.'

'Okay.' Ben raised his eyebrows, a look of intrigue passing over his face.

'I need some help. I'd like to paint the walls in my flat, and possibly some furniture too, and I'm not sure my skills are up to scratch to take on such a mammoth task singlehandedly.' She folded her arms across her chest and fidgeted with her dangling strands of hair. She didn't want her proposal to appear flirtatious, that wasn't her intention. But she needed help, and she needed a friend. 'What do you think? I'd pay you, of course. After all, I'd have the finest artist in St. Ives applying emulsion to my walls.'

Ben raised his chin. 'Well,' he began, his muscles relaxing and a warmth radiating from his cheeks. 'There are a few conditions.'

'Okay,' Kitty replied with hesitance.

'Well, I'm maxed out during the days at the moment, and so are you. So, I can only offer up my services during the evenings and weekends.' Ben poured himself a glass of lemonade, the lemon pith at the bottom of the pitcher clouding his drink. 'And in terms of payment, I know it's a bit cheeky, but instead of paying me for my time, would it be possible for you to hang up some of my work? Up there above the shelving would be great, a little extra wall space and exposure for my work wouldn't go a miss,' Ben asked, pointing to the left side of the counter above the wall of fabrics. He didn't particularly need the additional exposure, his paintings already doing a good job of selling themselves from off the walls in his studio, but he knew that Kitty's finances would be stretched having just opened, so this felt like the perfect solution.

'That seems like a fair trade, but you'd have to help me hang them. I'm not so great with heights.'

Ben held his glass. 'Cheers to that,' he announced, catching sight of what he concluded might just have been a mutual look of affection.

'Brilliant. Let's pencil in Friday, shall we?

'Perfect,' he said with a smile, allowing his gaze to briefly linger on Kitty's face. 'Well, I best get going, I've not locked up the studio yet. See you tomorrow, neighbour!' he said, leaving the shop and closing the door gently behind him.

Kitty turned off all the lights and grabbed her bag, hovering in the shop doorway and spinning the sign to *Sorry, we're closed.* She locked up and headed down towards the seafront, simply because she could. The novelty of going out at will felt wonderful, her feet itching to explore and experience all of life's offerings. She couldn't recall the last time she had gone for a walk alone, the last time she had admired the sunset, or a time when life felt so full of hope. After a few minutes of strolling, she reached the same bench that she had sat on the previous day. She wrapped her arms around her body and became a sunset spectator, admiring how the rusty colours departed, leaving behind a sombre skyline.

'I promise, I'm not following you. I come here after work if it's been a busy one, you know, to get some air into my lungs after a day of smelling nothing but paint fumes,' announced Ben, taking a seat alongside Kitty on the bench. Kitty smiled, secretly appreciating the company.

'It has been a busy day. I've lost count of how many times I've stabbed myself with a pin, or caught my finger in the till.' She looked at her hands before stuffing them into her pockets. 'Can't complain though, this makes everything worthwhile,' she added, looking out towards the sunset. Beneath the remaining daylight, she admired how the dotting of seashells beneath her feet sparkled like glitter, and briefly wondered where her engagement ring might be buried.

Ben spotted her taking off the brooch. 'I'm sure I've seen that before,' he said.

'It belonged to Peggy. She gave it to me today.' Kitty cupped the brooch in her hands, her thoughts replaying the conversation they had had the day before about her parents, about her mum's secret. 'I feel like I've known Peggy a lifetime, and yet we only met yesterday.' Kitty couldn't help but visualise her attic on Pembroke Road, combing through all her mum's belongings, resenting the thought that she may have left something so precious behind.

Ben turned and smiled. 'I felt like that when I first met Peggy. Although, in all the years I've known her, she's never talked much about her own life - life beyond the shop I mean - and it's never felt appropriate to ask for some reason.'

'She has a daughter who doesn't live at home anymore. That's about as much as I know. I'm just grateful she sold her shop to me.'

'It makes me happy knowing that she has a daughter. I wonder if she lives here in St. Ives? It'd be nice to meet her family, because to so many of us on the street, Peggy is part of our extended family.'

Kitty turned to look at Ben. 'I'm hoping she's going to keep popping in the shop, so maybe in the future we'll find out a bit more,' she replied. Kitty felt a great sense of guilt rattle through her bones the moment she acknowledged her underlying, selfish motivations for wanting Peggy to remain in her life, knowing that she alone knew her mum's dying secret.

19

'I THINK YOUR LAST CLIENT OF THE DAY IS HERE,' ANNOUNCED Pippa, watching Kitty loiter outside the frosted window. 'She seems a bit nervous.'

'I'll go and get set up. Bring her through when she's gowned and ready,' replied Charlie.

'Hello, is it Kitty?' asked Pippa when the door swung open.

'It is, yes. Hi.' Kitty walked towards the corner desk with a fixed look of apprehension on her face. Pippa confirmed which treatment Kitty had booked, before introducing herself properly.

'Perfect. I'm Pippa. If you follow me, we'll get you all ready and then I'll take you through to Charlotte. She conducted your telephone consultation, and she's the one who will be doing the treatment. Can I get you a drink at all? We have coffee, tea, orange juice, water, a selection of herbal teas, or maybe a drop of Champagne if you'd prefer?'

'No, I'm okay, thank you.' Kitty made her way through to the back of the building, nerves wrapping around her chest, causing her skin to itch.

'So, if you go behind this curtain, remove the clothes from your top half, and pop the gown on, then come through when you're ready. Is there anything you need?'

She shook her head. Behind the curtain, Kitty felt exposed. She kept her eyes on the ground, refusing to acknowledge the mirror. With reluctance, she removed her t-shirt and bra, and caught sight of her reflection whilst she leant down to grab the robe. Her body froze with the shock of witnessing the tattoo for what felt like the very first time. Beneath the professional studio lighting, the colossal tattoo shone in its full, gruesome glory. Her eyes swelled with heavy tears and she dropped to the floor, her body crumbling in a heap. She reached out and grabbed her mum's bag, pressing it to her chest for comfort, trying to inhale Delilah's strength. With fumbling hands, she grabbed the robe, wrapping it tightly around her body.

'Everything alright in there?' asked the receptionist, noting how long it had been since Kitty had started to change.

Kitty pulled herself off the floor and grabbed hold of the curtain. With an unsteady voice, she stepped out of the cubicle. 'Yes. I'm ready.'

'Perfect, just follow me this way,' guided Pippa, pointing with her hand through to another door. 'Charlotte, this is Kitty.' Pippa closed the door once Kitty had stepped inside the treatment room.

'Hi. Come in,' welcomed Charlie. Dressed in a charcoal tunic and wearing a warm smile, she encouraged Kitty to move further into the room. 'Please, take a seat up here.'

Kitty perched herself on the treatment table, her legs dangling.

'So, from the limited amount of information I could gain from our brief telephone consultation, I believe you have a tattoo that you'd like removing. Is that right?' Charlie studied her notebook, referring back to the comments she'd made from the previous conversation.

Kitty nodded in agreement.

'Okay. So, what I always tell my clients is that the success of the treatment will depend on how big the tattoo is, if any colours were used, the age and density of the ink and so on, and I think I explained this over the phone, is that right?'

Kitty nodded again.

'Wonderful. Well, I think the next stage is to have a look at the tattoo so that I can make a formal assessment and provide you with a better indication of what we can expect, plus the amount of time that will be involved, and the cost.' Charlie pulled on her treatment gloves in preparation for the examination.

'It's on your back, is that right?'

'Yes.'

'So, if you can just lie down on your front and place your head into this rest.' Kitty swung her legs up onto the table and positioned herself as requested.

'I'm just going to unfasten the tassels on the robe and then I can take a look. Sorry if my hands are a bit cold,' she apologised, pulling the ties free and exposing Kitty's back.

With her head in the rest, Kitty closed her eyes and awaited the anticipated reaction. Charlie temporarily froze as she digested the image that had been painfully marked out onto Kitty's back. She struggled to find any immediate words that would be suitable, and stumbled over her sentence, saying the first thing that came to mind. 'The bold letters dominate the design.' Charlie paused, becoming lost for words, her eyes scanning the length of Kitty's shoulder blades, examining every inch of the masculine tattoo that'd been carelessly scraped into the skin, the name *Stevie* surrounded by gothic-style hearts and roses. Even though she was drawing upon stereotypical comparisons, Charlie would never have imagined that hiding beneath Kitty's clothes was such a bold, unfeminine tattoo.

'Do you mind if I just have a feel of the skin, to try and gauge the extent of the scarred tissue?' she asked.

Kitty felt numb all over. 'No, that's okay,' she replied, bracing herself in anticipation of the touch of another human being on her bare skin.

Charlie pressed down gently with the tips of her fingers. 'I'm going to assess this side first,' she added, placing her fingers on Kitty's left shoulder.

With her head pressed firmly into the headrest, Kitty's blotchy face lay shielded beneath the table and she watched her shame drip onto the laminate floor. She sensed Charlie's reaction and a thickness built in her throat. Flashbacks flooded her mind and for a haunting moment, Kitty found herself back in the treatment chair the day she had unwillingly obtained the tattoo. She could hear the gun piercing her skin and smell the aroma of the room, bombarding her with a feeling of nausea.

Charlie ran her fingers across Kitty's back, assessing each drop of ink that Stevie had paid to be ingrained into his then fiancée's skin. He had exploited the fact that Kitty yearned for a memorial tattoo, a delicate flower with the name Delilah entwined within the design, and so planned a romantic weekend getaway to Edinburgh, all with an underlying mission. On the Saturday night, after frequenting numerous bars, Stevie suggested getting her the desired tattoo. In line with his plan, by the time he navigated her to the tattoo parlour, Kitty was so drunk that she couldn't walk in a straight line. Unbeknownst to her, Stevie had spiked each drink she consumed, all in a bid to ensure his plan would succeed. With the impression that she consented to a stamp-size tattoo of a daffodil with her mum's name, Kitty completed the paperwork, her signature nothing more than an illegible squiggle. After only a few moments of lying face-down in the chair, she had passed out.

'She actually really wants a full piece but wasn't brave enough, but now she's out for the count, we can make her wish come true. Can you do my name written in bold lettering across the width of her shoulders,' Stevie explained to the artist, pointing to the bold, masculine style of letters he desired. Being a back-street studio, the man accepted Stevie's bundle of cash and began the rogue design. Kitty stirred throughout the procedure, the sound of the inking gun reverberating through her ears, her shoulder blades burning beneath the constant puncture of the needle.

'Why are we still here?' she asked, a look of confusion appearing on her face when her eyes opened.

'Lie still and close your eyes, he's just finishing up,' explained Stevie each time she stirred, confused and disorientated, and feeling nauseous to her stomach. The design took hours and, upon completion, her shoulders and upper back were unrecognisable.

'Can I have a look?' she requested upon standing. Stevie helped to ease her top over her head.

'Later, when we get home. You're tired and it's late, this guy wants to shut up shop.' It wasn't until the following morning when the alcohol had drained from her system that Kitty recalled the events of the previous evening and caught sight of herself in the bathroom mirror whilst preparing for a shower.

'Oh, God,' she cried, covering her mouth with her hand, her body swaying. She steadied herself against the basin, her lungs only able to take shallow, shaky breaths. She blinked in a constant stream, sure her tired, bloodshot eyes were playing cruel tricks.

'What're you crying for?' asked Stevie upon entering the bathroom. 'You were the one who wanted one.'

'Is this a joke?' she asked, for once finding the courage to stand up for herself, all the while touching her skin and willing the ink to transfer to her hand. Her fingers remained clean, and the skin on her back burned at her touch. 'I wanted a daffodil as a dedication to my mum, you knew that.' Even when Kitty turned away, shielding her vision, she could still see the grotesque ink plastered all over her skin. 'Not this.' Her words began to fail, rendering her speechless.

The couple never once spoke about the tattoo after that morning, and every time Kitty took a shower, or soaked her body in a steaming bath, she scrubbed her skin and cried herself through the pain, pleading for the ink to disappear. Each time Stevie caught sight of his name sprawled across her back, he smirked with an accomplished sense of satisfaction. He had staked his claim and branded his possession, permanently, forever.

'The density of the ink on the periphery of the tattoo doesn't appear as thick as the ink used on the central design, which is good news,' declared Charlie, now running her fingers across to the right side of Kitty's shoulders. 'I'm nearly done.' In a moment of empathy, Charlie lowered her left hand and took hold of Kitty's, a silent offer of comfort and compassion. For Kitty, Charlie's touch served to acknowledge the barbarity and legitimise her pain, and her anger. Apart from Stevie, Kitty had kept her tattoo a secret, even from Millie.

'Right, you can sit up now,' explained Charlie, covering Kitty's back with the gown. 'To try and remove it all will take time, I want to make that clear, just so that I'm not misleading you in terms of what can be achieved.' She drew a sketch of the design, omitting the actual letters and replacing them with boxes. 'These parts here should be easier to remove, the ink quality is far less superior,' she explained, indicating with her pencil the floral, outer design. 'But I'm assuming these parts are more important to try and erase, am I right?' Charlie hovered her pencil over the boxes, each one representing the letters which spelt out Stevie's name. Kitty nodded, her eyes still studying the paper, avoiding eye contact. Her internal organs tightened, like they were being bound with string.

'So, these parts will be more stubborn and will take more time. But they will fade, Kitty, I promise you. Given time, they will fade.' Kitty acknowledged the statement with a hesitant nod.

'Thank you,' she whispered, lifting her head and making steady eye contact.

Charlie smiled. 'So, why don't we get started on the letters today and focus on the other parts another time?'

'Perfect.' Kitty lay back down, her arms tucked beneath her body.

'The sensation of the laser shattering the ink isn't nice, you won't need me to tell you that, but I can reduce the discomfort by using numbing cream, and before your next appointment, I would apply some yourself at least half an hour before you attend, okay?' Charlie rubbed Kitty's shoulders, her skin reacting to the cream. After a few minutes of prepping the equipment, Charlie began.

'How's that?' she asked. Charlie held the laser over the top part of the letter S for around fifteen seconds before moving to another part.

Despite the stinging sensation burning at her skin, Kitty bit her lip, determined. 'Just keep going.'

Whilst flashing Kitty's skin with the laser gun, Charlie attempted to distract her client. 'I love this time of year, don't you? All the buds on the trees developing, the weather warming up and the evenings getting that bit longer. Oh, and I love how snowdrops and daffodils appear everywhere, decorating little patches of land all over town.'

'Daffodils have such a vibrant colour. They're such a happy flower,' Kitty replied, appreciating the light-hearted conversation. 'They remind me so much of my mum.'

'Someone used to buy me daffodils at this time of year and it was always such a romantic gesture,' explained Charlie, thinking back on the memory with a level of fondness that she felt would never dwindle, despite the relationship having broken down.

'After my mum passed away, I used to pick daffodils from my garden, but they never lasted long,' Kitty paused at the hurtful memory before explaining. 'He just couldn't help himself,' she added. 'Stevie always made sure they didn't last the day, and I never understood how a person could act so deliberately cruel.'

'Well, he sounds like a truly horrible human being. I hope you've managed to get him out of your life for good.'

Kitty clenched her fists at the side of her body. 'I have left him, and I will never go back,' she replied with more defiance than she'd ever felt before. For the remainder of the session, neither one spoke, each taking comfort in the silence. Kitty kept her fists clenched and willed herself to suffer the pain without flinching, knowing that no amount of pain would ever be worse than what she'd already suffered.

'Right, all done, at least for today. Here, take a look.'

Kitty stood up, taking hold of a mirror.

'Now, don't get too excited, the white parts will only last for around thirty minutes, but it's a good sign and means the laser has broken down some of the ink.' Kitty looked in the mirror, the white parts of the tattoo now obscuring the letters and even though the name remained visible, the slow process of fading had begun. She bowed her head, her thoughts jumbled. 'Thank you.'

With a delicate embrace, Charlie wrapped her arms around Kitty, making sure to avoid her scarred shoulders. 'You're welcome,' she spoke softly. 'Take your time getting changed, there's no rush.'

Kitty walked out of the room and hid herself once again in the cubicle, before easing her top over her head. She wiped away her smeared mascara and applied a little gloss to her lips before straightening out her hair. With a renewed sense of confidence surging through her body, Kitty took out her phone, a moment of bravery urging her to call Stevie. From the safe distance of her faraway Cornish retreat, she finally felt able to fight back. Each and every moment of physical and emotional pain that she had endured at his hand felt ready to explode, and yet the moment she began to type in his mobile number, her bravery crumbled, and she cancelled the call. Allowing her emotions to trickle down her face, Kitty waited for the moment of vulnerability to pass. Revenge wasn't something that she felt her heart needed in order to heal, but releasing all her pent-up anger would go some way to aiding the process. For now, having taken the first step to having Stevie burnt off her skin felt like all the revenge she needed.

'Now go home and get some rest, give your body time to heal,' Charlie added, opening the shop door once Kitty had completed payment.

'Thank you again,' she said before stepping out onto the street. With a bounce in her stride, Kitty walked away feeling emotionally lighter having eliminated some of the remaining burden etched onto her shoulders. Across the street, she spotted a sea of daffodils in an otherwise dreary flower bed, a smile developing through her lips and she couldn't help but think of her mum. The floral display transported Kitty back to her childhood, and she admired the daffodils in a way her innocent eyes once relished, and for a moment, along with the ink, her haunting memories of Stevie had been erased.

20

*C*HARLIE PICKED UP HER PHONE FOR THE TWENTY-THIRD TIME that day and upon pressing the side button, flung the mobile across the kitchen when it failed to show any new notifications.

'Oi, watch it. I know there are loads of chips in the paint already but that doesn't mean I need any more,' said Pippa, jumping down off the island stool. 'I'm letting you stay here because you're my best friend, and because you're my boss, but that doesn't mean you can wreck my apartment.'

Charlie banged her elbows onto the countertop and hid her face in her hands. 'Pip, why hasn't he called or messaged me? It's been over a week since I last replied to the message he sent.'

'He's stopped messaging you because you've told him a hundred times to leave you alone. Plus, he's probably a bit put off by the fact that you've been ignoring him, we both have,' she replied, rummaging for her secret stash of pink gin, anticipating the brewing crisis. 'You told him to leave you alone. You told him it was over. You've moved out of your marital home and severed all forms of contact. You even left your wedding rings in his studio.' Pippa grabbed two glasses and poured them each a generous measure, downing one herself. 'And despite all that, he's still been chasing you for the past three weeks,' she added. 'And now that he's finally taken the hint and left you alone, you want him to call?' She sighed, and drank the second shot in one. 'It's no wonder guys tend to find women confusing.'

154

'Eh, thought that one was mine?'

'I've been living this ordeal with you for weeks now, so I need it more.' Pippa poured a third glass and drank that too. 'The fact remains, Charlie, you want a baby, and he doesn't. The hardest part is over - you've left him, you've moved out, so now it's time to move on. Can you imagine your life without a baby? If the answer to that is still no, then you've done the right thing. Ben wants to focus on his career, get the studio established. He doesn't want to start a family and he's been good enough to tell you that.'

Charlie covered her face with her hands. 'But I still love him, Pip,' she confessed, shaking her head. 'With or without a baby, I love him. I always have and I always will.'

Pippa wrapped her arm across Charlie's shoulders. 'If I was in your shoes, I wouldn't beg for him to take me back. I'd go to the studio and see if those rings are still there. You still have a key, don't you? The cost of those rings would pay for a deposit on a new house and get you out of here before you chip any more of my paintwork,' she joked. 'I'm only looking after your best interests,' she added before planting a kiss on the side of Charlie's face. 'I love Ben, you know I do. But I love you more, and he doesn't make you happy anymore, not in the way you need him to. So, I think you should stick to what you've done and find someone who *is* looking to start a family. And you can stay here for as long as you need, you know that.'

Although not much of a drinker, Charlie grabbed the bottle and took a mouthful, the fiery liquid burning the moment it trickled down her throat. 'It's so hard, Pip. He's always been in my life. And now I'm supposed to just forget about him and pick someone else to spend the rest of my life with, just like that?' said Charlie, clicking her fingers.

'I'm not saying to go out and find a new man today. I'm just saying you were the one who left Ben so there must've been a reason, a reason that hasn't magically gone away now that you're feeling a little lonely, and full of regrets. So, stop checking your phone every two minutes and get on with your own life, because it looks like he's now decided to get on with his.'

Although she appreciated her friend's honesty, Pippa's words stung, and a deep-rooted bitterness suddenly aggravated Charlie. Each time she sat down and had nothing to distract herself with, jealousy stabbed like a knife through her skin. She hated, more than anything, not knowing Ben's activities and who he might be with. 'I can't even check his Facebook or emails - he's changed the passwords.' Charlie grabbed her keys and phone. 'I'm off out, I won't be long.'

'It's half-seven on a Friday night, where are you going?' Pippa shouted out of the window, watching Charlie run up the street.

'I've got to go and see him. I don't have anything to lose.'

The streets of St. Ives were still alive with start-of-the-season tourists. Each person that Charlie passed had a carefree look painted across their face, stirring the feeling of envy that was festering in the pit of her stomach. The air felt notably warmer, a sign that the town would soon be a hive of activity as people flocked to the popular holiday destination. Charlie slowed her pace and strolled past the seafront, jealous of all the couples sharing romantic moments. She peered into every restaurant, checking each face. On a Friday night, she and Ben usually stayed at home with a takeaway and watched whatever was on TV.

'Hi Charlie. How are you?' asked Ruben, spotting Charlie lingering outside one of the best bars in town.

'Oh, hi, Ruben. I didn't see you there. I'm alright, thanks. Are you out with Ben?' The question came spluttering out, dripping with jealousy. She peered around, her heart thumping, expecting Ben to appear at any moment, and she immediately regretted her casual appearance, wanting to look nothing but amazing.

'No, he said he was busy tonight, so it's just me, Lily and Susie. Agnes is joining us later, I think.' An awkwardness hung in the air.

Charlie couldn't contain the question swirling through her mind. 'He's busy? Doing what?'

'Oh, erm, I'm not sure,' he lied, diverting his gaze.

'Ruben, you're his best mate, you know everything that goes on in his life, so I know you're lying.' Charlie crossed her arms, demanding the truth.

'I think he said he's doing some painting, that's all I know.' Not satisfied with the reply, she probed further.

'Has he mentioned me at all? I'm still his wife.'

Ruben peered down at his feet. 'Look, Charlie. I'm sorry about what's happened. I know it's hard, for both of you. But I'm Ben's best mate, like you said, and under the circumstances it doesn't feel right to betray his trust.' A rush of adrenaline surged beneath Charlie's skin and her eyes prickled with tears at the hopelessness of her situation.

The pitch of her tone raised. 'Under the circumstances?' she questioned.

Ruben jumped on the defensive. 'You moved out. He tried calling you for weeks, Charlie, but you never answered, did you? You told him it was over. You told him to stop calling. He was a mess, Charlie, a right state. I've never seen him like that. And you can't just expect him to sit around and wait, hoping at some point you'll change your mind.'

Charlie checked her watch and wrapped her coat around her body, the wind blowing her hair across her face. 'Well, I best get off. I'm busy tonight too, just meeting up with someone for a drink,' she concluded before walking off. Ruben knew she was lying; he'd known Charlie for too long. He knew she hated town on a Friday night because everywhere felt too cramped.

'Let's not fall out, this is hard enough for everyone as it is. Stop by the café and I'll whip you up some of your favourite blueberry muffins,' he shouted, but Charlie had vanished up the side street that led out onto Ladysmith Lane.

She lingered at the top end, on the corner just next to Crook Antiques. Her stomach knotted the moment her eyes fell on Ben's studio in the distance, and she set off walking towards it with a small sense of reluctance. Reaching the door and realising it was locked, and that Ben wasn't in the studio painting, she took out her key and eased it open. She didn't switch on any lights and crept up the stairs in darkness. The studio smelt familiar and seeing all of Ben's things made her produce a heavy, audible sigh. She noticed that some of the paintings he'd been working on before they'd separated were now complete. Her arms felt heavy, pulling her shoulders down, and she steadied herself against the wall, her back slipping all the way down until she reached the floor. With a pounding heart, she made herself peer around the space, searching in the half-light for clues. Empty coffee cups were scattered across the windowsill and a yellow jumper she didn't recognise lay strewn over a chair. The sight of the new clothing dragged her off the floor, temporarily freezing her emotions. Charlie always insisted that yellow didn't suit his complexion, and so nothing in his wardrobe resembled yellow. She pressed the material to her face, the smell of an unfamiliar fragrance clinging to the cotton.

Her phone buzzed in her pocket.

'Where are you, and what are you doing?' asked Pippa, omitting all formalities.

'He's not at the studio, despite the fact I bumped into Ruben who told me that Ben couldn't go out because he was spending the night painting,' she cried, the jumper falling free from her hand.

'So, where are you now?'

Movement coming from across the street caught Charlie's eye and with the phone pressed against her ear, she gravitated towards the window. 'I'm in his studio.'

'Charlie. This isn't doing you any good. You're hanging out in his studio alone on a Friday night. Just grab your rings if they're there, and come home.' Charlie could hear her friend's voice travelling through the phone, but Pippa's words didn't register.

'You bastard!' Charlie exclaimed, her temperature rising.

'What? What've you found?'

Her eyes squinted. 'I can see him, Pip.' Tension stiffened

Charlie's jaw, making her whole face ache.

'Who can you see?'

Charlie's posture seized. 'Ben. He's right across the street in the flat above the antique shop. He's with a girl.' Charlie felt her heart break, an unbearable pain coursing through her body that she had never before experienced. In her mind, Ben was her man, and always had been. She tried to focus her vision on Kitty, but couldn't quite make out her features from such a distance away.

'What? Who's the girl?'

Charlie clenched her stomach with her free hand and swallowed hard. 'I can't see her face. They're painting the walls together.'

'Come home, Charlie, please don't stand there and watch. She's probably just a friend and you're reading more into it.'

Charlie broke down in hysterics. 'I know all his friends, Pip, and I've never seen this woman before in my entire life.' Pressing the phone against her ear with her shoulder, Charlie pushed open the window. 'They're listening to music, I can hear it from over here.' On the other end of the phone, Pippa placed her free hand over her face.

'Charlie, please, walk away. Sleep on it for tonight, and then if you're still thinking you've made the wrong decision, phone him in the morning and sort it out.'

The more Charlie observed, the more devastated she felt. 'I drove him away, Pip. I've made him walk straight into the arms of another woman.'

'Charlie, if his head's been turned so soon, would you really want to have a child with him?'

Charlie felt her breath catch in her throat the moment Kitty's features suddenly became recognisable. 'Oh my God. It's the woman from work, what was her name?'

'Which woman?'

'The one with the god-awful tattoo I told you about.'

'Kitty something-or-other, wasn't it?'

'Kitty Twist. I held her hand. I comforted her. I told her I would erase the guy called Stevie who had apparently ruined her life,' cried Charlie through deeper and quicker breaths, her chest rising and falling in a constant cycle of shock. 'I don't understand. How do they know each other? I'm sure she'd only just moved to the area.' Charlie paused because her words were unable to make it past the jealousy that was now causing her to panic, tightening around her throat. 'She's so pretty, isn't she? All that gorgeous hair, a flawless complexion, and that figure.' Charlie slammed her back against the wall, hiding herself when Kitty looked up, peering out of the window. 'I think she might have just seen me.'

'Get out of there. You don't want to confront him, not now, not whilst he's with someone else.' The phone line went dead.

Charlie scrambled across the floor, creeping into the back office. Her rings weren't where she had left them. She stood up, ensuring her shadow remained out of sight from the window. She picked up a bottle of bubbly her and Ben had been saving for a special occasion and lunged it across the room, emerald shards scattering loudly across the floor like jewels. The moment she moved to leave, a sparkle caught her eye, and she noticed her wedding rings dangling off a drawing pin attached to a noticeboard. She reached out to take them back, but the sight of a pink post-it-note stole her attention, the paper stating simply, *Kitty 07663363363 xxx*

Moving with a sense of purpose, Charlie walked back through to the studio, this time not caring who spotted her shadow from outside. Jealousy raged through her veins upon seeing all the paintings, each one holding a cherished memory. Like the painting of a church - the canvas Ben had created whilst Charlie was planning their honeymoon. Or the lone sailing boat - a picture Ben had attempted to sketch whilst his then fiancée sat naked, doing her best to distract him. The paintings were full of memories of a life she once shared, a life she felt falling from her grip. Without thinking, she picked up the painting of the church and thrashed it against the wall, the canvas tearing upon impact.

She reached out her hand and grabbed the litre bottle of water resting beside a used easel, the paint brush next to it still wet. With angered movements, she unscrewed the cap and recklessly showered the entire room, ensuring splashes of water landed on each painting. Her hand released the bottle to the floor and she walked out, leaving the sodden artwork, now bleeding colour, behind her.

21

Until swathes of peak-season tourists arrived in St. Ives with their beach towels, flip-flops and bottles of sun cream, the shops on Ladysmith Lane remained asleep on Sundays – apart from one. For the past couple of weeks, Kitty had sought refuge at Flourish on her only day off. She convinced herself that tinkering with stock and getting a firm grasp on her new business without having to worry about seeing to any customers felt like too good an opportunity to miss. In reality, she just wanted to be somewhere that reminded her of her mum; a place that gave her a reason to smile.

'I love the new window display - very beachy,' shouted Ben upon catching sight of Kitty outside Flourish. He crossed the street whilst pushing a brimming wheelbarrow filled with paintings, all stacked up haphazardly.

Kitty turned her head upon hearing his voice. 'Thank you, I'm glad you like it. Do you need a hand?' she asked, watching the barrow wobble. 'I could have carried them over with you, I didn't know this is why you needed to borrow one.'

'I don't think I thought it through,' said Ben, leaning to grab a painting just before it fell.

'I was beginning to think that you weren't bothered about your end of the bargain, even though you did do all that wonderful painting at my flat the other weekend.'

'You're not getting out of it that easy,' he smiled. 'I'd actually planned on getting these over to you last Sunday, but something came up.'

'Oh?' she asked, helping Ben to carry all the canvases into the shop.

'An incident at the studio. Some pieces ready for shipping got damaged. So, I've been putting in the hours this week to try and get things sorted.' Once the last of the paintings were transferred inside, Ben took hold of the daffodils he'd bought and slumped himself on the floor, his back pressed against the shop counter. He released a sigh and ran his hands through his hair, his youthful appearance ransacked by heavy shadows beneath his eyes and a pasty complexion.

'Oh no, that sounds awful. Can I get you a cup of tea? And I'm sure there's some stale croissants in the back, which, if you dip into your drink, will still taste sublime.'

'Sounds good. I'm not sure I can physically climb a ladder without copious amounts of sugar beforehand. Oh, I've got these for you,' he explained, holding out the daffodils. 'They're for your window display. I've bought some for Lily, Susie and Agnes too. They're only a pound a bunch in the shop so I thought I'd treat you all.' Upon witnessing the seasonal flowers, the sight of the daffodils transported Kitty back to the unhappy parts of her past despite her recent best efforts to focus on the future.

'Don't you like them?' he asked, noting her blank expression. 'They brighten up the street when we all have them in the window. Look, you can see them across the road in Susie's place,' he explained, pointing to the teapot over in the window display at Past Times.

'Thank you,' she said, stretching out her hand. 'They're lovely. I'll just get something to put them in,' she said, heading through to the back. 'So, what happened at the studio? Was it a burst pipe or something?' she shouted above the sound of the kettle, trying to shake off her history.

'I wish,' muttered Ben, looking at the white line on his wedding finger where his ring had once sat, suspecting his wife's hands were at the root of the incident, knowing she still had a key.

Kitty appeared with the daffodil stems now swimming in a cool pitcher of water, placing them centre stage in her new shop display. The buttery daffodils stood tall with the natural elegance of swans. 'Sorry, I didn't catch what you said, about the damage,' she said, disappearing to tend to the boiled kettle.

'Yeah, just some water damage, but I've managed to salvage most of the stuff. Only a few couldn't be saved, so I reworked them this week – not my finest but the customer seemed happy enough, so nothing to fret about.' Kitty reappeared, carrying a steaming mug of pale, weak tea, and a single, crispy croissant.

'Thanks,' said Ben, taking hold of the tea.

Kitty lowered herself to sit alongside him on the floor. They both sat with their legs crossed, their feet resting on the door mat.

'This communal tea drinking is becoming a regular thing,' she laughed, trying to recall a day during the past week when the pair hadn't sat in the exact same position after work and eaten all the leftover cake crumbs from the countertop offerings, before Ben headed back to his studio and Kitty walked home to continue decorating her flat so that it began to feel like home.

'I must've put on at least half a stone since meeting you,' he joked, patting his solid stomach. 'But I'm so glad the business has taken off. We just need all your customers to eat the cake, so I don't eat it for them.'

'I don't think I even need the cakes, to be honest. Most customers politely turn it down, citing that they're watching their weight.'

Ben wiped his mouth after finishing a bite of the crispy pastry. 'So, where exactly do you think we should hang these?' he asked, peering up at the wall.

'Wherever you want is fine with me. My flat would still be looking a little too beige had you not helped, so I want to pay you back anyway that I can. My arms are still aching from the meagre bits I managed to paint.' Kitty stretched her arms, the tender muscles throbbing beneath her skin.

Ben stood up after finishing his tea and croissant and gazed around the shop, trying to figure out where to hang his paintings. 'I still can't believe you bought this place, plus the flat, without viewing them first. Who does that?'

'Me, I guess,' laughed Kitty, brushing off the enormity of what she'd achieved.

'Where did you say you used to live?'

Kitty stood up too. 'Why don't we get started? If we chat all morning, we'll never get anything hung,' she replied whilst taking hold of one of the paintings.

In the weeks that Ben and Kitty had known one another, Ben had come to notice her reluctance to talk about her life before St. Ives, and was now wondering about what it had held with a growing sense of intrigue. 'Sure, no problem,' he replied whilst hiding his disappointment. He yearned to discover more about the girl who he couldn't stop thinking about, his curiosity craving information. He had gone as far as doing some social media research on Kitty Twist, and yet failed when he couldn't locate any active accounts matching her profile.

Kitty crouched to admire the painting in her hand. 'These are incredible, Ben. You have such a natural talent. If you hung these in a public toilet, they'd still sell. No wonder that business guy who Ruben mentioned bought a bunch.' The canvas in Kitty's hand was definitely her favourite in the collection, depicting a stripped back portrayal of the beach. Simple in its composition, the canvas offered nothing but ripples of swell, billows of creamy sand, and a scramble of pastel beach huts, capturing their little strip of sand perfectly.

'Thanks. It's taken a while, but finally a wider audience may start to see my work.'

Kitty picked up the painting, standing with it aloft. 'How about we put this one here? It's the most striking piece, so it will act as a focal point, and then we can position the rest at either side.' She turned to look at Ben, 'What do you think?'

Ben took hold of the painting and began to climb the ladder. 'I call myself an artist, but I'm no gallery curator; I have no idea which will look good where so let's do whatever you suggest, you clearly have an arty eye for this kind of stuff.'

After a whole day of hanging, positioning, levelling and repositioning the paintings, the walls of Flourish were transformed, and the shop became part haberdashery, part art gallery.

'I think I'll take these ones back. If we hang any more, not only will it feel cluttered, but I may just accidentally hook myself against the wall.' Ben glanced at his watch, acknowledging his hunger levels for the first time since the morning croissant. 'Wow, I've kept you long enough, sorry, I didn't realise.' Kitty hadn't noticed the passing of time either, too content with spending time with one of the few people in the world she had grown to trust.

'How about we go and get a cone of chips? I think we've earned it,' she suggested, unable to suppress the rumble now brewing in her own stomach.

'If you help me carry these back to the studio, I'll pay for chips. How about that?'

'Deal,' she replied, picking up as many paintings as she could carry.

Outside, the lane was bare, with not a single person to be spotted. 'Can you manage?' Ben asked, watching Kitty follow him out onto the pavement cradling paintings in both arms.

'I'm okay. I can't lock the door but we'll only be a minute,' she replied, crossing the road and heading up the lane to the studio.

'Just one more step,' Ben said, navigating Kitty up to his studio. 'Just put them here, I can sort them out tomorrow.' Kitty took a fleeting glance around the room, ruined paintings lying abandoned on the floor. 'Thanks, you get back and lock up. I'll lock up here then come and meet you,' he suggested, trying to hide the severity of the water damage.

'I thought you said only a few got damaged? Ben, I'm so sorry.'

'It's worse than it looks, honestly. Most of the ones leaning against the walls were duffs anyway,' he replied, downplaying the situation. 'You get going, I'll be over in a sec.'

'Okay, see you in a minute.' Kitty strolled back across the cobbles, the lane still barren of life. She walked into the shop and grabbed her bag from behind the counter. She meandered through to the back office, turning out the lights and pulling the kettle plug out and coiling the wire, a habit forced upon her by Stevie that she just couldn't shake. She walked through to the sales floor, switched off the lights and opened the door, ready for chips with Ben. The flash of yellow at her window diverted her attention, and she looked to find her pitcher of gifted daffodils deformed. The once flawless, sunshine petals lay in familiar tatters on the floor. Her world fell still, the new life filling her sails only seconds ago now scared away, leaving her gasping for breath. She steadied herself against the wall, fearful she may actually collapse. The all too familiar churning in her stomach returned with vengeance, and she once again felt Stevie's ghost by her side.

Darting across the road, Ben appeared in the doorway. 'Right, let's go.'

Kitty shuddered, her body visibly jumping. 'Sorry, I didn't mean to scare you,' he apologised, witnessing the fright. The pungent, distinctive smell of Stevie's aftershave knocked Kitty off balance, her frame threatening to tumble. She felt a plume of vomit rising into her throat, and darted to the toilet in the back of the shop.

Ben remained hovering in the doorway, failing to spot the pool of damaged flowers.

'Are you wearing aftershave?' she asked upon returning, lingering at the back of the shop. She tried to see past the counter, ensuring her eyes weren't playing games. The daffodils remained scattered over the floor despite her willing the sight not to be true.

'Erm, yeah. But not to impress you or anything. I've been lifting and shifting all day and I don't want to smell, that's all.'

Kitty edged herself forward. 'I'll give chips a miss, if that's alright with you? I'm not that hungry after all, too tired to head into town after a long day of lifting.'

A look of disappointment and confusion appeared on Ben's face. 'Are you alright? Have I done something wrong? Please, tell me if I have. I have this awful tendency to put my foot in things without knowing I've done anything wrong.'

Kitty kept her thoughts solitary and instead, attempted a smile. 'Course not. I'm shattered, that's all. We've had a busy day.' She walked over towards the door and ushered him outside, shielding herself from the smell and leaving Ben no option but to stand alone on the pavement, bewildered.

'See you tomorrow, then,' he said, waving through the window. He walked away, turning back a couple of times, trying to figure out what he'd done so wrong. Kitty waited until he moved out of sight, spying until his silhouette turned the corner and vanished. She pressed her back against the door, closing her eyes. Her breath remained captive whilst she listened out for the faintest of noises, but not a sound could be heard - just a sombre, Sunday silence.

She dared to open her eyes, and burst into tears at the sight of the petals strewn across the floor. Only a handful of moments ago, her shop had been the place she had felt safest. Now, she couldn't help but feel vulnerable. She peered out onto the lane with suspicious eyes, terrified of finding Stevie's peering back at her. Outside, the streetlights flickered, a sudden clattering noise made by a stray Coke can tumbled across the cobbles, and Kitty felt immediately threatened by the street filled with darkened shop windows that stared back at her. With flushed cheeks and an uncontrollable heartbeat, she stared at the daffodils again, searching for alternative explanations. But upon closer inspection, the torn petals told her the act felt all too familiar, and deliberate.

Kitty stepped out onto the pavement and closed the shop door before locking it. She scurried the length of the street, reaching the door to her flat with a panting breath. Her shaking fingers rummaged in her bag to grab her keys, but once she pulled her hand free, she lost grip and the keys tumbled. She bent down and felt her heart jolt as she noticed the carpet of yellow daffodils lining the steps to her home.

22

OR THE RISE AND FALL OF FOUR CONSECUTIVE SUNSETS, KITTY remained imprisoned in her flat, huddled on a single chair next to the window. At sporadic intervals, she stood up and peered down to her doorstep, seeing nothing but a sparce scattering of yellow foliage. Every time someone lingered near her window, her skin flushed and she felt her jaw tighten. She felt her heart thump heavily, until the stranger moved away, and she could be confident that it wasn't Stevie who had found her. Having not returned to Flourish since fleeing on Sunday, all customers had been met with a locked door, and no offer of explanation.

'Still no sign of her,' shouted Lily, when she spotted Ben walking down the lane on Thursday evening. 'Do you have her number?'

Ben paused outside the salon to chat. 'I do, and I've messaged her loads. She's feeling under the weather, that's all she says. I've knocked at her flat, but she doesn't answer, and I know she's in because I've seen her at the window, but as soon as she sees me, she moves away.'

'Let's check the shop's alright,' she said, walking towards Flourish. Lily pressed her head against the glass. 'It's all a bit strange. Who buys a business without seeing it beforehand? And who moves house and leaves all their belongings behind? She only had a small handbag with her the day she arrived in St. Ives, did you notice that?' She pulled away and looked at Ben, who also peered inside.

'It doesn't make any sense, none of it does. I spent the whole day with her on Sunday and it was brilliant, we had such a great time. But then, just as we were about to go and get something to eat, something about her changed, just like that,' he explained. 'It was weird. She seemed scared, frightened by something. I could see it in her eyes.'

'Frightened? Of what?'

Ben shook his head. 'I don't know. She's very guarded about her past, like she has something to hide, or something she doesn't want me to know. And despite the amount of time that I've spent with her these past few weeks, I don't really know anything about her.'

'That's not normal, Ben,' warned Lily, shaking her head. 'Maybe you should take a step back. Don't get involved. Maybe there is something in her past, something or someone you'd be better not knowing about.'

Ben's tone of voice lightened and he offered a genuine grin, a facial expression that developed into a beaming smile. 'I'm already involved. I think she's wonderful, Lily,' he replied, maintaining strong eye contact. 'She makes me smile. She makes me laugh. She makes me forget about everything else whenever I'm with her. And I know it's a terrible thing to admit, considering my past, but I've never felt like this before and I don't know what to do.' Ben plunged his hands into his pockets and kicked away a stone.

Lily took in a cleansing breath, her shoulders loosening. 'And in all the years that I've known you, I can honestly say that I've never seen you so happy – you're like a different person. So, why are you still stood here? If you really feel that way about her, go and see her, make her come to the door, make sure she's alright. It sounds like she might just need a friend.' Lily drummed her hands against Ben's back before walking back towards the salon. 'You know what you need to do. Let me know how you get on. Text me later.'

A knot twisted around Ben's organs as he marched up the lane and knocked on Kitty's door. His eyebrows pulled together upon noticing the dead flowers on the step, and when no answer came, he knocked against the door for a second time. After he was met with nothing but silence, he stood back and caught sight of Kitty peering down at him.

'Open the window?' he shouted up, waving with an enthusiasm that Kitty couldn't ignore. 'Hi. Are you sure that you're okay? I haven't seen you for days and the shop is still closed,' he asked before Kitty had opened the window fully.

'I'm full of flu,' she replied, trying her best to cower out of sight. Ben caught a glimpse of Kitty's pale complexion and dark bags hanging beneath her eyes.

'Do you need any supplies? Food? Paracetamol? I can bring some stuff over, it's no bother.'

'Thanks, but I'm okay.' Kitty began to close the window.

'If you're feeling better tomorrow, I'd like to buy you dinner. Meet me on the bench down by the front at seven-thirty. If you're not there, I'll be bringing the dinner to you,' he said, before walking across the road and up to his studio.

Inside her flat, Ben's offer ignited something inside Kitty, stoking her resilience and warming her heart. She looked at her watch, realising the time, and so slammed the window shut before rushing to get ready. With a sense of haste, she grabbed her things, and scurried down the stairs before heading out onto Ladysmith Lane. Outside, the season appeared confused. The snappy bite clinging to the air felt more reminiscent of winter than spring. Kitty wrapped her coat so it fitted snug against her body, her folded arms securing it in place. Shadowed by her paranoia, Kitty headed towards Radiance for her second tattoo removal appointment.

Down on the front, the sea performed with an aggressive nature, a strong undercurrent throwing waves in all directions, dislodging even the hardiest of surfers. A brusque breeze ushered Kitty along until she became protected by a tunnel of slate-covered rooftops. A few chimneys already put to bed after the cold winter months were once again being re-stoked. Inside the curtain-covered windows, families huddled up close to the flames, their faces brushed with a warmth from the amber coals.

Whilst navigating the side streets, Kitty gave everyone a wide birth, as though a contagious virus lingered in the air. Her destination came into view, only another few hundred yards in the distance. The sound of footsteps followed her from behind, the stomp of each foot getting louder until her followers came into contact.

'Get off me,' she yelled, turning with a sudden movement and thrashing out her hands, expecting to see Stevie. The group of lads who were innocently kicking a ball up the street laughed at her outburst, an amplified succession of giggles following their trail. Out of breath from jogging the final stretch, Kitty pushed open the door to Radiance, regaining her composure.

'Hi. Is it Kitty?' asked the receptionist.

'Yes. Sorry, I'm a bit early.'

'It's no bother at all. Charlotte is just setting up, so go through and change into a gown, then she'll be ready for you.' Once behind the safety of the changing curtain, Kitty exhaled, like she'd been holding her breath the entire journey. She pealed back the clothes from her upper body, her head turning in slow anticipation, fearful to witness her reflection. The moment her tattoo came into view, her hopes flew away like confetti in the wind, the letters still appearing bold, black and dangerous. She covered her face with her hands, trying to eradicate the crawling sensation covering her skin. Taking hold of a tissue, she wiped away her tears and stepped out into the hallway.

'Hi, Kitty. Come in,' encouraged Charlie, closing the door before taking a seat. 'How are you? How's it been since I last saw you?' Charlie pulled her stool closer to the treatment table, getting her gloves out ready.

'Good. I feel like I could see a real difference at first, but under your lighting, the tattoo looks darker than when we started, like the ink is returning to the surface.'

'Let's take a look.' Kitty lay down and untied the gown, exposing her back. 'There are areas of improvement,' Charlie began whilst inspecting the tattoo, running her fingers across the damaged skin. 'But I can see why you're disappointed, because in some areas, where the ink is more stubborn, it hasn't faded quite so well.' Kitty pushed her face into the headrest.

'I just want it gone.'

'And it will go, I promise. It's just going to take time,' encouraged Charlie, taking hold of the laser. 'Shall we get started?' Kitty manoeuvred her head just enough for the go-ahead signal to be seen.

'Great. Just relax if you can,' she suggested, holding the laser in her hand. 'So, have you begun to settle in St. Ives?' Charlie asked, making small talk. 'I'm sure I recall you saying you've just moved here.'

With her eyes closed, Kitty replied. 'It seems a nice place to live, although I haven't really had chance to explore properly yet.'

'There are so many places to visit that you'll be spoilt for choice.' The laser hovered right over Kitty's left shoulder blade. 'We'll concentrate on some of the areas around the main tattoo today, give the letters enough time to heal before we have another go at them.' Kitty remained still.

'Do you work in town?'

'I own a shop. It's only been open a couple of weeks, at least it has with me as the owner.'

'Oh right, which one? I'll have to pop by and have a look.'

Kitty felt the intensity of the laser, her skin throbbing beneath its power. 'I work on Ladysmith Lane, it's one of the quirky little side streets.'

'I know Ladysmith Lane, but on my days off I prefer to stay away from here and venture somewhere that doesn't remind me of work.' Charlie paused the gun, sensing Kitty's discomfort. 'Are you okay? I can stop if it's too much?'

Kitty clenched her fists. 'No, please, carry on.'

'I like going for coffee and mooching around galleries. I'm no art expert or anything, but there's something so relaxing about admiring paintings, it's like being transported to someone else's hidden world.'

'If you like art, have you been to the little gallery on Ladysmith Lane? It's above a shop called Pebble & Sand. The artist is really talented - not that I know anything about art, but in my eyes, his paintings are pretty wonderful.' Kitty smiled at the thought of Ben, a new, automatic reaction. Even during the past four days she had spent hiding from the world, she had still found herself peering across the road to his studio, wondering how it would feel to be snuggled up on the other side of the street, protected by the embrace she felt sure Ben would offer, even just as a friend.

'I might have to take a look,' Charlie replied. 'What's his name? Maybe I'll have heard of him.'

'It's Ben. Ben Fox.' Charlie couldn't see Kitty's blushing face beneath the table, or the first grin she'd developed in days.

'Do you know him well? I'm only asking because if I do like his work, maybe you'd be able to get me a discount.'

'Well, no, not really. I've actually only known him for a few weeks. I met him on my first day here in St. Ives.' Kitty paused.

'I can sense a little something in your voice, am I right?' probed Charlie in a playful, coaxing manner.

'Well, he's asked me out for dinner,' she blurted. 'It's not a date or anything,' she felt quick to add. 'When we first met, I made my situation clear, or at least I think I did.'

'But maybe you are interested?'

'At this exact moment, all I'm interested in is to feel happy and not have to answer to anybody. I've been unhappy for so long, and I won't allow myself to enter another relationship like that ever again.'

'There's nothing wrong with that,' Charlie replied. 'Will you feel more open to new love once we get rid of this tattoo, once we get rid of whoever Stevie is?'

Kitty took a moment before replying. 'Who knows, maybe. I've actually forgotten how wonderful life can be, and now that I'm single, I want to experience everything. I want to be able to walk out of my flat wearing nothing but a pair of shorts and a t-shirt, and feel the rain on my skin. I want to be able to dance in a bar and drink until I can sing in tune. I want to be able to jog along the beach with my bare feet, getting my clothes sodden and sand on my face. I want to be able to go out for tea on any weekday evening and order whatever I fancy, and chat to the waiter about which wine to choose. I want to be able to talk to total strangers without fear, come to think of it, I actually want to be able to talk to anyone without fear. I want to be one of those people who just hops on a bus and travels to an unknown destination, just for the sake of it.' Kitty paused and allowed herself to imagine a life full of possibility. 'I don't want to have to clean my flat like some crazy person. I don't want to have to iron someone else's clothes in any exacting way. I don't want to have to watch sports all weekend. I don't want to have to remember how someone else likes every single thing in their life positioned. I don't want to have to organise the contents of my life into threes; three apples in the bowl, three cups in a line, three books piled together, three pens in a pot, three bloody eggs on a plate.' Kitty took a moment to compose herself. 'I want to live *my* life instead of just existing in someone else's, and above all, I don't want my body to hurt anymore. That's all I really want.' Kitty's pained stare fell to the floor and her restless fingers fell agitated by her side.

Charlie paused the treatment. She bent down and handed Kitty a tissue. They locked eyes for a few seconds, sharing a mutual look of understanding. Having gained an insight into the person who had ingrained their name into her client's skin, all Charlie wanted to do was cast aside her own feelings, and wrap her arms around Kitty. 'So, the only question is, when is this dinner date, that isn't a date, but is just dinner?' Charlie picked up the laser and carried on with the treatment.

Kitty smiled. 'It's tomorrow.' The moment the laser powered up, her entire body flinched and her skin screamed. As the intensity increased, she found herself almost unable to remain still.

'I'm sorry,' apologised Charlie. 'These stubborn bits just need more focus, but we're nearly done for today if you can try and keep still.'

'Sorry, I'll try,' she replied, grinding her teeth through the discomfort.

'You're going to have to tell me all about this dinner engagement when you're next here,' said Charlie, finally turning off the laser. 'Perfect, all done for today. Let me go and get my diary so that we can pencil in your next session. Take a look at today's results.' Charlie left the room, allowing Kitty to admire her shoulders in the mirror. Segments of the tattoo appeared blistered, frosted skin bubbling on the surface. She stepped closer to the mirror, her disappointment expressed through her deflated body, and wished she could skip the weeks of painful treatment and just rip her skin away and start fresh.

'Here we are,' announced Charlie, diary in hand. 'We're making progress, don't get disheartened. It's a broad tattoo, hefty with crude ink, but it will fade,' she added, upon catching sight of Kitty's facial expression. 'How about next Thursday for your next session? We can work on other areas, like here,' she pointed, touching an area that hadn't yet been treated.

'That would be great. Is after work still okay, around half-five?'

'Perfect, I'll see you then,' she replied, opening the treatment room door to allow Kitty to leave. 'Pippa will sort you out now. See you next week.' Kitty got dressed then walked through to the waiting area. She rummaged in her bag, pulling out her purse.

'How much do I owe?' she asked, stood at the reception desk. Something in the periphery of Kitty's vision grabbed her attention, and she turned her head in a slow, reluctant manner. A surge of adrenaline invaded her nerves, placing her whole body on pins. She felt her temperature rocket as the soles of her feet became nailed to the spot and her eyebrows crumpled. The colour in her face flushed, and the churning sensation whirling in the pit of her stomach encouraged her bubbling emotions to erupt.

'Are you okay?' asked the receptionist, noting Kitty's sudden change of stance. 'If you need a moment to sit after the treatment, that's no problem, and I can get you a glass of water. It is warm in here today.' Kitty failed to register the comment and instead glanced around the room, her grimace unyielding.

'I didn't notice the daffodils when I entered,' she began through a stutter of words, her heart still in a tailspin.

'Oh, I'm sure Charlotte said a client bought them as a gift,' she replied, walking over to the jug of flowers adorning the window. 'They look a bit dead now though, don't they?'

Kitty watched her pick the flowers off the floor, which, just like they had in Flourish, appeared deliberately scattered.

'I'll leave this here,' advised Kitty, placing her money on the countertop. 'See you next week,' she concluded, wrapping her fingers around the door handle and pulling. Outside, jet-black clouds lingered above, and she felt the ghost of Stevie Best walking in her wake.

23

'Hi Kitty, are you feeling better?' asked Lily, upon entering Flourish around lunchtime on Friday. 'I've missed you this week. Have you been poorly?'

'I've just been feeling a bit under the weather, but I'm fine now, thanks for asking.'

The smile plastered across Lily's face refused to dwindle. 'I hear you and the lovely Ben are going out for a meal together. Very nice,' she commented, adding a wink to punctuate the end of her statement.

'We are, but it's just tea, nothing, erm, you know, formal,' she replied, struggling for a suitable explanation. 'He's just a friend.'

'You don't need to explain to me, Ben told me that it's just dinner, nothing more. It doesn't mean that you can't get excited though,' encouraged Lily, giving Kitty a playful nudge.

'Hello, Ladies,' Ruben announced as he entered the shop.

'Well, I best get going. I've got one more customer to sort out before I can ditch the dryer for the day. I'll catch up with you tomorrow, Kitty,' concluded Lily as she pushed past Ruben, turning back to give Kitty an encouraging thumbs up.

'Something I said?' asked Ruben, sniffing his armpits the moment Lily walked away.

'I can't believe you've walked all the way over here without bringing coffee. You can't turn me into an addict and then not supply the goods,' laughed Kitty, checking the lane before sitting behind the desk.

'Apologies. I'll make up for it tomorrow.'

'That's more like it. Can I set up a tab or is it strictly pay as you go?'

'Well. How about we exchange goods?'

'I didn't have you down as the sort who's in desperate need of a chintz cushion or a reel of pink organza,' Kitty replied, pulling down the ribbon reel dangling above her head and wrapping it around her neck like a scarf.

'Not quite, but I could do with some curtains for my bedroom. My neighbour is fed up of seeing me walking around the house naked.'

'I bet.'

'I'll bring in the material, if you can do the rest? That should see you sorted on coffee for ages. What do you say?'

Kitty held out her hand. 'If you throw in the odd cinnamon swirl, I'd say it's a deal.'

'Excellent, I love a bit of bartering. Now for the real reason I'm stopping by. I wanted to discuss your initiation onto the lane.'

'Right?' Kitty cast a dubious look.

'There's a bit of a tradition that we're keen to carry on, despite Peggy no longer being at the helm,' he announced, flour still dotting his hair. 'Each time a shop opens on the lane, we've got the lovely Ben to draw a caricature, which is then hung in the shop, as a kind of good luck charm. It's worked for us lot so far, so we want to continue with the tradition.' Ruben looked around, noticing all the artwork that'd been hung, failing to recall if it'd always been there.

'Oh, and here he is now,' Ruben added, opening the door for Ben. Kitty felt a wave of nerves, her body overrun with a subtle bout of shakes. 'Just explaining to Kitty about the caricature you're going to produce, which she can then hang amongst these beautiful specimens,' he added, pointing to the mini gallery decorating the walls. 'Or, you can hang it in the toilet,' he whispered into Kitty's ear.

Ben pulled his torso back and brushed his shoulder. 'You'll be begging for some of my work when Sotheby's are knocking down my door.'

'I can't see any distinguishable gentlemen, or women for that matter, knocking on your door right now,' Ruben replied, peering up the street towards the studio.

'Give them time. First, I'll conquer Cornwall, and then I'll take on London.'

Ruben raised his eyebrows. 'Anyway, I know finding time to produce this commission will be tricky given that you both work, but it's Friday which means I shut early, so I'll come over and hold down the fort, whilst Ben draws the masterpiece over at the studio. What do you think?' he asked, peering at Ben, then Kitty.

Ben looked sheepish.

'Is there something I've missed. And why are you here anyway? You can't be in need of a pair of curtains too.' Ruben spotted Ben fidgeting. 'You're messing with your hair. This means he's embarrassed or uncomfortable, or maybe both,' he explained, before taking a glance at Kitty, witnessing the same level of discomfort. 'Is someone going to tell me what's going on?'

'I'm meant to be taking Kitty out for dinner tonight and I was just calling over to make sure she's feeling better, and to confirm a time.' Kitty didn't know where to look, wanting to shake off her embarrassment.

Ruben washed away the awkwardness. 'Tell you what then. I'll come over in a little while when I've locked up, that way you'll have time to go over to Ben's, strike your very best pose and still have time for your evening plans. That's if you'll still want to go out with him when you've seen his interpretation. Mine was hideous,' laughed Ruben, pulling an unflattering face.

'Sure,' agreed Ben. 'That's if you're willing to trust this moron with your business, having only known him a handful of weeks.'

'All good with me,' Kitty replied.

'Well, I best go and get my best pencils sharpened,' Ben added, looking at his watch. 'See you in a bit.' He dashed out of the door and back up the street, both Ruben and Kitty spotting the visible, child-like spring in his step.

'So, is he taking you anywhere nice?'

Kitty tried to look busy. 'He hasn't told me.'

'Well, don't expect too much. He's not great at romance, he's always been that way. And I should know, having been his best man.'

Kitty's heart plummeted. A look of surprise showing through her makeup. 'I didn't know he was married.'

Ruben stumbled over his words. 'Oh, erm. Yeah. But they're separated,' he explained, fidgeting with the scissors on the desk. 'Should never have gotten married in the first place, but don't tell him I said that. Touchy subject.'

'He never mentioned anything to me,' she replied, her body language reflecting her moment of disappointment.

'Have you told him everything about you?' he asked, recalling Ben's comment a few days ago about her secretiveness. All the skeletons in Kitty's closet screamed, desperate to be heard. Whilst she was willing to let her new friends into her world, she somehow felt there was never the right time to share her story.

'I've never been married, thankfully,' she whispered, the admission creeping out amongst a deluge of relief.

Ruben captured her gaze, 'You're not really bothered though are you, about him being married? Because you're just friends, right?' he asked, a smirk spreading across his face, suggesting he knew better.

'That's right, we're just friends.'

Ruben saw the disappointment hanging from Kitty's posture. He lent his elbows on the counter, speaking with a genuine tone. 'Let him tell you in his own time, but I can assure you, Kitty, Ben's marriage is over.' Kitty locked eyes with Ruben, a meek smile breaking through the surface, followed by a nod of acknowledgement.

'Anyway, I best get going. I'll be back in a bit to take over.' Ruben made a fleeting exit, running up the road. Just as the door closed, Kitty's phone rang in her back pocket. Still not used to having a mobile of her own again, it took her a few seconds to acknowledge the buzzing sensation vibrating against her skin.

'Hello?'

No reply came.

'Hello?'

Kitty heard muffled noises at the other end, an intense breathing pattern, and yet nobody spoke. She ended the call and stood in the shop window, scanning for anyone lingering along the lane.

Her phone buzzed again.

'Hello?'

Still no reply.

With the phone pressed against her ear, she scanned the street, searching for his face. 'Stevie?' Saying his name aloud left a bitterness, a stinging sensation in her mouth. Someone knocked at the back door, startling Kitty's already fraught demeanour. She walked away from the window and ended the call.

'Who is it?'

'I've got a delivery for a Miss Kitty Twist,' the man's voice on the other side announced. 'I need a signature.'

Kitty eased the door open. 'Who is it from?'

Taken aback by the unorthodox question, the short-tempered man demanded her signature. 'Who knows, sign here.'

After the delivery driver had obtained Kitty's squiggle, he set off, stomping on the acceleration. With the box in her arms, the package felt light; empty. She heard the jingle of the shop door opening, but when she reappeared, the premises remained empty, the door hanging ajar.

Her phone buzzed again.

Her finger hovered over the cancel icon before pressing it to decline the private number. She placed the box on the counter and took hold of some scissors, tearing the tape and allowing the box to open. She pulled back the flaps, and felt a pained expression spread across her face as she was met with a sea of yellow.

An immediate cramping knotted her stomach, a wave of unsettling nausea threatening her composure. Kitty's stare fixated on the contents of the box, each individual daffodil petal torn so that no floral integrity remained. The sight of the contents made her muscles tense and she backed away, stumbling over the stool. She ducked behind the counter, her heart turning inside out, and she pressed her face into her palms, restraining her fear. Her shaking hands pulled out her phone, her finger hovering over the emergency call icon. But then the doorbell jingled and her body braced in anticipation, her lungs ready to release a deep-rooted scream.

'Hello?' a female voice announced. Kitty stood up, taking the lady by surprise. 'Oh, gosh. I didn't see you there, you made me jump,' said the customer, placing her hand over her heart.

'Sorry, I was just looking for something. How can I help?' Kitty asked, moving herself away from the parcel.

'I'm looking for a pair of sixteen-inch feather cushion inserts. Do you have any?'

'Of course, they're just here.' Kitty completed the sale in a daze, her mind focused on the parcel. 'Have a lovely day,' she concluded, watching her customer close the door. With the box still placed on the counter, Kitty examined it from afar, trying to identify a sender's address, but the outside remained unmarked. The writing on the label wasn't Stevie's, that she felt sure of. She took out her phone again, urging herself to call the police, and for almost an hour she debated in her mind the pros and cons of getting them involved.

She paced the circumference of the counter and peered out of the window every few seconds. With weary legs, she crouched behind the counter again, the central island becoming her fortress. Through a sense of defeat, she rested her head in her knees and prayed for help.

'Hello?' announced Ben upon entering the shop, seeing that it appeared empty. 'Oh, hi. You scared me,' he added when Kitty popped up from behind the counter like a jack-in-a-box. 'I didn't see you down there.' Kitty wanted to fling her arms around his broad shoulders and never let go. She had prayed for help, and there he stood, the very man for whom her heart pined.

'Sorry, I was just rummaging around for something, you'd think I'd know where everything is by now.' She attempted to conceal her beads of anxiety, pretending to fix her hair whilst strategically wiping her clammy brow.

'I can still never find the right sized paint brush when I need it, it's like there's a paint brush thief living in the studio,' Ben mocked. 'Or maybe it's Ruben pulling a prank, you know, hiding cameras so that he can laugh at me turning the place upside down every day.'

A mobile phone began to ring.

'Are you not going to answer that?' questioned Ben.

'Could you? I'm desperate for the loo,' she said before handing Ben the phone and scurrying through to the toilet. She secured the lock and pressed her back against the door, the room spinning. She leant over the basin and closed her eyes, splashing water over her face, washing off the sickening expression haunting her features.

'Who was it?' she asked, returning to the shop a few moments later. Hesitation held her towards the back, where an exit was within reach. With heightened senses, she heard the sound of chattering out on the street and spotted the postman walking up the road, before noticing the flapping string of bunting wrapped around the lampposts. She could smell the tray of chips that someone carried as they walked past the shop, and she sensed the group of ladies that were now peering into her shop were about to enter, the vibrant window display enticing them in.

'Oh, must've been the wrong number because they just hung up,' explained Ben, placing the phone on the counter. 'I'm all set up and ready at the studio and Ruben said he could come over now, to give us a bit more time.'

Kitty felt flustered. 'I don't feel I'm in any way ready,' she admitted, having not ran a brush through her hair all day or applied any lipstick. 'Give me one tick,' she said, scurrying through to the back.

'No rush,' he replied, lingering near the counter. He spotted the open box on the desk, the writing on the handwritten address label striking a chord of familiarity, the accentuation of the letter *s* unusual.

'I'm here,' announced Ruben, barging through the door and taking his place behind the counter, his abrupt entrance throwing Ben off his trail of thought. 'Right, what do I need to know?' he asked Kitty when she appeared at the exact same time. 'But don't muddle me with complicated till procedures,' he added, noting the fancy cash register.

 'Write down anything you sell on this piece of paper,' Kitty instructed, thrusting the pad and pen into his hands before grabbing her bag. 'Everything is priced, and if you get stuck, take details and I'll call people back.' Kitty walked towards the door and stepped out onto the lane with nervous feet. 'Thanks again, Ruben,' she expressed with a worrisome expression.

'He'll be fine,' commented Ben, upon noting her visible display of nerves, her head turning every few paces to peer back at her shop. 'Listen, if you're uncomfortable, we can do it on a Sunday when it's closed, or even one evening.' Kitty stood shoulder to shoulder with Ben, allowing her arm to brush his, the proximity offering a fleeting feeling of protection. She took one last glance over her shoulder, witnessing the lane dying down.

'And miss the opportunity to one day be auctioned at Sotheby's? No chance - let's go.'

The moment Ben and Kitty disappeared, a waiting customer pushed open the door and walked into Flourish.

24

BEN HELD THE STUDIO DOOR OPEN. 'AFTER YOU,' HE GESTURED with his hand, allowing Kitty to enter first. He couldn't help but watch her, noting how her fingers navigated the bannister, how her feet climbed each step whilst standing on tiptoes, plus the way her fair-haired curls draped the length of her back, a sweeping plait fixed in place by a single, silver-star hair grip. She paused at the top of the stairs, allowing Ben to guide her further.

'You'll have to excuse the mess. I didn't have time to tidy,' he apologised, opening the door.

Kitty admired the vibrant and eclectic display of artwork, strolling around the perimeter of the room the way a person might peruse the art in an established gallery. The skylights flooded the room with an abundance of natural light, the fair, Cornish weather providing the perfect backdrop for artistic inspiration. Her eyes drank in each piece, admiring the local landscapes and the use of contrasting colour palettes. Many of the paintings she admired were the ones which encapsulated a whimsical, seaside image; an abandoned pink boat named Bobbie-Juliet, a sunbathing couple sporting retro-style costumes, and the abstract painting of an abandoned beach umbrella.

'You were right, with these I'm sure you'll soon conquer any market.'

Ben adjusted the stool he'd placed in the window, obtaining the perfect angle from his vantagepoint. 'I hope you're right. I'm not sure about the umbrella one though.'

'I love it. It's simple yet effective. It grabs your attention, and you can't help but think who it belongs to, where've they gone, why they've left it alone and whether they'll come back to look for it the next day.'

'That's exactly the feeling that I wanted to evoke. And yet everyone I've shown so far hasn't got it. People keep suggesting I add in a person, or a boat, or something to add more interest, more depth. And yet you've grasped the inclination to perfection.'

Kitty turned and smiled, eyeing up her perch. 'So, where do you want me?'

'Just here, please,' he indicated to the stool. 'And all I need you to do is sit down, just as you naturally would, there's no need to pose or feel like you can't blink.'

Kitty took her position in the window. 'That's good to know, I'm not sure posing is one of my strengths.'

'Perfect,' he replied, noticing how the sun brushed over her features, accentuating her natural, pronounced cheek bones and soft, blue eyes. He took his place behind the easel, his hand quivering when holding the pencil. He unfastened the button on his t-shirt collar and took a gulp of water, attempting to eradicate his dry mouth. 'Right, let's crack on.'

Kitty spotted his left eye twitching each time he manoeuvred his head to take another look at his model, an endearing trait she was happy to observe as he studied her features. Behind the locked studio door and whilst in Ben's company, all the tension fell from Kitty's body, her limbs relaxing on the stool. She felt her neck loosen and her lungs became able to draw in longer breaths. With a strong sense of determination, she forced all lingering demons to the back of her mind and worked hard to erase the unexpected events of the day, plus all lingering thoughts of Stevie.

'I hope you're not going to give me a really big nose, or a giant forehead,' she commented. 'Be kind.'

Ben poked his head around the canvas. 'Well, I can't promise anything,' he commented, sneaking another peek from above the easel. 'Rest assured, it won't be as exaggerated as Ruben's, he didn't speak to me for a whole day after I sketched his. He hung it in his toilet just to make a point.'

'He told me that you're married.' The statement was blurted from Kitty's mouth. In the seconds which followed the statement, she wanted to jump down off the stool and capture all her words before they landed in Ben's ears. 'Sorry, ignore me, it's none of my business.' A visible layer of emotion clung like static, her body shimmering with vulnerability, her new complexion ready to be captured on canvas. She held her breath, waiting for a reply.

Ben's internal organs pumped with excitement at the prospect of her interest in his marital status. 'He's right, I am married.' The room fell beneath a spell of silence; neither one of them speaking.

Upon hearing the truth, Kitty worked to retain her composure, masking the disappointment radiating with more warmth than a roaring fire. Inside, she felt silly, and naïve. She had allowed her heart to fall for someone quickly, and for a man already married, at a time in her life when she should act more guarded than ever.

Ben broke the room's silence. 'But only legally,' he added in a matter-of-fact tone. He remained hidden behind his easel, not wanting any hurt to be evident on his face. 'We're separated, and I'm in the process of filing for a divorce.'

In that moment of hope, Kitty realised how much she cared for Ben. 'I'm so sorry.'

'Please, don't be, it's fine. If I was honest with myself, it wasn't right from the start and I knew it, even back when we became engaged.' He shook his head. 'Blimey, that sounds awful, I know it does. But I don't care anymore. It's the truth, and I'd rather be true to myself than be seen as a liar, or live a lie.' He took a breath and peered around the easel, eager to witness Kitty's reaction. He shook his head when he saw that she'd manoeuvred herself away, her body now facing towards the window.

'I hope Ruben is coping,' she commented, changing the subject.

'He can charm his way through pretty much any situation, he'll be fine. And if anything, he'll be talking your customers into buying more than what they actually need.' Ben stood at the side of his easel. 'Now, unless you want me to sketch the back of your head, you're unfortunately going to have to face this way.' He didn't really need to study her face in order to complete the portrait, already able to recall every feature from memory. He knew the curvature of her eyes and the way her dark eyebrows framed her face. He knew that the fullness of her lips tended to be accentuated by lip gloss, like cherry or strawberry, a smell he now associated with her. He knew the exact way in which Kitty often braided her hair around the side of her head, the strands interlocking with effortless precision. But mainly, he knew the exact shade of her eyes, a mixture between his favourite colour represented on his artistic palette, cornflower blue, and the vibrancy of pure sapphire.

'I think it's starting to look good,' he commented, breaking the moment of silence that no longer felt awkward or strained. 'Just need to work on your ears a little more,' he joked, peering to catch Kitty's reaction.

'Maybe work on them with a rubber if they're looking enormous,' she mocked.

'Tell you what, if you don't like it, you can forgo our plans for tonight and I won't be offended.'

'Deal,' she agreed, although she'd already thought about what their evening might entail.

'All done,' he announced, clasping his hands and encouraging himself not to keep working on something that he already felt looked perfect. He hesitated for a moment before moving away, reviewing his work from another angle. His sweaty palms took hold of the canvas. 'Are you ready to take a look?'

Ben's nerves transferred over to Kitty. 'Sure.'

He closed his eyes the moment he turned the canvas around to face her. 'I can never bear to witness the first impression, I think someone should be allowed to express a moment of disappointment if they wish, without the risk of offending.' Kitty stepped down from the stool. She took a few paces closer, inspecting the drawing.

'I thought you were doing a caricature?' she asked, allowing her eyes to digest the drawing.

Ben's sketch portrayed Kitty's real-life portrait, capturing her facial expression and each shadow created by the sun resting on her skin. He had captured the way her hands settled in her lap and the way her hair dangled in curly waves over her relaxed shoulders. On canvas, her lips were parted, allowing her thoughtful expression to be evidenced in the sketch. The pencil strokes were delicate and drawn with a finesse which couldn't help but express the artist's admiration.

Ben opened his eyes. 'I changed my mind, I needed to practice my portraits,' he explained. 'And anyway, those ears of yours wouldn't have fit onto the page with a caricature interpretation.'

Kitty tilted her head. She allowed herself to dive into the portrait, and for the first time since her arrival in St. Ives, she saw how the outside world viewed her new appearance. She couldn't see any element of her old self in the sketch. The dark shadows once ingrained beneath her eyes were no longer visible. The haunting face of someone whose life was ruled by fear had vanished.

'I don't know what to say.' Her skin blushed, her cheeks warming the entire room with a natural glow. She locked eyes with him, witnessing a reciprocated sense of affection. She wanted to find out how it felt to wrap her arms around him, and to be held close. She yearned to take hold of his hands and see how his skin felt against hers. But instead, the tender moment encouraged her to leave.

'I best get going, check that Ruben hasn't fallen asleep behind the counter, or eaten all of his own cake.'

'Sure, here, take this. It's yours,' said Ben, handing over the canvas. 'Place it wherever you see fit. The toilet is absolutely fine,' he joked, lightening the suddenly awkward atmosphere. 'You can forgo dinner plans, my deal still stands.'

'I'll meet you at the bench in half an hour,' she smiled, taking hold of the picture before heading out of the studio.

Ben's grin illuminated the room. The moment he heard the studio door bang closed, he peered around the empty room. Methodically, he turned around each of the shielded canvases leaning against the walls and resting on easels, each canvas decorated with a sketch of Kitty. In some, he'd drawn her sitting alone on the beach, whilst in others, he had captured her mid-laugh, highlighting the way her smile radiated. Detailed sketches of the woman now ingrained on his memory hung off every wall, a private dedication to the one who'd captured his heart.

Outside on the lane, Ruben closed the shop door and locked it. 'I was just on my way over. Everything is turned off. I had a little rush this past hour.' He handed Kitty the keys when she approached. 'No need to go in and check anything until tomorrow morning, unless you want to. I've even tidied up and emptied the bins. You'd left a box of dead flowers on the counter so I've thrown them away too, and I swept the floor and tidied all your displays. So, I suggest you get yourself off and enjoy your date with Ben, though don't expect anything more than a pub meal paired with a side of conversation about paintings.'

'It's not a date,' she replied. 'But thank you for looking after the shop.'

Ruben caught sight of the canvas dangling in her hand. 'From the look of that, I'd hedge my bets that it turns into a date.'

'What do you think?' she asked, holding it up for him to admire. 'Worthy of more than a toilet wall?'

'I think he's smitten and even if you can't see it, I can.' He pulled out the box wedged under his arm. 'Oh, and this came for you,' he said, shaking the box. 'Doesn't feel like there's much in it though.' The sight of the box pulled Kitty out of her romantic bubble, her carefree feelings replaced with a sickening sense of dread. She peered over Ruben's shoulder, then up the street.

'Was it delivered by the postman, or a delivery driver?'

'A delivery guy, just asked me to sign for it. Here, I'll help you to your flat,' he offered, noticing how Kitty was struggling to carry both the box and the canvas. Kitty scrutinised her surroundings with each step, paranoia weighing down on her shoulders.

'Are you okay?' asked Ruben, picking up on her sense of distraction.

Embarrassed, Kitty forced herself not to turn around. 'Thought I'd dropped something,' she explained. 'Well, thanks so much again for looking after the shop, I really appreciate it. Just leave the box there,' she said, indicating with her foot once they reached the door to her flat.

'Enjoy tonight,' he hollered from his side of the street. 'And I'll be over in the morning with that coffee ready to hear about how it's all gone, and then I can compare your version with Ben's,' he added, waving from inside the café.

Kitty opened her front door and placed the canvas inside, before going back to retrieve the parcel. Once in the kitchen, she spotted the familiarity of the handwritten address, and could already picture the dead flowers likely to be revealed inside. She grabbed the kitchen butchering knife and sliced apart the cardboard, lowering in her hand and pulling out a handwritten note.

25

KITTY REACHED FOR HER PHONE AND ONCE AGAIN DRAGGED STEVIE'S mobile number from out of the depths of her long-term memory, tapping in the digits before pressing the phone against her ear.

It began to ring.

Her muscles tightened, reaching an unpleasant rigidity. Her internal temperature rose, and her jaw cast itself into a single, set position.

On the third ring, still no answer came.

She pictured Stevie in her mind, and grew sick at the mere thought of seeing him again, and the prospect that he was close by, watching her.

Forth ring, still no answer.

No amount of time could have prepared her for what she would say, or how she would feel upon hearing his voice. She peered at the note which simply read 'I'm watching you', before looking out of the window, searching for his stature, knowing that only he could have written something so cruel. The sight of Ben's studio stole her attention, and she became all too aware that her dinner date was fast approaching.

The answer machine took control, luring Kitty into a false sense of security by thinking Stevie had answered. Her heart fell to the floor upon hearing his voice. *You're through to Stevie Best. I'm not available at the moment, so leave a message and I'll get back to you.*

She didn't think before speaking, her words forcing their way out. 'Leave me alone, you sick bastard. I'm not afraid of you anymore and I'll scream if you come anywhere near me.'

She hung up.

She positioned herself in front of the mirror, double checking her composure before grabbing her bag and leaving the apartment.

As soon as she stepped outside, her body instinctively braced. Her persistent plea to be left alone flickered in the breeze, and her initial feeling of freedom began to waver. The lane looked quiet and the usual bustling hum had dissipated, all the shop shutters now down. Pausing on the safety of her doorstep, she took a deep inhale of fresh, salty, sea air. Before she had time to change her mind, she stepped down onto the pavement and strode towards the seafront, her pace quickening. In the early evening breeze, she was glad that she'd worn a chunky cardigan, wrapping her body within its warmth. Her wavering confidence craved the safety of numbers and as soon as the crowd scattering the front came into view, she dove into its epicentre and sought camouflage. She stood on tiptoes, trying to see past the commotion to spot Ben at their meeting point. Pressed against her thigh, she felt the vibration of her phone and when she took it out, saw that she had received twelve missed calls since leaving the flat, all from a private number. Her insides rattled the moment the phone rang again.

'Hello?' There was no reply. 'Who is this? Stevie?' She could hear breathing again and muffled background noises, what she thought sounded like ringing. The phone went dead. She looked up, searching for Ben and catching sight of their meeting point. Her phone rang yet again; private number calling. 'You're a coward, you bastard,' she proclaimed in a moment of bravery upon answering. 'Hiding behind a phone and bunches of dead flowers. If you want me, then take me,' she concluded, ending the call. In the distance, just by the bench, she saw Ben raising his hand in acknowledgement. She navigated the winding cobbled path down to the bench. 'Hi.' She spotted what looked like a picnic blanket and basket under his arm. 'I'm not late, am I?'

'No, I've just arrived myself,' he replied, wanting to engage in a welcoming hug, but instead, his arms fidgeted, making the initial greeting awkward.

'Looks like you've come prepared.'

'I thought we'd have dinner alfresco. It's a little cool but I've brought an extra jumper in case you get cold.' His thoughtfulness warmed her heart.

'Great, which way do you think is best?' she asked, scanning the beach and seeing a bustle of tourist activity; children selecting their favourite flavour of ice cream, families brushing sand from between their toes and water sport companies packing up their equipment.

Without thought, Ben pointed to his right. 'I know a quiet spot. It's not too far to walk, if that's okay with you?' He held out his arm, offering to assist her down onto the beach. Kitty reached out and took hold of his hand, landing her feet on the pebbles. 'I'd leave your shoes on for now. When we reach the sand, take them off so that it's easier to walk,' he advised, leading the way. The pair followed the curvature of the coast, leaving in their trail all the noise emanating from the bustling restaurants and bars.

'So, did the shop survive under Ruben's temporary management?'

'I haven't been in to check, but it hadn't burnt down,' she replied, displaying a wide grin. Upon reaching the sandy stretch, the pair eased off their shoes, the sand clumsy beneath their feet, with broken, abandoned sandcastles creating an uneven surface. The beach in front became calmer, and to the right, sheltered by the protruding landscape, Ben spotted his secret, secluded spot.

'Not far, it's just over there,' he pointed. The sand in the cove appeared fresh, like it hadn't been meddled with since the last tide. 'Here we are. How's this?' asked Ben.

Kitty paused, admiring the backdrop and drinking in the sense of peace it offered. She helped Ben with the blanket. 'Great little spot. How do you know about it?'

Ben held out his hand, imitating pulling out a chair in a restaurant, offering Kitty the opportunity to sit down first.

'Thanks.' Kitty sat crossed legged, looking out to sea, the loose strands of her hair blowing in the wind. She took out her phone from her back pocket, tossing it towards the front of the blanket. Six more missed calls flashed up on the screen.

Ben sat down alongside her, bending his legs and resting his arms on his knees. 'I've lived in St. Ives a long time, so I've come to know a few little nooks that the majority of tourists don't stumble across.'

For Kitty, the seclusion of the spot felt safe; shielded. Out amongst the dying waves, a sprinkling of sunset surfers attempted to ride the last waves of the day, providing free entertainment to those acting as a shoreline audience. A collection of boats sailed in, making their way to a mooring, the bobbing buoys guiding them home.

Ben spotted her phone illuminate. 'Your phone's ringing.'

'It'll be a nuisance call. Best to ignore it.' She reached out and with her finger swiftly ended the call.

'Now, I wasn't sure what you liked, so I've brought a bit of everything,' he began, taking out traditional picnic items, the blanket soon brimming.

'Looks wonderful, thank you so much. Did you make it all yourself?'

'Absolutely not,' he was quick to admit. 'I didn't want to risk giving you food poisoning.' He picked up a sausage roll, scraps of flaky pastry clinging to his lips the moment his teeth sunk into the tasty morsel.

'If it's alright with you, I'll start with pudding first. I'm always scared that after a meal I'll be too full to enjoy all my favourite bits,' she added, spotting the fresh fruit.

Ben took out some slices of the prepared watermelon. 'I was going to bring some of Ruben's cake, but I forgot to order it and he'd ran out by the time I asked, so this was second best.'

Kitty took hold of a slice. 'I'm not sure how I can eat it without making a mess,' she laughed, her hands already covered in the fruit's juice.

'Making a mess is the best part,' he replied, taking a sizeable bite from a slice of quiche.

For Kitty, the experience of eating alfresco felt so liberating; allowing the sweet, cool juices to dribble down her face and not caring about the unsightly mess. 'Delicious.'

'I aim to please,' he began, at which point her phone rang again.

Kitty's heart plummeted. She watched the screen flash, her heart pumping beneath her clothes, and she willed the phone to stop ringing, the sound of the ringtone cutting through her nerves. 'There's something I need to tell you,' she began, casting her gaze down at the sand.

Ben carried on eating his sausage roll, his deep swallow forcing the food past the lump that'd appeared in his throat. A gust of apprehension suddenly came over him, a sinking feeling immersing his insides and stealing his appetite.

'I didn't leave my home up North just to start a new life down here,' she began, scooping sand into her palm and allowing the grains to trickle through her fingers like an hourglass. She didn't look at Ben, fearful to witness his reaction. 'If I was to be really honest, I sort of escaped, I guess,' she added, at which point she took a sneaky look at Ben out of the corner of her eye, spotting how his arms rested on his knees. She could see that he was biting the inside of his lip through his cheek, and frowning as he buried his feet in the sand.

She looked back down, searching the sand for answers. 'I was engaged,' she continued to explain. 'And at first the relationship appeared great, perfect even, and he made me believe that *he* was perfect.' Kitty paused and raised her head, her gaze cast out towards the sea. 'But he didn't turn out to be quite so perfect. It was all just a lie,' she admitted, dropping her gaze once more whilst her toes dug themselves into the soft grains of sand. 'I learned the hard way that he's a dangerous man.' Kitty's muscles tensed and the stack of memories she had worked so hard to leave behind in Perth surged through her mind.

'And one day, I decided I couldn't take anymore, and so I left. I snuck out during the night so that he wouldn't try and stop me, or know where I'd gone.' Her confession hung in the air, and she cried, covering her face with her hands, the enormity of her troubled past flooding her emotions. 'I didn't leave home just to start a new life somewhere else, I escaped.' Kitty's tears fell heavily, and she finally felt the relief she had been craving at sharing her secret, embracing the moment of vulnerability.

Ben took out a tissue from his pocket and placed it in her hand. Driven by his own instincts, he nudged his body closer to Kitty, only a slither of daylight separating the two of them. His caring gesture encouraged Kitty to continue.

'My parents passed away not too long before I met him, and I felt so lonely, so utterly alone in life, that when he came along, I accepted the distraction,' she confessed, trying her best to conceal the look of embarrassment clinging to her face. 'I felt so ashamed that I'd let someone treat me so badly, and I just didn't know what to do. I felt embarrassed of my life, and how I must have looked to the outside world.' She shook her head at the words she wanted to say next, already humiliated by her own behaviour. 'So, I did exactly what he wanted, and I locked myself away like some sort of prisoner.' With Ben's tissue, she wiped her nose and took a breath. 'I know it sounds ridiculous, me allowing someone to treat me that way, and for so long. I just felt like there was no other option.' She sighed and produced a meek smile, trying to break the heaviness weighing down over the conversation. 'He used threats, making me believe that I couldn't leave, like I was his property, and always would be.' Kitty stopped talking and turned to look at Ben, offering him an apologetic look. 'I'm sorry to burden you with all this mess. I bet you wish you'd never met me now, and I really wouldn't blame you.'

Ben looked up, meeting her gaze. 'I could never regret having met you, Kitty,' he began, his hand reaching out and taking hold of hers. 'I knew you were keeping something from me, I just didn't know what,' he added, wiping away a stray tear from her cheek. He stroked her hand gently with his thumb. 'I can't imagine how awful life has been for you. I'm so sorry.' Already brimming with a desire to protect, he shuffled closer to her, eliminating all space between them so that their arms touched. 'I now understand why you refused to talk about your past, and why, on some days, you appeared on edge,' he began, shaking his head with disappointment. 'I'm so sorry for all the times I've been trying to get you to talk. I just wanted to get to know you, that's all.'

'It's not your fault, really. I was trying to act like none of it ever happened, like I could just become a new person, but obviously it's just not that easy,' she shrugged at her own naivety. 'Nobody knew what was happening, not even my best friend. You're the first person I've told.'

'It sounds like he should be reported to the police,' he said, his shock evidenced in his words. Ben looked at her phone. 'Do you think he's followed you down here?'

Kitty nodded. 'I don't know how else to explain what's been going on. I'm getting these calls to my mobile where nobody speaks, yet I know someone's at the other end because I can hear them breathing. And a delivery arrived at the shop, nothing but a box of dead flowers - something he used to do all the time back in Perth.'

'Dead flowers? Why would he do that?' Ben questioned. Kitty's shoulders rose then fell back down.

'It was sick way of trying to intimidate me, and it worked - it's still working. How could it not, when dead daffodils appear on my doorstep?'

'He's been to your flat?' Ben was quick to ask, the sound of shock wrapped around his words.

Kitty nodded with reluctance. 'I found more flowers on my doorstep, torn daffodil petals, like always. Plus a note saying I'm being watched.'

A look of horror washed over Ben's face, his heart pumping. He held her hand with a tighter grip, the strong emotions he felt towards her pressing against her quivering palm. Both Kitty's and Ben's eyes followed the hypnotic crescendo of each incoming wave, their minds processing the situation whilst simultaneously trying to seek comfort. Their hands remained joined, a unity that Kitty hadn't experienced since losing her mum. She relished the warmth of his skin, learning once again how it felt to be touched by a sincere hand. The mobile phone that had been cast aside buzzed once more in the sand.

Kitty glanced down at the private number calling her phone again. Ben could feel Kitty's entire body quivering. 'Hello,' he began, reaching out and pressing the phone against his ear. 'Ben speaking.' He too could sense someone on the other end, a vigorous breathing pattern audible. The person hung up and Ben tossed the phone back down. 'We should call the police. He's dangerous, you said it yourself. And if he's found you, you're in real danger, Kitty, and the police will be there to protect you.' Their hands remained entwined and the wind rushed into their secluded cove, a swell of shivers scattering all over Kitty's body.

'I can't, and I don't expect you to understand why.'

'Try me,' he replied, tightening his grip on her hand, squeezing so that their fingers interlocked.

'I'm scared that if I tell the police, he'll be so furious and he won't stop until he's got revenge. He'll want to hurt me, and the only way he'd know how to do that is by destroying my house in Perth, or at least the things inside that belonged to my parents. He knows how much all those items mean to me,' she began picturing in her mind all the treasures hiding in the attic. 'There's something I need to find, something so important to me, and I can't take the risk of that being stolen or destroyed.' Kitty thought back to the conversation with Peggy. 'Before my mum passed away, she tried to tell me something, something she wanted me to know or find out, and until I uncover what it was, I just can't rest, and I'll never feel at peace with what happened,' she added, turning to look at Ben, waiting for his reaction. 'I know all of this sounds so crazy, and I don't expect you to understand, but I feel like I owe you the truth.'

'It does make sense,' he replied, nodding to add emphasis to his words. 'And you're sure that this thing you're looking for is back at your home in Perth?'

'It must be, my entire life is back in Perth. You saw me that morning on the bench with just a shoulder bag. That's all I brought with me,' she explained. Like she had done so many times previously, Kitty closed her eyes and tried to hear her mum's words. 'She told me to look in something, I just don't know what. She couldn't get the words out,' she replied, smiling at the hopelessness of her situation. 'Before I sold the family home, I turned it upside down and left nothing untouched, I even got a company in to lift the floorboards. I needed to be sure that I hadn't missed anything, knowing that I wouldn't be able to go back and check.' Kitty turned to look at Ben again, her wide eyes overflowing with emotion. 'And the rest of her belongings are in my attic, the things I couldn't bear to part with after she passed, all the things that meant the most to her. I wanted to bring them all down here with me, but I knew that I couldn't, not without Stevie getting suspicious.' Kitty took a breath, her body feeling cold all over. Her free hand fumbled and she pressed it against her chest, trying to dislodge her pain. 'Those belongings were precious to my mum, so her secret must be hidden with them.'

Ben tucked a few stray hairs behind Kitty's ear and watched her emotions fall, her cheeks reddening. 'I do understand why you don't want to tell the police, at least not yet.' He wrapped his arms around her body, trying to shelter her from the increasing bite of the wind. 'You'll find what you're looking for, I know you will. How can I help? Tell me, I'll do anything.'

Kitty wiped her cheeks with the back of her hand. 'I need a

favour,' she began tentatively. 'And you can say no, because it's a lot to ask given that we haven't known each other long, and that you've already painted my flat,' she laughed, her smile soaking up the few straggling tears now trickling down her face.

'What is it?'

'I need to go back to Perth, back to the house, but I'm scared to go alone.' Kitty watched the early evening sunset take command of the sky, the blushing canopy reminding her so much of Delilah. A vacancy appeared in her eyes and her body released a long, slow sigh. 'You know, it's crazy, but on some days, I swear it feels like I only lost my mum and dad yesterday.'

Ben cast her a reassuring smile. 'I'll go with you, back to Perth I mean. And if he's there, he'll have two of us to face this time.'

Kitty turned to Ben, a wave of guilt flooding her conscience. 'He's dangerous and I have no idea what he's capable of. He won't stop until he gets what he wants,' she said, her chin pressed into her chest.

Ben released his grip and, with his palms, framed her face, holding it close to his so that their noses were nearly touching. 'Nobody is going to take you anywhere if you don't want to go, and nobody is going to hurt you. I'll take you home and you will find what you're looking for.' His words were defiant. 'That I can promise you.'

Tears welled behind Kitty's eyes again. 'You do realise that Perth is in Scotland, don't you? I'm not sure if I'd mentioned that before. That's my hometown,' she confessed. Ben held her cool cheeks again, permeating her skin with his warmth.

'You could be from Perth, Australia, and I'd still go with you.'

Kitty held her breath, raising her eyebrows to offer a questioning gaze. 'Are you sure? I'd want to go this weekend. You can walk away, or at least wait until I've managed to sort my life out before you get involved. I won't be offended, or think any less of you, I promise.' She leaned into his palm, resting the weight of her head against his hand, a warm tear smudging onto his skin. She found herself growing greedy for his company, and yearned to feel the bellows of his skin. Her ears craved the soothing tones of his voice and her lips became thirsty for his. Her lungs inhaled his intoxicating scent, the aroma dancing inside her body.

Ben realigned her face, making sure their stares met. 'The first day we met I could tell by the shadows in your eyes that you were holding something back. I didn't walk away then, and I won't walk away now.' He combed away more of the stray hairs draped over Kitty's face, easing the blonde strands back behind her ear. 'Something's been missing from my life for so long, and I didn't know what it was, until I met you.' Ben noticed the white mark on his wedding finger where his band had once sat, and he felt a surge of relief. 'I thought I loved someone before, and that's why I got married, but I now know I wasn't in love.' He paused, scared to lay his feelings bare. 'The problem was, I had nothing to compare my feelings to, so I didn't know what being in love felt like.' His vulnerability showed through his words, and his voice went quiet beneath a shallow trickle of breaths. 'But, after just a few weeks of knowing you, I'm beginning to understand what love is, and I'm scared that if I let you go, I'll never find you again.'

The tide began to teeter towards the shore, swallowing up the once dry sand and washing away every footprint that the day had left behind. The evening breeze mellowed, and the sea became limp, with not a surfing wave to be spotted. The sunset crawled beneath the horizon, indicating the end of daylight hours. Ben and Kitty rested their heads against one another and Kitty allowed herself to indulge in the view, drinking in the melting sky.

'Can we stay here forever, right here in this secret nook where nobody knows where we are?' Snippets of Ben's burly physique became visible beneath his t-shirt and tank top, his arms able to wrap around Kitty and lock into place.

'We could, but sea critters would feast on our feet whilst we sleep,' he jested, relishing the moment, he too realising it couldn't last forever. 'But we can come back tomorrow, and every other night if we want to.' He held her close, his touch delicate.

'Do you promise you won't tell anyone? In this life, the life I'm making for myself down here in St. Ives, I want to be known as Kitty Twist, the owner of Flourish, not the Kitty Twist I once was, the person I allowed myself to become.'

'Of course. Come on, let's get going before we get washed out to sea and I have to do the gallant thing of trying to save you, despite the fact I'm a nervous swimmer.' Packing up the picnic and vacating their spot, their bodies left indentations in the sand, before the incoming, ravenous tide erased all trace of their moment.

They meandered across the beach, back towards civilisation, the wind assisting from behind. Ben took out the spare jumper he'd brought.

'Here, put this on,' he said, helping to ease his polo top over Kitty's head, their eyes locking when her head popped through. Looking into his eyes, she gained the strong impression that he wanted to press his lips against hers. He eased his face forward but Kitty looked away, pretending to straighten out the jumper.

'Thanks, I didn't realise how cold I felt,' she said, evading the romantic moment, nervous to take the next step so soon.

Leaving behind a trail to their hideaway snug, Kitty and Ben meandered back across the beach, neither one in a hurry. Her hand dangled at the side of her body for just a moment before Ben swept it up, engulfing her delicate fingers within a warm embrace. The cluster of restaurants speckling the front were doing a bustling trade; flickering table candles wavering against the swirling breeze.

'I still can't get over the fact that you're Scottish,' Ben commented, helping Kitty up the steps that led to the winding, main road.

'Well, my mum originated from Canada and my dad was Irish, so that resulted in me having an accent that didn't really belong anywhere.'

'And now you belong in Cornwall.'

Kitty looked up, the sky turning on its spotlights; the black background now inundated with illuminating stars. The pair made their way back to Ladysmith Lane, meandering through the winding streets, never letting go of each other's hand.

Kitty's front door came into view. 'Well, thanks for tonight,' she began, pulling her hand away to dig in her bag for the door key. 'It felt like a special date,' she whispered.

A silly grin appeared on Ben's face. 'So, it was a date then, and not just dinner?' He watched Kitty place the key in the door.

'It started as dinner, but ended in something else I think,' she said, turning back around.

Ben eased himself a little closer, joining her on the steps and taking back hold of her hand, unwilling to let it go. 'I think you're wonderful, Kitty Twist. You have this way of making me smile, and you don't even need to say anything,' he began, looking down at their entwined hands.

She followed his gaze, his touch feeling more delicate than silk. To her wounded heart, his words acted as thread, stitching together her injuries. She tightened her grip, examining his hands with her fingertips. 'And your eyes make me feel giddy.'

He opened his eyes wide in a playful way. 'Thanks.'

The more Ben spoke, the more Kitty felt her wilted insides blooming. 'Are you always so caring?' she asked, stricken by his constant kindness.

He leant in, pausing near her ear, his hair tickling her skin.

'I can't help it when I'm with you. You're just adorable.'

Kitty smiled, feeling the warmth of his breath against her skin. Whispers of sensuality danced down her spine, acting as a reminder of how it felt to be loved.

'I best get going, busy day ahead tomorrow,' she explained, pulling herself away.

'Are you going to be alright? Alone, I mean? Are you safe in the flat? I can check it out before leaving.'

'I'll be fine,' she replied, releasing his hand and easing the door open.

'If you need anything, ring me. I'm not far away.'

'I'll be fine, please don't worry.'

Ben sensed her attempt at lightening the mood, her words doing little to ease his mind.

'I'll just pop over in the morning then, drop off a coffee, and we can start to plan our trip up to Perth. How about Sunday, is that soon enough?' Ben felt drawn towards the open doorway, his instinct urging him never to leave Kitty's side.

'Perfect,' she replied.

An awkwardness lingered, and his clumsy actions showed his hidden collection of nerves. He cleared his throat and, through a shaking voice, bid her farewell.

'Good night, Kitty.' He leaned in and delivered a gentle kiss to her cheek, before stepping away, sensing the perfect moment to press pause. 'See you tomorrow,' he concluded, smiling to himself as he walked across the road. He fumbled in his pocket, pulling out the studio keys and feeling his phone vibrate. He took it out to see a message from Charlie, her two simple words stealing the life out of his lungs.

I'm pregnant.

26

THE WIND CHIMED THROUGH THE TAWNY TANGLE OF BRANCHES, early season petals decorating them like miniature cotton buds. In the background, the fresh breeze made the surface of the sea quiver. Charlie stepped out of the door and zipped up her polka-dot anorak, concealing her freezing body beneath. With spring awakening, a fine dispersal of blossom delivered a floral pungency to the air. The sky murmured with birdsong and the warming rays of early morning sunshine rested on Charlie's skin, encouraging her to smile.

She made her way over to The Cherry Tree, walking slowly to give herself some time to practice what she wanted to say to Ben. During the walk, she imagined how it would feel waking up the following morning nuzzled against her husband's shoulder, the swathes of duvet concealing their entwined limbs. She anticipated how it would feel to once again prepare Ben some breakfast, producing brimming bowls of honey-infused porridge, before sneaking back beneath the covers and snuggling until late in the morning.

'Morning, Beth,' announced Charlie upon entering The Cherry Tree, the quaint café nudged in at the far end of town. The low ceilings and exposed beams offered a rustic ambience to visiting patrons, the aroma of fresh bread enticing customers who hadn't yet experienced the internal charm. To Charlie, the café held special significance because it was where she and Ben had celebrated all their special occasions.

'A cup of my usual, please, and the same for Ben. He shouldn't be long. We'll have two slices of your almond strawberry cake, too. Thanks, Beth.'

'Take a seat, Charlie, I'll bring it over.'

Charlie perched herself in one of the window seats, the leather folds moulding around her familiar contours. The rising heat of the morning beamed in, tempting her to remove her coat. She adjusted her baggy, grey jumper, easing it off one shoulder to show just a bit of skin. Ben had always adored the simplicity of the knitwear, the jumper that more often than not Charlie refused to wear, arguing that it wasn't fashionable or favourable to her slim physique. Today, she had concluded that the jumper was the perfect choice, knowing that it might just help her in winning Ben over.

The waitress paused at the table, leaning down with a tray in hand. 'Here you go, Charlie, two espressos, and two slices of cake.'

'Thanks, Beth.'

'I haven't seen you and Ben in here for a while.'

Charlie flicked her sachet of sugar between her fingers. 'We've been having a few issues, but nothing to worry about. After today, we'll be back here topping up your till whilst expanding our waistlines with your delicious cakes.'

'Good to hear. Let me know if you need anything else,' Beth offered, before walking away.

Charlie eased herself into the seat and found herself drawn to the face of each passerby in eager anticipation of her husband's arrival. It wasn't like Ben to be late, and their arranged meeting time had already been and gone. She checked her phone, but was disheartened to find there had still been no message or missed calls. Sipping on her coffee, she allowed the caffeine to settle her nerves.

After another handful of minutes, Ben pushed open the door, taking a prolonged intake of breath upon seeing his wife sat in the window. 'Hi,' he announced.

Charlie stood, ready to accept a welcoming embrace. 'Oh, hi. I didn't see you, you must've come from a different direction to the way we usually walk.' She noticed Ben's hands remained hidden in his pockets, whilst also picking up on the lemon-coloured jumper beneath his coat, and the unfamiliar scent of a new aftershave. His stubble looked more pronounced, which she hated, and his hair style, too, appeared ruffled. Despite all of these irregularities to his appearance, she'd forgotten just how good looking he was. 'Do I not even get a hug?'

Ben remained at a distance with his hands still hidden out of sight.

His evasiveness stoked her fire. 'Is this really how a husband greets his wife, the mother of his unborn child?'

He pulled over a stool, no longer wanting to rest in the warmth of the familiar, leather chairs. 'I haven't come here to fight, Charlie. Please, sit down,' he requested, indicating with his hand for her to take her seat. Charlie's plan scrambled, she quickly lost the composed trail of thoughts that she'd intended to deliver. She crossed her legs and folded her arms over the jumper which she now regretted wearing.

'This feels strained, like we're strangers all of a sudden,' she said, searching for glimmers of familiarity in her husband.

Ben noted the drink and cake, just the sight of the food turning his stomach. 'You walked out on me, Charlie, and we haven't spoken in weeks. It was never going to be easy meeting up again.' Ben rested his arms on his thighs, drooping his head and running his fingers through his hair. 'When you left me that morning, my world fell apart. You wouldn't answer my calls, you wouldn't reply to any of my messages. You didn't even let me know that you were okay. All you did was deface my studio, for reasons I still don't understand.'

'I went to the studio to get my wedding rings, I wanted them back where they belong, on my finger. But I bumped into Ruben beforehand in town and I got all flustered, thinking you were out having a great time without me, so…' Charlie paused, unsure of how to explain herself.

'So?'

Charlie bowed her head, embarrassed of her childish behaviour. 'I'm sorry. I shouldn't have done what I did. I felt upset, and angry.'

Ben shook his head with frustration. 'I didn't leave the flat for days, Charlie. I couldn't eat, and all I thought about was you, and how badly I'd acted that morning you came to tell me about the ovulation test. I should've been more sensitive to how you were feeling and I'm sorry for how I behaved.' Before Charlie could respond, Ben continued. 'But in the weeks after you left, refusing to talk to me, it forced me to admit that things weren't right between us, and hadn't been for a while. Longer than I cared to admit.'

Charlie's hands began to sweat and she leaned away from the table, easing her body back into the comfort of the chair. 'What are you saying?'

Ben forced himself to look up. 'You did the right thing by leaving. You deserve someone who can provide you with the life you want, and that person isn't me.'

Charlie felt flustered beneath the strength of the sun, its rays casting an uncomfortable brightness over her face. 'I'm confused. Are you saying that we're not right for each other anymore?' Her frown lines multiplied, and her body stiffened.

Ben fidgeted on his stool. 'I love you, Charlie. I always have done,' he paused. Grabbing a moment of relief, Ben allowed his eyes to admire the couple strolling past the café, the elderly pair walking in perfect synchronicity whilst their fingers remained interlocked. He inhaled a wave of bravery. 'But I'm not in love with you, not anymore.' Once spoken, the words refused to die, their aftermath clinging to the air like a pollutant, poisoning the threads of hope spinning in Charlie's heart.

Her bottom lip quivered. 'You're not in love with me?' she repeated, the notion unfathomable, and one that she hadn't predicted.

Ben didn't reply, choosing instead to leave the truth dangling like an axe above their marriage.

'What about the baby - our baby?'

He held back the intrinsic, paternal instinct that had unexpectedly flourished since he'd learnt the news, desperate for it not to cloud his judgement. 'I can't stay married to you just because of a baby. It wouldn't work, and it wouldn't be fair on any of us.'

Charlie held out her hands, having played her last card. 'So, that's it? It's over? Our marriage is over, just like that?'

Ben's silence answered her question, his defeated body language acting as final confirmation. 'I'll do my best to be the perfect dad, and I want to play my role in all of this, if you'll let me,' he said after an extended pause. He leant in, offering Charlie a tissue. 'I'll do everything I can to support you, and the baby, but it doesn't change our situation.' He watched Charlie sipping on the espresso, questioning in his mind her choice to consume caffeine when all of her pre-natal research had advised against such beverages, especially during the early stages. 'I'd like to come with you to the doctors' appointments, if you'll let me.'

Charlie threw the tissue on the table. 'You want to support me, when what you're actually saying is that our marriage is over?' Her cheeks became blotched as the anxiety firing beneath her skin rose to the surface. 'I made a mistake, Ben. I lost my temper that morning at the studio and I stewed over it for far too long, and now it feels like I'm being punished. Why can't we just pretend that it didn't happen? We always have these silly rows and we always make up, that's what we do.'

'I'm not punishing you, that's not what I want. But we can't just go back in time and pretend that all this didn't happen. You made the right decision by leaving me.' Ben's insides crumbled, his heart flatlining beneath the pressure of causing another human being so much emotional pain. 'If you thought you'd made a mistake, you wouldn't have left it for so long. You'd have answered my calls, or you'd have come home. But you didn't, Charlie, and you didn't for all the right reasons.'

Charlie noted the absence of his wedding ring. 'You've met someone else, haven't you? I saw you with someone; a blonde woman.'

Ben shook his head in a defeated manner. 'This isn't about anybody else, it's about you, me, and our baby.'

'Our baby? How can you call it our baby when you're abandoning us?'

Ben's movement lacked energy, his eyelids feeling hot and his throat scratchy. 'I'm not abandoning anybody. I'll always be there for the baby, but I can't do it as your husband. Things have changed. I've changed.' The moist slices of cake on the table began to dry, the heat permeating through the window causing the fresh, cream cheese icing to turn. Charlie reluctantly let go of her romantic notion of a Sunday morning reunion as she felt her marriage slipping away.

'I made a mistake, Ben. I didn't want to leave you. I was just upset and felt frustrated by your indecision.' Her eyes searched the floor in an attempt to conceal her shame. 'I thought I could manipulate the situation by walking out. I thought that, given enough time, you'd want me back. We've had fights like this in the past and I've spent a few days on Pip's sofa, but we've always sorted things out.' With a defeated tone, Charlie asked the question she'd been mulling over. 'Why have you never told me before that you didn't want to start a family with me?'

An extended silence lingered heavily over the table.

Ben couldn't maintain eye contact. 'I have, you just didn't want to listen.'

He attempted to take hold of Charlie's hand, but she pulled away, and began to sob.

'You're my entire life, all my memories include you.'

'This isn't easy for me either,' he said.

Charlie shook her head. 'I'm sorry I ever met you. I'm sorry I ever fell in love with you and I'm sorry I ever married you,' she concluded, before getting out of her seat and walking away, her saturated tissue falling with a heaviness to the floor.

Ben held his head in his hands, and despite feeling the urge to run after her, he forced himself to remain seated. He stared at the tissue on the floor, knowing how much pain he'd caused. The cosy chair retained Charlie's impression in the leather, the material warm from the heat of her body. He felt someone place a hand on his shoulder.

'Are you alright?' asked Beth. 'I couldn't help but hear.' She took a seat by his side, witnessing the glossy nature of his eyes.

He shook his head. 'It's over.' He wiped the tears away on the back of his sleeve, embarrassed. 'I never wanted to hurt her.'

'I know,' replied Beth. She wrapped her arm around his shoulders. 'Life is too short to waste. If you weren't happy, you've done the right thing.'

'Thanks, Beth,' he said before pulling himself away from the little café nook, the home to so many memories. He hovered in the doorway with an air of uncertainty, torn between his past and present. He looked up and saw a fracture appear in the clouds, the cumulonimbus mass rolling in with the swift gust. The sun bled through and in the distance, a rainbow dripped down from the sky, splashing a pool of colours onto the horizon. The image made Ben think immediately of Kitty, and her suggestion on the very first day they had met that a rainbow would make a wonderful sketch. In that moment, he knew where his future lay.

27

At the opposite end of town from The Cherry Tree, splashes of vitamin D seduced exposed snippets of skin, and whilst she hung her head out of her bedroom window, Kitty's senses awakened. She admired the rainbow in the distance, the natural phenomenon encouraging a smile to stretch across her face. Her thoughts remained secluded in the romantic beach bubble she and Ben had created the previous evening. She recalled how it had felt to be held, and revelled in the aftermath of his shower of affection. Across the street she saw his studio, and felt disappointed to witness no signs of life.

Making her way through to the kitchen after a dip in the bath, Kitty caught sight of the scribbled note that'd been delivered to the shop the previous day, grabbing hold of it and tossing into the bin. She flung open the curtains in the lounge and allowed the new day to enter. Across the street, she caught sight of Ruben opening up Legumes, and the moment he caught sight of Kitty, he scrambled with an impatient foot back out onto the pavement.

He signalled with his hands for her to open the window. 'So, how did it go?'

Kitty threw a jumper over her head before opening the lower half of her double-hung window. 'Shush,' she begged, pressing her finger against her lips, her face flushed with embarrassment.

'Sorry,' he apologised, sinking his shoulders and scouring the lane to see who may have overheard. 'I didn't know it was a secret.'

Ruben could tell what kind of night it had been just from the silly grin plastered across Kitty's face.

'I don't tend to announce my personal business across the street,' she giggled through an infectious smile, relaxing after noting the quietness of the lane.

'He's not up there with you, is he?'

'No,' she corrected. 'We just had dinner.'

'Really?'

'Really,' she proclaimed. 'I was back home and in bed by ten-thirty.'

Across the street, Ruben rolled up the shop blinds, frustrated by the lack of detail. 'That's so boring. I wanted you to tell me about the sparks, the fireworks… At least tales of his awful chat up lines!'

Kitty checked the street again, signalling for Ruben to cross the street until he stood below her window. 'There might have been a few sparklers, but I'm not saying anything else until he tells you his side. I don't want to look pathetic if he doesn't feel the same.'

'I'll report back later. He hasn't replied to the ten messages I've already sent him asking for an update.'

This news alone caused the butterflies dancing in her heart to pause. 'Maybe for him there's nothing much to say?'

'I'll let you know when I find out. Best get going, customers to feed.'

'I've got to actually put in a full shift today too. Could you bring me a coffee over, around ten, if you can? I might need a pick-me-up to see me through the day.'

Ruben replied with a thumbs-up before dashing back over to his side of the street.

In under ten minutes, and with hair that was still damp from her morning shower, Kitty stepped out onto the street, a half-eaten banana in one hand and her portrait in the other. She walked a handful of paces down the lane, pausing outside Lily's salon. She tapped on the window, sticking her thumb up when Lily saw her. 'I'll come and chat to you later,' Kitty mouthed through a gap in the door, her naturally quiet voice struggling to be heard above the din of the dryer.

'Make sure you do,' replied Lily. 'I want to know everything.'

Upon arrival at Flourish, Kitty pushed open the door and switched on the lights, locking the door behind her before tossing the keys onto the desk. She hadn't made it beyond the doormat before sensing some form of irregularity. A befuddled expression took residence on her face whilst she peered around the shop's interior. Her quick glance confirmed no obvious sign of a break in, but something felt out of kilter. In an attempt to shake off her neurosis, knowing Ruben had taken charge of the shop the previous afternoon, she cast aside her inkling and turned to face the door, flipping the sign over. The street, although it was still early in the morning, began to stir. The fifteen-degree temperature boasted on the outside thermometer promised a warm day. A congregation of early-bird tourists dotted the street, each loaded with arms full of beach paraphernalia.

Kitty turned back around, witnessing the interior with fresh eyes.

The fog that had clouded her vision a few moments prior lifted and she paced backwards, her body pressing against the wood of the door, which stood to block her escape. In her next breath, her heart plummeted. Her frame froze and yet her insides trembled.

Her eyes fixated on the three pencils purposefully aligned on the desk, military precision having gone into their placement. Then her stare flickered towards the balls of yarn, all now arranged in groups of three. She looked at the bobbins of ribbons dangling above the desk, each reel hanging alongside two others. Everywhere she cast her gaze, she witnessed nothing but an infestation of threes; the entire room poisoned with a sickening familiarity.

The door pushed against her back. 'Are you open?' a woman asked, stripping the life from Kitty's lungs. The woman noticed the *Open* sign, a disgruntled face emerging the longer she remained on the pavement.

Kitty shook her head.

'But your sign says you're open?'

Kitty flicked the sign back around and prayed that the customer would leave without a fuss. Her attention gravitated back to the interior and her chin quivered, sending ricochets of fright coursing to her extremities. A sabotaging pain collapsed her posture. The thought of Stevie being inside her shop sent shivers down her spine. She envisaged how his shadow must have manoeuvred past the desk and she traced his steps, his trail of bitterness hanging heavy in the air.

She wrenched out her phone, her trembling fingers pressing the emergency call icon.

A knock on the door made her entire skeleton seize, and the phone fell to the floor with a thud. She turned around to see Charlie waving.

'Are you open?'

Kitty fumbled over her words and tried to regain a sense of composure. With no way of ignoring her, Kitty unwillingly replied after an unorthodox delay.

'Yes, come in.' She pulled the door ajar. 'Sorry, Charlotte. I'm not quite with it this morning.' She failed to notice Charlie's blotchy face, her pockets brimming with used tissues. 'I'm glad that you're my first customer.'

'Are you feeling alright? You look a little pale.'

Kitty closed the door. She picked up her phone and cancelled the emergency call without speaking, placing the phone back in her pocket. 'Just a little tired, nothing a coffee can't fix.'

'Oh, Kitty, what a charming little shop. The way you described it really didn't do it justice.' Charlie moseyed around the interior, admiring the eclectic collection of crafting treasures. 'So, tell me everything. How did the date that wasn't quite a date go last night?'

'We enjoyed a picnic down by the beach.'

Charlie leaned on the desk in a casual manner. 'Now come on. Really? Is that all, just a picnic? I haven't made the journey over here to see how your skin is healing, or to buy some buttons – I need all the juicy details.'

Although touched by Charlie's interest, Kitty failed to share her excitement. 'The picnic tasted delicious,' she replied, her distracted mind making a mental note of everything misplaced, ready to relay to the police, if she could summon up the courage to call again.

'I wasn't really enquiring about the food, Kitty, I meant the company. Did he flirt with you? Was there a nightcap afterwards? Is there a date number two lined up?' Without realising, Charlie had stepped into Millie's shoes, asking all the questions Kitty's best friend would have done given the opportunity.

Kitty hesitated, and through a strained voice replied. 'Who knows?' She took hold of her portrait, hoping to divert the embarrassing line of questions. 'He did draw this for me, and we mentioned maybe spending some time together tomorrow, but I don't think it's a date,' she added, taking hold of the drawing and holding it aloft, allowing it to be examined by Charlie's keen artistic eye.

'Wow.' Charlie gravitated towards the canvas, her fingers tracing the pencil lines. 'Well, you might not know how he feels, but I sure do from looking at this.' She edged away after admiring Kitty's portrait. 'I wonder if he'd draw mine? Nobody has ever offered such a romantic gesture for me before.' A snippet of jealousy rolled off Charlie's tongue. 'I'd say he's really smitten with you.'

'You can ask him yourself about a portrait, he should be popping over anytime. I actually thought he'd have been here by now.' Kitty peered up the street, noticing the studio lights still weren't illuminated. 'He promised to bring me a coffee, but I actually haven't heard from him yet this morning, so maybe last night didn't go as well as I thought.'

'Well, I best get going, I've got a busy day at the spa - it appears that everyone in St. Ives is after a little dose of pampering.' Charlie edged towards the door. 'I'll be back to purchase some material soon; I think the spa could do with its own fabric facelift. See you at our next session, Kitty.'

As soon as Charlie had left, Kitty took out her phone, but her moment of bravery wavered, and she found herself now unable to make the call. She lingered in the shop window with her forehead pressed against the glass and admired the sky, envious of the free-spirited birds bathing in the early morning vermillion.

A police car pulling up at the end of the lane drew back her attention. She watched as a single officer stepped out, heading on foot towards her shop. She spotted him speaking into his radio, his eyes checking the door numbers. Kitty scurried away from the window and sat behind the counter.

'Can I come in?' requested the officer, peering through the window and spotting Kitty lingering in the background.

Confused and wary, she approached the door. 'I'm not opening for another twenty minutes,' she replied.

'I'm not here as a customer. Please, open the door.' Kitty released the lock, allowing the policeman to enter.

'How can I help?' she began, placing herself behind the desk.

'We received an emergency call made from this location, but the person hung up,' explained the six-foot-something, heavily-built officer. In her previous life, Kitty had hoped and prayed that a police officer might one day knock on her door, and yet now that he was here, she found herself unable to speak.

'It's policy to follow up every emergency call.' The officer meandered, inspecting the back of the premises, the office cubbyhole, and the toilet.

'I made the call,' Kitty announced when he reappeared.

'Okay. And what was the problem?'

She walked away, trying to shake off her rigid posture. 'I'm scared,' she blurted, unable to add any context onto the end of her statement.

'Scared? Of what?'

'Of my fiancé.' The officer's face transformed, his initial demeanour at the prospect of having wasted time on a nuisance caller now replaced with a genuine look of concern.

'Why? What's happened?' he asked, taking out his notebook.

Kitty took a moment, trying to pick the correct words to surmise, noting the placement on her hands where bruises were once visible. 'He's hurt me.' Her brave admission set about a chain of protocols in the experienced officer's mind and he manoeuvred himself towards the door. 'Do you mind if I lock this, just so that we won't be disturbed?'

'Okay,' she replied.

Noticing the officer's look of concern, the guard that she had constructed for herself crumbled and Kitty permitted herself a moment of weakness, cowering into a corner and lowering her body to the floor. She pulled her knees into her chest. 'I escaped from him, but now he's found me, I know he has,' she whispered. Her body began to shake.

Assessing the physical and mental state of the woman sat in front of him, the officer's keen eye spotted faded scars on Kitty's arms. He witnessed the avalanche of fear depicted through her eyes, a look that was impossible to fake. He crouched by her side, softening his initial stern tone. 'You're safe. The door is locked, and he can't hurt you whilst I'm here. What's your name?'

'My name is Kitty. Kitty Twist.'

'Kitty, my name is Sam,' confirmed the officer, reaching out and offering a supportive hand to her shoulder.

She flinched, cowering further into the wall whilst shooting the officer a probing stare, directly into his eyes.

'I'm not going to hurt you, Kitty.' Sam witnessed a broken soul, a disturbing vision he'd seen too many times during his career. 'You're safe now,' he reiterated, retracting his hand. 'And we can get you some help. But I need you to tell me your fiancé's name.'

Kitty planted her stare towards the ground, spitting out her reply. 'Stevie Best.'

'Can I come and sit with you? Would that be alright?'

Kitty indicated her consent with the merest of nods, allowing the officer to sit shoulder to shoulder with her.

'You did the right thing making that call. For someone in your position, it's the bravest thing you could have done.' He nestled his body up close, right next to hers, so that their arms were touching.

Kitty didn't back away or flinch at the invasion to her personal space. Instead, for the briefest of moments, she felt comforted.

'Are you hurt right now, Kitty? Do you need to be medically assessed? I can ring for an ambulance and we can get a female nurse to look after you.'

Kitty shook her head, the majority of her external wounds having healed, the remainder mostly internal, invisible scarring.

Although Sam already knew the answer, he asked the question for confirmation. 'Has he ever physically hurt you?'

Kitty recalled the brutality of her first beating and how her limbs had ached for days, her ability to walk reduced to a feeble hobble.

'Yes,' she whispered, ashamed and embarrassed.

Kitty felt the officer's arm wrap around her shoulders, his reassurance filling her bones with a strength she seldom experienced. She closed her weary eyes. 'Thank you,' she said, 'For coming to help.'

Sam waited and then looked into her eyes. 'So that I can do my job properly, I need you to help me, Kitty. Do you know Stevie's location or phone number?' She took out her phone and showed the officer his number. 'But I'm pretty sure he's been using a different number to torment me from, a private, withheld number.'

'Where does Stevie live?'

'In Perth, Scotland.' The officer took a moment to send a message on his mobile, waiting for the immediate reply he knew would come.

'But you suspect he is here, in St. Ives?'

'He was at my flat a few days ago, and only yesterday, he was right here, in my shop,' she replied.

'Whilst you were here?'

Kitty shook her head. 'No. A friend watched the shop for me yesterday.'

Sam flicked over the page on his notepad. 'Can you describe him for me, or do you have a photo?'

'I don't have any photos, but he has active profiles on social media.'

'I'm going to get you some help, Kitty, but it can take time.' He got himself up off the floor, pulling Kitty to her feet. 'So, is there somewhere you can go? Somewhere that you will be safe until we can track down Mr Best and bring him in for questioning? I don't want you staying here.'

Kitty nodded. 'I have a friend who I think will help.'

'Brilliant, I'll drive you there, and I suggest that's where you stay until I can update you. I'll need an officer to come and talk to you, to take a full statement and collect all the information we need so that we can offer you some real help. Would that be alright?'

She allowed her head to rise and she looked Sam straight in the eye.

'I have a diary of every time that he beat me, and my injuries.' The officer wrote something in his notebook whilst Kitty shielded herself, wrapping her arms around her waist. Her words were barely audible, her lungs having difficulty drawing in a deep breath.

'We're going to help. But, until we find Mr Best, my main priority is to keep you safe. So where does this friend of yours live?'

'He owns an art studio just across the road.'

The officer took some personal details, relaying them back to the station. 'Take everything you need. Is there anyone else who can keep the shop open?'

Kitty thought about calling Peggy, but decided against the idea. 'No, not really. It's my business, I don't have any hired help yet. I'll just close it temporarily.' She grabbed her bag, turned off the shop lights and made her way outside with Sam.

Out on the pavement and in front of the eyes of the world, Kitty felt people gawking. The officer escorted her across the road, just as Ben arrived at the studio.

'Is everything alright?' he asked, a concerned expression

spreading across his face. He inspected Kitty, ensuring she wasn't hurt, and took hold of her hand.

'Can I stay with you? They're going to try and find Stevie. He's been in the shop; he's definitely found out where I am.' Kitty buried her head into Ben's chest, allowing him to put his arms around her trembling frame.

'Of course,' he replied, kissing her head. 'But how do you know he's been in the shop?'

'Everything's been moved. He's arranged all my things so that I know he's here, so that I know he's found me.'

Ben turned to look at Sam. 'She'll be okay here. We're going back to Perth tomorrow to collect some of her belongings, but we'll be back in the evening if you need any further details or require access to the shop. Is that okay?'

'I can't guarantee your safety until we know the exact whereabouts of Mr Best, and that may take time. You say that you think he's now down here, but that doesn't mean that going back to Perth will be safe. If you say he's a dangerous man, then I would avoid any situation that would put either of you in harm's way.'

Kitty lifted her head from Ben's embrace and looked at Sam. 'I need to go back,' she cried. 'It's important.'

'It's your decision, and I can't stop you, I can only advise. I'll contact you on the number you've given me, but should anything happen in the meantime, call the police and state this number.' The officer gave her a victim support identification card with a series of handwritten digits scrolled onto the back. 'Keep safe, Kitty, and I'll be in touch.'

Overwhelmed with gratitude, Kitty hugged Sam, taking him off guard. She whispered into his ear. 'Thank you so much.' Sam smiled and walked away, leaving Kitty and Ben alone on the pavement.

'Come on, let's go up to the studio, you can help me do some paintings today. I spotted a rainbow this morning and want to get it down on paper before I lose the image I had in my mind,' suggested Ben, taking hold of her hand and helping her to navigate the steps. 'Or you can just sit and chat to me whilst I do all the work,' he laughed, easing the studio door open.

'I'm not so great with a paint brush,' she replied, her body gravitating towards the window once upstairs. Ben eased her away.

'Come and sit down. You're safe here, with me,' he encouraged, standing behind her and wrapping his arms around her waist. His embrace felt warm and she leant into his body, supported by his sturdy frame. 'I don't want you watching for him, you'll go crazy.'

'Do you promise?' she mumbled.

'Do I promise what?' Ben eased her body round until their eyes met.

'That I'm safe here.'

Ben placed his hands on her face. 'I promise. He's not going to take you anywhere whilst you're with me,' he whispered into her ear. 'Now, sit here and talk to me about anything. I usually only have the radio as company so you're a real treat.'

'You might want to message Ruben. He's been trying to contact you, he told me this morning.'

Ben took a glance at his phone. 'I'll text him now, otherwise he'll carry on hounding me all day.'

Just before Kitty sat down, she spotted a stack of canvases facing the wall. 'What are these?' she asked, turning each one around in turn, her face awash with shock. Canvas after canvas presented a painting of herself, each one showing a different angle or pose.

Ben ran his hands through his hair. 'Please don't think I'm some kind of weirdo. I'm not, I promise you. It's just that when I find a subject that captures my creativity, I just have to go with it and allow my brush or pencil to do all the work. It's like the beach umbrellas. I've painted dozens and dozens of the things. It just so happens that you were my next subject, and I needed to practice doing some portraits, having not done any for a while.'

Kitty picked up one of the paintings, marvelling at the petit, slender legs of a dancer, accentuated by a pair of ballerina shoes.

'That's a random one I know. But during one of our many chats, I couldn't forget the way you described those shoes to me and the way they made you feel as a child. I wanted to try and have a go at capturing the emotion, and the memory. I know you've left so many memories behind and I wanted to try and create some new ones for you.' The painting transported Kitty right back to her childhood and to the Saturday mornings spent with her mum at ballet. She could feel the tightness of the shoes around her feet and the ruffles of the tutu that had always made her feel like a princess. She could feel the softness of her mum's skin against hers as they held hands, and remembered the way her mum had admired from the side, watching Kitty in the mirror.

She turned to look at him. 'I don't think you're a weirdo,' she began, her eyes looking back to admire the intricacies of the design. 'I think you're wonderful,' she added, reaching out to take hold of his hand. 'Don't let me disturb whatever work you had planned for today, I've caused enough disruption in your life without ruining your career too. I'm going to make us a drink, if you have a kettle, and then I'm going to sit and make a list of all the places I need to double check when I get back to Perth. I'm going to find whatever it is that my mum left for me.'

Kitty spent the afternoon perched in the window, sipping on cups of tea, Ben having given up on trying to encourage her to move away. She sat and watched the afternoon pass by, spotting every person who approached her shop, unable to tear her eyes away. She formulated her list, recalling as many items as she could that had belonged to her mum, all of which were tucked away in the attic.

'They're locking up across the road, it must be getting late,' she said, hearing Vera's music silence and the shutter slamming. She turned to look at Ben. 'Will you stay with me tonight?'

Ben stepped down from his stool and walked across the room. 'Of course I will,' he replied, kissing her head, the scent of her shampoo fragrant and now familiar. 'Let's pack up here and get going. I've done enough work for one day.' The pair turned down the lights, grabbed their bags and walked the ten paces across the road, Kitty's hand gripping Ben's in a manner indescribable.

'I need to tell you something,' he muttered upon stepping through Kitty's front door. 'And I've wanted to tell you all day, but I've been too scared that it'd ruin what I think we might have found together,' he added, hanging his head low. 'And you've got so much to deal with already, I feel I'd be adding to your troubles, not helping.' Ben sat half-way up the stairs, the weight of his news causing his shoulders to sag.

Kitty remained facing the door, her fingers clutching the chain, her forehead resting against the wood. 'I need honesty in my life right now, Ben. I can't cope with surprises, or lies. I need to know where I stand, and who I'm choosing to stand with.' She turned to face him. 'So, if there's something you need to tell me, then just say it.'

Ben couldn't raise his head, fearful of witnessing the reaction to his confession. 'I'm going to be a father. Charlie told me this morning that she's pregnant.' He fell quiet as the statement hung in the air. 'I had no idea.'

As the news digested, Kitty held her heart in her hands. 'That's wonderful news. Congratulations,' she offered as a reply, forcing the words past the tension that was causing a lump to lodge itself in her throat.

'I want you to know that it doesn't change how I feel about Charlie, and I've made that clear to her already. I'll be the best father I can possibly be, but I can't remain trapped in a marriage that has already died.' Ben looked up, his heavy eyes clouded with sadness, the glossiness of tears stealing their usual vibrancy.

Kitty edged towards the stairs, kneeling in front of him. 'It's amazing news.' She waited for Ben to look up before she continued. 'Will there be enough room in your life for me?' she couldn't help but ask, her emotions bleeding through her laboured tone of voice.

'There's always been room in my life for you, it's just taken me twenty-seven years to find out where you've been hiding.' He stroked her cheek, relishing the softness of her skin. 'But the real question is, will there always be space in your life for me?' He scanned her eyes for the answer.

Kitty took hold of his hand, aligning her palm against his. 'It took me travelling the length of the country to find you, and I know now that everything in my past happened for a reason.' She scratched the aggravated scab smeared across her back, wishing she could peel away one of the remaining barriers which she now felt stood between her and a flourishing new relationship. 'Had I not been forced into a situation where I needed to escape from Perth, I would have never uncovered my new life down here, with you.' Kitty let go of his hand. 'But I come with baggage too, you know that,' she added, allowing her gaze to fall. 'I'm scared to even go outside by myself. I'm scared of going back to Perth. I'm scared of what I'm going to find. I'm scared of what I might not find. I'm scared of everything, apart from you.' She gulped back her emotions.

Ben stood up and rested his forehead on hers, feeling at home for the first time in years. He soaked up the warmth radiating from Kitty's flushed features and, despite her fears sabotaging her smile, he sensed the person inside waiting to break through to the surface. 'You don't have to be afraid anymore. You're not alone in this.' He took hold of her hand and guided her up the stairs.

'I'm so tired, I feel I could sleep for days,' Kitty muttered.

'Get straight in bed, it's going to be a really early start and a long day tomorrow,' he replied, navigating her towards her bed. 'I'll stay up and make sure we're all set for the morning flight.'

Kitty collapsed onto her bed fully clothed and her heavy eyes closed within minutes, her brain sinking into the depths of a sound night's sleep.

'Good night, Kitty,' Ben whispered, kissing her on the cheek once she had fallen asleep. As the hours passed, he forced himself to stay awake, not wanting to miss their 5am departure. He sporadically peered down onto the lane, watching for any loitering figures. A great sense of responsibility weighed down on his shoulders having promised to keep Kitty safe, his own fear of the unexpected rattling his usually calm composure. The moment he tossed an empty crisp packet into the bin, he spotted a handwritten note at the bottom. He took it out and held it in his hands whilst walking towards the window, the lamppost outside acting to illuminate. The words *I'm watching you* caused his insides to tumble, and a great sense of apprehension stole his breath. With the imminent trip to Perth in mind, it felt like he was about to walk into a lion's den.

28

'KITTY, WE'RE HERE, WE'VE ARRIVED IN SCOTLAND,' BEN whispered. He kissed her hair and slowly eased her head from his shoulder. Kitty blinked in a rapid succession, allowing her eyes to become accustomed to the light. She peered out of the window, spotting the familiar sights below.

'I'm ready,' she replied, taking hold of Ben's hand and entwining her fingers in his. 'Thanks for coming with me.'

'I'd go anywhere with you,' he replied, pulling her hand to his mouth and placing a delicate kiss on her fingers.

The moment the airplane door opened, Kitty saw that the idyllic, Cornish sky had declined the opportunity to board the first flight of the day from Newquay to Glasgow. Upon disembarking, Ben and Kitty zipped up their coats, the cool air whipping around their bodies. The Glaswegian air felt smog-heavy, and the surrounding hum of commuter traffic thrashed like a migraine in their ears.

'It's going to be alright,' Ben reassured, witnessing Kitty's fear and watching her eyes scanning their new surroundings. 'Like I told you last night, I won't let anybody hurt you.' He kissed Kitty's forehead and, with their hands glued, navigated her through the awakening airport and security checks.

'Perth, please,' Ben requested, holding open the taxi door.

Splintered by unseasonal high winds, the taxi ride from Glasgow to Perth took about an hour and a half. The heavy tree branches cast away foliage, the roads and pavements covered by a rustic, natural blanket.

'It feels so strange to be back. I spent so long dreaming of leaving this place and now here I am, choosing to return. I must be mad,' Kitty commented, watching the views scurry past her in a constant trail of blurred visions. She spotted familiar landmarks of the place that had once felt like home, the buildings now standing tall, like imposing strangers.

Ben looked out of his passenger window. 'You're not mad, Kitty, you just want answers, and anybody else in your position would do the same,' he began, turning to face her. 'You need closure, and I know that this is the only way you can achieve it.'

The car whizzed past Hedgerow, a secluded park Kitty and Stevie had visited in the early stages of their romance.

'Are you okay?' Ben asked, noting her body become tense. She turned to give him a nod before turning back to face the skeletons dancing outside her window, sinking back into her past. She recalled the time Stevie had shoved her so hard that she crashed to the floor, smashing her skull against the wall.

'I knew he was bad from the start, I just couldn't admit it,' she muttered. Now a spectator peering in on her old life, Kitty could see the warning signs clearly for what they were. 'I was too numb from losing my parents to feel any of his pain, and I couldn't accept the reality of the situation until it was too late.'

With their fingers linked, Ben applied pressure to her hand, stealing her attention away from all the bad memories. 'He can't hurt you now,' he reassured, fixing the collar on her coat. 'Where shall we go first? Did you say you wanted to visit the church?' he asked, the pale pink roses that he'd purchased from the airport resting on his lap.

Kitty nodded. 'I wonder if they've found him yet? I wonder where he is?'

'They'll find him, I promise, just give them time,' he reassured.

'Then what? It'll be his word against mine. What if they just let him go?'

'It's all going to be okay. Let's just do what we need to do here, and then we can deal with everything else once they find him.'

The church appeared in the distance, the steeple appearing to touch the clouds. Kitty peered out of every window of the taxi, watching for signs of Stevie's car or anybody on foot. The early morning hour meant the streets appeared deserted, making it easy to spot anybody lurking.

The taxi pulled up.

'Let's go,' encouraged Ben, passing Kitty the flowers and opening his door. 'Can you stay? Just keep the clock running,' he requested to the driver, before walking to open Kitty's passenger door and taking her hand, easing her body from the safety of the car.

Kitty's eyes flickered from one direction to another, her heightened senses remaining on guard. 'The grave is just over there, to the right,' she pointed. They walked hand in hand through the cemetery gate, Kitty recalling the last time she'd visited her mum's grave, on Mother's Day the previous year.

'You go, I'll stay here and keep a look out,' Ben offered.

Kitty took a few tentative steps alone, like a child walking into school on their first day, missing the comfort that came from holding their parent's hand. She passed all the names lining the path to her parents' shared grave - William Farrow, Elizabeth Grace McNamara, Albert Richard Benson, Sylvia Forster.

The grave of Delilah and Ernest Twist came into view, the familiarity of the arching stone bringing tears to Kitty's eyes. She fell to her knees and crouched.

'Hi, Mum. Hi, Dad,' she whispered, wiping away her tears with a tissue that Ben had subtly stuffed in her pocket.

Kitty's ears closed off to the world and all she could hear in her mind was the soothing tone of her mum's voice and her infectious giggle. Kitty noticed the bunch of fresh flowers already placed on the grave, a card popping out of the wrapping. Kitty took hold, reading the words aloud, *I miss you both, and I miss Kitty. Love always, Millie.*

Kitty held the card to her chest and admired the selection of tulips. She loved Millie like she was a sister, and thoughtful gestures like this made her realise just how much she missed being a part of her best friend's life. The pair once lived in one another's pockets, and now, because of Stevie, Kitty and Millie were more like strangers. She placed Millie's card back on the grave and unwrapped her own bunch of flowers, sorting them into an elegant arrangement, the specks of colour adding life and love to the grave.

'I miss you both, so much,' she began, lowering her head and clasping her hands. 'I miss hearing your voices. I miss not being able to talk to you both. I miss not hearing you bicker,' she smiled. 'I miss everything.'

She closed her eyes and pictured her mum, the way she looked before the cancer had stolen her sparkle.

'I miss the smell of your perfume, Mum, and the touch of your hand. I miss the way your skin felt against mine. I miss hugging you, so much. I miss the way you always made me feel, like everything would be okay.'

Kitty opened her eyes, making herself read the words on the stone, forcing herself to believe the horrible reality that still felt new to her.

'I've left him, Mum, and I promise I won't go back. I'll never go back to him.' She looked over at Ben, admiring how his eyes scoured the area. 'I've moved away and I'm making a new life for myself down in St. Ives, just like you and Dad planned for me. I just wish you were both here to live it with me. You would love St. Ives and the life it offers.' She adjusted the flowers for a final time. 'I might be living far away now, but I think about you and Dad every day.' She rose to her feet and took a step back.

In the distance, with his heart in his mouth, Ben watched Kitty walking back towards him, a sense of relief filling his body. He hadn't thought through his actions should Stevie make an appearance, but he could feel his anger brimming just beneath the surface, anger that would make him face any confrontational situation head on. 'Are you okay?' he asked when she neared, holding out his hand for her to take. 'Why don't you stay a bit longer? There's been no sign of anybody, it's just you and me here.'

'I know it wasn't part of the plan for today, but can we go to Millie's?'

'Of course we can. Let's go,' Ben encouraged, the pair getting back into the taxi.

Kitty looked at Ben. 'I need you to go into Millie's and order a coffee, she'll be the only one serving at this time. Once she's taken your order and you've paid, whilst she's preparing it, pretend to be on the phone and just as you pick up the coffee, could you say into the phone, just loud enough so that she can hear, *during a storm, search the sky for rainbows.*'

'Why don't you go in? Seeing Millie will make you feel so much better.'

'It's not safe until they've found where he is. I'd be putting her in harm's way and I'd never live with myself if he hurt her too. He'll have been hounding her, Ben, I know he will, and if he thinks she knows anything, anything at all, he'll do whatever it takes to shake it out of her. I just want her to know I'm alright, so she doesn't worry.'

'So, what would you like, a latté or cappuccino?'

Kitty smiled, gratitude lingering on her lips. 'Any, you choose.'

'Okay. Wait here, I'll be two minutes,' Ben said, once the taxi had come to a halt near Millie's. He skipped across the road and into the café, leaving Kitty in the taxi around the corner. The café looked empty and Ben could hear the sound of boxes being opening in the back room. He stomped his way to the counter, alerting her to his presence.

'Morning, what can I get for you?' asked Millie, carrying through what looked like a tray of warm, oozing apple turnovers.

'Hi. I'll have a regular cappuccino to take away, thanks.'

'Great, £1.95 please.' After handing over the money, Ben took out his phone, pretending to speak to a fictitious person at the other end, watching Millie prepare the drink. She placed it on the counter.

'Here you go, sugar is just over there so, please help yourself.' She carried on with filling the cake stands, a little disgruntled that someone could be so rude as to speak on the phone whilst being served.

Ben's heart galloped. The pressure to perform his one line made his mouth feel dry. 'Yeah, I've heard that during a storm, it's best to search for rainbows,' he spoke into his phone, just before reaching the door. He heard Millie drop whatever she was holding and just before he walked out of sight, he peered into the shop, throwing a reassuring smile towards Kitty's best friend.

'Let's get going,' he insisted, climbing into the taxi.

'Was she there? How did she look? What did she say?' Kitty questioned.

'Well, from the description you've given me previously of Millie, I'm pretty sure she served me. She had wild-looking hair scooped into a bun on top of her head, washed-out dungarees, and a bright pink top underneath.' Kitty rested back in her seat, grinning with a warm familiarity.

'That sounds about right.'

'I said what you asked me to, and I know she heard because she dropped something the moment I spoke.'

A warm feeling rushed through Kitty's veins and the niggling seed of regret that had been growing in her mind wilted now that she had learned that her best friend was safe and well.

'It's time to go to the house,' she announced. 'Our last stop.'

Ben turned and nodded. 'Okay then, let's go.'

29

'CAN YOU TAKE US TO PEMBROKE ROAD, PLEASE?' KITTY ASKED the driver.

'What number?' Ben asked.

In the distance, Kitty caught sight of the house and was relieved to find no sign of Stevie's car. 'It's there, number sixty-seven. Can you drive a bit slower?' she requested, the driver easing off the accelerator. 'It's that one there,' she said, pointing. The moment they drew level, she heard her own screams and saw a vision of herself slumped behind the door, hurt and begging for help.

'Are you ready?'

Kitty continued to stare at the gate. 'What if he's in? Then what do we do?'

Ben cleared his throat. 'Then we'll ask him politely to leave whilst we collect your things. This is still your place too, remember, you have just as much right to enter.' Kitty turned around and positioned her hands at either side of Ben's face, placing a tender kiss on his lips. The moment their skin touched, her heart skipped, and a topsy-turvy sensation swept through her veins. His lips felt warm; tender pillows filled with passion. She felt his hands reaching out, reciprocating her affection as he placed them on her flushing cheeks. They both opened their eyes at the same time, each displaying a strong, yearning expression.

'Let's go,' he replied, opening the door and taking a deep breath. 'The curtains are closed. Could he still be in bed?'

'I wouldn't have thought so, not at this time,' she replied, easing the gate open. The creaking sound turned her insides upside down. She took out her key and twisted the handle, the door easing itself open.

Bottom-of-the-ocean darkness drowned the hallway.

'Here, let me go first,' encouraged Ben, leading the way and trying his best to push away his own set of fraught nerves. 'I thought you said he liked things tidy,' he added, noting the upended state of the lounge the moment he stepped inside. Kitty followed, spotting the absence of Stevie's regular pair of shoes by the front door. She felt a wave of relief pass over her as she noticed his wallet and keys were also gone.

'He must be out,' she whispered, flicking on the hall light and peering through into the empty lounge. She listened for movement, but no sound came from the creaky upstairs floorboards.

'Something's happened,' she whispered, noting the disarray of the living room. 'The kitchen is down here,' she said, taking the lead and guiding Ben along the hallway. She spotted the milk carton on the floor, the sell by date having passed weeks ago, and a worrying smell of stale food permeated through the entire house. 'It's the same in here,' she added. She sidestepped the mess and opened the fridge, catching sight of the last lunch box she had prepared for him.

'I don't think he's been here since the day I left,' she commented, turning to face Ben. 'I'm sure of it.' Kitty's face fell to the floor. 'Do you think he's been in St. Ives all along? How did he know where I was? How could he possibly have known? I was so careful and hid everything so that he would never find out.'

'He's not here, that's the main thing. So, let's start looking for what you've come for,' suggested Ben, his heart beating irregularly. Kitty stepped back over the mess and headed up stairs.

'It's all in the attic,' she explained, peering up the stairs with each step. She pushed the bedroom door open wide until it banged against the wall. The contents of the room had been scattered like litter in a hurricane. 'He's definitely not here.'

Ben peered into the bedroom, gaining an impression of the man who'd instilled so much fear in the woman he now felt himself falling in love with. 'Thank god you left him,' he said, taking hold of Kitty's hand and pulling her back onto the landing.

'Wait, there's something in here I want to take too,' she said. Kitty walked into the bedroom, stepping across the strewn duvet in search of her photos. Tears welled when she saw the broken frame lying on the floor, the precious photo beneath having been trampled over. She took hold of the crumpled photo, admiring her parents' faces for the first time in weeks. She plunged her hand into the drawer of her bedside table, searching for their wedding rings.

'What are you looking for?'

'A jewellery box. I've always kept it in here.' On her hands and knees, Kitty scoured the floor and as the seconds passed, her fluster turned into panic, her senses playing tricks, making her believe she could hear the front door creaking.

'Did you hear something?'

Ben walked out of the room, peering down the stairs. 'There's nobody here, I promise,' he said upon re-entering the room. 'Let me help,' he offered, crouching on the floor.

Ben looked under the bed, catching sight of a black box. 'Here it is,' he exclaimed, handing it to Kitty.

'It's empty. They were in here. Their wedding rings have gone. This is what I was fearful of.'

'We'll find them, don't worry. Just keep looking.'

'Did you hear that?' she asked, the sound of the creaking gate echoing through the bedroom window.

'I think it's your mind playing tricks on you,' said Ben, reaching out and placing a hand on her back. 'You're not on your own this time. I'm here with you, and I won't let anything bad happen.'

'Would you take a look, just to make sure?'

He stood up and walked towards the window, easing the curtain aside and spotting the moving gate. He looked down towards the vacant front doorstep.

'Is there someone here? Is it him?' Kitty asked, her heart jumping into her mouth, all colour draining from her face.

'I can't see anyone, but the gate is open. Must have been the wind.' He drew the curtains back and allowed the natural light of the morning to flood into the room. 'Let's carry on, I'd rather leave as soon as we can.'

Something sparkly caught his attention.

'Is this what you're looking for?' he asked, picking up Delilah's wedding rings, the early morning flecks of sun reflecting off the chiselled diamond.

Kitty stood up and scurried over, taking hold of the rings and clenching them in her fist. Her emotions poured down her cheeks, and she nodded her head in confirmation.

'Oh, thank goodness. These were my mum's, and this one was my dad's,' she replied. 'At least I've found these,' she said, slipping them into her jeans pocket. 'Right, let's head up into the attic where all the other stuff is stored.'

Ben walked through to the landing and pulled down the ladder that led up to the hatch, a cool breeze whooshing down along with a fine sprinkling of dust.

'I'll go up first. Is there a light up here?' he asked, stepping into the boarded attic space.

'Just above your head,' Kitty replied, following in his footsteps.

Ben reached out his hand and pulled the cord, the single bulb illuminating the gloomy crevice. 'Blimey. Where do we start?' he asked. He peered around, the dingy space filled with a collection of cardboard boxes.

'I guess we start at one end and make our way through. Anything that I want to take I'll put in a pile over here, then we'll see if we can manage to carry it on the plane, or maybe we'll just get a courier to deliver it all. I don't want to ever have to come back here, and all I care about are my parents' things. I can replace my own belongings.' Kitty paced across the dusty attic, overwhelmed by the number of boxes. 'I don't recall there ever being so many,' she began, a scattering of frown lines appearing across her forehead. Like so many times previous, Kitty peered out of the window, gazing at the world with fresh eyes.

'I spent so many hours sat up here alone, waiting for the right time to leave, and now here I am.'

Ben walked over and put his arms around her waist, encouraging her to turn around.

'It's different now. You've come back to collect your things, that's all. You're not staying here this time.'

Kitty looked at all the boxes. 'I was frightened to throw anything away, just in case, and so I stored everything up here, knowing he'd never come looking. A space like this is his worst nightmare.' Kitty sat down at the far end of the attic and took hold of the first box, pulling open the flaps and revealing the contents.

Ben followed. 'I know it's going to be hard, but I'm here too,' he replied, squatting down by Kitty's side and wrapping his arm around her shoulder the moment he spotted her falling tears. 'We're going to find what you're looking for and then you'll be able to move forward with your life.' He wiped her saturated cheeks. 'Even though I never met your mum, or your dad, that's what they would have wanted, for you to be happy.'

Kitty came across her own personal diary, her fingers flicking through each thumbed page. After only a few seconds, sadness flooded her eyes as she recalled each painful memory that she had documented within.

'What's that?' Ben asked, noting Kitty's slight shake of the head.

She took a moment before replying. 'It's a diary that I kept, you know, something to prove what went on, what he did to me.' Ben wrapped his arm around her once again, kissing the side of her face. 'I'm here if you want to talk about it, you know that, don't you?'

Kitty looked into Ben's eyes. 'Maybe one day I'll talk to you about it, but I can't right now, not here,' she explained. 'I want to try and put all this behind me, and that's how you can help,' she smiled, taking in a deep breath. 'Let's keep searching,' she suggested, placing the diary to one side and continuing to rummage through the box. She pulled out a collection of her mum's handbags, feeling the soft leather and recalling the associated memories. 'It feels like I'm invading her privacy by going through all her belongings like this, her last piece of dignity taken away by her own daughter,' Kitty began, looking inside and finding old lipsticks, used tissues and worn hairbrushes. 'The thought of someone going through my personal belongings is just awful. I know she's not here to bear witness, but I still feel like it's an intrusion.' Kitty looked at Ben, her wide eyes glossy with a sheen of vulnerability. 'When I'm gone, I hope someone just throws my stuff away. Be done with it.'

'Your children might have something to say about that. That's if you're even thinking about having a family in the future.'

Kitty smiled. 'When I was little, I rummaged through my mum's wardrobe for something to dress up in all the time, and she hated it when I would spill some tomato ketchup or get something sticky down her best top, which happened a lot, but she never stopped me. She never stopped me from doing anything, if I was having fun, not really. And I hope that's the kind of mum I'll be if I ever have children of my own.'

Ben opened a box to his left, reaching his arm in and taking hold of an item. 'She sounds like the perfect mum, if you ask me. Tell me about what she said to you, or what she was trying to say, you know, before you lost her.' Ben handed Kitty a new tissue and placed a hand on her thigh, the warmth from his palm penetrating her jeans.

'She said that she wanted to tell me something, that she wanted me to know the truth. She said that she loved me, and that she always would, and that I needed to remember that, no matter what,' Kitty began, recalling the harrowing last few hours she had spent alongside her mum. 'At the time, I didn't encourage her to talk, I wanted her to rest so that we could have a better chat when she felt stronger.' Kitty pressed the tissue against her eyes. 'I didn't know it was the end.'

Ben wrapped his arms around Kitty, securing her in the kind of embrace that felt wonderful. 'And she didn't give you any other clue about what she wanted to tell you, or where to look?' he asked.

Kitty shook her head. 'No, not really. She said to look in something, I just don't know what that something is,' she replied, raising her hands to indicate the boxes that surrounded them both, before resting the one closest on her lap. 'Did she want me to look in a drawer, look in a cupboard, look in a box? Who knows? There are just so many things she could have meant.' Kitty looked through all the handbags in the box before reaching for the next. 'Before I sold the family home, I looked everywhere. I searched and searched for days, weeks even, with Millie's help. I felt exhausted and emotional, yet came no closer to finding out the truth. I needed to sell the house, otherwise I'd have spent every day searching, I know I would. I wouldn't have been able to let it go, just like I haven't been able to part with all of this.' She shook her head, overwhelmed by the enormity of the task. 'All the things in these boxes have pockets and zips, easy to hide something in, so I couldn't bring myself to get rid of them without having a good look through everything again.'

'So, you're thinking this something that we're looking for is small?'

'I honestly don't know what to think anymore,' she replied, sifting through a jewellery box.

'Isn't it enough knowing that she loved you, and that she would always love you? Some people are left with so much worse after a loved one dies. Some people don't even get to be there, Kitty, or to say goodbye, and yet you were able to experience all that with your mum. You were there for her when it mattered the most, so what more is there?'

'I know, and I'm so grateful, in many ways. But it's just the way she said it, Ben, the way she looked at me, and the timing of the whole conversation,' she replied, her emotions welling each time she spoke. 'She knew she was dying and whatever she was trying to say must have meant so much to her, and therefore it means something to me too.' She carried on sifting through the items, checking that she hadn't missed or overlooked something.

'What about this one?' Ben asked. He reached out and grabbed a smaller box that had been pushed into the corner. 'This box is sealed, and it doesn't look like it's been opened recently.'

Kitty looked over. 'Oh, that's just some of my things from when I was little, it's not my mum's stuff. It's silly to keep it really but I've always had this romantic idea of passing some things on to my children if I'm ever blessed with a family of my own.'

'I don't think it's silly. I wish I'd kept some treasures from my childhood to pass on,' he replied, his thoughts wandering to Charlie and their unborn child. 'I know that we've only known each other a short amount of time, and that this isn't the ideal time or place to lumber with you with any other emotional baggage, but I think I need to tell you something,' he explained before pausing. 'I *want* to tell you something,' he added, his heart pounding. 'I've learnt that I should say how I feel and not wait for the perfect time, as the perfect time inevitably never arrives.' He paused again and drew in a deep breath. He reached out and took hold of Kitty's hand, feeling the warmth of her skin against his. 'I love you, Kitty. And I know that it's so soon to be saying it, and I don't want to scare you off. But I do love you, and since meeting you, I know now how it's meant to feel when you really love someone, when you find true love. And I don't want you to reply or say anything, I just needed to tell you.' He let go of her hand and turned back around. 'Now, let's carry on before we miss our flight,' he added, busying himself with tearing open the box and pulling out the contents. He could sense Kitty staring, his heart secretly willing her to offer a reply.

Kitty knew what she wanted to say and yet she couldn't produce a single word. The longer the pause in conversation continued, the harder it felt to express anything at all, so she remained painfully silent, and the tender moment of vulnerability which she had wanted to share came and went.

Ben broke the ice, clearing the emotions from his voice beforehand. 'I know you said that this stuff didn't belong to your mum, but shouldn't we check anyway? What's there to say that she didn't hide this secret in your belongings?' Ben took out a pair of faded, petite ballet shoes. 'How long did you say that you took ballet classes for?'

Kitty smiled. 'Judging by my ability at the time, you wouldn't have been a fool for thinking I was just a beginner, but I actually did it for many years, right up until I left primary school. I had all the enthusiasm and dedication, and yet I had no sense of balance. I seemed to fall over more than I was ever on my feet,' she laughed, recalling the fond memories. 'But I loved going, and that's where I became friends with Millie. We were in the same class. When we both started secondary school, we found new interests, I discovered my love for textiles, and Millie began her baking obsession, and so we both abandoned our ballet shoes.'

Ben pulled out an old black and white photo. 'And who's this?' he asked, passing the photo to Kitty.

'Oh, I'd forgotten about this. It's a photo of my mum. She did ballet too when she was a young girl, and I always remember wanting to look just like her, so elegant and beautiful. But I never managed it. Her tutu looked perfect in that photo, mine was always a little lopsided and dirty from spending so much time on the floor. This is why I was so desperate to do ballet and why I never wanted to give up, I wanted to be just like my mum.'

Ben reached into the box and took hold of a stuffed toy, pulling out a tattered ballerina. The doll's hair looked ragged and the dress was dirty and torn. 'It looks like you played with this a lot,' he commented, blowing on the toy to remove some of the dust.

'Oh, I did. She went everywhere with me, and at night, once I'd fallen asleep, my mum would slide it from out of my bed and wash it, placing it back in my arms by morning so that I was none the wiser,' Kitty explained, her mind recalling the fond snippets of memories like they had occurred only yesterday. She looked away and carried on rummaging through the box by her side, looking inside each item and ensuring there wasn't anything hiding within.

Ben pressed his fingers into the fabric and felt something hard inside. 'Well, it certainly looks loved. Is there a zip or something on it?' he asked. Kitty hadn't registered the comment, too engrossed with the bunch of letters in her hand. Ben examined the back of the ballerina, pulling up the dress to reveal a press stud.

'I think there's definitely something inside it,' he added, pulling the fastener apart to reveal the stuffed inners of the toy. He took hold of a piece of paper. 'Kitty,' he began, his hands starting to shake. He reached out his free hand and placed it on Kitty's shoulder. 'There was something hiding inside here. This could be what you're looking for.'

Kitty looked up, her eyebrows bunched together in the middle of her forehead. She reached out and took hold of the paper.

'What is it?' she asked. Whilst her eyes scanned the paper, Ben's fingers rummaged back inside the ballerina, taking hold of a faded, crumpled photograph. He didn't recognise the young woman in the picture, who was positioned in what looked like a hospital bed, and cradling a new-born baby in her arms.

'There's this too,' he added, handing it to Kitty. She took hold of the photo with trembling hands, and as soon as she set eyes on it, she was overcome with emotion. Tears streamed from her eyes as though they might never stop, and every memory she once held dear threatened to shatter in her mind.

With a worried expression, Ben moved closer. 'Kitty, what is it? Talk to me.'

She released the photo and piece of paper, both cascading through the air before landing amongst the disarray. Her hands gravitated towards her chest, applying pressure over her aching heart. With reluctance, she turned to face Ben, her face awash with a haunting expression. 'I've seen this photo before,' she finally said. 'And I now know what my mum wanted to tell me. I know the secret,' she added. 'We need to go home. I need to go back to St. Ives.'

30

A JUMBLE OF QUESTIONS TUMBLED THROUGH KITTY'S MIND, making her brain ache. She squinted in an attempt to block out some of the striking brightness provided by the early morning dashes of sunshine. Due to a lack of sleep, her eyes were stinging, and dark bags pulled down her usually vibrant facial features. For the past twenty-four hours, her thoughts had remained in a fog, making her feel lost and alone. She peered down at her watch, noting her early arrival at the meeting point. She felt her phone vibrate in her pocket, the message from Ben flashing on the screen, *Good luck xxx*. He had offered to go with Kitty and provide support, but she had insisted on going alone.

She peered around, checking her periphery for anyone approaching. The longer she waited, the more nervous she felt, a nauseous feeling rumbling deep in her stomach.

'I might just leave,' she blurted when Ben picked up his phone. 'I don't need to put myself through this, do I?'

'I think you'll regret it if you leave. You have so many questions that need answering, Kitty, questions that will never go away.'

'I've already erased parts of my past, like certain things never happened. And, if I've done it before, I can do it again.' Kitty turned her head at the sound of footsteps approaching from the distance. 'Too late, I think she's here. Got to go.' She turned back to face the hospital, maintaining a discrete eye on the person who was walking towards her, her nervousness making her lips feel dry.

'Hello, Kitty,' announced Peggy. Kitty couldn't see the tears welling in Peggy's eyes, the sun providing a natural camouflage. With her hands fidgeting by her side, Peggy remained standing, her feet unwilling to move any closer, leaving a few metres separating the pair.

'Would it be alright if I come and sit with you?' she asked, awaiting her invitation.

Kitty nodded but continued to stare at the building before her, the collection of windows reflecting various shapes and shadows from the surrounding picturesque gardens, the secluded grounds at St. Mary's Hospital flourishing with seasonal beauty. Despite scents of lavender rippling through the air and the sound of bees bobbing from one source of nectar to the next, Kitty couldn't do anything but loath her surroundings, and the reason for her visit.

Peggy took a seat at the opposite end of the bench, also keeping her gaze fixed forwards, although her instinct told her to turn and look at Kitty.

'I've been waiting for this day for so long, my entire life,' she began, her hands now hiding in her pockets, a crumpled tissue nestled into each palm. 'And although you asked me to come, I still wasn't sure that you'd be here, waiting for me.'

Without asking any questions, Kitty tried to piece the puzzle together in her mind, and yet each time she came up with a plausible hypothesis, it only created more questions. 'Why did you request for us to meet here?' she finally asked after an extended pause, keeping her arms crossed tightly across her chest.

Peggy took an intake of breath, drinking in as much courage as her lungs could hold. 'This is where our story began, Kitty. This is the place where I let them take you away from me, and this is the place where I'm going to ask for a second chance.'

Kitty frowned. 'So, I guess what I've found out is true then? I haven't made all this up, or misunderstood. You really are my biological mother?' she replied, craving verbal confirmation in one breath, yet frightened to receive it in another. Without turning her head, Kitty sensed Peggy's body shift.

'Yes, Kitty. I'm your biological mum,' Peggy announced, turning her body so that she could admire the side of Kitty's face, craving to be accepted by her own flesh and blood for the very first time.

Kitty digested the words and repeated them over and over in her mind, and even though she'd told herself that she wouldn't, she cried, the confirmation that Delilah wasn't her real mother stabbing at her heart, leaving her feeling breathless and hurt.

'Please, don't,' Kitty requested, the moment she sensed Peggy moving closer, her hand ready to offer a tissue. Peggy retreated back to her side of the bench and bowed her head, resting her hands in her lap.

'I never wanted it to be like this, Kitty.'

Kitty released a sharp, audible sigh. 'Really? Then how come I have gone my whole life without knowing anything about this,' she muttered.

'I know you're upset, and angry, and that's okay. But, until you've heard my side of the story, you don't know what really happened.'

'I know that because of you, I'm questioning my entire life. Do you know how that feels?'

For the first time since Peggy had arrived, Kitty turned to face her. She scoured Peggy's face for traces of familiarity, and although they'd met previously, Kitty looked at the person before her in a whole new light. She didn't want to spot any traces of herself in the person sat beside her, she wanted to be able to believe that she and Delilah were biologically related. And yet similarities appeared, like their similar elongated faces, their shared slender fingers and skinny wrists with protruding bones.

'I remember when I was younger, I once asked my mum why I didn't look like her, or my dad for that matter. My mum had very fine, straight hair, and they were both pretty short and stocky. You wouldn't have matched us together, as a family I mean. Obviously

now I know that my suspicions all those years ago were right.'
Kitty felt a pang of guilt seeping into her veins, a feeling of betrayal
that made her body quiver beneath a sickening sense of loss. 'But
they will always be my parents, regardless of DNA,' she added.

'Of course, they will,' Peggy felt quick to add.

'Only it's not really that easy, is it? I feel like I've been living a
lie, like I've been living someone else's life. I feel like I don't know
my own history because I don't come from where I thought I did.'
She paused and drew in a painful breath. 'But the worst part is the
feeling that my family has been taken from me all over again, like
I've lost them for a second time. Do you know how that feels?'

Kitty's head thrashed from side to side and she avoided looking
at Peggy, the truth too hurtful to face.

'This doesn't change anything, not for me. Delilah was, and
always will be, my mum. They were the only parents I've ever
known, and you can't take that away from me, nobody can.'

'I don't want to take that away from you, Kitty, that has never
been my wish, or my intention,' Peggy began, her eyes examining
the hospital building before her, a sickening feeling rising inside
her. 'Your mum wanted to tell you the truth, she felt that you
deserved to know, and although this wasn't the way that she'd
anticipated you discovering, she'd be happy that the truth is out
now. She knew you'd be strong enough to cope, and she knew
that in your heart, she'd never be replaced.'

A question sat on the cusp of Kitty's lips. 'Why did you give
me away?' The question fired like an arrow and pierced Peggy's
heart, her entire body paining beneath the burden of the question.
Peggy's hair danced in the gentle breeze, the same as it had done
over twenty-five years previous, when she had sat on the same
bench, heartbroken at being forced to give away her only baby.
She turned to face Kitty.

'I didn't give you away, Kitty, but at the same time, I didn't
fight hard enough to keep you either.'

'I don't understand.'

Peggy took out a tissue and dabbed her cheeks. 'I was so young when I found out I was pregnant, and my parents weren't supportive, they were furious,' she began to explain. 'They were ashamed of me, and embarrassed.' Peggy's stomach twisted in knots as she recalled the hurtful events of her past, something she'd learnt to avoid thinking too deeply about over the years.

'I wanted to keep you, Kitty, more than anything in the entire world, and I didn't care how hard it was going to be, I was just ready to become a mother. But without the support of my parents, it just felt impossible. I was still in school. I had no job, and I would have been homeless.'

Peggy looked down at her lap, her deep-rooted sense of regret pulling down her features until only the most harrowing look of sadness remained.

'I believed what the people around me were saying, that it was selfish to keep you, that it was cruel to let a baby have such a terrible start in life. And back then, I was too young to realise that the material things didn't matter. I had so much love for you, which would have made up for the lack of material things. That's all a child really needs; unconditional love.' Peggy pulled up her head and looked at Kitty, the pair locking eyes. 'I loved you from the very moment I found out I was pregnant, and I have loved you every single day since.' Peggy looked pained, her body folding over on the bench, the burden of her memories pressing down on her frame.

Much of the anger and resentment Kitty had brought to the reunion blew away with the wind as she made space in her heart for empathy. 'I'm so sorry,' she began, pulling out a tissue from her pocket and handing it to Peggy. In that moment, she felt the urge to offer a hug, and yet she couldn't. 'I've only been thinking about how all this affects me, and I'm sorry for that, I'm sorry for being so selfish.' Kitty spotted the way Peggy bit her bottom lip, just like she did herself when feeling nervous or anxious, and she couldn't help but feel a flicker of hope that, given time, maybe they would become friends.

'You don't have to apologise.'

Kitty shifted her body to one side so that she could now face Peggy. 'I do, and I need to explain. It's just that when I read the adoption certificate, I felt so scared,' she began, looking Peggy in the eye. 'I was so scared to hear that you didn't want me, or that I was a mistake. After everything that I've been through, I just didn't feel strong enough to deal with any more pain.' Kitty lowered her head, searching the floor.

Peggy reached out and took hold of Kitty's hand. 'I always wanted to be your mum, you have to believe that, and I'm just sorry that I didn't fight hard enough to keep you.' Kitty looked up, gazing into Peggy's eyes.

'Seconds after they came to take you away, I managed to get out of bed and I threw myself against the door, screaming for them to bring you back. But you'd already gone.' Kitty squeezed Peggy's hand.

'I'm so sorry, Peggy.'

'This isn't your fault, there's no need for you to be sorry.'

'I feel guilty in so many ways. I feel guilty that I experienced such a wonderful upbringing with parents who adored me, and yet you had to live with this every day. And I feel guilty now. It feels like I'm betraying my parents by even speaking to you, like I'm doing it behind their back.'

Peggy smiled. 'You're not doing anything behind their back. Your mum reached out to me before she became poorly because she wanted me to be able to have some sort of involvement in your life. That's why they were moving down here.'

'And you were happy to wait so long to be a part of my life?'

'I had no choice. Part of the adoption agreement ensured that I had no contact. I wasn't allowed to have any details about you, who your parents were or where you lived,' Peggy explained. 'But there hasn't been a single day when I haven't thought about you, wondered where you are or what you're doing.'

'So how did you come to meet my parents?'

'One day, several years ago now, your mum traced my details and gave me a call, and just like that I was back in your life, if only in a small way,' she explained, a beaming smile radiating from her face. 'She talked to me about how you were doing, and she would tell me what a wonderful young lady you'd developed into. They were the most magical conversations, and I'm just so grateful that she found it in her heart to contact me. It was your dad that remained hesitant, which I can understand, but as the years passed by, your mum insisted on you knowing the truth.'

Kitty gazed at the sky, like she often did when thinking about Delilah. 'She was a wonderful person, and such a special mum,' she replied, a raft of memories flooding through her thoughts, each one centred around Delilah. 'And I miss her so much. Some days it feels like I've only just lost her.'

'She had so many hopes for your future, Kitty, and owning the shop was just one of them. She knew you'd feel happy here, and I'm just sorry that we can't all share in this experience together. For so many years, I pictured the four of us reuniting and becoming great friends.'

'And what about my dad? I mean my biological dad.'

Peggy tilted her head. 'After the day I told him the news, I never heard from him again. He and his parents moved away, they didn't want anything to do with me, or my baby, and that was that. I've never heard from him since.'

Kitty shrugged off the news with a sense of triviality. 'Well, that's his loss, I guess.' She smiled. 'Some children go through life without any loving parents to speak of, and all along here I was with three. How lucky am I?'

Still holding hands, Peggy moved a little closer. 'I knew that one day we'd be sat here together, or at least I prayed for as much. After they took you away, I came out here and sat for hours. I couldn't bear the thought of returning home without you. And so, I stayed in this very spot and allowed myself time to cry, time to feel like I was still a mother despite having no baby.' Peggy admired the garden which had offered her some distraction during the most difficult time of her life, now able to recall each variety of flower and shrubbery by heart. 'And on every single one of your birthdays, I have returned. This is the only place in the entire world where I felt a connection to you, the only place where I felt like a mum.' Peggy took out the photo that had been taken of her and Kitty when they were in the hospital, moments after the birth. 'Our room was that one over there,' she explained, pointing to a second-floor window on the far right-hand side.

Kitty nudged herself along the bench so that the pair were now sat side by side, taking out the exact same photo from her pocket, along with her adoption certificate. 'This is the photo that I saw in your house, isn't it? The one next to your chair.'

Peggy nodded. 'I have always kept it close to me. This is my only photo of us, and I've looked at it so many times that I can picture it in my sleep. It was my one concrete reminder that I was a mum.'

'You are a mother, Peggy, and nobody can ever take that away from you.'

'I've never felt like one, until today,' she replied, cupping Kitty's hands into hers. 'Now that I can hold your hands, I know that you are real, and that I really did give birth to a beautiful baby girl.'

Kitty relished Peggy's touch, her warmth radiating. 'I don't feel so alone anymore, or like I don't belong to anybody,' she added after a few moments. 'After I lost my parents, I experienced such a terrible feeling of loneliness knowing that I didn't have any family. But now I have you.' Peggy smiled with a genuine happiness for the first time in her adult life.

'And I no longer feel so alone either, knowing that I have you.' The pair sat in silence, both of them savouring the moment without feeling the need to talk any further. In a moment of tranquillity, Kitty watched as a flourish of surrounding wildlife re-emerged and brought the garden back to life. She admired how the butterflies fluttered from one flower to the next, how a squirrel foraged beneath some bushes, and how a cluster of birds swooped through the tree branches above, dislodging delicate cherry blossom that fell to the floor like snow. It felt like her heart had been brought back to life, and she appreciated the world through a fresh pair of eyes.

'I'll carry on calling you Peggy. You're part of my family now, but I don't think I could ever bring myself to call someone else Mum. I hope you'll be okay with that.' Peggy placed her finger underneath Kitty's chin to raise her head the moment it dropped.

'I have you back in my life, that's all I've ever wanted.'

31

'WHY DON'T YOU STAY OFF TODAY? ANOTHER DAY AWAY FROM the shop isn't going to hurt,' said Ben as they both lay in bed. He watched Kitty's eyes begin to open, admiring how, even first thing in the morning, she still managed to look radiant. 'I think we were talking for most of the night about Peggy, so you must be shattered,' he added, a string of yawns sounding from his mouth. 'And we haven't had an update from Sam yet. Stevie could still be down here, watching you, and that makes me feel very uneasy, especially if you're on your own.'

Kitty rolled her head along her pillow until she met his gaze. 'You're looking out for me, which is adorable,' she began, placing a delicate kiss on his warm lips and stroking the side of his face. 'But I'm ready to get on with my life now, my new life, down here,' she explained, sitting up. 'I've been hiding inside for way too long and I'm so excited to go to work and make a success of the business. I'm excited about going on dates with you. And I'm excited to do all the little mundane things in life like nip to the supermarket, go for a walk, tinker with my flat, learn how to surf maybe,' she said, smiling.

Ben raised his eyebrows. 'Surfing?'

'Okay, well maybe not surfing. But I want to do everything else, and I'm not wasting a single second hiding away up here, just because I feel scared.'

'You're so cute, do you know that?' Ben sat up and took hold of her hand. 'And it upsets me hearing that you feel scared, because you shouldn't, not anymore. So, you should go to work and enjoy being in the shop, and I'll arrange when and where to take you out for dinner.'

'There's something I've been meaning to tell you,' Kitty began, looking down at their entwined fingers. 'And I wanted to do it when we were in Perth, but for some reason I couldn't, it just didn't feel right,' she began, sensing the natural blush of her cheeks. 'I love you, Ben Fox,' she declared. 'And I'm sorry I didn't say it when we were in the attic, because I did feel it.' She leaned in and delivered a tender kiss to his lips. 'I love how caring you are. I love your thoughtfulness. I love that you're a bit of a geek about paintings,' she mocked, covering her eyes. 'But, most of all, I love the way that you love me, a way that nobody has ever done before.'

Ben leaned in and delivered a kiss. 'I guess that means we love each other,' he laughed, his internal excitement shining through his broad smile. 'It would be nice to just hide up here for a while, pretend that everything is perfect,' he said, running his hand down the contours of Kitty's back.

She looked across the room towards the window. 'It would be lovely, I can't deny. But I would much rather walk down the street holding your hand, or stroll down the beach with you before sunrise, feel the cool sand on my feet and hear the waves breaking on the shore, maybe sit on our bench and snuggle to keep warm. Now that's a place I'd stay with you forever.' Kitty closed her eyes and imagined her new life. 'I want to experience life with you, Ben, but not just within these four walls.'

Kitty turned her head away from the window and maintained eye contact. 'I can't waste any more of my life being scared. The police might never find Stevie, and whilst I'm hiding away up here, my business is going under and I'm missing out on sharing a life with you.' She paused and wiped her eyes with her t-shirt sleeve. 'My business means everything to me now. It's all that remains of my parents' inheritance and I can't just let it slip away. I feel like I'm living their dream, and making my own dreams come true.'

'Let's go and get on with our life then, shall we? We'll just deal with Stevie as and when he shows up,' said Ben, smiling at Kitty. 'Shall we go and wash Perth off our skin?

'Sounds good to me.'

'Great, come on then,' he smiled.

Ben helped Kitty off the bed before leading her into the bathroom. He turned on the shower, the power of the spray soon filling the enclosed cubicle with billows of steam. Without thinking too much beforehand, he took off his boxer shorts and t-shirt, and stepped inside, relishing the heat, the water dancing over his face. 'Ah, this was one of my better ideas,' he said without turning around, allowing Kitty some privacy to undress.

Kitty pressed her back to the door, hiding her scars from the man she loved. She allowed her underwear and t-shirt to fall to the floor before grabbing a towel the moment she felt exposed.

Ben spotted her apprehension out of the corner of his eye. 'I'll only be two minutes and then you can go after me, if you'd prefer. I'm a terrible singer in the shower and I wouldn't want you to suffer unnecessarily,' at which point, he began to hum and wash his hair.

Kitty let her towel drop, opened the shower door and stepped inside, manoeuvring herself in front of Ben and facing the shower head. She closed her eyes and let the water saturate her hair, revealing her back to him for the first time. His carefree humming stopped.

'I was drunk at the time,' she began, still facing the water. 'I'd agreed to a single flower in memory of my mum, but he'd got me so drunk that I passed out. When I woke up it was too late, it'd already been done.' She wiped her face, removing a mixture of tears and shower spray from her eyes. 'I've been trying to get it removed, but it isn't that easy.'

Once he'd digested the shock, Ben carried on humming. He lathered up his hands and with the most delicate of touches, covered her back with pearly soap suds, his fingers brushing over the scars. 'You have a perfectly sculpted spine. Did you know that?' He ran his hand slowly along the length of her back, pausing when he reached her waist. 'And so many freckles that you'd make a great dot-to-dot drawing.'

Kitty turned around, wrapping her arms around his neck. 'You really are amazing.'

With passion lining his lips, Ben kissed her, his hands cupping both sides of her face. 'You enjoy the steam and I'll go and make us breakfast.'

Kitty appeared in the kitchen ten minutes later, dressed ready for work, and turned on the television before wrapping her arms around Ben's chest, pressing her head into his back.

He buttered some toast with a generous hand. 'You can't leave without anything inside you,' he said, turning to offer her a bite of toast.

Kitty switched on the kettle. 'I'll be much better equipped for the day with a coffee inside me.'

The television played in the background, the weather presenter wrapping up the regional segment before handing back over to the national anchor.

'It has just been confirmed that the driver of a car who knocked down and killed a thirty-one-year-old pregnant woman, has died after spending many weeks in a coma. The driver's identity has now been confirmed by Police Scotland as Mr Stevie Best. Mr Best's car was travelling at twice the legal limit the day the accident occurred. Mr Best knocked down and killed expectant mother Megan Foster, who was walking to work the morning of the accident. Her family have asked for privacy during this difficult time.'

Above the sound of Ben's humming, Kitty caught a snippet of the news presenter's statement. 'What did she just say?'

'Kitty, careful, you're spilling it,' Ben called out, watching Kitty's hand continue to pour the boiling kettle into an already brimming mug. She placed the kettle down without looking and walked towards the TV, crouching down right in front of the screen, her eyes staring at Stevie's face.

'What's wrong?' Ben asked, following her. 'Kitty? What is it?'

Without turning her head, she responded. 'Stevie is dead.'

Ben watched Kitty's frame crumble, her lungs deflating and her shoulders collapsing into her chest.

'What?' Ben took hold of the control and rewound the programme to replay the segment. He crouched besides Kitty, placing his arms around her shoulders, preventing her from falling. He took a long, hard look at the only person in the entire world he hated, the image of Stevie's face making his blood boil.

Kitty broke down. 'I can't believe it. That poor woman and her unborn baby.' She covered her face with her hands, blocking out the photo released by Megan's family. 'How could he?' A photo appeared on the screen of Stevie's car immediately after the accident, the mangled metal located just around the corner from Millie's Café, the date of the accident flashing up on the screen. 'That was the day that I left him. He'd have been desperate to ask Millie if she knew where I was,' Kitty bawled, her hysterics heightening. She buried her head into Ben's chest.

'I'm so sorry, Kitty,' were the only words he could think to say.

'That poor woman and her baby lost their life, and all because of me.'

Ben pushed Kitty's head away from his chest so he could look her in the eye. 'Kitty, you didn't cause that accident. You weren't the one driving the car. You weren't the one speeding. You can't take responsibility for someone else's actions.'

Kitty shook her head, tears leaving a trail across her face. 'He was driving so recklessly because of me. He killed that young woman and her unborn baby because of me.'

Ben made strong eye contact and sighed. 'It's a tragedy, but that doesn't make it your fault, Kitty. If you could ask her family, they would tell you the same. And they'd be right. Stevie was driving the car. He was the one speeding. He was the one who knocked that poor woman over, not you.' His finger produced some sharp movements, jabbing towards the screen at Stevie's picture. 'He killed that girl, not you.'

'I know but-'

His brow furrowed, and he spoke in a steady, low-pitched tone. 'No, Kitty. There are no buts. You can't make yourself suffer because of him anymore. You're a victim, too. He abused you, Kitty, and you decided to leave him. That's it. That's all you did.'

'She had her whole life ahead of her.'

'You're right, she did. But it wasn't your fault. None of this is your fault, and I need you to hear me and understand what I'm saying.' He leaned in closer to maintain eye contact. 'It's not your fault.'

Kitty's phone buzzed.

'Hello.'

'Hello, is that Kitty Twist?' asked Sam, the familiar voice of the local police officer ringing in her ears.

'It is.'

'Kitty, I have some news about Stevie,' he began.

'I've just seen it on the news,' she cried. 'Is it true? Did he really lose his life in the accident?'

Sam offered Kitty all the information he knew, confirming that on the morning she escaped from Perth, Stevie drove to Millie's. After a short conversation, he sped away and failed to stop at a pedestrian crossing, killing an innocent young woman and her unborn baby.

Ben stood up and walked across to the window, peering down onto the lane. 'Kitty, do you realise what this means?' he asked the moment she put down her phone.

'What?' she replied, turning to look at him standing near the window.

'Stevie has been in a coma since the day you left Perth, right?'

'That's what they're saying, yes.'

'So, he couldn't have been at the shop. He couldn't have been here, in St. Ives. He couldn't have sent you those parcels.'

Kitty walked across to the window, following Ben's gaze down onto the lane. 'Then who did?'

32

CHARLIE PLUNGED A KNIFE INTO AN APPLE. FOR OVER AN HOUR now she had found herself scrunched into an armchair, her knees pressed tightly against her chest. Her finger robotically scrolled through the hundreds of photos captured over the years of her and Ben. She shook her head at each forgotten memory, stirring up a mixing pot of fiery emotions. Denial felt like her new best friend. Then, she opened up Ben's Facebook page, searching for updates on his recent activity, and found nothing. She hated the way it felt to scroll through his posts as an outsider, no longer knowing what he was doing, or who he was doing it with.

And then her tired eyes spotted the conformation that made her heart combust, the update to his relationship status now reading *Single* instead of *Married*. The slow-burning embers in her mind ignited like a bonfire and her shoulders hunched over.

'What are you doing?' Pip asked, having been awoken by a strange noise coming from the lounge. 'It's a bit late to be sat in here, you'll be shattered in the morning.'

'He's updated his Facebook page,' she cried through an outpour of hysterics, 'to single.'

'Oh, Charlie. I'm so sorry,' she replied, sitting on the side of the chair, scooping her friend into her arms.

'He vowed to always love me, Pip. He vowed to remain married to me through the good times and through the bad.'

'I know he did. And you've tried your best to apologise and

261

patch things up, but you need to start thinking that you're better off without him now.' Pippa grabbed a tissue, wiping away her best friend's trail of sadness. 'He didn't want children, Charlie, and you do. More than anything else in the world, you want to become a mother.'

'I wanted to raise a family with him, I thought that's what we both wanted.'

'He should have been honest with you from the start, Charlie. But you can begin a fresh start now, find someone who wants the same things in life that you do.'

'I need to go over to the flat. I need to try one last time. He owes me another chance.'

'It's late and you're too emotional, too hurt and too upset. You'll end up saying something you'll regret and making things even worse.'

Charlie threw her hands in the air. 'How can things possibly get any worse? Look at me, I've lost everything; my husband, my home. I've lost everything.'

'Let me come with you then, at least walk you over there. It's late and not safe for you to be out alone.'

'Please, go back to bed. I'll text you when I get there. I'll be alright, I promise. I need to do this on my own.'

'Well, it looks like I have no choice,' she replied, watching Charlie rummage for her coat. 'Text me when you get there, okay?' Pippa requested, before walking back into her bedroom.

Charlie searched under the cupboard beneath the sink, pulling out a carrier bag. Still dressed in her pyjamas, she zipped up her trench coat and scooped her hair beneath a cap before heading out of the door. The sky appeared heavy with black clouds, each one eating up the stars, until nothing but a dark sheet remained. The streets appeared deserted, only a faint noise coming from the seafront as the final restaurants packed up after a busy night of service.

Charlie looked up to see the lights in her and Ben's flat were switched off, so she took out her key and unlocked the door. The flat felt cold and unlived in. A few days' worth of mail scattered the doormat, and an unwanted smell of gone-off milk lingered in the air. She knew he wasn't home and hadn't been for a while, maybe a number of days.

'I've arrived,' she said when Pip answered her phone. 'Now go to sleep and I'll see you in the morning,' she said before hanging up.

Charlie crept upstairs, searching through Ben's drawers and wardrobe, noticing that some of his clothes were missing. The watch she had bought for his birthday last year remained hidden in his drawer, the inscription *Together Forever* now meaningless. In the bathroom, the toothbrush holder stood empty. Bitterness brewed in her stomach, vengeance pushing away any lingering strands of sadness. She checked the contents of the carrier bag clenched between her fingers and headed back out into the night.

OVER ON LADYSMITH Lane, Ben and Kitty sat surrounded by pictures, his studio providing the perfect backdrop to an evening spent on a stakeout. Huddled by the window in complete darkness, with only the streetlamps outside illuminating the studio interior, the pair looked down onto the lane.

'It's getting late. My eyes are tired and every inch of my body aches from spending the night on the floor,' admitted Kitty, resting her weary head against Ben's shoulder. 'We've been hiding up here for three nights now, watching the shop, and nothing has happened. Isn't it time we move on?'

Ben remained silent, watching over the lane like a sniper.

'This is the last night we're doing this, Ben,' Kitty added, becoming uncomfortable after so many consecutive hours spent crouched on the floor. 'No more daffodils have arrived, there's been no more phone calls, so let's just assume that it's over with now, shall we? Whoever was doing it has stopped, isn't that the main thing?' She looked at Ben, who was still refusing to divert his stare.

'I just have this feeling that it isn't over, Kitty. It doesn't make any sense, but I need to be sure.'

'And you still think that someone's going to turn up in the middle of the night? I got those other deliveries during the day. So, why don't we just wait to see if anything else happens whilst I'm at the shop?'

'Let's just give it a few more nights and if nothing else happens, brilliant, it's over, like you said, and we can put it behind us and carry on with our lives.'

A black cat crisscrossed the cobbles the moment the hour brushed past midnight. As he sat on a chair pushed up against the window, Ben's eyelids became heavy. Kitty lay curled up on the floor by his feet, her eyes having closed hours ago. Her head was rested on Ben's foot, causing his leg to go numb and become riddled with pins and needles. Exhausted, he rested his head on the windowsill and closed his eyes, just as someone walked down the lane, heading towards Flourish.

Outside, the prowling black cat scurried from the approaching stranger, it's entire spine stiffening. The person paused and checked that the street remained deserted. The rustle of the carrier bag drove the cat away and Charlie carried on walking towards Kitty's shop, taking a glance up at Ben's studio, failing to see his head resting on the windowsill. She looked in through the shop window, spotting the portrait of Kitty hanging as part of the new display, Ben's signature inked into the bottom left-hand corner. Tears trickled down her cheeks, anger-infused jealousy igniting within her bones. She unscrewed the cap on the bottle of gin that was clenched in her hand, and took an extended drink.

Back inside the studio, Kitty's body juddered, causing Ben to stir. It took him a few moments to register his surroundings, his mouth agape and drool seeping down his cheek. After a few seconds, his eyes focused. He peered back out onto the lane, his heart racing at the sight of somebody lingering outside Flourish. He eased Kitty's head off his foot without waking her and snuck down the stairs, peering down the lane from the studio door. With his nose touching the glass, he watched the person outside Kitty's shop push something through the letterbox. He unlocked the door, leaving it wide open, adrenalin encouraging him to bolt down the street.

Before the person realised his approach, Ben bellowed. 'What the hell are you doing?'

He reached out and grabbed the person's arm. Unexpectedly, a female voice shrieked, making him release his grip.

Charlie turned around.

'Ben! You scared me, what are you doing?'

'What am I doing?' He looked into the shop, witnessing the dead daffodils scattered on the door mat. 'I don't believe it.' His head dropped and he placed his hands on his hips.

Through a slurry of words, Charlie rambled. 'I love you, Ben, and I want you back,' she cried. 'I made a mistake by leaving. I love you more than anything and I want to save our marriage.'

He flung his arms into the air. 'You want to save our marriage? Look at yourself. You're creeping around in the middle of the night pushing dead flowers through letterboxes. Only, this isn't just any letterbox, is it?'

She grabbed her cap and tossed it away, allowing her hair to cascade. 'I wasn't trying to hurt anyone, I just wanted her to go away because I felt like she was taking my place in your life. I'm still your wife, Ben, and all I see you doing is flirting with some other woman instead of trying to sort things out with me.'

Ben shook his head. 'I can't bear to look at you right now, Charlie. Of all the scenarios I came up with about who could have been behind all of this mess, it never entered my mind that it could've been you. I didn't think for one second that you could be that crazy.' Ben recalled the hand written note that he had spent so long studying, plus the address label on the box he had seen in Flourish. 'It was your writing,' he nodded to himself, shaking his head and casting his arms in the air. 'I knew it seemed familiar, you tried to disguise it, but it was written in your hand.'

Charlie reached out her hand, taking hold of Ben's. 'I just want things to go back to normal, how they were before.'

Ben cast her away. 'Kitty didn't deserve this. Have you any idea how much fear you've caused? Have you?' Ben looked away, his eyes blinking through a fog of disgust. 'She had the courage to escape from a horrible life and instead of finding safety, she stumbled into the hands of another crazy person.' He forced himself to look Charlie in the eye. 'Whether Kitty came into my life or not, this marriage would never have worked. I don't love you anymore, Charlie, and I know it's hard to hear, but why can't you understand that?'

Charlie struggled to stand still, her body swaying. 'You don't mean that. I know you love me, Ben, you always have, and you always will.'

'I feel sorry for you,' he said, watching her struggling posture, the bottle of gin in her hand almost empty. 'There was never a baby, was there, Charlie?'

Charlie shook her head. 'I just wanted you and I to get back together, and I'm sorry, I know it was a stupid thing to do.'

'I don't even recognise you right now,' he said in disgust. 'How can you play with people's emotions like this? Don't you have any conscience?'

'I didn't mean to hurt anyone.'

'You made me believe I was going to be a father. What part of that isn't an attempt to hurt me?'

Charlie stood with makeup smeared over her face, blotches of black mascara running from her eyes. 'I'm sorry, Ben. I really am.'

Ben thought back to the one thing that always niggled away in his mind. 'I didn't propose to you in Venice, did I?'

The question hung in the air.

After a pause, Charlie shook her head and broke the silence. 'No, you didn't.'

Ben thrashed his foot against the wall. 'I knew it.'

Charlie walked over to him and wrapped her arms around his neck, pressing her head into his shoulder. 'We can work this out. I'm willing to try, whatever it takes.'

Ben took hold of her arms and released her grip. 'I'm not willing to work anything out. This is over, our marriage is over and you need to start listening to me for once in your life.'

Charlie fell to the floor, her body crumbling. 'Do you love her?'

Ben walked a few paces away. 'It doesn't matter if I love her or not, why can't you see that? Kitty isn't breaking up our marriage, Charlie, I am.' Ben peered inside the shop again. 'How do you know about the daffodils? How did you know about Stevie?'

A noise sounded in the distance and Kitty came scurrying down the street. She saw Ben, before spotting Charlie on the floor. 'Ben, what's going on? Are you alright?' she shouted, peering at the shop. As she crossed the street and drew closer, a lamppost illuminated the scene. 'Charlotte? What are you doing here?' she asked, a confused expression adding to her befuddlement. Kitty bent down, following her natural instinct to help Charlie to her feet.

Frown lines added unwanted character to Ben's face. 'You two know each other?'

'This is Charlotte, she's been doing the laser treatment on my tattoo.' Kitty looked at Charlie, making sure she wasn't hurt. 'Are you alright?' she asked, moving Charlie's hair away from her face, some loose strands saturated with tears.

'So, that's how you know everything,' he muttered, directing his statement at Charlie. 'Kitty, this is Charlotte Fox.' Kitty's facial expression froze.

'What?' She released her grip of Charlie's arm and stepped away. 'Your wife?'

Ben nodded and walked over to take hold of Kitty's hand. 'It was Charlie who delivered those parcels to your shop, not Stevie.'

Kitty took a few seconds to absorb the news. 'It was you?' she questioned, looking at Charlie, her eyebrows raised. 'You're the one who sent me the daffodils? You're the one who's been watching me, and who's been calling my mobile?'

Charlie remained silent.

'And she isn't pregnant, she never was,' Ben interjected, his bitterness firing through the air.

Kitty turned to face Charlie. 'How could you use everything that I'd told you in confidence against me?' she began, her anger mounting the more her mind processed. 'You could see how vulnerable I was, how scared I was of him, and yet you made me believe he'd found me. Why?'

Charlie's expression grew dark. 'Ben is *my* husband. When you met him, we were still married. We are *still* married,' she spat.

Kitty flung her arms in the air. 'You were the one who left him. I had nothing to do with your separation, or the breakdown of your marriage.'

'Had it not been for you, our marriage might have survived.'

Kitty lowered her tone and composed her emotions. 'He doesn't love you, Charlotte. It doesn't make any difference if I'm here or not.'

'You encouraged something to happen between the two of you when you knew he was still married.'

Kitty shook her head. 'I feel sorry for you, Charlotte. It's easy to see why Ben doesn't love you anymore.' Kitty didn't give Charlie any time to reply. Instead, she turned her back on the woman and headed back up the street. 'Stay away from me and my shop, otherwise I'll have you arrested,' Kitty added, before opening the door to her flat, and closing it behind her.

Charlie turned to Ben and watched as he also began to walk away, following in Kitty's footsteps.

'Please, Ben, don't leave me.'

Ben stopped in his tracks and turned to face her. 'I want a divorce, Charlie,' he began. 'You can have the flat and any savings. I don't want any of it,' he explained, fumbling with his keychain. 'I just want Kitty,' he concluded, as he tossed his key to their flat through the air.

33

THE SOUND OF THE FRONT DOOR CREAKED, AWAKING KITTY FROM a deep sleep.

'Where've you been?' she quizzed, upon catching sight of Ben entering the room. Early morning snippets of sun spilled in through the crack in the bedroom curtains, stinging Kitty's eyes and encouraging them to open. 'Have you been out all night?'

'Maybe,' he replied.

'It's seven o'clock in the morning. Where've you been?'

He walked over and perched on the end of her bed. 'Well, for the past three weeks, I've been working on that big commission I told you about, and I just needed to add the finishing touches.'

'What, all night?'

'Yep, and I'm finally happy with the results,' he explained. 'So, get dressed, there's something I want to show you,' he requested, grabbing the duvet and flinging it back.

Kitty retrieved the covers and threw them back over her shivering body. 'What, right now?'

'Right now.' Ben's grin stretched the width of his face, his happiness infectious.

'Could it wait? It's Sunday morning and I'm cosy in here. Why don't we have a day of unpacking. Your stuff is still in boxes and I'd like it to feel like you actually live here. Then, later on, we could pop out and you can show me these wonderful paintings.'

Ben ripped the covers away and held out his hands. 'This

cannot wait.'

'Can I at least shower first? I must look a right state,' she said, wrapping her arms around his waist and kissing him good morning, still savouring the way that his lips felt against hers.

'You look perfect to me,' he replied, fixing the strands of hair that were tangled around her ear.

With unbrushed hair and one of Ben's oversized jumpers thrown over her bedtime t-shirt, Kitty sunk her legs into a pair of trousers. 'Have I ever told you that I'm not a big fan of surprises?'

'I think you'll like this one, but I need you to put this on first,' he explained, taking out a blindfold and placing it over her eyes. 'Perfect, now let's go.'

'Can I not just promise to keep my eyes closed?' she requested.

Ben grabbed hold of a gift bag that was hidden beneath the bed, before navigating Kitty down the stairs. 'Nope. I want to make sure this is a complete surprise.'

The pair set off on foot down Ladysmith Lane, Ben guiding the way. The freshness of the day whipped through her hair, completing the process of awaking her senses. Pearly petals of summer blossom showered down like champagne over the pavement.

'This must look a bit odd. I bet everyone's staring,' she said, the sound of her flip flops echoing through her ears.

'It's not even seven-thirty in the morning and the street is deserted. There's nobody staring,' he lied, smiling over at Agnes, Susie, Ruben and Lily, who were all waving from across the road, each one having been let in on the surprise.

'I'm trusting you, Ben Fox,' she replied.

'Keep walking,' he encouraged, now half-way to his intended destination.

'Where are we going, exactly? I assumed you'd be showing me some pieces in the studio if that's what you've been working on.'

'So many questions – can't you just trust me? I promise you'll like it,' he insisted, guiding Kitty down Ladysmith Lane until they reached Flourish.

'I bet you're taking me for breakfast somewhere because it was your turn to cook this morning,' she jested. 'Have you prepared another beach picnic at our hideaway cove?'

'No, but that's a great idea, we should do that next weekend.' Ben pulled on her hand, making her pause.

'Are we here? That was quick.'

Ben took out the shop keys from his pocket and opened the door. 'Right, take one step up,' he requested, helping Kitty to navigate her way into the shop. 'Now, are you ready?' he asked, switching on all the lights.

'Ready as I'll ever be.'

Ben untied the blindfold and remained behind Kitty in the doorway. 'Okay, now you can look.'

Kitty's hand was drawn automatically to her mouth, her breath stolen from her lungs at the sight of the shop. She looked to the left first with wide eyes and shook her head with disbelief, the transformation rendering her speechless.

'Well?' he asked tentatively, fretting for a second that maybe he'd made a terrible error in judgement. 'What do you think?'

A response wasn't forthcoming as Kitty hadn't even heard the question, too caught up in her own world. Through wide eyes, she soaked up every detail of each painted rainbow decorating the walls of her shop. Her skin tingled at the tribute, and she felt so overwhelmed by the thoughtfulness that had gone into every brush stroke.

'I remember you telling me about your childhood, and how your mum encouraged you not to be scared during a storm, and to look for rainbows instead, and that even now, rainbows remind you so much of her.' The montage of individual paintings that had been hung on the walls formed to make one large piece of personalised artwork. Ben stood back, urging a reaction. He knew she still hadn't seen what he considered to be the best bit and so, from behind, he placed his hands at either side of her head and arched it gently upwards. 'Don't forget about this,' he said, his infectious smile still stretched across the width of his face.

A mural of pastel-coloured rainbows decorated the entire ceiling. For Kitty stood beneath, the impact felt greater than if stood inside the Sistine Chapel. She admired the vibrant collage, witnessing how Flourish had been brought back to life with a new radiance. Kitty's eyes released a torrent of tears and she finally released her hand from her mouth and turned to Ben. 'Did you do all this?'

Through a more understated smile, he nodded. 'I've been working on the canvases for weeks during the evenings, and then last night, Ruben hung them whilst I worked on the ceiling.' He turned her around so that she could see everyone across the road, waving and shaping their hands into hearts.

'I couldn't have done it without Ruben's help.'

Kitty waved to everyone before turning back. 'So, this is the commission you've been talking about? I thought it must've been part of that big hotel project you landed.' Kitty admired the shop, her eyes spotting something new with each glance. In the intricacies of the designs, all she could see was her mum, and all she could hear was Delilah's voice. Memories from every part of her upbringing flashed through her mind. She heard the laughter that had filled the garden on her seventh birthday when Delilah had dropped her three-tier princess cake. She relived the moment she and her mum had held hands, running into the choppy sea off Brighton Pier in a moment of summer holiday madness. Kitty could smell her mum's cooking, the aromatics that infused Delilah's famous Sunday lunch, and she could hear the crunch as her teeth sunk into one of her mum's crispy roast potatoes. She could feel the warmth provided by her mum's lips, and in her mind, Delilah remained by her side, placing a kiss on her forehead like she had done thousands of times before.

'Ben, I don't know what to say.'

'My motivations are purely selfish,' he began. 'I knew that if I filled this shop with something special to you, with memories of your mum, that you'd never want to leave St. Ives.' Ben stepped inside the doorway, standing by her side and taking hold of her hand. 'I know that your mum and dad wanted to retire here, and I hope in some small way you feel like they're still a part of your journey.' Ben placed his hand over his mouth and coughed twice, the kind of cough that grabbed attention in a room. The sound of a door creaking made Kitty turn and peer towards the back of the shop. 'But it wouldn't be full of all the things you love without these two people being here too,' he commented, holding his breath as Millie and Peggy appeared from out the back where they'd been hiding.

Kitty covered her face with both hands, capturing all the tears that had immediately broken free. She ran towards Millie, wrapping her arms around her best friend like they had been separated a lifetime. Lost for words, neither one could speak, their prolonged, tight embrace conveying so much more than words, their heads buried in one another's shoulder.

'Are you okay?' Millie whispered in her friend's ear. She could feel Kitty's body trembling and the erratic beating of her heart.

'I'm sorry for not telling you, I just didn't know how,' Kitty mumbled, still buried in the nook of Millie's neck.

Millie squeezed tighter. 'I'm sorry for not doing more. I knew something was wrong, but I didn't do enough. I didn't do anything, and I should've. I made a promise to your mum, and I failed to keep my word.'

'It's not your fault. You couldn't have done anything to stop him. I was just so ashamed and I didn't know how to tell you.'

'Listen to me,' Millie began, parting their bodies so that they could look one another in the eye. 'Don't ever feel ashamed. None of this was your fault.' Millie took a tissue out of her pocket and dabbed Kitty's blotchy skin. 'All I care about is that you're safe.' She wiped Kitty's cheeks and beamed, happy at the fact that she could finally speak face to face with her closest friend. 'It's all over now and you have all this to look forward to,' she said, gesturing around the shop. 'Plus, you've got this wonderful man, who I know is going to treat you right because I've already put him through an interrogation.'

'It's true,' Ben laughed. 'She actually has. She knows more about me than I know about myself. I did pass the test though, didn't I?'

'You did,' she replied, before turning back to Kitty. 'And look at your wonderful new look, I almost didn't recognise you,' she added, stroking Kitty's hair and admiring her new, quirky clothes. Kitty then wrapped her arms around Peggy before making formal introductions.

'Millie, I'd like to introduce Peggy Maltby to you. Peggy is my biological mother,' she explained. 'But I'm guessing that you've already met, having been in on this whole surprise together.' Kitty turned to look at Peggy. 'I'm hoping that with a little help from Peggy, I can continue to make this shop a huge success.'

Peggy gave Kitty a hug. 'I'll come and help you whenever you need it, you know that,' she whispered in her ear.

Whilst they hugged, Kitty turned to look at Ben and mouthed, 'Thank you.'

'Millie and I have organised a whole day of pampering, so the three of you can spend some quality time catching up.'

Kitty raised her eyebrows and turned to Millie. 'Oh, you have, have you? When we spoke on the phone last night you told me that you were giving the café a deep clean today.'

'What can I say? I lied,' she replied with a sense of satisfaction.

'So, Millie and Peggy are heading over to the country club now, just to put a few finishing touches to the day, and then I'll take you over in a little while once everything is in place. Does that sound alright with you?' asked Ben.

Millie whispered into Kitty's ear. 'Savour this moment because I'm going to want to know all the details later on.' Millie zipped up her coat and gave Kitty a subtle wink before walking towards the door. 'Right, let's go, Peggy.'

Kitty watched Millie and Peggy walk away until they were out of sight, still not quite believing her eyes.

Ben walked over to Kitty. 'Don't worry, they're not going far. I just need you alone for a few minutes.'

Kitty pressed her finger against his lips, requesting silence before he could continue. 'There's something I need to tell you.' She took hold of his hands and slipped her fingers in between his. 'Even if you hadn't decorated this shop, I will never leave St. Ives. This is where I belong,' she began, wrapping Ben's arms around her body so that she could release her hands and place them on his face. She paused, looking down and taking a deep breath, before lifting her gaze. 'And if it's alright with you, I'd like to spend the rest of my life here in St. Ives, alongside you, and our baby.' There was a moment of silence whilst Ben absorbed the news.

'What? Really?' His face beamed. Kitty took hold of his right hand and placed it over her bellybutton.

'Really,' she replied, tears trickling down her face. 'And I know we didn't plan this, and that it's so early for us to be thinking about babies, but it's happened and I kind of feel that it's just meant to be.'

Ben kept his hand pressed against her stomach, a feeling of contentment radiating through his palm. 'I never wanted a family of my own until I met you, and now I couldn't think of anything more perfect.' The pair rested against each other, both looking down at Kitty's tummy. 'Will you come down to the beach with me? I have one last surprise.'

'How can you possibly have any more surprises?'

'Last one, at least for today,' he joked, guiding her out onto the street before locking the shop, the gift bag hanging from his fingers.

She noticed the bag. 'What's that?'

'Never you mind,' he replied, shielding it behind his back.

For Kitty, St. Ives in early summer felt wonderful. The wind took on a timid nature and offered warmth as it tickled across her face. The blue sky felt tropical, shades of summer blue comforting like a blanket. Salty nuggets direct from the sea clung to the air like invisible diamonds, minute crystals landing on Kitty's lips, a constant reminder of her new seaside home. She strolled hand in hand with Ben down towards the seafront, blossom petals sticking to her flip flops.

'Any idea where I'm taking you yet?' he asked, their bench coming into view.

She peered around, spotting the early morning walkers and swimmers that dotted the beach. 'Not really. I'm just hoping that it's not for an early morning swim, or surf.'

Ben navigated the few steps down onto the sand, guiding Kitty, who followed behind. 'Here we are,' he said. 'Remember this bench?' Ben placed the gift bag next to his feet.

'Of course, I do,' she replied, recalling her memories with fondness. 'I'd been in St. Ives for less than an hour, and yet I found myself sharing this bench, and this wonderful view, with you,' she explained, pointing to the romantic horizon acting as their backdrop. Sand trickled onto Kitty's flip flops and she recalled how the cool grains had felt beneath her toes on her very first day.

'I was so lost that morning. I'd run away from such an awful situation and I didn't know what life down here had in store for me, and yet it felt so right, even during that very first hour,' she explained, turning back to look at Ben. 'And within the space of a few months, I now find myself sharing a home with you, my boyfriend, a man I love more than life itself, and I have a baby on the way.' Kitty paused and placed her hand over her chest. 'And if all that wasn't enough, I have Millie back in my life, and I'm growing closer to Peggy.'

Ben scrunched his face. 'Boyfriend? I feel a little old to be called your boyfriend,' he explained. He dug his hand into his pocket, taking out a silver, square jewellery box. He bent down, resting on one knee, and took hold of Kitty's left hand.

'Kitty Twist, in such a short space of time, you have come to mean everything to me. Every day that I wake up by your side, I realise how lucky I am to have met you, and how grateful I am that the world delivered you into my life.'

He paused for a moment, drawing in a deep breath and collecting his emotions. 'You make me smile, you make me laugh, and you make me happier than I ever knew was possible.' He took a moment to ease open the box, taking out a dainty engagement ring. 'And, if you'll do me the honour of being my wife, I will make it my job to ensure that I make you happy for the rest of your life.'

He took another breath before continuing.

'Kitty Twist, will you marry me?'

Kitty nodded without any hesitation, tears winding their way down the contours of her beaming face. 'Yes, of course I will,' she replied.

Ben slipped the delicate ring over her finger, witnessing how the cluster of tiny diamonds sparkled. He stood up and placed his hands at either side of her face, kissing her delicately, before wrapping his arms around her body and lifting her off the ground so that her feet swung in the air. 'I love you, Mrs Kitty Fox to-be,' he whispered into her ear before easing her back down.

'I love you, too,' she replied. She held out her hand and admired the ring, the band fitting snugly around her delicate finger. 'How did you know my size?'

'Never you mind,' he laughed. 'Now, I have one last surprise for you.' Ben leaned down and took hold of the gift bag. 'I've bought these for you,' he said, taking hold of a brand-new pair of ballet shoes. 'They're not identical to your old ones, but they're as close as I could find,' he explained, indicating with his hand for Kitty to take a seat on the bench. 'Now, I know that it's been a while, but you talk about ballet with more passion than I talk about paintings, so I thought it's about time you brush up on those forgotten skills and do something that you really love, something that makes you happy.' He removed Kitty's flip flops, and eased her feet one by one into the new shoes, securing the ribbons in place around her ankles.

Kitty's legs tingled the moment her feet eased their way into the new shoes, the material soft and striking a chord of familiarity against her skin. The tautness of the tassels wrapped around her ankles, plus the snug fit of the shoes caused a nostalgic sensation to sweep through her entire body. She closed her eyes and allowed her mind to drift, and for a moment, she was once again dancing alongside her mum in the back garden of the family home.

'Okay, how do they feel?' he asked, taking hold of her hands and assisting Kitty to her feet, her radiant smile silently answering his question.

'They feel wonderful,' she began, taking a moment to compose herself, her bout of giggles and radiant smile infectious. 'Now, get ready to catch me if I fall,' she laughed, glancing over at Ben. 'It's been that long that I'm not sure if my feet will remember what to do.'

Kitty took a few paces towards the sea, her feet easing into the soft sand. With the specs of early morning sun warming her back and the beach acting as a natural stage on which to perform, she eased herself up on to tiptoes and with her arms outstretched, twirled, strands of blond hair trailing in the wind. Ben admired his fiancée whilst his artistic mind took a mental snapshot of the poignant scene. In that moment, he realised that the image of the lone ballerina dancing on the beach was destined to be displayed on gallery walls across the Cornish Coast.

The End

Printed in Great Britain
by Amazon